Eden's Heat

By

Evelyn Starr

For lovers everywhere.

Made to Love Her

By

Evelyn Starr

This book is a work of fiction. Names, characters, places, and incidents either are products of the author's imagination or are used fictitiously. Any resemblance to actual events or locales or persons, living or dead, is entirely coincidental.

Eden heat

ISBN: 978-1-55487-160-5
Cover art and design by Martine Jardin

Published by eXtasy Books 2003
Look for us online at:
www.extasybooks.com

Library and Archives Canada Cataloguing in Publication

Starr, Evelyn, 1952-
Eden's heat / Evelyn Starr.

ISBN 978-1-55487-160-5

I. Title.

PS3619.T372E34 2008 813'.6 C2008-906741-X

STARING DOWN AT HIM THROUGH A LONG AND QUIVERING MOMENT WHEN THEY BOTH seemed to be waiting for something that might not yet happen, Claire laughed. Suddenly. Unexpectedly, the sound of it bubbling from her lips the way it had in other days, better days. The kind of spontaneous laughter she knew had been hers before, because her heart kept telling her it had.

"Show me," Eli whispered, his eyes glittering more feverishly...glittering indescribable brandy-rich as the plain deep brown faded from their depths and the fire crept in to claim them.

"Show you?"

Laughing along with her, his teeth shone perfectly white and deliciously perfect.

Pale morning light infused their bedroom with a soft-blue stillness flung like a veil over the warmer gold of walls and curtains and satin-smooth polished floor. A stillness so real Claire felt she could hold it in her hand should such become necessary. And in the midst of it, his eyes dared her to go on.

Dared her to *do* it.

Whatever he thought she might be about to do.

Moving smoothly as if she'd practiced for years and years, Claire rose off the thighs she'd held captive beneath hers. Leaning toward him, she fell to hands and knees, her breasts dangling free within easy reach of hands he didn't immediately lift from the pillows upon which he'd propped himself. Her breasts were fuller now, rounder since she'd had the twins, as was her entire body. Fuller, rounder, more lush and, she knew just from the way he looked up at her, more desirable.

Taking her time, she moved toward him. Slinking like the lovely cat she sometimes imagined herself to be, she moved slowly. She'd fixed her gaze upon him in the same way that hungry beast might regard a delicious morsel. And she never let it waver.

Still motionless, seeming almost mesmerized, Eli stared back.

He wanted to lift his hands. Claire could *feel* the want hovering in heated summer morning air between them. She could feel the ache of it in her own hands. The hardened, burning ache of hands that needed to lift. Needed to graze her breasts with peaked knuckles, to lift their weight with sweat-slicked palms. Hands that needed to...

A fevered wind swept through the open window a few feet from the bed, bringing with it inspiration that seized her in the same instant Eli's hands managed a feeble twitching.

She should deny him.

Chapter One

SNOWFLAKES RIMMED TALL WINDOWS ON EITHER SIDE OF THE MASSIVE FRONT DOOR. Scratching softly against the leaded glass, they dropped, piling in gentle scallops along the edges of each small pane. More flakes drifted down every second, blurring the old and familiar outlines of objects and erasing them, only to create all new and even more fantastic ones as they gently, inexorably, worked to cloud all view of the outside world.

Claire Hardistique glanced once over her shoulder at the pale marble hallway. Deserted and glittering, it lay as empty as it had been from the first moment she'd set foot in this most peculiar of houses. Shuddering, shivering, she grasped the brass door handle and let herself out into the night.

Beneath her long white velvet cloak, silvery soft fur brushed skin left bare by the skimpy and inadequate garments she'd been forced to wear. It was some kind of long haired fur. *Fox,* she thought, though she had no knowledge of fur other than a vaguely formed notion that it somehow seemed cruel to kill animals for no other purpose than to adorn herself.

The corset into which she'd been laced by a grim-lipped, unspeaking maid, fit tight. So tight, with steel stays digging deep into her flesh, that Claire worried she'd be unable to drag in the next breath. Or the next.

Why are the clothes men consider sexy always so uncomfortable? she wondered, shaking now inside her cloak as she picked her way carefully down stone steps beneath an enormous porte-cochere.

The corset was all she wore beneath the cloak. All she'd been given to wear, other than the pair of finest white silk stockings she'd fastened to ribboned garters and calf-high white boots with torturously high heels and painfully pointed toes.

Shivering again, shuddering with anticipation of the unknown that awaited her in the snow-swirled darkness, Claire descended carefully to the bottom of the steps, mindful of the precarious shoes and the mask that covered her face, inhibiting her vision. Like the corset, the mask was white. Satin. A jeweled and feathered thing that had been laced so tightly that no part of her face or her hair showed. Her mouth, her chin, her brow, and the thick bronze-brown hair she'd always considered her special glory, had all been rendered nonexistent by the smooth and tight covering. Nonexistent. As if they'd never been important at all.

She could see clearly only when she cast her gaze down. The odd placement of the eye slits made it possible to look only at her feet and the floor directly in front of her. She supposed the thing had been designed that way...a heinous contraption meant to humiliate the wearer and force her even deeper into submission than she'd gone already just by agreeing to be here.

Vision compromised, seething a little at the indignity, Claire somehow made her way safely to the bottom of the steps and across to the very edge of the porte-cochere and the gathering, swirling snowstorm. There she waited as she'd been instructed to do. Standing perfectly still, her covered head lifted, chin tilted slightly up, not quite ready to relinquish the last shreds of her pride or her dignity. Her shoulders were equally proud and straight as she awaited the whims of the man she'd been ordered to regard as her master. She clutched her cloak together with one white-gloved hand, looking neither to the right nor the left. Looking nowhere but straight ahead into the snowlit night, refusing to give Eli Eden the pleasure of seeing her cowed. Even if fear had already filled her heart and made it all but impossible not to run back into the hard and uninviting sanctuary of the mansion at her back.

The sleigh appeared after a few minutes. Burgundy dark in the soft golden light from the enormous iron lantern that hung beneath the porte-cochere, it was drawn by a pair of magnificent horses, black and splendid, even to an eye as untrained as Claire's. Their harnesses jingled softly as the heavily cloaked and top-hatted driver drew the vehicle to a stop. Harnesses as perfect and as deeply red as the sleigh itself glittered with polished studs. White and burgundy plumes fluttered as the horses stamped their feet and tossed their heads, clearly impatient to be off.

Claire hesitated, though she knew it was forbidden to hesitate. Knew she was expected to follow instructions immediately and without question. To go to him immediately. But for the moment she could only stare at the man who sat in the back of the sleigh.

He was as resplendent as the horses and the carriage. Deep burgundy highlights in his curly chestnut hair matched the sheen of the carriage's finish.

His eyes shone dark and demanding, and he wore formal evening clothes, complete with top hat.

For a long, long moment, nothing happened.

Even the snow seemed to hesitate, the wind to pull back the faintest yet most significant bit, and all the soft and mysterious rustlings of the moonless night to silence completely.

Then the man…Eli Eden, Claire knew even though she'd never set eyes on him before…held out his hand. His white glove flashed in an impatient, beckoning gesture as his jet eyed gaze met hers, and he spoke.

One word.

"Whore."

I'm not. Claire felt tears well in her eyes, and she blinked them back quickly, fearing to let them flow, fearing that if she soiled the perfect, pristine white of the mask she wore, Eli Eden would hold her in even more contempt. He might even punish her.

The mask belonged to him. The cloak and the corset and the gloves belonged to him, as did the house, the sleigh, and everything else around her. *As do I.* He permitted her to have nothing here. To possess nothing.

I shouldn't even be here. Wouldn't be, were it not for her own dire circumstances and the princely sum Eli Eden had offered. The fifty thousand dollars which waited somewhere, locked in a safe, probably, inside the forbidding marble mansion.

His white-gloved hand moved again, and Claire hastened to obey.

I've been summoned.

I'll be paid handsomely.

I have no other choice. I must do my duty, whatever that is. Must do it, and try not to think too much about it. Must remember only what lay ahead at the end of the ordeal.

The money. For her mother. To keep her mother safe.

All else was incidental and of no importance. Only her mother mattered.

Eli Eden shoved back the dark lap robe that covered the lower part of his body, and Claire saw that he'd readied himself for her. His shaft stood exposed, a gleaming and pale alabaster column, enormous and rearing, straight and strong against the darkness of his clothing and the shadows that filled the bosom of the sleigh. Alabaster. Or maybe it had been sculpted of the same icy white and inhospitable marble from which he'd constructed his mansion. It seemed lifeless. Waiting only for gratification.

For her.

It waited for her. It was intended for her.

Trembling inside, though she made every effort to conceal this from the man who waited impatiently, Claire accepted the offered hand. White glove met white glove, and he assisted her into the sleigh, directing her movements with a practiced ease and an economical strength that made it clear he knew what he wanted and what he expected. Directing her with motions rather than words, he wanted her. In position over him and before him with her feet on the seat, one on either side of him.

Then he made her squat. With her fur lined cape thrown back, her bared breasts and tightly corseted midsection were exposed, her most private parts below the minuscule garment revealed to the wind that had resumed and the snow that once again swirled in wild and fantastical patterns around her. Around them. Showing her where to place her hands, where to wrap quivering and suddenly weak fingers around a thin silver rail that topped the back of the seat, he forced her to descend. To lower herself until she touched him, only in that one place. Only at the tip of that long and waiting alabaster shaft. Forced her to halt there and hover with the exposed flesh between her legs brushed against the very tip of him, barely touching him yet firmly in contact in a way that made her face heat. That made her glad for the cover of darkness and the mask she wore. Because it would keep him from seeing the flush of humiliation that stained her cheeks, her brow, her throat.

"Remain so," he ordered, his voice a deep snarl in the back of his throat, his handsome face set in hard and emotionless, even cruel, lines.

Touching him, her legs folded tight against her steel constricted sides and tucked high beneath her armpits, her flesh already separating slightly to accommodate him and allow him to penetrate at his slightest whim with the merest lift of his hips or the slightest jolt from the sleigh, she did as she'd been ordered. She hovered over him. Waiting, as he had seemed to wait for her scant moments before. Waiting, with that most intimate of contacts made and yet unfulfilled. Uncompleted. Once again, she was grateful for the mask when she felt her expression change to one that had to be...could only be...a look of utter loathing and distaste.

Looking past her as if she'd ceased to exist, Eli Eden shouted to the coachman who still sat motionless and apparently oblivious atop his box at the front of the sleigh "Drive!"

Claire heard the crack of a whip. And they were off. Flying across hard-packed snow and into rougher terrain away from the house. At first she fought the sleigh. Its motion unfamiliar and hard to predict, its swaying and bumping threatened to move her away from the single point at which her flesh was required to touch his. But she soon learned, rebuked whenever she allowed herself to stray from him by even the slightest degree, that the contact was indeed not to be broken. No matter the pain in legs that had already begun to cramp from the strain of holding her position, no matter how her arms ached or her shoulders burned with the effort of clinging to the railing behind his broad shoulders, she must do what she'd been commanded. She must do it without a word. Must hold herself perfectly positioned against that loathsome, that threatening and intimidating instrument, until...

What?

"Do you understand our arrangement?" Eli Eden asked after a time, his hands held strictly away from her, down at his sides so that he would not have to touch her in any other way.

So he won't have to contaminate himself with me?

Claire could not see his gaze. Not with her own turned forcibly downward by the narrow eye slits. But she imagined it fastened upon her. Imagined it piercing through her, dark and stern like the coldest rapier blade of hammered steel. Or ice-pale and cold like the shaft that all too soon would certainly pierce her and impale her, driving itself into her with a force that even a rapier blade...

"I asked you a question. I expect to be answered when I speak to you."

"Yes, Sir." *Speak only when spoken to. Address him as Sir.* That was how she'd been instructed to behave if she expected to receive the money she needed so desperately.

"You understand that you will be paid if, and only if, you do as I say?"

"Y...yes, Sir." Her voice was muffled. Indistinct behind its wall of satin.

"Only if you do it without hesitation?"

"Yes, Sir." Fear clotted Claire's voice, and she could only hope he didn't hear it.

She had no idea what would be expected of her other than that she was to indulge him. Indulge his fancies. She'd been told that much, but no more. She'd been given an idea, if somewhat vague and unarticulated, that the fancies and fantasies would be for his benefit rather than hers. Beyond that, she'd had no clear idea what her duties would entail, and why he would place her in such a position or why he would choose to torture her now.

"Fine. Then lower yourself onto me and fuck me."

Claire closed her eyes.

He would not be able to see her eyes.

He would not know if they were opened or closed. Or maybe he wouldn't care. But she cared.

Drawing in the deepest breath she could manage against the constricting corset stays, she closed her eyes and pushed herself down. Forced her cramped leg muscles to tighten even more against her sides, and used all her strength to grip the railing as she forced her tight and unprepared body down onto the harsh enormity of the shaft she'd held so carefully beneath her. As if it was the one, the only, precious jewel in a new universe that seemed built to revolve specifically, entirely, around Eli Eden.

He was large. Larger than he'd appeared in the scant moments when she'd been allowed to see what he had planned for her. And she was small.

Soft tissue, never before plumbed, tore inside her. It gave way painfully beneath the thankless pressure she exerted. Only with the greatest reluctance did her virginity give itself up to him.

Had Eli Eden known she was a virgin?

Claire suspected he had. She'd been asked all sorts of questions by the *representative* who'd hired her. All sorts of prying, sometimes indecent and embarrassing questions about her life prior to this. About her relations and her contacts. All sorts of questions that led her to suspect she might have been chosen from all the other women who were or had once been in Eli Eden's employ for just that reason.

His hands took hold of her. When she moved too slowly, he made a sound of rude impatience and grasped her hips with strong, gloved fingers that bit deep into her flesh. Hands that shoved her body down farther. Much farther and with more aching and tearing, until she'd taken all of his enormity into her, the length of him forced deep, deep, deep into tender and unready softness at her core.

Claire bit back a cry of agony and panic.

To cry out was forbidden. She'd been ordered to make no sound, show no emotion, display no feeling at all. If she wanted ever to see the payment she'd been promised.

An instant after they lowered her, the hands at her hips lifted her again. But there would be no relief from the searing pain of the invasion of her body, for he stopped short of allowing her to escape completely. Tightening, his arms and hands held her for a moment with the head of him just inside her opening. And then he pulled her back down, jerking her into the second penetration with new force and new brutality.

"This is what I want you to do," he commanded.

"Yes, Sir."

His gloved hands released her. "You will continue to do it until you are told to stop."

"Yes, Sir." Claire hated him more with every second that passed. But the promise of cash, of release from all her worries and her nightmare fears loomed just beyond her grasp. Tantalizingly close, yet still too far away.

Eli Eden's cash would save her mother and herself from terrors too horrible to be considered. From hunger and eviction and almost certain death on the streets or in some nameless, heartless shelter somewhere.

She hated him, but she did as he wished. Muscles tortured and protesting, she levered her body up and down along the uncompromising shaft that had been meant explicitly to punish her. Squat and release, hold for a moment and then repeat. She urged her body to comply long after it had lost even the smallest and most reluctant wish to comply. As she lowered and raised herself in the rhythm he had taught her, Eli Eden grew ever larger. Riding him, sometimes aided by the swaying motion of the sleigh and sometimes hindered by it, Claire took the greatest, the most enormous care to ensure her flesh never left his.

He would not tolerate separation.

Instinct told her so.

"Faster," he ordered.

"Yes, Sir." Trying hard not to grimace, even though he could not see her mouth, she squeezed her eyes shut even more tightly. Her hands tightened, too, around the silver rail that was so perfectly placed and so well oriented for this activity that for the first time she wondered if it hadn't been designed and installed specifically for the purpose.

How many other women has he handled this way? she wondered. *How many other hapless and hopeless victims of circumstance has he forced to work the way I work now? To satisfy him. To make real his unreasonable fantasies, with no thought to my dignity, my feelings, my needs and sensibilities?*

Around them, snow continued to swirl, coming down harder now that the sleigh had hurtled away from the sheltered areas around the mansion and plunged at breakneck speed into darkness unrelieved by any light. Darkness so choked with the ever-falling snow that Claire began to fear they would lose their way and never be able to return to the marble mansion.

And if they didn't? What then?

Squat, release. Hold, accept, release. Penetrate, release. Strength failing, she continued to work diligently over him even as she allowed her mind to wander into sometimes reassuring and other times frightening paths.

If they didn't, if they were unable to return, will I be required to service him this way until the moment I die, my bare flesh frozen solid in the depth of this bitter storm?

Sleigh runners squeaked faintly upon freshly fallen snow. Sounds of the horses' breathing rumbled faintly far ahead, and Claire let her mind drift, imagining tall plumes of steam rising from their nostrils.

No other sound intruded upon the absolute quiet. None until Eli Eden spoke again.

"Faster." His mouth had moved close to her ear. She felt the sting of his breath heating the thin and tight layer of satin that confined it.

Opening her eyes, Claire tried to see the face that loomed so close to her own. But it was beyond her range of vision. No doubt this, too, had been a purpose of the mask. To prevent her looking at him. To dehumanize her even more and prevent her making the connection that a woman should...that she had a right to make when she'd joined herself to a man in just this way.

Her legs ached with a hot, deep pain that would surely never go away. Her body ached as well, in all of the places where she'd been made to impale herself upon him.

No, not made, she corrected herself immediately, seizing at anything, any thought, to divert her from the business she'd undertaken. No one had forced her to do this. No one had kidnapped her and dragged her to the marble mansion on the mountain.

She had come to this place, had come to Eli Eden by her own choice. Of her own free will. She had sold herself to him, knowing full well that she would be required to do things of this nature, and for that she had no one to blame but herself. No one to hate but herself.

Picking up her speed, applying her body to his with more vigor, she felt a new wetness. A new ease in the motion that allowed her to glide with less effort. To take him and then discard him so much more gracefully. Her vision began to blur a bit, and her head spun when she heard him make a low noise in the back of his throat.

That was it. One small growling that might have been approval, but might just as easily have been complete and utter dissatisfaction. But he hadn't rebuked her, and she took that as a good sign.

Perhaps if I satisfy him now, the other fantasies he'll expect will be more...

A new sound broke the stillness. A faint and plaintive twittering that seemed not to belong here. That seemed startling when heard here, though it was a familiar sound and a perfectly normal one in the world from which she'd come.

Eli moved then. Reaching inside his midnight black evening jacket, he pulled a cell phone from some hidden inside pocket and flipped it open with a well-practiced motion. "Yes," he said into it at the same time that he motioned with his free hand, indicating she was not to stop what she was doing. She was not to falter or hesitate.

His shaft had begun to move inside her. Had begun to torture her anew, growing and swelling in amazing ways, filling her in ways she'd never dreamed possible. It even, incredibly, had begun to please her.

"I'm with her now," he said into the phone and she imagined him looking at her, his dark eyes glittering like cold and lifeless coals. The short statement was followed by an even shorter silence and then, "She's adequate."

As if I'm not even present!

As if I don't even exist.

Very suddenly, Claire wanted to scream. Almost did scream and shatter the fantasy he'd built at her expense. But the money, and the memory of her mother's frightened white face in the hours after she'd suffered the stroke that could have killed her but mercifully hadn't, kept her quiet. Kept her pumping with legs that had long since gone beyond pain or suffering.

Claire wanted only for this to end. If she could bring him to climax...

In the last few minutes, she'd sensed something building inside him even as a similar thing built inside her. Impossible as it was to imagine, she felt her body beginning to be stimulated by the motions he'd ordered, though she felt certain he'd never meant to give her such slow and spiraling satisfaction. Such moistened pleasure between her thighs, such a shimmering of heat given to her with each successive plunge and lift along the surprisingly delightful hardness that had taken her prisoner.

Wondering if she'd be chastised for her actions, Claire dropped her hands suddenly from the silver railing onto his broad, black clothed shoulders. Digging in with gloved fingertips to gain a better grip, she clung to the hard knots of muscle and sinew she found there and used them as she had used the railing. To lever herself upward and downward, all the while biting back the forbidden cries that now would have expressed nothing but a sheer need to feel Eli Eden come inside her.

Chapter Two

STUNNED AND STARTLED, ALL BUT PARALYZED BY WHAT SHE'D DONE TO HIM SO FAR, ELI HAD TO give her credit. *This one was good. Better than good.*

She'd been a tight-assed and disapproving virgin when they'd started out on this little adventure. Tight-assed, tight-muscled, and hating him. He'd felt the hatred roll off her in waves. And he'd wondered, right up until the very first, absolutely spectacular and quiescent parting of her body opening to take him in, if she would actually do it.

So many of them arrived here with grim eyes or sometimes eager eyes, hoping to catch the brass ring. Hoping to win the prize and leave with the riches, only to fail.

He'd sent so many of them packing on the first night of their service. After they'd failed to satisfy him. After he'd decided he couldn't bear to spend another second fucking them, much less the week he required them to stay if they expected to be paid.

But this one was different. This one was interesting.

She'd been a virgin, as many of the others had not been. And still she'd consummated the beginning of her agreement with him. She'd done what he'd ordered obediently and without question. She'd done it silently and compliantly. And by God, now that she was riding him like a real pro, her little tight-assed, corseted body rising and falling faster than he'd have dreamed possible given the posture he'd forced her to assume, thrusting with strong and healthy legs that could only be a wonder and an amazement, she'd loosened more. Relaxed more.

Tucking the cell phone back into the inner pocket of his jacket, Eli lifted his arms and knotted his hands at the back of his neck, always taking the greatest care not to touch her in any way other than the one for which she would perhaps, if she could keep this up, eventually be paid.

He'd been a little startled when she put her hands on his shoulders. A little startled and more than a little outraged.

Touching meant intimacy. Intimacy meant familiarity. And those were things Eli Eden could not allow himself. They were things he could not afford, things which he'd forbidden for quite some time now.

She'd gone beyond what he permitted her to do. Eli knew his man had made the parameters perfectly clear when he'd first contacted the woman. When he'd first made the proposal and invited her to come here for Christmas week to give Eli what he so desperately wanted and needed, but which he never would have unless he bought and paid for it.

Nothing had been offered to her beyond the fifty thousand dollars.

No actions had been allowed her unless Eli specifically ordered them. And for a minute he thought about punishing her for her disregard of his rules. Of maybe even sending her away with her contract broken and unfulfilled. But then she'd started to come. And that was an interesting development. An unprecedented one.

Eli couldn't remember that any of the other women he'd brought along for the sleigh ride had ever come so unexpectedly or so lusciously before.

Always, he'd felt hatred. Only hatred and loathing for every miserable, disgusting thing he was and had become. He'd come to expect it. But the strange mixture of seething hatred and helpless attraction that poured from this woman's body as effortlessly as cum had begun to steam from between her legs...this fascinated him.

This time, he thought, fighting to stifle a sudden burst of laughter, *I might find a woman strong enough to last the full week.* He might actually have found one who would actually earn the cash and deserve it. After all of five years, the possibility of that happening had seemed remote. Doubtful. Improbable. But this one might do it. She might actually walk away with the prize he'd dangled so temptingly for so long and claim it where all others had failed.

For a fleeting instant, he wondered what she looked like beneath the snowy white, featureless mask that covered her from the throat up. He wondered how her voice would sound if he invited her to speak. Then he grimaced. He knew how it would sound. Knew what she would say, the names she would call him and the way in which she would say them if he ever gave permission.

All in all, it was better to keep the women faceless. Nameless. To keep them at the distance the mask commanded. Maybe this year, this time, he'd have the added bonus of not finding himself alone on Christmas, sitting in his enormous mansion with only wishes to keep him warm and imaginings to bring him the peace that seemed the birthright of every other last, goddamned man, woman, and child on the planet.

The woman had begun to slow down. She was tiring. Eli could see it in the way she moved. He could feel it in the tremors that had begun to shake her tight, compact body. She was wearing herself out to please him. Usually that was his cue to order the sleigh turned around. To head back to the house and release her to a few hours alone in the bedroom he'd provided. To allow her a few hours' rest and a chance to regain her strength for the next fantasy. And he would find the bottle of brandy that always waited, ready to drown his inadequacies and his pain with its ruby-amber magic.

More often than not, though, he would have lost his fascination with the woman who serviced him by this time. Usually he would have headed back and told her to leave for good.

But not this time. Not tonight.

He decided to let this one continue.

He wanted to see how good she was. How much stamina she had and how long she could last.

"Fuck me," he growled into her ear, suddenly aware that she wore perfume. A sweet scent, flowery like the terraced gardens that surrounded his palace in the summertime, mocking him with their nearness that would forever remain off limits and unattainable.

None of the others had worn scent.

He'd never expressly forbidden it. Hadn't even thought of forbidding it. But the others had always, invariably, come to him smelling of soap and antiseptic. As if they'd prepared themselves for surgery instead of a night of fantasy aimed at granting *him* sexual release, granting *him* satisfaction.

The woman sighed. She'd been forbidden to speak or groan, forbidden to make even the smallest of sounds while in his presence. That had been made clear to her along with all the other conditions of her employment. She'd been forbidden to do anything other than service him in silence. But Eli felt generous. So much so that he couldn't fault her for the sigh that might have merely been a breath too hastily expelled. Might have been completely understandable, given the way he'd trained Estella to lace his women into the corsets he liked them to wear and the physical activities he forced them to undertake once they'd been trussed up that way.

Perfectly understandable.

The woman moved around him. Moved on him, stroking his cock, his over-sensitized, demanding and seldom satisfied cock with liquid fire that felt even hotter because of the frigid air around them.

Gooseflesh stood out on her arms. It dimpled the tops of her bare breasts that stood erect, thrust out by her rigidly engineered costume. Her nipples were tight, dark buds against flesh so white and luminous it might have been formed from the snow itself. But she exuded warmth. Eli felt it, even though he didn't permit himself to touch it.

He never touched them. To touch was to invite...

To his complete astonishment, he realized his hand had lifted itself to her breast. Had cupped it, the thumb beginning to stroke gentle circles across and around the hard nub of that enticing nipple.

He felt the tremor of the touch ripple all the way through her body in the same instant that it rippled through his, and he caught his breath.

Of her own accord, the woman had increased the speed of her up and down motion. Shimmering and shivering along the length of his aching cock, she exuded an urgency that had begun to approach his own. Moist and tight, she surrounded him. Seemed to swallow him up with her fragrance that turned sultry when she began to come.

Beneath her jeweled white mask, Eli felt her grimace. He saw the tight and gleaming fabric shift slightly as her expression shifted, and he wondered again how she would look. How she would taste if he ever had the nerve to try to kiss her. If he ever had the courage, the sheer, unimaginable, inconceivable *guts* to look straight into her eyes and know by their look what she was thinking and how she was feeling.

He felt her grimace as the waves of astonishing, steaming orgasm poured over her and from her.

As ordered, she still made no sound though it was obvious she wanted to and needed to. And he almost wished she would. Almost wished for the intimacy it would afford him...afford them both. But intimacy was not a part of the deal, and she seemed to have taken that fact to heart. Seemed to have realized without being told that life had decreed long ago that intimacy of any kind, any degree, was expressly forbidden and that that was one rule Eli Eden never broke. Because he'd suffered enough. And would suffer no more.

For him, women would remain as they'd been for these five years. Faceless, nameless objects. Masked and anonymous bodies whose only attachment would be the clutch of their tight, wet flesh upon his. Whose only purpose would be the release of the pent-up desires he harbored, sometimes for far too long, before he could locate one of them and convince her to sell herself to him.

Someone groaned, softly.

For a minute, thinking she'd done it, Eli tensed. Ready to reprimand, or maybe to pinch the bit of breast and nipple that remained in his hand even long after he'd ordered it to let go.

Then he realized the groan had come from him.

His cock was responding to her in ways it usually didn't. It was responding to something she'd done or might be about to do with the unflagging, increasingly spasmodic and desperate movements of her body as it rode his.

Up and down. Up and down. Diligent as no woman in his memory had ever been, she worked at him. Worked on him. Did her damnedest to satisfy him. To truly and honestly go beyond the physical mechanics of the act she was performing and give him pleasure.

She was different, all right. And he felt the first very real, very rare, stirring of desire in nearly as long as he could remember.

"Whore," he murmured again, using the insult as a tool to help him push the attraction to the back of his mind. Because even more than intimacy, desire and attraction were dangerous. Were arguably the most dangerous emotions of all, leading as they did to pain of kinds worse than any he'd had to endure so far. Worse than any he'd imagined he'd have to endure. Attraction was intolerable. Desire was intolerable. "Fuck me faster," he demanded, using that as a tool, too.

Incredibly, she managed.

And she was no longer silent. "Ohhhhhh." Her breath escaped in one long, sibilant and low moan that almost, if he hadn't known better, sounded like a moan of delight.

He decided to let the infraction slide. This time. He was that curious to see what was going to happen next.

Her hands tightened on his shoulders. White-gloved and small, her fingers dug deep into the flesh beneath and around his collarbones. Eli thought for an instant that they would snap, and he shuddered a little as she began to inflict pain upon him, perhaps in retaliation for what he'd inflicted on her earlier when she'd torn herself thrusting onto him. She'd begun to inflict pain, and to his surprise, it felt wonderful. Felt invigorating and enrapturing. Stimulating, thrilling, mind-boggling. In a lifetime that seemed never to have been filled with anything but pain, he'd never thought pain could be so delectable.

His cock throbbed. It began to thrust with its own separate and distinct motions that seemed deliberately designed to insinuate his length deeper into her than she'd so far been able to insert him into herself.

He strained, wanting to lift himself to meet her. But of course that was impossible. He only had her to rely upon. Her strength and her agility.

Lifting his hands to her waist, he wrapped his fingers around it and marveled at its smallness. Its tight compactness. That would be the corset, of course. Because no woman was so small in reality. No woman he'd ever known anyway.

"My God." Moving his mouth next to her ear, he lifted her away from him, using the strength of the muscles in his arms to aid and encourage that which had begun to fade from those in her legs. Her feet still remained on the seat, positioned correctly on either side of him where he demanded they be positioned. Her legs had to hurt by now. Had to hurt like hell. But she showed no sign of giving up. And now, with him to help her, she had no reason to give up.

"Fuck me," he whispered again, the words uttered so much more gently and with so much more meaning than he'd uttered them before. "Please, fuck me. Please keep on fucking me. Please."

She said nothing.

His lips searched for the sweetness of her ear, only to find their way blocked and their desire thwarted by the layer of satin.

Impenetrable barrier. Unattainable delight.

His cock gave another deep throb. An alarming one.

This is the end. This has to be the end. And she brought me here!

Incredibly, she had awakened his cynical, uncaring, unresponsive body.

Once again he groped with his mouth, searching desperately for the sweet morsel that lay so near and yet so far away, as impossibly distant as the flowers in his garden in the summertime, inside its casing of white satin.

He'd loved the mask because it made her anonymous. Now he loved it even more because it denied him. Hiding the color of her eyes and the set of her expression, denying him the color of her hair and the feel of it against his hands and his face, it kept him out. Kept him at his distance.

"You can speak," he murmured, his voice trembling against that gleaming white barrier. "You can…"

She didn't.

True to their agreement and their pact, she remained silent except for the small, labored and whistling sighs of her breath burning against his shoulder.

"Christ almighty."

She seemed not to hear. Not to care that her small and pistoning body had done to his what he had set out to do to hers. That she had possessed him, and that he was in this instant, her slave and would do whatever she ordered him to do. Whatever he was able to do. That she had brought him to the edge of the cliff and was just about to send him plummeting into the abyss, his sanity and his separate self lost for all eternity.

Deep inside him, something rolled again. It had been gathering steam before, gathering strength. But now it was terminal. Now it would not be ignored.

His cock gave a sharp and warning stab.

Catching her hips, he used all his strength to hold her still. To push her down harder onto him. And then harder still. "Stop," he ordered, holding her tight on the jerking and seeking length of himself.

Slave that she was, slave that he'd bought if only for a little while, she did as he commanded. Instantly, she came to complete, wet and suffering stillness atop him while he shuddered. While his cock shuddered for an instant before it released as he couldn't have expected it to release. As he never remembered it releasing before, with a sudden rush of draining warmth that shimmered like light in the midst of cold and snowy darkness. Light that shone inside, illuminating every insecurity and inadequacy and ugliness and made him ashamed of the way he'd behaved.

"God." He sought her ear lobe again and then, still denied it and denied her ruby-red lips, claimed the soft and tender flesh of her shoulder below the place where the mask ended.

She was sweeter than he'd imagined. Sweeter than he'd dreamed.

She remained absolutely still, crouched atop his aching and surging, screaming and thrusting cock. She allowed him to explore at will, divining the taste of her from the scrap of skin he nuzzled and suckled. And all the while she did nothing that would either stop him or encourage him.

"Touch me?" he breathed. This time it wasn't a command as much as a question. A plea.

She did as he asked.

Asked, Eli told himself on a sudden note of wonder.

Her fingers lifted to his face. She ran them across his cheekbones, his mouth, his parted lips. Feeling her way like the blind woman he'd nearly forced her to be, she touched his mouth with a quick and darting motion. For an instant her gloved fingers left it behind and then, when they returned, he parted his lips. Catching the tips of the marauding fingers, he allowed them to enter and closed his lips around them to suck eagerly and hungrily, tasting the rich and slightly tart flavor that seeped through the thin silk. A flavor that must be, had to be, uniquely hers...that could only be a pale imitation of the taste of the lips he'd locked away from himself.

She came again, joining him as at last, at sweet, too long delayed last, the dam broke and he spilled himself into her. The exposed softness between her legs returned a hundredfold what her mouth and her tongue could not. Moist and warm around him, she returned every ounce, every iota, every scintilla of what he gave her in those few eternal and burning seconds.

In vain, Eli tried to look into her eyes. Tried to see if she was as shaken by this unexpected turn of events as he'd been shaken all the way to his core. But the mask was cleverly designed. The small twin slits sat low on her cheeks instead of directly over her eyes. Wearing it, imprisoned inside it, she would never be able to look directly at him. She would be forced to look down, her gaze lowered in humble obedience. It was a double-edged blade. One that cut him to the quick because impossible as it was for her to look up at him, it was equally impossible for him to look at her. To look into her eyes. And as much as the idea, the sheer mystery of it, enticed him and aroused him, he wanted to see. Wanted to *know.*

Depleted though it was from its exertions, his cock gave another half twitch. As if it thought it might still have some life left.

The woman had begun to weep softly.

He had shrunk within her and slipped out of her. She still crouched over him, her legs shaking visibly. And she'd begun to try to wipe away the tears that filled eyes she could not touch.

Eli's arms closed around her. Urging her to sit, he lifted her off him and swung her around effortlessly so that she could extend her legs and ease their cramped agony. Placing her sideways across his own legs, he pulled her long cape close around her half naked and shivering body, her satin-covered face pressed against the hollow of his shoulder.

"It's all right," he murmured as he'd never murmured to one of the women before. Then, voice shaking, he called out to his coachman. "Home. And make it damned quick."

Chapter Three

SHE'D BEEN LEFT ALONE IN THE LARGE ROOM, A SUITE OF ROOMS, REALLY, THAT SHE'D been assigned at the side of the house. Huddled in the wide bed, her body aching and exhausted, her mind still reeling from the strange mix of emotions with which she'd been bombarded during a sleigh ride that had been either pure evil or pure delight depending upon how she looked at it, Claire wrapped herself tight in golden satin sheets.

Expectant and nervous, she jumped at every small sound in the unfamiliar house. She doubted Eli Eden would come for her here, doubted he would call her back to *duty* this evening.

The maid, Estella, had informed her she was free to take a bath. She'd said she would be bringing up a dinner tray in a little while, since Mr. Eden preferred she not leave her room when she wasn't in his company.

Claire had found that a little odd. Just like she'd found odd the insistence that she bring no baggage or money or personal items other than the clothes she wore. Everything would be provided for her, she'd been told by the man who'd hired her.

Now, in another minute or two, she would take that bath. She would take a long, long one and luxuriate in the soothing warmth of the water. She would relish the chance to scrub away, if she could, all memory of the bizarre events in the snowy darkness.

But in the meantime, while I've got these few precious minutes to myself...

Moving slowly and painfully, grimacing when even the slightest hint of motion set up a burning ache in the overworked flesh between her legs, Claire rolled onto her stomach and lowered the upper half of her body over the side of the bed. Leaning down until her forehead nearly touched the deep blue carpet with its pattern of tiny gold fleur-de-lis, she scrabbled at the bottom of the box spring, searching for the ripped place where she'd hidden her cell phone.

It had seemed important to hide the phone. There had been that insistence, subtle but unmistakable though it had been, that she wasn't to bring anything with her to the mansion. And she hadn't wanted to take any chances. Then, when she'd arrived and Estella had asked to take her coat and had inspected the pockets none too covertly for any sign of contraband personal effects, she'd decided she'd been right to hide the phone in the waistband of her jeans beneath her bulky sweatshirt.

She hadn't been surprised to discover that the *everything* Eli Eden would provide for her use during her visit didn't include a phone. She'd seen none in the few brief minutes she'd been permitted to spend downstairs and there was none in her suite of rooms, none in the hallway for as far as she'd dared to venture in either direction. So she'd slipped the cell phone out of her waistband at the first opportunity, before the maid had a chance to manhandle her clothing and find it, and secured it in the spot beneath the bed.

Palming the phone, Claire levered herself back up into the bed and eyed the wide doorway that opened into the hall. She wished it had a lock. Wished any of the doors in her suite had a lock.

She'd laughed at herself in the first hour after her arrival. She'd called herself paranoid and suspicious, even crazy.

But not now.

Not anymore.

There was something just a little odd, maybe even a little sinister, about the arrangements in this house. And she thanked heaven she'd thought to provide herself a means of contact, no matter how tenuous it might be, with the outside world. A way to check in with her mother. It had been a little more than three years since her mother had had the stroke, and though it hadn't been major or irrecoverable, it had frightened Claire half to death. It had also left Marie Hardistique weak and unsteady. Enough that Claire worried about her, about being absent from her for more than a few hours, and about something happening to her.

Eyeing the door again nervously, she lifted the phone and punched in her home number.

The phone at the other end rang three times before her mother picked it up. "Hello?" she questioned in her soft, slow and lyrical voice, her speech so nearly back to what it had been before that even Claire had a hard time believing it had ever been impaired.

"Mum."

"Ah. Claire!" As always, Marie sounded delighted to hear from her. As if they hadn't talked at length no more than twelve hours ago. As if Claire had traveled to the ends of the earth instead of just a couple of hundred miles away. "How is your new job shaping up, dear?"

"It's fine, Mum."

Claire hadn't told her mother anything about selling herself to Eli Eden. That was too shocking, too humiliating. Even without the stroke and all the worries that had come along afterward, it was the last thing Claire would ever reveal to her mother.

"Is the house beautiful?"

"Breathtaking."

Her mother laughed softly. "And the people? Are they nice?"

"I've only actually met Mr. Eden," Claire replied carefully. "And a maid. And a driver." She frowned, thinking back on the silently rigid shouldered men or man who'd driven the limousine that brought her here from the pickup point at the subway station in downtown Pittsburgh, and then the sleigh that had carried her to her shame. "Or maybe it was two drivers. I'm not too sure about that."

"But…I thought you said there would be guests?" Her mother sounded doubtful, and Claire cursed herself silently.

Of course she does.

She'd told her mother there would be a big house party at the mansion. That she'd been referred to Mr. Eden by a fictitious employment agency with which she'd registered. That she was going to serve as a temporary social secretary for the week right up through Christmas. Kind of a landlocked cruise director to take care of the houseful of guests he expected.

It had been a plausible lie. A convincing one.

And her mother had believed it.

"The guests are due to arrive tomorrow," she improvised.

"Oh." Marie sounded relieved. "Should I call you on this phone then? In case I…"

Claire steeled herself to deliver this piece of bad news. "I'm afraid not. Mr. Eden doesn't approve of his staff receiving phone calls. He's made it clear that my priority is to be his guests and seeing to their needs. He's already told me I shouldn't have brought the phone with me."

"I…see."

"But don't worry. I'll call you as often as I can," she promised quickly. "Hopefully every day."

"Sounds like a strange arrangement."

Claire allowed herself a small laugh, struggling to keep any hint of bitterness or hysteria out of it. "Mr. Eden is something of a strange man."

"Well, I guess." Her mother still sounded doubtful.

"It's going to be all right. This is a good opportunity for me. I'll earn some good money this week, and then we won't have to be so afraid."

She heard only silence from the other end of the line.

"Mum?"

"You just be careful, Claire." That was her mother talking. The one who'd set such high standards for behavior through Claire's youth, yet had gone to bat for her without a second's hesitation whenever it looked like the world had been even slightly less than fair in the way it treated her. The one who'd protected her the way a tigress protects her young.

Closing her eyes, Claire bit back a groan.

How the hell did I ever think I could fool Mother? Even for a minute?

"I'll be fine," she murmured and then, jerking her head up when some small noise from the hallway beyond the closed door made her back stiffen and her heart begin to pound, she clutched the phone tight in a suddenly sweaty hand. "I have to go," she whispered urgently, turning her face close to her pillow so that she wouldn't be heard.

"I love you, Claire."

"I love you, too, Mum."

"I won't know what to do on Christmas day without you."

Claire sighed. "I'm doing this for us. We'll have Christmas later. I promise. I'll be home on the twenty-sixth, and we'll have Christmas then."

"This little tree you set up looks so..."

The door handle rattled. It moved.

"Goodbye, Mum."

Hand jerking so badly she could barely control it, Claire shut the phone off and thrust it beneath her mattress in the same moment the door swung open and Estella strode in, a steaming tray of covered dishes in her hands.

"Dinner, Madam." The maid stood motionless on the threshold, her thin face pinched and suspicious.

"I..." Claire looked around for a place to set the tray, but she needn't have bothered.

Apparently deciding Claire hadn't been up to any kind of mischief, Estella strode briskly into the room and deposited the tray on a small, round table next to a window. "You were instructed to take a bath," the maid said, turning to glare at her again.

"I'm sorry. I didn't..."

"Mr. Eden is very particular about this. You are to take a bath immediately upon your return from your sessions with him. You are to wash yourself carefully. And you are to wash your hair. Always."

Sessions?

Claire almost laughed. She might have, if the maid hadn't looked so stern. So humorless and even a little ferocious.

"You are to have a bath," she repeated, turning toward the private bathroom adjacent to the enormous bedroom.

"Wait!" Unsteady, clasping the gold satin sheet even tighter around herself to hide that fact that she was completely naked, Claire staggered to her feet.

Wordless, the maid turned and stared at her.

"I just..."

Lord in heaven, what am I supposed to say now? Stomach tightening into a knot of anxiety and despair, Claire resisted an urge to scrub her sweaty palms against the thin fabric that only just managed to conceal her body. *What the hell can I possibly say that anybody will listen to in this out-of-kilter-household?*

Estella waited half in and half out of the bathroom, her expression growing impatient.

"I need to talk to Mr. Eden."

Claire thought she should have been gratified at the maid's expression. At the horrorstruck way the woman's eyebrows seemed to want to shoot off the top of her head and the way her mouth dropped open for a fraction of a second before she closed it again into the old, grim, forbidding line. "I'm sorry, Madam. That isn't done."

"I need to talk to him about our...arrangement."

"Your arrangement?" The maid looked suspicious again. Worse than suspicious. "I believe everything has been made perfectly clear."

"I have questions." Lifting her chin, Claire glared back at the woman.

"Perhaps if you will allow me, I can answer them." Clearly, she'd rattled Estella. Clearly, no one...Claire had no doubt now that there had been others invited to partake in this little *arrangement*...had ever made such a demand.

Estella didn't seem to know quite what to do.

"The arrangement is between Mr. Eden and I," Claire shot back, reveling in her small victory. "I'm afraid that any questions I have are between him and I as well."

"Well, then." Estella hesitated in the doorway, rocking a little on her feet. "I'll draw your bath while you eat. Perhaps after you bathe, if you still feel such a need to make a nuisance of yourself, I can find someone who—"

"I have a better idea." Sitting in one of the chairs placed next to the table, Claire tucked the sheet a little more securely around herself, sarong style, and lifted the silver cover off the largest of the plates.

Salmon. In dill sauce. With new potatoes and asparagus.

Maybe it wasn't going to be completely bad staying here, after all.

"What idea is that, Madam?"

Claire didn't look up. She didn't want to give Estella the satisfaction. But from the corner of her eye she could see the maid's shoulders stiffen, could see her fold her hands in front of herself and make an effort to contain her obvious and mounting outrage.

"Why don't I eat dinner and get dressed while you go downstairs and tell Mr. Eden that I want to talk to him immediately? Tonight?"

The maid's shoulders sagged. "Very well, then. But I can't promise he will agree to this...atrocious request."

At last Claire looked up, her expression one of deliberately sunny innocence. "I can't imagine why he would be think it atrocious," she murmured, "to discuss a business arrangement. After all, he hired me to do a job. And I have questions about how he expects me to do it. If I'm to do my best—"

Abruptly, Estella turned and disappeared into the hallway.

Frowning, Claire watched the open doorway for a few seconds. Then she scrambled to her feet and hurried, as fast as she could considering the awkward slipperiness of her improvised toga and the aching discomfort between her legs, to the enormous armoire that took the place of a closet. It took no more than two minutes to slip into her own blessedly warm and concealing clothes. She'd lost her underwear somewhere, bra and panties both, so she contented herself with jeans and sweatshirt, socks and battered running shoes.

She had no idea what she meant to say to Eli Eden. No idea what she wanted to say. The whole thing had been completely unplanned, the demand purely spur of the moment and instinctive. But the maid didn't have to know that. And neither did Eli Eden.

She would be ready when the maid came back. If he agreed to see her, and there was no guarantee that he would, she wanted to be ready to go downstairs immediately.

And if he didn't agree?

Returning to the bed to hide the cell phone inside the ripped box spring, Claire shrugged a little.

That one was simple.

Whether Eli Eden agreed to see her or whether he didn't, she was going to go downstairs. She was going to look for him.

The salmon hadn't cooled by the time she made her way back to it. Neither had the vegetables or the single cup of tea, inexplicably her very favorite brand, or the plate of hot rolls she discovered beneath another, smaller, silver cover.

It was only fair that he should talk to her, she decided as she stared through the window at swirling and agitated snow. It was the only civil thing for him to do. She'd expected that much courtesy at least, before she'd had to get down to her...duties. And since he hadn't offered it, since it apparently hadn't even occurred to him that she might deserve a little civility and respect, she was determined to force the issue. To drive the point home and make sure he understood where she was coming from. Why she was here and what she expected from this *arrangement*. Satisfied that she'd

made all the plans she could make at the moment, reconciled to having to play the rest of it by ear, Claire sat back in her chair and munched on a roll, staring thoughtfully at the night beyond the window.

The snowflakes were larger now. Heavier. Falling in thick and screening masses, they tapped at the windowpanes like the crazed fingers of someone who wanted desperately to get her attention. To call it to something she should have noticed by now and should have considered, but hadn't. Something strange and...

Leaning closer to the glass, the roll held forgotten halfway to her mouth, Claire realized another house stood close to this one. Strangely close, since the location was so remote and the estate so vast that the two could have been built miles apart without the slightest difficulty.

Snow blurred the outlines of that other house just as it blurred everything, even the golden circle of light from the pole set in the narrow space that separated the structures. But she could see enough to know the other building was much smaller. Much older. Unlike the stone and marble palace in which she sat, it was a frame house that sagged a little along its roofline. Its windows stared back at her, dark and lifeless, and its shutters drooped dispiritedly, its every spindle and rail and bit of decorative woodwork long unpainted and dark with age.

It was an odd set up, all right. An odd thing that once the new house had been finished nothing had been done about razing the old.

Her forehead all the way against the icy window, Claire frowned.

There was an answer here somewhere. To a question she hadn't asked, hadn't even been aware she should be asking.

Chapter Four

SEATED NEXT TO THE WINDOW IN THE SMALL DINING ROOM OF HIS PRIVATE QUARTERS ON the first floor, Eli turned his head at the sound of a sharp knock on the door.

He'd been drinking his brandy. Basking in the glow of the evening he'd just spent with this latest woman. He'd been just about to admit to himself that he'd made a good choice this time. One of the best choices in a lifetime that only recently had seemed more prone to exceedingly bad and disastrous choices.

Another tap at the door and he frowned, ready to speak harshly. The staff knew better than to interrupt him at times like this. They knew he expected to be left alone for the short time he would be at peace with himself and the world following one of his encounters with the women.

They'd been instructed never to do such a thing except in the most extreme of emergencies.

His back stiffened and his voice was hoarse when he called out, torn between irritation at the intrusion and a cold, stark, unreasonable fear at the possibility he might be about to learn something *had* happened.

"Come."

The door swung open and Estella walked in. Planting her feet deliberately, nearly stomping, she looked even more morose than usual and far more grim and disapproving. Obviously something had outraged her. And that sent another little dart of impatient annoyance through him.

"Well?" he demanded, surprised that she of all people would dare to intrude. Estella's emergencies were not any concern of his. They didn't qualify as extreme at the worst of times, since she had charge of the house and had full authority to deal with whatever might arise. But even so, something about the way she… "Don't you look like a thundercloud."

Estella stopped a dozen feet away. Openly afraid of him.

Most of his employees feared him to some degree or another.

It had never annoyed him before, but it sure as hell annoyed him now.

"Well, speak up!" he barked, reaching for the brandy bottle on the table next to his chair. "What is it? A burned roast? A misplaced telephone bill? What's so damned important that you felt you had the need to—"

"It's her, Sir." The housekeeper folded her hands tight against the front of her dark blue sweater.

"Her?"

She nodded once, jerkily. "Your…the woman."

"Don't tell me. She's left." The idea sent a pang through him. A vague yet sharp one. He'd enjoyed her so. Enjoyed her like he'd never enjoyed any of the women before. Already he'd been planning, considering. Wondering which of his favorite fantasies he should enact next. Wondering which would take the best advantage of her and all of her undeniably astonishing talents.

If she leaves me now…

"You know she can't leave, Sir. You know she has no way to leave this place without your knowledge and approval."

"Yes." Eli relaxed back against the cushions of the chair, straightening his tired back a little so it wouldn't ache so horribly. *How the hell could I forget such a simple thing? That we're miles from anywhere, and the woman is at my complete mercy?*

Shit. He must be worse off than he'd thought. A hell of a lot more rattled than he'd believed.

"So what's the problem, Estella?"

"Well, for one thing, she didn't bathe."

Frowning, Eli felt impatience rise up again. "Damn it to hell. Do you mean to tell me you interrupted my evening…my quiet time…to complain because some little bitch wouldn't get into a *bathtub*?"

He had to give Estella credit. She was afraid. He saw it flicker in her eyes. Most of his other employees, his female employees, would have run for the door by now. They'd have been looking for a place to hide, trying to think of a way to deflect the annoyance he never bothered to contain. But the housekeeper stood her ground. Chin high, her hands and shoulders held rigidly under control, she betrayed her fear only through that fleeting look in her eyes.

"It's not only the bath," she said quietly.

"What else?"

"She wants to see you."

Eli felt his heart drop to the floor. Felt it plummet like a lead brick released from the top of a hundred-story building.

"She insists upon it immediately. Tonight. I don't believe she's going to take no for an answer, Sir."

For a second, Eli thought he was going to crush the snifter of brandy between his suddenly quaking hands.

"What's this about?" he asked and lifted the snifter, his first but most definitely not his last of the evening, to his lips.

"I believe it's about the terms of her employment. I believe she's going to try to weasel out of your agreement."

Eli's eyebrows lifted. "Impossible. Only I can break the agreement. She knew that before she came here. She has no say in the matter now, and she—
"

"I don't believe she cares, Sir. I don't believe any of that matters to her."

No. Swirling the bright gold liquid around in his glass, astonished that he hadn't gulped it straight down by now, hadn't finished the three or four he would have normally consumed by this time on any given evening, Eli swallowed a sigh. "And she won't tell you what she wants?"

"She won't tell me anything, Sir. I've only deduced that's what she wants, but for all I know—"

"Very well, then." His words surprised him a little. *Why the hell am I agreeing to this? Why the hell am IU thinking it's a good, or even an intelligent one, to agree to this? And why the hell, since I really think it's the sheerest, most criminal kind of insanity, am I going to go ahead with it?* "Bring her to me." Tilting his head a little, he turned his face to the window. Ignoring his reflection in the polished pane, the reflection he hated and refused to acknowledge except on the rare occasions when the truth forced itself upon him in ways he couldn't deny, he peered beyond it. Peered at the wide sweep of meadow at the front of the house. "But give me ten minutes. No, make it fifteen."

"And should I…"

Lifting the brandy again, he didn't look at the housekeeper. "Should you what?"

"Should I prepare her, Sir? Is there any special thing you might…"

"How is she dressed right now?"

"I don't believe she's dressed at all."

Eli almost chuckled. "That sounds interesting. No, Estella. Don't do anything special. Just bring her to me the way she is."

Mistake. Something screeched inside his head in the same second that he commanded it to shut up and leave him alone. *Big, big mistake!*

Hell. He was starting to think this whole plan, this whole ill conceived and misbegotten plan with this particular woman on this particular Christmas week, might in reality have been the biggest mistake of them all. But he was going to go through with it.

Turning back to the window as the housekeeper left the room and shut the door quietly behind herself, he scowled again.

He was going to do it because life had ceased to be interesting a long, long time ago. Had ceased to be anything but a dreary monotony on that afternoon, right out there beyond the reach of the most distant of the security lights...

Covered with snow, the meadow sloped down through the clearing night air toward the dark band of woods that lay nearly invisible at its perimeter.

That damned field. Eli could close his eyes or, given the right amount of brandy and the correct hour of the night, keep them open and see his life being lived out right there in that field. He could watch and relive at his leisure and occasionally his extreme peril the best of his memories. And the worst of his nightmares.

I should be getting ready.

The woman would be here in fifteen minutes or less than that now. And he had a lot to do to be ready for her. Halfheartedly, he set his brandy on the table.

So many things to do. And still his gaze seemed riveted on the snowy meadow and his hands gripped the arms of the chair, knuckles white, fingers tense and already aching with the strain of fighting to survive a winter that had invaded his soul as surely as it had swept across his meadow.

Eli disliked winter. Disliked it intensely. Even at twenty-nine, winter caused a deep down aching inside him that would never leave...a throbbing and bone crushing ache that only the oblivion of his treasured brandy had any real power to relieve. And even then the pain could only be eradicated completely when he'd rendered himself stuporous with drink.

Winter was hard on him. Much more so than any other season.

He preferred the summertime when the meadow lay green and undulating. Summertime meant baseball, and that was the one thing he'd always loved. The one thing he'd always depended upon to carry him through the worst of times and even to shield him in some incalculable way from them. Summertime and baseball. He smiled. For a moment he had a vision of the way life was in summers long past, when he'd had nothing better to do than play an impromptu game with friends. A vision of running free and easy across soft green grass. Of reaching up, his arm outstretched and his body taut and lithe as he moved easily and without hesitation. A vision of the prize, the baseball, dropping neatly into his glove and the following swing...the long, hard lob that would send it to the base sure and sweet and true, eliminating the opposing player who'd never had a chance.

Eli reached for the snifter. Frowning. His father had never approved of baseball. He'd called it a *waste of time*. Thinking himself something of a country squire though he'd never had the kind of money he'd needed to really pull it off...never had much beyond two nickels to rub together until Eli found his niche in the software industry and hauled in more nickels than any one man could ever rub together...Howard Eden had declared fox-hunting a more appropriate sport for his son and only child.

This time when Eli's hand met the snifter, he grabbed it up and took a long, deep swig of the liquid golden courage inside.

Fox-hunting.

Horses.

He wanted to spit. Almost did.

As much as he'd loved baseball, he'd detested the horses. Those enormous, ill-tempered brutes his father had insisted he learn to ride and ride well. How he'd detested the long afternoons he'd sat for hour upon hour in the saddle under the old man's critical eye, his back ramrod straight and his riding crop held at just the right angle. Those long afternoons when summertime was running out, and with it, his chances to play baseball.

Then there'd been the pink jacket.

Eli took another gulp of brandy, draining the snifter dry.

Above everything else he'd detested that horrific thing. He'd felt like a fool wearing it, when he'd understood as the old man never could that wearing it flew in the face of all etiquette. That he didn't deserve the privilege of wearing the pink jacket because he hadn't *earned* the privilege.

Eli reached for the bottle.

He'd hated his old man. Almost as much as he hated himself for letting himself be pushed around. But he had no time for hatred now. No time for brandy, or wallowing in self pity. The woman was coming to him for reasons he couldn't imagine. She was on her way and he needed to be ready.

Grimacing, he scowled at the empty snifter and poured another stiff shot anyway.

The woman can damned well wait until I'm ready for her.

Estella wouldn't let her come into this room, wouldn't let her come anywhere near this room, until he was damned good and ready. And right now...

His hand left the arm of the chair and gravitated to his cock that had begun to stir restlessly beneath the black tuxedo pants he hadn't bothered to change.

Some of his best enjoyment...his *true* enjoyment...happened right here. On nights just like this, when he'd lock himself into his private world where no one could intrude without his permission. When the door was shut and the outside world only a dim and distant memory. When no one could see him and he could feel free to be himself.

Beneath his fingers and the layers of fabric, his cock leaped. It hardened nicely, growing ready as the first soft, immediate stirrings of arousal shimmered through it.

The woman can wait, all right.

While I think about her. While I consider her.

Freeing his cock from the confines of slacks grown suddenly and perilously too tight, he ran his fingers expertly along its expectant length, then wrapped his hand around it and settled back more comfortably into his chair, thinking again about the woman. About her hair. How it would smell. How it would curl, maybe, in soft and fragile ringlets around her face. He wondered about the shape of her face and the color of the eyes he'd never seen because he'd been just too goddamned chicken shit to let himself see. He wondered what look would come into those eyes when she saw him...*really* saw him as he was...for the first time.

The woman would be coming to him soon.

And he'd have to plan something for her.

Not now, not in these few minutes he had to work up his courage and get ready to face her, but later.

Already he could imagine her naked, her breasts catching the soft light from golden fixtures, poised maybe on a satin sheet or on a slab of dark marble. Or maybe somewhere else. He hadn't quite decided.

For now he would go along with her insane and foolish need to talk to him. But in return, he'd demand something extra special. Something new and never before tried, perhaps.

Something delicious.

His hand moved faster along his cock, rubbing it until the old familiar heat and the accompanying weakness crept over him. Tender flesh, expertly stroked. He sighed. Smiled at his reflection in the window. Shifted a little, nudging his legs apart a little more with the hand that never ceased its slow and rhythmic motion.

His balls felt heavy. Uncommonly heavy, as they hadn't felt in the longest time. In almost as long as he could remember. They'd begun to send out the first warning shivers in response to his careful stimulation, and he set the unfinished brandy down at last. He didn't think he would need the rest of it. Not tonight. Devoting both hands to himself, he lifted his balls with one, marveling briefly at their full weight before he began to massage them. His sack was already full. And even so it continued to swell with every second that passed. Not yet at that delightful, aching stage where it cried out for release, it was nevertheless coming close. Perilously close.

His other hand continued with his cock. Stroking vigorously, he urged it ever closer to frenzy before he backed off to trace insidious patterns with fingertips that barely made contact.

It would be an interesting experiment, seeing which excited him more. His own attentions to himself or the woman's attentions to him.

In the end, he thought it had to be a dead heat.

An even match.

No fox bagged, no success to brag about.

Just the steady building and the steady stoking of the fire he'd kindled within. Staring out at the snow-clotted night, Eli smiled again.

For now it was the woman's turn. She'd made her demand and he would honor it. He would listen patiently to her, as patiently as he could and with as much interest, to whatever she had to say. And then it would be his turn. Then he would summon her. He would wait a little while...until midnight, perhaps, when she would believe herself safe for the night in the enormous bed with its carved cherub headboard. He would wait until midnight, and then he would send Estella to prepare her for him.

Releasing his grip on his cock, he tucked it away again, almost regretfully and turned away from the window.

He would have to wait. *Until midnight.*

Chapter Five

He sat sideways on a loveseat the color of new butter, his long legs stretched out and crossed indolently at the ankles. He still wore his evening clothes, at least partially. He'd discarded his top hat and jacket and loosened his cuffs, turning them back to expose strong wrists and a rich sprinkling of dark brown hair on muscular forearms.

Claire had to forcibly restrain herself from licking her lips.

All men looked good in evening clothes. But this one…

She'd entered the room determined to hate him, but he looked good enough to drive a woman to drink. His hair shone a richer and deeper chestnut than it had before, under cover of night. Softly wavy and shoved back carelessly, it drooped across a wide and smooth forehead to throw the slightest, almost imperceptible shadow across eyes that were dark brown, too, and rich…as deep and smooth as melted chocolate. He could easily be the most handsome, the most absolutely delectable and desirable man she'd ever seen. If only he would smile.

But he didn't. Glaring at her across the distance that separated his loveseat and the door, he looked as mean spirited, as grim and unfriendly, as he'd ever looked in the sleigh when he'd seemed intent upon humiliating her.

This time, Claire did lick her lips. Casting a furtive glance at the glass he held in one large hand, she wished she could have a fortifying sip…just a tiny one…of whatever liquor it held.

"Well?" he said after a minute or two, when she still hadn't gathered her courage to speak. "You were damned insistent you had to talk to me. You made such a fuss that…"

Claire felt her back stiffen in automatic reaction. Instinctive reaction. She'd never liked being accused of doing what she hadn't done. And even if the stiffening wasn't a good sign…was, in fact, a very, very *bad* sign considering the kind of situation she'd gotten herself into…she couldn't help herself. No more than she could help the defensive words that popped out of her mouth before she could even think about holding them back. "I did no such thing."

The mean look left his face in a rush. "Excuse me?"

The dirt speaks. That was what his new expression said, and Claire didn't much like that either.

"I said I did no such thing," she declared, striding into the room with a show of unflappable confidence that had nothing to do with the soft and queasy, shivery melting she felt inside.

I made love to this man. Well, okay, maybe she'd be stretching it by calling it making love. Because it hadn't been love. Not in any traditional or generally accepted sense. But she'd had sex with him and not so long ago either. Pretty wild and uninhibited sex as she recalled. It had left her shivering outside now as well as inside.

She'd started the evening determined to hate Eli Eden for everything he was, everything he stood for and especially for all the lousy ways he'd treated her and taken advantage of her. She thought she genuinely did still hate him for the terrible choice he'd forced upon her…for the offer he'd made when he'd known she was at the end of her rope…terrified, desperate, and hardly able to refuse.

Fifty thousand dollars.

She'd once heard that everyone had her price. And now she guessed she knew hers. Fifty thousand. It wasn't much, not in the grand scheme of things. But it was a vast and unimaginable fortune to her. It was enough to have turned her head and made her cast aside every last one of the principles her mother and the Sunday school and all of her teachers had tried so hard to instill in her. Because fifty thousand would let her slide a little longer. It would let her hope a little more that one of these days one of the ads she answered in her unending quest for a job to replace the one she'd lost would actually pay off, and someone would hire her to do legitimate work in a legitimate way.

Eli Eden was watching her with luscious, deep-set eyes that hinted maybe he wasn't everything he appeared to be on the surface either. That besides being handsome enough to die for and rich enough to buy whatever…whoever…he wanted, that besides being as smart and as successful and as savvy as the few interviews he allowed the business journals said, there was something else about him.

It glimmered in his eyes right now. A look that said he'd had very few choices himself. That said he'd been backed into his own kind of corner and was busy fighting his way out right now. Busy fighting for something he tried to conceal, but which should be obvious if she would only try to see. Try to understand.

Very suddenly, Claire felt a connection with him. One that went beyond what he'd paid her...or would pay her at the end of the week. And damn it, a connection was the last thing she'd wanted to feel. A connection would ruin everything.

"I feel...confused," she murmured uneasily, wrapping her arms tightly around herself as she advanced a few more halting steps into the room.

Eli didn't move except for the eyebrows he lifted another notch. "It's immaterial to me how you feel," he grated, then paused to take a slow sip of the liquor. "And as for being confused..."

Licking her lips again, Claire heard a low, strange buzzing begin at the back of her head. A sound not unlike some fire alarms she'd heard inside buildings as she'd passed them on the street, a low and muted warning. Muffled, but nonetheless important to heed.

She wanted to kiss him, and the realization almost sent her to her knees on the gleaming, uncarpeted floor.

She wanted to kiss Eli Eden for no good reason that she could name. Wanted to lick the sweet-sharp residue of whatever he'd been drinking off his lips, wanted to know what he would taste like once that residue was gone. Wanted to know if the amber liquid in the glass could be half, or even a quarter, as intoxicating as she suspected the man himself would be.

She almost turned. Almost ran. But then he spoke again and she forgot all about running. All about kissing, or intoxication, or anything else.

"We had a deal, Miss..."

How the blazes can he not even know my name?

"Claire," she snapped. "Claire Hardistique. Do you always force-fuck women without knowing their names?"

His eyebrows lifted again, for just a moment. "Touché," he said, holding his glass out to her in mock salute. "But no one has force-fucked anyone here. Not tonight and not any other night. You've been free to say no any time you wanted, Miss...Claire."

Is it my imagination, or did his gaze just flicker a little? Did he just show more than a little interest in my lips? Is it my imagination, or could this man be thinking about kissing me too?

Impatient, she shook off the thought.

"The fact is, Claire, I only brought you to the sleigh. What you did after that was your business. You were free to refuse anything I suggested. You were—"

"You did a little more than suggest!"

He shrugged again, eyes glittering as he continued to watch her. "You fucked me," he said, and her heart sank because that was one fact she couldn't argue...one distinct and irrefutable fact.

He had ordered her to do what she had done. But he had never actually forced her. Instinct told her he never would have. So whatever had happened in that sleigh, whatever she had done or not done...

Her face flooded with sudden heat as the memory came back to her. Of herself, bare breasts exposed above the torturous satin skimpiness of the corset she'd *agreed* to wear, her body crouched over his, her legs spread wide as she pumped herself up and down, up and down. As she plunged herself onto his shaft rather than the other way around.

It all came back to her in hot and horrid detail, and she wanted to die. Just literally die. Or at the very least, to find someplace to hide. Someplace dark and warm and secure, where she'd never be found again. Never have to come out until the blackest of nights, when she could just slink away to...

"So." Eli moved at last, a little awkwardly as he turned and set his glass, empty now, on a sturdy, inlaid table next to the loveseat. "Now that you understand that no one is forcing you to do anything or forcing you to stay, I hope you'll be good enough to understand that I value my privacy. Especially after such a long and exhausting evening."

Claire's breath came in short, hot gasps. So *he'd* had a long evening, had he? Hot words of retort and disgust sputtered on her lips. "I don't understand why it's necessary to play games," she spat. "I understand that you want sex. That for some reason you feel you have to buy it rather than going out and finding it honestly." She ignored the sudden hurt and lost, even terrified, look that flashed across his face for half a second. "I guess maybe I don't understand that after all. But I'm willing to live with it because I'm in a corner myself right now. And as much as I'd have liked to tell you to just go to hell with your stupid fifty thousand, I couldn't afford to do that. So...look. I really don't understand why I have to wear your degrading costumes and perform your degrading..."

"As I said before. We had a deal. A legitimate business deal. One we both entered willingly, with the full understanding that you were to indulge my fantasies for one week in exchange for..."

"Christmas week!"

HE SHRUGGED AGAIN. "THAT isn't my problem. I don't care for Christmas. I don't observe it and frankly, I didn't even think about it." Something twitched inside him when he told the lie. Something old and denied and so deliberately forgotten that it surprised him to find it still alive inside himself. *Not care about Christmas?* How the hell could he say that and keep a straight face? A memory floated to the surface. Just one quick and fleeting memory of Christmas in the old house. His father's house that still stood right beneath the eaves of this marble monstrosity because when it came right down to it, he hadn't had the heart, or maybe the guts, to tear the place down. He remembered the feeling in his heart, the soft and sweet sigh of recognition when he'd opened that one box on that one long ago Christmas morning and lifted out the Louisville Slugger…

If winter was the hardest season for him, then Christmas was always the hardest day. The pain always seeped closest to the surface then. Sometimes it came all the way to the surface, if he didn't do something to keep himself occupied. Like bring a woman…one of his paid women…into the house to indulge him and satisfy him and keep him from thinking too much. Remembering too much.

"You're free to leave whenever you want, Claire." *Damn it to hell. Why'd the woman have to go and tell me her name, anyway? Why the hell did I let her…why the hell did I listen when she did?*

By now he could to know that knowing her name would only complicate things. Would only…

"I'll be more than happy to call the car for you. All you have to do is say the word." *And I'll be more than happy to get rid of you if you're going to make a nuisance of yourself, too.*

Claire paused, staring back at him, her lower lip caught between her teeth, indecision plain in every line of her.

Looking at her mouth, he decided he loved it.

Loved the soft and full, pouting shape of it.

Loved the way it promised all sorts of delights he would never dare sample.

He knew it had been a mistake to look at her face to face without the mask he always required. Because the mask hadn't ever been for the woman's protection or punishment as much as for his own. It was there to protect his heart. Because no man could fall in love with what wasn't real, what was only an anonymous body doing anonymous, if highly incendiary and erotic things.

No man could love a woman who had no face, no eyes, no way to express her emotions or her spirit.

He'd known that for a long time. For all of five years. So why the hell had he let this woman, Claire, ruin it by coming here in her snug-fitting faded jeans and her not-quite-baggy Steelers sweatshirt, her short brown hair mussed as if it had been carelessly combed? Why the hell had he let himself look into that strong-featured face, devoid of makeup and shining fresh and clean as a schoolgirl's?

Because I'm a fool. A helpless, hopeless sap of a fool who'd never given up believing…not really…that he stood as much chance of loving and being loved as any other poor and defenseless sucker on the planet.

"Should I call the car?" He reached for the cell phone in the jacket he'd thrown across the back of the loveseat. *Don't tell me to call the car,* his heart begged, astonishing the shit out of him. *Don't show me how beautiful you are, how really gorgeous and strong and honorable, and then ask me to call for the car to send you away. Please don't!*

Biting her lip again, Claire twisted her hands together until it seemed like the fingers must surely snap off. "I'm going to have to wear more costumes?" she asked finally, staring at him.

Without hesitation, Eli nodded. *It's the only way.*

"But you will pay me when the week is out?"

He frowned. "Is the money that important to you?"

She didn't answer. He knew she wasn't going to answer, but that was okay.

He'd already had the answer to that one quite a while ago.

Of course, the money was important. She wasn't a hooker. Wasn't even slightly loose, definitely wasn't what his mom would have called a slut or a tramp. She was good. Decent. Trapped.

Above all, trapped.

He'd known all of that from the start. From the minute he'd been looking over some old records from one of the companies he owned and spotted her name on a roster of employees he'd had laid off when he'd decided the company wasn't making enough money for him. The name had jumped right out at him, its vague Frenchness just slightly provocative, its slight rowdiness more than a little promising. His cock had leaped to attention, and he'd checked a little farther. Had learned she was twenty-six, just about the perfect age for his tastes. More importantly, she was single, and she hadn't found another job. Not even after a search so prolonged that she'd already had to move once, from an inexpensive apartment in a good neighborhood into a dirt-cheap efficiency in a not-so-good one. He'd instructed his representative to make the offer without knowing if she would accept. Without knowing if she would come to him, or exactly when she would come. He hadn't even known which one she would be when and if she did come. Because he never knew specifics. Like names. When the women arrived, he never wanted to know.

The way he knew now.

The way she'd made him know.

"Are you staying?" he asked, resenting her for that. "Or going?"

"I'll—"

"More importantly, if you do stay, will you agree to the terms and conditions of the deal? All of the terms and conditions?" *Good.* He breathed a sigh of relief. *We're back to business now. Strictly business.* And he meant to keep it that way from now on. Meant to make sure she kept to her room when her services were not required. And for damned certain, he meant to refuse ever to see her again unless she'd been properly prepared, properly masked and made anonymous.

And if I really think any piece of satin is going to conceal what she'd already revealed, I'm an even bigger fool than I thought.

What he should do, and do right now, was fire her ass. Fire her on the spot and...

"I want you to stay." Christ almighty! Was that him saying that? Was that him holding out a hand that wasn't quite steady, reaching for her the way he'd never...at least not in recent memory...reached for anyone? *Christ almighty.*

Luckily, she didn't take his hand. She didn't come near him.

She saved him that humiliation, and he loved her for it.

No, he quickly amended, feeling the heat of confusion rise in his face as he dropped his hand back to his lap. *Gotta respect her for that.* There was a difference between love and respect. And that was all he was ever going to do. Respect her.

"Do we have a deal?"

She hesitated for a fraction of a second longer. "We have a deal," she said, no longer looking at him, her face flushed the same deep red he felt creeping into his.

"Fine. Then if that's all..." He wanted to reach for the brandy bottle he'd hidden behind the loveseat. He could hear it calling to him right now, hear it demanding he give it a little more undivided attention. But he wouldn't do that. Not in front of Claire or anyone. He felt sure the household staff knew how much he drank and when he drank it. After all, somebody had to buy the stuff for him. But they knew it was none of their business to notice, none of their business to notice a lot of things. Unlike Claire, who noticed everything and seemed to have no compunction about commenting on what she'd noticed.

That should be a warning to him. That he should be doubly careful...triply careful...in his dealings with her. He should do everything humanly possible to make sure she didn't notice too much. Didn't notice the wrong things.

I should fire her ass.

She'd started to back toward the door, and he'd actually started to breathe a sigh of relief. But then she stopped again. Her expression turned questioning and her too delectable lips opened halfway, ready to ask some other question. Something he knew he wasn't going to want to answer. Wasn't going to be *able* to answer, because it was going to get him into all the trouble he'd sought to avoid by bringing completely anonymous women to the house in the first place.

"What?" he barked, doing his damnedest to sound fearsome and rude.

"I was wondering—"

"If you're going to start in about the costumes again, my mind's made up."

"No." She turned even redder. "It's about the house."

"What's wrong with my house?"

"Nothing. Well, okay. It's cold, and it's heartless. And did you ever hear of Christmas decorations? Maybe a little bit of tinsel or an evergreen bough or two?"

"Christmas." He wanted to spit. "I don't believe in it."

Backing off another step, Claire studied him for a second. "Well, I guess that's none of my business. And that wasn't what I wanted to ask you anyway."

"Oh, really?" He just kept growing more and more belligerent, more and more defensive. And there didn't seem to be a damned thing he could do about it. "What, then?"

"I didn't mean this house. I meant the...other one. You know, the one right outside my window? The one that just about touches this one? I was wondering—"

"You were right, Claire. That house is none of your business." *Damn. I should have had the old white elephant torn down. Years ago. Right after I finished building this one.* And he *would* have it torn down. The minute the snow cleared in the springtime. He made the vow to himself right then and there, and he damned well meant to keep it. "Now, if there's anything else—"

"No." She'd reached the door. "There's nothing."

"Fine. And Claire..."

She turned back just as she'd been about to leave. "What?"

"Stay in your room whenever you're not with me."

She nodded again in that tiny, not-quite-subservient way that saddened him as much as it sent roaring, warning thunderbolts of alarm all through him.

She'd no more stay confined to that room than the cow would really jump over the moon.

He should fire her. Get her the hell out of here.

Several long and silent minutes after she'd left him and shut the door quietly in her wake, he moved. Finally. Slowly. Feeling every last damned one of the snowflakes in his too-old-much-too-soon bones and joints, he leaned over a little, ignoring the sharp and stabbing pain in his back and reached for the house phone he kept tucked out of sight behind the tailored skirt of the yellow loveseat.

He dialed three digits and waited for the other end to pick up.

"Yes?" Estella said. He had no idea if she'd been asleep or not. That was of no importance to him, and she knew it. She knew the score, knew he could call at any time and knew she was expected to be there whenever he did.

"Get her ready for me."

Chapter Six

HER GOWN WAS PINK. A DEEP AND DUSKY SHADE OF RASPBERRY PINK, THOUGH IT really wasn't a gown at all, just a variation of the white getup she'd worn earlier in the sleigh.

Hesitating a dozen feet from the closed, carved double doors, Claire glanced at herself in a mirror mounted on the wall across from them.

What a mistake, she thought, and felt herself blush the same robustly furious pink as her costume.

It was another corset...another too-brief device of torture that constricted her waist painfully and left her breasts firmly thrust out, absolutely bare and just begging to be handled. It left everything beneath her navel exposed, too, beneath its steel reinforced scrap of lace.

She had no cape this time, no gloves or high-heeled boots in which she could barely stand, much less walk. Now her hands were bare, her wrists circled by twin, shimmering bracelets that probably were, considering who owned them, diamonds worth more than she would earn for her entire week of misery. Her feet, clad in soft and flexible raspberry-bright slippers, made no sound as she strode forward again as boldly as she could, her shoulders thrown back so that her exposed breasts thrust themselves forward even more forcefully. It wasn't a gown, yet it was in a way, because the dark pink corset featured a train, yards and yards of foaming, floating pink and silver lace that skimmed the floor behind her, a full six feet in length. And of course she wore the mask. Deep pink satin this time, covering her face as completely as she wished she could cover her body.

Once again, she found herself all dressed up and ready to take part in something in which she was supposed to have no part, in which she was meant to be nothing more than an object to be used for Eli Eden's exclusive gratification. But this time, to her complete and utter surprise, she was actually looking forward to it. Was that statement too strong?

Don't try to deny it, she told herself sharply, reaching with a strangely unsteady hand for the door handle. *You got your pleasure out of that last little episode. You didn't want to, but you did. Fifty thousand dollars or no, you wouldn't still be here, dressed this god-awful way at this god-awful hour of the night if you hadn't.*

Pleasure. From Eli Eden's little fantasy. No matter how she tried to tell herself...and she did try...that it had all been for her mother, so her mother would have a place to live and enough to eat for at least a little while longer, she knew that was only the half baked voice of reason kicking in. Trying to keep her initial outrage alive at the same time it tried to justify what still seemed vaguely wrong to her, no matter how much unexpected pleasure it had started to give.

Well, whatever the voice was trying to do, it wasn't working.

As nervous as she'd been the first time, she felt more nervous now. Because she had some idea what was in store for her. And she *was* looking forward to it. Was already tingling between her legs and beginning to moisten in anticipation of whatever dream scene he'd cooked up in his delightfully twisted and downright seductive imagination.

Breathing hard, her body fighting the constriction of the corset, Claire yanked her hand back from the handle as if the touch of it had burned her skin black. Pressing the palms of both hands tight against the outsides of her thighs in an attempt to blot their sudden moisture against her pink and silver lace stockings, she hesitated.

"Go in," Estella hissed at her back and gave her a little shove.

Seizing the handle, Claire gave it a sharp turn. The door swung open, and she saw him.

He sat straight ahead in a carved chair at the head of a long, long dining table. Black and polished wood gleamed with ruby highlights in the dim glow of a single chandelier, an immensely long surface upon which, she guessed, she was expected to lie.

He didn't frown. Didn't smile. He merely held out a hand as he had before, commanding her to come to him.

He isn't calling me any insulting names this time either, she realized through the strange and sultry swimming inside her head. Once again she appreciated the mask. Appreciated the way it hid the slow burn of embarrassment mixed with something that must very closely resemble anticipation that she felt slithering across her face.

Obeying his command, she stepped forward with the maid trailing along silently behind her to keep tabs on the train and make sure it went where it was supposed to go. Which, Claire wondered more nervously with every step she took forward, was...where?

Slowly, she made her way to the end of the table. Stopping next to the chair where he sat motionless, she stared down into darkly deep eyes that looked as unaccountably expectant as her jittering and titillated heart.

"The clothes," he said in a quiet, deep voice devoid of the snarling note she'd endured at their first meeting. "Are they to your liking?"

The question, the way in which it he asked it and the inexplicable look that swept through his eyes as he did, took Claire's breath away. For a moment, though she'd loathed everything about them...the color, the fit, and most of all, what they stood for...she nodded mutely. Giving her approval and her consent. Then, remembering the honesty he'd allowed when he'd agreed to meet her in his private quarters, she opened her mouth to tell him no, that they didn't meet her approval. They weren't what she preferred or anything she intended to tolerate again after tonight.

She was thoroughly surprised to hear herself breathe "Yes, Sir," in a shaky and acquiescent little voice.

What the hell was I thinking? She screamed silently at herself, almost jerking from the shock of hearing what she'd said. *What the hell got into me all of a sudden?*

"Good." Smiling, his eyes still gleaming in that inexplicable way, Eli patted the table in the bare space between an array of plates spread out before him.

"Sir?" She stood absolutely still, not understanding. Or maybe she didn't want to understand, since instinct kept insisting she did and impulse kept singing at her to do it. Just *do it* and see what happened next.

Impatience flickered in his expression. "Up you go," he said and patted the table again, harder.

"Up?"

Slowly, he nodded, and Claire's heart began to jerk with true, unbridled wildness inside her chest. Attracted by that gleam in his eyes, not the least terrified by the unknown it represented even when she told herself she should be absolutely and utterly terrified, she took a halting step or two toward the table.

Eli still didn't move. Not a muscle. He simply watched her with incalculable, unreadable eyes.

Shivering, Claire brushed her train aside and swung herself up onto red-highlighted wood that matched her gown as perfectly as if the silken lace had been chosen especially to compliment it and shimmer against it.

Rather than harden her heart against him as she might have expected, the idea only made it melt more. Made her legs quiver and made it difficult to do as he demanded…take her place on the table, her posture strangely demure in comparison to her costume, her knees folded before her and pressed tightly together to hide what she knew he would all too soon insist she reveal.

The gleaming wood—mahogany?—felt cold beneath her bare flesh. Energizingly cold. Behind her, Estella arranged her train, straightening it so that it lay in foamy mounds and heaps along the table's length. A backdrop for Claire. A backdrop that would highlight her and make her seem to sparkle in the same way the color and texture of the wood worked perfectly with the color and texture of the lace.

Eli waited a moment, then flicked his hand. Only once. But Estella took the cue and retreated. Claire heard the door click shut softly at the far side of the room and then, for another very long moment, nothing happened. She continued to sit, demure and yet anything but demure with her knees clenched tight against her bare and suddenly eager breasts, her arms crossed and her hands pressed against erect nipples, hiding them from him. Hiding the true extent of their eagerness. Hiding everything and, she feared, hiding nothing at all.

Then Eli touched her. He pressed the flat of his hand against the outside of her thigh, and a soft sizzle of something electric shot through her. Something she couldn't deny, didn't want to deny because it was almost audible in the eager and expectant silence that had sprung up between them. The touch of his flesh burned the place where it met hers above the sheer lace of glittering stockings.

"Like this," he said, grasping her ankles and urging her legs to part. Placing one at the very edge of the table on either side of him, he pushed gently at her knees to spread them wide. He urged her to move toward him until she sat at the very end of the table, almost off its edge with her legs pulled up high and tight against her sides and her most intimate parts displayed for him, within his easy reach. Now she understood why she'd been given soft slippers to wear instead of high heels.

The slippers allowed her to grip. Allowed her to curl her toes around the beveled edge of the shiny and slightly slippery wood. Allowed her to steady herself for…

"Feed me," Eli murmured, and when he lifted his chin to gaze up at her, his face remained completely calm. Completely dispassionate, even though his eyes had begun to burn.

"What?" Dazed, shivering uncontrollably, Claire could only stare back at him, mesmerized. Thanks to the angle at which she sat in front of and slightly above him, she had a clear view of his face this time through the narrow eye slits of her mask.

"Feed me," he said again, lifting a hand to nudge a plate of strawberries centered with a small cup of clear and fizzy liquid closer to her hand. Then he dropped his hand back to his lap and made no other move except to part his lips slightly, tantalizingly. Just enough to reveal strong white teeth that had also parted in anticipation. Just enough to soften the mouth that only hours before had seemed hard, set, and incapable of ever softening.

In the dim gleam of light, eyes closed, lips parted and expression expectant, Eli Eden was the most beautiful, the most incredibly, desirably, unspeakably handsome man Claire had ever seen. Her insides shook with a silent, sensuous earthquake as she murmured, so softly she almost wondered if he would hear, "You want me to..."

He nodded. That was all.

Her insides convulsed. Her hand, too, as she picked up a strawberry and dipped it into the liquid. Champagne, she realized, even as she offered it to him.

Eli didn't move. It was up to her to lean forward the slightest bit, gripping hard with her toes to keep herself from toppling straight forward into his lap and onto his hands that seemed almost to anticipate and wait for just such an occurrence.

Her face burned beneath the protective covering of satin. He sat so close. So tantalizingly close. Her exposed flesh had begun to moisten in earnest. It had begun to hum, as if it wanted nothing more than for him to touch her and caress her.

Eli opened his mouth a little wider, seeming to sense her hand as it moved toward him.

Trembling so badly that she could barely control the movement, Claire placed the strawberry between his lips. But when she tried to withdraw without touching him in any way, he caught her fingers between his teeth. Suddenly, she had no desire to withdraw. Fascinated, she wanted only to watch those delicious, perfectly formed and undeniably kissable lips surround her fingers and suck gently, drawing them deeper into the incredible, wet and steaming depths of his mouth.

He moved his tongue across her fingertips, pressing them down hard on the berry until she felt a sudden release of the juice he'd crushed from it. Inside herself, Claire shuddered and cried out. Even though she wasn't supposed to cry out, she couldn't help herself when a sudden and unbelievable tide of heat and anguish and mounting need rocketed through her.

A strawberry?

How the devil could a simple strawberry, even one crushed beneath a man's tongue, be such an explicitly sexual and unnervingly arousing experience?

Claire had no idea. But it was. Had been. There was nothing in the world now except the smooth and unbelievably soft lips that held her fingers, nothing except glittering eyes that had opened again to gaze straight up at hers, seeming suddenly desperate to see hers. Nothing but the tongue stroking her fingers and cleansing them of the last remnants of the berry he'd swallowed.

She shuddered, and Eli released her fingers.

"More," he whispered, and nodded toward the plate.

The second berry was even more delightful than the first. At the brush of her fingers against his lips and the inside of his mouth, a more confident brush now that she'd realized she wanted only to touch and keep on touching, a shimmer of pure light sliced through her. Pure white, incredibly shimmering light that left her body soft and pliable, nearly at the point of collapse. Made her shamelessly exposed flesh relax and then quiver, almost pulsing in its desire to have him look at it, have him touch. Have him invade it because it *needed* to be invaded.

He didn't do any of those things. Didn't try to do any of them or even glance at that part of her. Head tilted back, mouth opening again to receive what she offered, he kept his gaze strictly on her covered and hidden face. Moving his head a little to the side, looking almost curious, he once again pulled her fingers into the depths of him with lips that closed around them. His teeth grazed her skin a little harder this time, strong, sharp teeth that skimmed along the length of her fingers, mesmerizing with their threat to bite, but only seizing the berry she held.

Eli looked rapt. Transported. Hypnotized.

His tongue moved slowly, and then still more slowly, as if he wanted to explore her fingertips. Explore their possibility as if they…she…were the real prize. The berry momentarily abandoned and forgotten, he stroked with silken softness, silken strength, his lips opening so that she could see the way his tongue moved across her fingertips. Opened enough that she…

Moisture gushed between her legs.

Embarrassed, mortified, Claire wished she could close them. Wished she dared. Wished she possessed the strength, the ability, the dexterity. Instead she cried out. Again. Unable to stop herself or to care that she was to make no sound in his presence.

The skimming of lips and teeth along fingers that had grown super-sensitized in the last fraction of a second, the stroking of his tongue against them and the way he pulled the fingers deftly deeper so that he could suck again, harder…all were more than she could bear. More than she would *ever* be able to bear in silence.

If he noticed what she'd done, he gave no sign.

Releasing her at last, he smiled at her. And it was a smile she recognized not so much from personal experience, which before today had been extremely limited, as from the late night movies her mother loved. The late-night love stories.

It was a dangerous smile. A sensual, inviting, forbidding, intoxicating, enticing, enslaving one. Nevertheless, she moistened again beneath its warmth. Moistened and began to hum in that strange, soft way that she felt suddenly certain he could hear.

The flesh he hadn't yet touched or even looked at came suddenly alive. Became suddenly urgent, suddenly desperate and aflame with the need to feel him inside her. Some part of him, any part of him. To know the miraculous, stroking and searing wonder of his tongue against the innermost parts of her.

Slowly, Eli moved, and Claire tensed.

The flesh she now offered up so willingly, clinging tight with her toes to the edge of the table as she wished she could move forward to press herself against his hungry and smiling mouth, moistened yet again. She could feel the moisture shimmer from her. Could feel it moisten her thighs and the wood upon which she sat. She felt her opening flex automatically and instinctively, without conscious input from a brain that had begun to simmer and smoke, incinerating itself alive as her body issued its eager and unmistakable invitation.

And still Eli paid no attention.

He hadn't been reaching for her at all, she realized with a sudden pang of disappointment. He'd made her spread herself for him, made her offer up everything she had, the most precious thing she had, and then he'd ignored her. Completely.

She wanted to cry. Closing her eyes, she told herself she'd be foolish to cry. Foolish and silly. She reminded herself that she'd been hired to do a job. That, incredibly and inexplicably exciting as it might be, it was *only* a job, and that the man who sat before her and tormented her was only her employer. That she was an idiot to have ever expected anything more.

Eli's fingers closed around her wrist. Gently, insistently, he forced her hand to rise again, not toward the champagne centered plate of strawberries, but toward something else. Something he pressed against her fingers, murmuring "Take this," in a hoarse and not entirely steady voice. "Use it."

Dimwitted with desire, barely able to form a conscious much less a coherent thought, Claire looked down. She held a small crystal bowl, elegant and heavy, filled to the brim with white and fluffy mounds.

Whipped cream.

Just as gently, forcing her to remain upright and to balance herself precariously, dependent entirely upon her toes now to grip and hold her in place, Eli brought her other hand up from the table. He refused to allow her to lie back as she wanted, speaking sharply for the first time this evening as he ordered her to sit.

Still dumbfounded, still unable to comprehend though somewhere at the back of her mind consciousness insisted she *did* comprehend, Claire stared stupidly at the bowl, watching as Eli plunged her fingers deep into its creamy white contents.

"Use it," he ordered again.

"I..."

"Spread it thick."

Still Claire didn't move. Almost didn't breathe.

"I'd like a nice little piece of tart for my dessert," he murmured, his smile returning with slow seductiveness. "And I like tart with whipped cream. Lots of whipped cream, so I can lick it away before I bite."

Gulping as she came, abruptly and without even the slightest quiver of a warning, Claire scooped away a small mound of cream on two fingers and, shaking, touched it to herself. Barely touched it to the wet and shrieking place between her legs.

"More," he said, never looking at the fingers that dipped into the cream or the place where they spread it. He seemed to focus exclusively on her face and seemed frustrated when he couldn't see it.

Scooping another, larger mound of white, Claire touched it to herself and marveled that the heat of her steaming body didn't turn it instantly to milky, misty moisture not unlike the milky and misty stream that flowed within her.

"I want it all over you," he whispered dreamily, at last lowering his gaze to watch her fingers massage slowly and carefully, spreading whipped cream around her opening and over it. "I want it on you. I want it *in* you."

Shuddering, Claire scooped up a handful of cream, an enormous gob of it, and shoveled it onto herself with the flat of her hand, kneading it into hair and flesh. Coating her body with soft, smooth cream that heaped into cool peaks which did nothing at all to cool what lay below, nothing at all to ease the discomfort of flesh gone suddenly, incandescently wild with the need to be cooled.

There was so much of it. So much whipped cream, and Eli kept urging her to use more, kept expecting her to use all of it.

When she'd mounded the area between her legs, saturated it and spread the cream so thick that her body could accept no more, Claire began to spread it across her thighs. She covered the moisture of her body that coated them, covered every inch of flesh. And still there was more cream. The small crystal bowl seemed magically and inexplicably to replenish itself even as she worked to empty it.

Dipping two fingers into the undepleted white cloud, Claire moved them toward herself as slowly as was humanly possible. Watching Eli's face, she wondered what he would do if…when…

Carefully, she touched herself again. Plunged her fingers through the creamy mass that covered every millimeter of her now and paused, slowing her pace so that her fingertips could part herself. Could move into her slit one aching millimeter at a time. Could carry cooling, unnerving creaminess from the outside to the inside, against all the dictates of nature or reason. Straight in. Slowly, but without hesitation.

Eli groaned, and it was a groan of pure need. Pure and unadulterated want.

Slowly, Claire maneuvered her fingers inside the tight canal. Smiling a little, aware that he couldn't see the smile behind the mask, aroused by the idea that he could only sense it, she twisted them back and forth. Back and forth and back and forth. Slowly. Teasing him. Teasing herself.

Several times she withdrew, each time eliciting a sharp and ragged breath from him. And each time she returned after only a second, her fingers laden with a fresh serving of cream. Each time she inserted her fingers deeper into the cream-glutted parts of her that lay hidden and gorged beneath the white and foamy mass.

At some point she'd begun to move her body in an undulating rhythm. Massaging the inside of herself, she stroked and coated, then caressed and recoated. Her shoulders swayed provocatively from side to side as, unable to control the impulse, she leaned forward as far as the constraints of her corset and her precarious perch would allow to try to press her body to his mouth.

Entering and retreating repeatedly, she moved her hand in slow and widening circular motions. She pulled at herself, pushed at herself, and ultimately brought herself to a climax so sharp and heavy that, looking down into Eli's stunned and rapt face, she laughed a little.

Very softly.

With sheer exhilaration.

Chapter Seven

OH, GOD. OH, CHRIST. ELI'S COCK HAD NEVER BEEN SO HARD, AND HIS BODY HAD NEVER FELT SO leaden, so useless. His breath had never felt so ready to choke him and smother him.

Claire had taken over.

She'd taken his fantasy and made it her own. Their own, he amended through a dim and persistent pounding that filled his head as he tried in vain to see the expression on her face.

She'll never wear another mask. Never again deny me the pleasure of seeing her.

That was a vow, and he made another one quickly, right on top of it. He vowed to keep that vow. *God. I want to reach up right now and rip away that filthy, peatureless, disgusting pink thing.* But he couldn't move. Not his legs, and not his arms either. He couldn't even move his mouth to form the words that would beg her to stop this torment. That would beg her to please, oh dear God, please*...*

He did manage to move one arm enough to pull the nearly empty bowl of whipped cream from her hand and fling it away with one swift, sure movement of his strong pitching arm.

Crystal shattered on the marble floor. Bits of Baccarat bounced and skittered with a thousand, maybe a million, tiny, scratching noises reminiscent of icy bits of sleet trying to claw their way into his senses and his heart. Corresponding diamond flickers of light ricocheted around the room, across the ceiling and across the waiting, willing flesh spread so temptingly in front of him.

Paying no attention to the destruction, Eli watched, his breath solidified to strangling lump in the base of his throat, as Claire stroked herself. As she massaged gleaming white mounds of cream into the flesh around her glistening, wet opening. She sat close to him. Purposely close, just as he'd planned it, with her legs spread wide inches from his face. So close that he saw every sinuous, circular, stroking motion of fingers that played with the cream and teased it into sculpted peaks. So close that he could only watch mute with fascination as she applied cream to herself carefully, deliberately turning herself into a prize buried so deep beneath foaming and opaque mounds that even if he searched for it, he knew he might never find it. Might die trying to find it.

Then he almost did die when she suddenly plunged her fingers, two of them, heavy with the sweet, sweet stuff, into herself.

It looked like she plunged them all the way in, but Eli couldn't tell. He couldn't really see anything now except the length of those fingers disappearing into white mounds that almost immediately swallowed her entire hand.

His cock surged. A long, low groan ripped from his throat, and he tightened his hands together in his lap, needing something to hang on to, something to keep him grounded and a part of the real world when she pulled her hand back out and immediately thrust it in again.

He'd always made it a point never to react to anything the women did. Never to relinquish control by letting them know if they'd pleased him. He'd made it a specific point to react only when they displeased him. Which they usually did. And then he'd made it a very special point to take everything from them, everything they were willing to give and as much more as he could steal, while never ever giving anything in return. But this time…this woman…this Claire…

Groans ripped through him, a series of them.

His cock ached, burned. It struggled for release, struggled to be free of the rigid confinement of tuxedo pants that had suddenly turned sixteen sizes too small.

He ignored it, or at least he tried to.

Because what she was doing, the way she was plunging her fingers into the sweet white mass that hid her just as sweet and delectable flesh, the way she kept on plunging and releasing, plunging and releasing, twisting her upper body back and forth and swaying gently with each successive, deeper plunge…

Goddamn.

She leaned toward him. Her body undulating in that slow, maddening and enticing way, she leaned right over him, her bare tits almost brushing his face. Delighted, he looked up, into her eyes. *Tried* to look into her eyes, but saw only satin. Saw only one of the masks he'd ordered made so they fit purposefully tight, allowing only the barest hint of the features they concealed. Bright jewel lights flashed from the scrolled pattern of silver and dark red beads and stones embroidered onto the cursed thing, a distraction meant to keep him from focusing on any hint that someone human might lurk underneath. A distraction that had been one damned hell of a piss-poor idea now that he knew there *were* lips beneath, now that he wanted only to take them with his. Now that he wanted to kiss them and kiss them and claim their sweet softness for his very own.

Groaning again, louder, Eli lifted his hands. For a second he thought he'd been about to cover his face with them. But instead he slipped them behind her and held her white and silky cream-coated thighs as far apart as she could spread them. Then he leaned into her even as she continued to work at herself with those thrusting, searching fingers that got in his way and denied him the sweetest treat of all.

Releasing her just long enough to grab her hand and pull it away from her, Eli lowered his head at the same instant. Catching a breath, he plunged into the deliriously sweet mounds and swirls. He extended his tongue to lick, but came up with only a mouthful of cream, a mouthful of whipped air that tasted infinitely less sweet than would the woman beneath. Less sweet than would the moisture that flowed from her to mix its essence with the cream and add to it. To make it musky, delicious, addictive.

He'd told her to spread the stuff on thick. And by God, she'd done exactly that. She'd mounded it onto herself and into herself, smearing and massaging until he'd lost her. Lost track of her.

Pressing his face deeper into the white and concealing cloud, he extended his tongue again and found nothing. *Christ.* Nothing but more cloud. More white. More cream.

Claire's hands grasped the back of his head. Her fingers found the roots of his hair and secured themselves there. Once she had a grip, once he sensed she'd satisfied herself that he wouldn't be able to escape, she pulled him all the way in. Pulled him so deep that he was aware of nothing else. Nothing but cream that filled his eyes and nose, that only through the most wondrous of miracles, didn't completely inhibit his ability to breathe.

"Eat me." Her voice trembled in unseen air above him. It ordered, and he felt compelled to obey.

Extending his tongue yet again, he found his prize at last. He found it and he licked, trying even as he knew he was doomed to fail to remove all trace of whipped cream so that he could see Claire, could see where she was and what she looked like, see the flesh he wanted so desperately to...

"Eat me," she whispered, moving her body in that impossibly arousing way again and tightening the grip of her hands to pull his face closer still. Pull it all the way to her.

She'd said that before, but he hadn't believed it was anything but a dazzled part of some crazed dream that couldn't be real. Or maybe he'd thought it some weird figment of an overstressed mind that had reached its breaking point at last. But it *was* real. It...the hands that now cupped the back of his head and held it in place so that he could do nothing but continue his licking, probing, searching...all of it was real. All of it was happening to him.

Pain rippled through Eli's back and side, a small warning that he was about to overdo. That if he wasn't careful he'd damage already damaged tissue and end up suffering for it.

Well, shit? Aren't I suffering already?

At last he cleared her opening and removed enough of the cream by swallowing it, since there was no other reasonable way to get rid of the damned, fluffy, clinging stuff to clear a path to what lay beneath. At last he fastened his mouth greedily around and over flesh that tasted not exactly sweet, but fruity. Flesh that had the sweet tartness of a peach. A plum. A ripe strawberry, plucked straight from the vine.

Remembering the way she'd handled those berries, dripping shimmering juice and champagne, the way she'd inserted them between his lips and how he'd sucked the juice from her fingers, he came.

In one massive and painful jerk, he felt cum explode from his body. Hot and wet, it filled his pants and kept on flowing. On and on. Endlessly, as his cock thumped madly with repeated, straining bursts that quite literally made his balls ache all the way to their roots, every single ounce of life and vitality and essence drained from him.

God, he was throbbing. So badly that he wanted only to rub himself. To commiserate with himself and try to ease the burning, steel-trap torture that showed no sign of abating. That had only begun to build again the very second when it had eased.

But he couldn't let go of Claire. His hands, coated with a fine and sticky layer of melted whipped cream, seemed glued to her thighs, the fingers twisted by some severe and sexually incited stroke into claws that would be locked there for the rest of his days.

Slowly, slowly, he moved his tongue. He swept it in wild lashes, working industriously to clean every fold, even the most miniscule and hidden, of the flesh she'd given him.

Somewhere far overhead, so incredibly and distantly far that it might have been on another planet, he heard her scream. Heard the sudden crash as she fell backward onto the table, unable to hold the impossible position he'd demanded of her. Then he heard his own scream, muffled and made indistinct by the press of flesh against his lips and the cloying foam that once again tried to fill his mouth and cut off the taste of her.

Eli swirled his tongue around. In ever widening circles, he darted it into her and found even more sweetness, more whipped cream, more of the natural, raw and smoked-peach flavor of the juices that flowed from her.

She screamed again, weakly, and again he paid no attention.

His mouth had closed over her. It had surrounded her and taken in the soft whorls of flesh. Sucking on them, he thrust with his tongue. Thrust and thrust, vainly trying to reach the bottom of her and see if she tasted any different there. See if she tasted any less wonderful than what lay nearer the surface. But his tongue was inadequate. No matter how he strained, no matter how he plunged and moved, he could never reach the bottom. Because she was bottomless. She held hidden delights he would never know. Never be able to know.

And he thought, as another long and desperate moan of torment tore from him, that it would break his heart.

At some point, Claire had released his head. She'd pulled her hands away, too involved in her own twisting and writhing torment on the table he'd set for himself with her as its centerpiece, to be able to cling to him. He heard dishes fall as she swept them aside. Heard china shatter and silverware rattle against unforgiving marble.

He heard, and didn't give one good goddamn about anything but her and what she had done to herself, what she had done to him.

"Jesus!" Claire screamed as her hips lifted all the way off the table, almost knocking him back in his chair and out of it as her feet found his shoulders. Wrapping her legs around his neck, she tightened every muscle. She joined herself to him so completely and so inextricably that he couldn't have moved away even if he'd wanted to. She joined herself to him in a way that made his entire world collapse and fade until nothing remained but the tight, steaming, wet flesh that flexed and flexed against his lips. Flesh that tightened around his inserted tongue and tried to trap it. That *did*, for a moment, trap it.

Somehow, he escaped. Pulling back, he felt the taut and irresistible strain of the upper part of Claire's body lifting away from the table. He heard her cry out more distinctly this time.

"Oh, Eli, don't stop. Pleeeeeeease..." The word dragged on and on into one endless and pulsing wail that seemed to have no beginning and would never reach an end.

Don't stop.

No woman had said that to him before. Not in these last five horrific years anyway. None of the ones he'd paid to turn themselves into whores for him. None of the ones who'd tried to do the things he demanded and had failed because they'd lacked what he was looking for, the innate sexuality, the acceptance of their own bodies and understanding of them, that allowed them to be completely at ease. Completely uninhibited.

But Claire...

"Oh, God." Lifting his head momentarily, he dragged in a deep and shuddering breath. "Claire."

Lifting her head, she glared at him.

He knew she glared, even though the thin slits of the mask allowed no eye contact.

He could feel the heat of her glare.

"Don't stop," she hissed, and he realized with a start that she was indeed now the one in charge.

He swiped a mess of melted whipped cream from his face with one hand, running it back over his forehead and shoving most of it into his hair. It had splattered the front of his tuxedo and had ruined it. But tuxedoes were a dime a dozen. He could buy them by the dozen if he wanted. Other details demanded his attention right now, other things that had once seemed unimportant had suddenly become vital. Details like Claire. Like her feet that continued to grasp his shoulders, trying to find a better grip so that she could tighten the arch she'd made of her body. So that she could lift herself to him in a way that seemed utterly and inarguably to defy every law of gravity and human physiology as she pressed her greedy and demanding opening against his mouth.

Laughing softly, he touched her again, with his thumbs this time. Laughing harder when she began to curse him in terms he'd have thought more appropriate for a sailor or a dockworker, he began to stroke the flesh around her opening. Unable to see her face or her expressions, unable to relate to her directly in any other emotional way, he studied the small, tight rosebud.

Studied as he stroked, marveling as the strawberry pinkness barely concealed by matted and drenched hair moistened again immediately.

"Mmmmmm," he murmured, focusing all his attention on what lay so close…so intoxicatingly, unimaginably close. "Has it happened yet?"

She twisted at his touch. Gasped when his thumbs skimmed over her and whimpered when they departed.

"I don't understand what you mean," she whispered and then cried out, her body arching against him again as it got itself ready.

"So, it hasn't."

"Hasn't…what?"

He touched the tip of his tongue to her again. Just the tip and just for a second. But that was enough. That was all it took.

Screaming, she arched higher, and a thin jet of moisture escaped her.

"You haven't orgasmed."

"Christ almighty!" she screamed. "What the hell do you *think* I've been doing? What the hell do you think I'm doing right now?"

"Oh, you've been playing at it." Laughing again, Eli slipped his arms beneath her thighs and around them. Lifting her close to his shoulders, lifting her ass and holding it tight, he pinned her to him as thoroughly and inescapably as she'd used her legs just moments before to rivet herself to him.

"Playing?" She sounded angry. And she tried to lift her head and shoulders off the table. But he'd given her legs a little twist. An expert and carefully exerted one that would hold her helpless in her place without hurting her.

"Playing," he agreed. "You've had a little orgasm." Touching his tongue to the whorl of her opening again, he caught the next thin jet of moisture with a quick, lapping motion. Caught it and instantly licked his own lips, transferring the fresh and still warm taste of her to himself. "Maybe you've had two or three. But you haven't really had one yet."

"I beg to differ."

"I've just got you warmed up," he murmured, and laughed again when she twisted, struggling this time to extricate her body from the rigid strength of the arms that held her. "I've got you to the place where you're just about ready. Not quite, but almost to the place where you're close to having the orgasm you've been living for."

"Excuse me?" she struggled again. "Let me go!"

Not on your life.

"You're not ready to be let go."

"How the holy, freaking hell do you know what I'm ready for, Eli Eden?"

He didn't answer. He just tilted his head forward and kissed her. Softly. Gently. First on the flesh between her legs, in the place where it had literally begun to pulsate with need and desperation. Then he kissed her thighs. One and then the other, and so on. Back and forth and back and forth, releasing her a little so that he could brush a trail of kisses along the inner curve of each trembling and quivering leg.

He trailed them down at first, tormenting himself as much as he tormented her, his body as ready as hers for the impending climax. Then he trailed them back up, retracing the path he'd blazed while seeking out new and untried territories at the same time.

He kissed her. Nuzzled her. Laughed softly when she called him another long string of highly insulting, deeply despicable and most likely true names. Laughed and inserted his tongue into her again, more slowly than he'd ever inserted anything into any woman. Inserted it and held it there, delighting in the soft and swollen surge of her body around it.

Chapter Eight

HE WAS ABOUT TO DRIVE HER MAD.

Or maybe he already had. Lying on her back on the unbelievably long dining room table, the train of her gown crushed beneath her, the metallic lace forming a thin, prickly mattress that made her skin tingle in the strangest ways, Claire could no longer hold back the cries, forbidden though they might be, that erupted from her.

Eli had begun to do the most incredible things to her. He had begun to touch her...really touch her, with tenderness and something that almost seemed like a genuine interest in giving her pleasure.

She'd been shocked, even dismayed, when he'd first ordered her to cover herself with the whipped cream. It had seemed uncomfortable. Pagan somehow.

Then she'd felt it against her skin. Smooth and thick, it had seemed to cool and soothe, delicious against burning flesh that had been overused during the encounter in the sleigh. So soothing that she began almost without realizing it to massage the concoction into herself. Then suddenly, without warning, craving the chill relief even more, she'd inserted her fingers into herself, the first time she'd ever done such a thing. She'd even inserted the cooling cream there.

And Eli's reaction?

That had been a marvel in itself.

Crouched before him, clinging to the edge of the table with her toes, she'd watched his eyes widen as her fingers disappeared into the creamy mounds with which she'd carefully concealed herself. Watched them as she'd penetrated her own body. He'd gasped. Or had she?

No. It had been him. It was forbidden for her to gasp.

Though she had gasped later, of course. Long after he'd first leaned close to her. Long after, seeming almost to move in slow motion, he'd inserted his tongue into the creamy concealment and searched her out with unerring accuracy.

She'd gasped when the tip of his tongue brushed against her as if by accident. And gasped again when it returned to begin a soft motion that swept it around and around, alternately exploring her flesh and then darting quickly, coyly forward. Gasped every time his tongue retreated before it had done more than stir the outermost folds of her flesh.

He'd taken great care to clean her, first on the outside with swift and sure strokes that removed the cooling coating and replaced it with sheer, wet fire. Steaming fire that set her to throbbing as even the feel of his hard and unrelenting shaft sliding into her earlier had not made her throb.

Now, lying on her back on the dark wood table, the train of her gown bunched beneath her hips and shoulders as if it had been intended for just such a purpose, to pad the discomfort of skin against the unyielding hardness of wood, she could no longer gasp. At some point, she had no idea when, she'd lifted her legs and slipped them across Eli's shoulders. They lay there now, trying hard to wrap themselves around him and hold him. But they were too weak. *She* was too weak.

Eli's tongue still probed. Still diligently worked to remove every trace of the whipped cream. Only now it worked inside her. Worked hard, thrusting to depths she wouldn't have imagined possible. Thrusting and turning, wet and lithe and agile as no man's swollen shaft could ever be.

His lips were soft as they cupped the outside of her, and as he explored the inside, murmuring soft sounds of approval and delight at the back of his throat.

Tilting her head back so that her chin jutted up, the pink satin mask pulling painfully tight around her mouth and throat, Claire concentrated on breathing. But it was difficult.

Almost *too* difficult.

Every stroke of that unbelievably soft tongue made her want to scream again. Empty her lungs anew in the longest, most primitive shriek of pain and delight and discovery she could summon. But she clenched her teeth. She bit down so hard that her jaws ached, and concentrated upon dragging in one shallow, jagged, halting breath after another.

She'd been holding his head earlier, urging him forward at first and then forcing him forward. Pressing his greedy mouth tight against her own flesh that had grown just as greedy. Just as painfully and shockingly eager to continue the fantasy. To see it go on and on and on. Fantasy without end. World without end. Amen.

To her horror, Claire realized she *had* screamed. Aloud. Defying orders she'd let it escape…a long and wordless wail that seemed to bounce off the dark gold walls of this torture chamber he'd made for her. It seemed to hover in the air above them, to color it a faint crimson as it surrounded them and broke over them again and again and again.

Claire couldn't tense. Her body had lost all ability to tense and her muscles, save for those enormously precious few that surrounded the marauding tongue, had lost all ability to respond to any command her brain might try to send.

Limp and gasping, she jerked spasmodically and cried out when Eli's mouth left her.

"No!" she whispered, struggling to raise arms that lay flung out at her sides, useless hands trailing into empty space at either side of the table. "Please, Eli, no."

Below her, close enough that she felt his breath scoring sweet trails across her thighs and the exposed flesh between them, she heard him laugh. *Felt* him laugh.

"Oh, God." Her voice wasn't even a whisper now. Wasn't even a whisper of a whisper. "Please…don't…"

He took his time about getting back to her. His own sweet, deliberate, mocking, maddening time. When he touched her again, it was to run the tip of his tongue, just the very tiniest tip, along the inside of her thigh to replace the white froth he'd removed with long and lacy swirls of moisture that shimmered against her skin and then right through it. That imprinted themselves all the way down to her bones and then even farther, all the way down to the aching, liquefied marrow itself.

Laughing, he teased her by touching her. He swept his tongue along every part of her flesh she *didn't* want him to touch and circumvented carefully and deliberately the flesh she did want touched. In that instant, breath tearing at her lungs as if it meant to rip itself free by gouging great and gaping holes in her chest, she wondered if he'd set out purposefully to drive her mad.

She wondered if that hadn't been a part of his plan all along, to entice her with money she needed so desperately, only to use her and abuse her. Repeatedly, so that he could eventually finish her off as he was about to do in this moment or maybe in the next, before she'd had a chance to live up to her end of their bargain. Finish her off not by killing, though even that seemed a good bet at this particular moment in time, but by driving her utterly, completely, irreconcilably insane.

She screamed again. "My God! Don't do this to me! You've got to...please, please...*please*!"

His laughter came again. Soft. Tantalizing. And then, so did his tongue.

Gently, he licked.

Carefully, he stroked.

Repeatedly, he prodded and teased, never quite entering her and yet never quite remaining on the outside of her either.

He wandered across her. Lazed, meandered, drifted.

With every whisk of his mouth against her, she felt a corresponding flicker on the inside. Flames sprung up wherever he touched, whenever he touched. They flared and ebbed, but never completely faded, were never completely extinguished. Because once Eli had ignited her, he proved incredibly adept at banking the flames, at making them simmer and effervesce, always promising the final relief, but never quite allowing it to happen.

Claire's stomach tightened. Deep down inside she twitched and felt it turn hard with the strain of merely surviving the things Eli Eden was doing to her.

"You're enjoying this," he murmured, and she scarcely recognized the voice as his. Gone was all the hardness of earlier, the slight hint of cruelty when he'd called her names he'd had no reason to call her. When he'd made demands in a way that let her know his pleasure was paramount, his pleasure was all that mattered. There was something different about him now. Something softer. Kinder. Something she almost might describe as tender in the way he fitted his mouth to her and began, once again and in earnest this time, to penetrate her.

"Oh, you're enjoying it all right," he murmured between thrusts, his breath threatening to scorch a hole right through her.

"Eli..."

"I wonder if anyone's ever truly enjoyed this the way you're enjoying it?"

"Please?"

"What do you want, Claire?" His tone turned softer. Teasing and playful, in a way she wouldn't three or four hours ago have imagined he could ever be playful.

He had a beautiful voice. A deep voice. Deep and rich, with a solid timbre when it rumbled in his chest.

Claire wanted to hear more of it. She suddenly, desperately needed to hear more. As much as she needed him to concentrate the entirety of his lovely, persuasive mouth on her.

"Pleeeeeeeeease!" Tilting her head back again, straining with neck muscles and shoulder muscles and abdominal muscles to lift herself away from the table, she felt the word physically rip from her in a long, shattering and rending burst of agony that knew no relief because there *was* no relief.

Eli laughed. He brushed the tip...again only the barest, almost ethereal tip...of his tongue across her. And in response, she flexed. Tried to pull him in, even though she knew it couldn't be done. Knew she couldn't hold him even if he'd already been inside, knew she could do nothing on this earth to force him to enter her.

She was helpless. Utterly helpless in the face of this new, most delightful and delicious thing that had ever been done to her. She'd begun to twist her body now. To rock her hips and her shoulders back and forth. To sway, flat on her back, in lithe and sinuous motions that expressed better than any words or cries could exactly how she felt.

Wonderful. Delirious. Dizzy. Lightheaded and lighthearted.

"Do you want me, Claire?" Eli had to pull away from her to ask, and that gave her the strength to move her hand at last. To swing it in a jerky, not quite coordinated arc around and down, in search of him. Finding his hair, his slightly long, dark hair that curled in enticing waves around the nape of his neck. She wrapped her fingers around it and through it and found it not soft as she'd imagined it would be, but sticky and clotted with the melted remains of the whipped cream that had transferred itself from her body to his. The stickiness made it easy to grip. And grip she did, with fingers that convulsed into the roots and around them. Fingers and a hand that forced him with one sudden, final, manic burst of strength to come to her.

Come to her, damn it, and give her what she wanted.

Still he resisted.

"Tell me, Claire. Tell me, or by God I'll make you suffer this way all night. I'll drag your torture on and on. I'll make you— "

"What?" Managing somehow to lift her head, she tried to see him. But her vision had blurred. Had turned dark, dusky, grayish tinged with pink. Or was that only the mask, slipped slightly out of position as she'd gyrated in her struggles to have him? "Tell you...what?"

"Do you want me, Claire?"

"Yes. Oh, God, yes. Please. I only— "

"Then say it."

"I w...want you. Want...you. Please, Eli, please. You don't have to pay me, you don't have to...I only want you. Please. Now. Ple...aaaaaaaaaaaaaaahhhhh!"

Her scream echoed bright and feral through the torture chamber as Eli closed his mouth around her roughly. As he found the opening with one quick and agile stroke, and shoved his tongue deep into the seething, churning mass that occupied the very center of her. He shoved and shoved, twisting his tongue and turning it so that no portion of her went untended, no portion was left neglected or had reason to feel slighted. He closed his mouth around her and he suckled, hungry for what she had to offer. What she had to...

Her back arched, her body touching the table now only at the back of her head, the majority of her weight centered upon her thighs, braced against his shoulders and around them. She arched higher and then still higher as a suddenly intolerable pressure welled up inside her. As a dam readied itself to break with only the last, the final and slightest bit of urging.

Eli groaned. A groan as long as any either of them had uttered so far. A groan of sheer, unabashed animal hunger.

And that was it. That was what she'd waited for.

Her body gathered itself together one last time. Muscles that had already tightened grew tighter still, tight beyond their capabilities and rippling with the strain. And then began the softening. The simultaneous tightening and tensing as relief hovered, lingering only seconds, infinitesimal, immeasurable and unsurvivable seconds, away.

Eli thrust one more time, determinedly.

And Claire's body let loose with a rush.

She came with all the force of a volcano or a geyser. Came as she'd never thought it possible to come. And still the shivering, simmering waves poured from her. Poured into the mouth that cupped her, seeming almost starved for the sustenance she gave.

Groaning again, more deeply than before, Eli drank in the essence of her. His fingers tightened around the flesh of her thighs and dug in so eagerly and so deeply that they must surely leave bruised imprints.

Claire didn't care.

She didn't care about anything now except the man who held her prisoner, a delighted, delirious, destroyed prisoner. She cared about nothing except the mouth that continued to cover her even now, even long after she'd drained herself dry. Long after she'd lowered her back to the table and lay motionless and shuddering, struggling for breath that would not come into lungs that would not expand.

"Eli," she managed, very faintly and after a very long time.

Releasing her, he collapsed forward. His arms still twined around her legs and his fingers still splayed against her thighs. But he'd gone limp, too. As limp as every part of Claire.

"My God," he murmured, his voice muffled, his face buried against the inside of her thigh.

"I..." She swallowed hard. Tried to speak and found she couldn't. No matter how hard she tried.

"That was..." Eli pushed himself away from her at last. And she was too tired to protest. Too drained to do anything but lie as he'd left her, with her legs splayed wide and her every muscle still aquiver from the effort of the orgasm that had surely and certainly shaken the entire world. "I've never felt anything like that. It was...Claire?"

"What?" She could barely make herself heard.

"It was...beautiful."

Tired as it was, expended beyond any rational hope of recovery, her heart nonetheless lurched. And began to pound in the strangest, uneven and thoroughly unfamiliar rhythm. "I'm glad you—"

"Shhh. Don't talk. Don't do anything. Just lie there for a minute."

But she had to do something. Had to move.

Slowly, using up the very last of her strength, she pulled herself back from the edge of the table. Beneath her ear she heard lace rip, and didn't care. She was too tired to care. Exerting one final, superhuman effort, she forced herself to roll onto her side so that her legs could close at last. So that she could curl up in a fetal position, her knees rising to meet her chest and the torn wisps of lace from her train floating over her to cover her in glittering, gossamer, sheer yet opaque folds.

Gradually the ringing in her ears began to subside. And she became aware of other sounds. The soft chiming of a clock somewhere far off in another part of the enormous house. Two chimes, then three.

Three o'clock in the morning?

She became aware, too, of the soft snap and hiss of snow brushing against unseen windowpanes behind drawn gold curtains, a sound as gentle and persistent as a kitten's claws struggling to gain traction on those smooth and polished surfaces. And she heard Eli. Heard him breathing. Heard the soft, sharp rasps as each intake of air gradually begin to ease and finally to relax into softer and deeper rhythms.

"Eli?" she asked after a very long time. "Are you asleep?"

"No," came the immediate answer. "But I thought you were."

"Maybe I was. For a little while. And...I meant it, you know."

"Meant what?"

"You don't have to pay me."

"We had a deal," he replied. "And I mean to honor it. Except..."

When he didn't finish, Claire rolled over. Rolled onto her back and pushed herself to a sitting position. Trying to see him, she struggled a little to nudge the mask back into a position that would allow her to see anything.

"Except for what?" she asked in a small and automatically wary voice.

"Except that I don't want to see you wear another goddamned mask. Ever."

Chapter Nine

"YOU CAN GO NOW." ELI SURPRISED HIMSELF...NO, DAMMIT, HE *SHOCKED* himself...when he heard himself dismiss her so coldly. So callously. After what had just happened, after she'd turned the tables on him and made his simple fantasy into something else entirely, something more arousing and erotic than anything he could have dreamed up on his own. How in the hell had she done that anyway?

He'd expected to have her feed him strawberries.

Expected her to dab a little of the whipped cream on herself when he ordered her to. Or to not dab it on.

Then he'd expected to take her and have his way with her without any help from her. Or any participation.

He'd never expected her to slather herself with the stuff. To spread it in layers so thick, so choking and impenetrable that he'd nearly drowned trying to find her beneath the suffocating clouds of it.

But find her he had. And he'd enjoyed her. More than he'd enjoyed a woman in his life. *Ever.*

So why was he being so rude now? So abrupt and curt?

His goddamned cock.

That was why. Because it hurt. Just flat out hurt, with a physical agony so real, so penetrating and pounding it nearly had him on the floor.

He was dismissing her without warmth because he hadn't gotten to live his part of the fantasy. And it was *his* fantasy, dammit. His! But it hadn't done one single, goddamned thing to relieve his sexual tensions. The ones the fantasy had been set up to relieve in the first place.

Still confined to his pants, never touched in all that wonderful, wild and crystal-shattering episode of shrieking and thrusting and groaning, his cock had never really had a chance to satisfy itself. Untouched, but yearning for a touch or a caress, for just a little attention that would ease its suffering, it screamed at him. Literally screeched, as hard as rock and twice as big as it had ever been, demanding that he *do something about it*! Do it now.

He was dismissing her because he felt just a little cheated. Just a little upstaged and, if he was to be completely honest with himself, just a little pissed that she'd thought she could do that. Even if it had been the single most enjoyable moment of his life.

For a minute Claire sat on the edge of the table, her body and her satin costume smeared with the remains of their encounter. She just sat, her feet swinging a dozen inches from the floor, and he imagined she stared at him though once again, to his extreme annoyance, he couldn't see anything about her expression. Couldn't see the set of her mouth or the look in her eyes, whether they gleamed with hatred or with something closer to what he was feeling.

"Damn it to hell," he growled. "Will you take that infernal thing off your head? So I can *see* you?"

She didn't move. Not a muscle. Even her feet stopped their swinging. "The mask was your idea."

"I know, but I've changed my mind."

"You insisted."

"Claire! I've changed my mind. I want it off."

She continued to sit, continued to, he imagined, stare at him. "Then take it off me."

He twitched a little. As much from frustration as from the continued pounding, throbbing demands being sent out from his groin.

That's going to be a problem. Isn't it?

For reasons he didn't care, didn't dare, to explain, taking it off her was one thing he could never do. Not without her aid and cooperation.

He could never use brute force to make a woman do anything. Never again. Not after what had happened five years ago, out there on his father's goddamned rolling meadow, not after…

"I said you could leave," he growled between gritted teeth, wondering if she was ever going to obey.

At last she slipped down from the table. She was a little unsteady on her feet, he noted with a slight rising of pleasure. When she walked toward the door, she staggered a little, keeping her legs wide apart as if she couldn't bear the feeling of her own flesh rubbing against itself. As if she was sore as hell.

Good. Let her suffer even half of what she's made me suffer.

Eli didn't realize he was going to miss her until the door swung shut behind her. Until he heard the latch click into place with a sound that resembled nothing as much as a gunshot to his heart. He didn't miss her until she'd gone and left him alone amid the mess and debris of what she'd done to him.

"Estella!"

Instantly, another door opened. The door that connected the dining room to the kitchen.

The housekeeper strode into the room briskly and stopped a few feet away, her hands folded in front of her waist, her eyes questioning but not surprised by anything she saw. That was what he paid her for. Good old Estella, who'd been his father's housekeeper and on-the-side fuck when Eli's mother hadn't been looking. Who'd no doubt be willing to continue on as Eli's full time fuck if he hadn't needed something a little more exotic…okay, something a little more imaginative and a little more stimulating…than anything he thought the old girl could handle. But she did her job. Did it well and without question. Without comment.

"Get me a phone."

It took her only a minute, vanishing behind the screen and through the swinging door only to reappear before the door quit swinging.

Wordless, she handed the cell phone to him.

"You can go," he growled in much the same tone he'd used to dismiss Claire. But unlike Claire, Estella gave no sign she'd been offended. She gave no sign that she felt anything at all. She just turned and went as ordered.

Eli punched buttons almost blindly, more from memory of their positions on the keypad than from actually seeing them. He punched with fingers that shook so badly he wondered exactly who he'd end up calling and if they'd even come close to who he wanted to call. And while he waited, listening to the ringing at the other end of the connection, he slid his zipper down with his free hand and released the angry and roaring beast that had been just about to rip through his pants. Wrapping his hand around it, he gave it a small squeeze. A gentle one, meant to reassure and calm at the same time that it assessed the damage the she-devil had wrought.

Just as he'd thought, he was big. Enormous. His skin throbbed hot and anguished beneath his palm, and he had no trouble feeling the deep and wounded pulse that hammered deep down inside.

She's practically killed me. All without touching me!

He groaned a little as he began to slide his hand along the swollen and suffering length. Groaned, because it seemed there could never be any relief from something so…

He groaned right into his lawyer's ear.

"Burton here," the man said and then, after pausing to hear Eli's long and protracted sound of sheer and unadulterated misery, "Eden? Is that you?"

"It's me," Eli replied. Never ceasing the careful stroking and caressing that would eventually calm his enraged cock to the point that he'd be able to live with it for a while longer, at least until the next time he called Claire to him, he struggled to keep his actions from showing in his voice.

"You sound like hell. Pardon my French."

"I feel like hell."

"What is it? Are you ill? Do you need—"

"If I was ill, goddammit, I'd have called a doctor."

In reply, Eli heard only silence.

"Burton, it's about that woman."

"The woman? The one I sent to you yesterday?"

Yesterday? Eli wanted to groan again. Wanted to laugh. Or maybe to cry. *Christ in heaven, was it just yesterday? Has Claire really turned me so upside down in less than twenty-four hours that I'm sitting here with my cock shuddering in my hand while I talk business with my lawyer?*

Shit, yes.

She'd made a real mess of things. And he wasn't just thinking of the whipped cream that had ruined his tux and come damned close to ruining the entire dining room either. He wasn't thinking of the shattered Baccarat bowl or the bone china plates. He was thinking of his life, dammit. His precious, fantasy riddled and grievously damaged life

"…not working out?" the lawyer was saying. "Last night you said she was adequate, but if…do you want me to find another? I can check, and possibly have someone else up there to you by mid-morning tomorrow."

Hell, yes. That was exactly what Eli wanted. Someone a little…make that a *lot*…less stressful. Someone who wouldn't make shit of his brains by playing games with him and getting him so riled he didn't know which end was up any longer.

"Hell, no," he growled, and couldn't quite believe he'd said it. Couldn't believe what came rolling out next either. "I want you to double her money."

A long pause echoed at the other end of the call. And that was good, because Eli was going to need a long pause or two to get his heart started again as well as his breathing. To convince his fingers to unclench themselves from around a cock that had started to howl now in earnest because he'd locked it in a squeezing vise grip that in another minute would surely wrench it from its socket and leave him an even poorer excuse for a man than he was already.

What the hell did I just say? What the living hell did I just do?

Apparently, Burton was wondering the same thing.

"Excuse me? Did you say—"

"Double the money?" All the fury left Eli's voice. All the command and the energy, too. "I think I did."

"Correct me if I'm wrong. Because I don't really believe I heard...you want to give this woman a *hundred thousand* dollars?"

Eli groaned again.

Shit. He wanted to give her more than that. Wanted to give her so much more. So many things, all kinds of things that she would never, ever take once...if...she learned the truth about him.

Shit.

"I think a hundred thousand would be appropriate. Yes."

"For having sex with you."

"That's right."

"She must be one hell of a piece."

"One hell," Eli agreed, so tired now that he wondered how he could still sit up, much less massage the cock that suddenly, having apparently decided it was just too tired to care anymore had begun to deflate like an old balloon. *Damned thing's going to have to have release sometime,* he thought grimly. *That pressure isn't going to go away by itself. But...* "You'll call the bank and arrange the payment, then?"

"First thing in the morning. One hundred thousand dollars, to be paid to Claire Hardistique on December twenty-sixth."

"No. I've reconsidered." Eli's head had started to throb as badly as his cock had just a minute or two before. *I want to go to bed. Alone.* Wanted to wrap himself around his pillow as if it was a woman who loved him, but wouldn't hurt him. A woman who really and truly loved him in spite of everything. He wanted to sleep. Until he reached the end of his life and then he wanted to slip away quietly. In his sleep. Without any fuss, or bother, or...

"What?" His lawyer's screech of agony jerked him up from the edge of dreamland. "Eden, for God's sake! You're not going to up the amount again. You're not going to—"

"No. A hundred thousand will do." *For now.* "But I want you to pay her right away. Tomorrow."

Now Burton fell silent. Completely, dead, stone-cold silent.

"I want you to have the check delivered here. To the house."

"This isn't good," Burton said quietly. Almost morosely, and Eli almost laughed. Did laugh a little, though it was more like a silent shaking of shoulders that had begun to slump with sheer exhaustion.

Not good?

Hell, if the man only knew the half of it...

This was worse than not good. This was the single worst thing that could have happened to Eli right now, in this time and this place. This had all the makings of a nightmare. Of a catastrophe that might...not even might, but would...do him in finally and for all time.

For better or for worse...*for richer or for poorer?* his mind wanted to know with a sarcastic jeer...he had just tumbled to one terrible, one inconceivable truth that he wouldn't dare confess to anyone. Ever.

For better or for worse, and yes, for richer or for poorer, until death did them part, he had just realized he was head over heels in love with Claire Hardistique.

Chapter Ten

The wind had picked up. Blizzard driven snowflakes whirled madly against Claire's window, blotting out everything but the light that stood between the marble mansion and the smaller frame house whose mention had seemed to upset Eli so terribly.

She didn't understand the man. Didn't understand herself for wanting to understand him. But she'd seen that something she still couldn't explain. That something in his eyes that said there was more to him than what he'd first appeared. Something much more than the cold and callous rich man who seemed to think he could take advantage of others' misfortunes. Who seemed to think that by offering them money and forcing them to play games he could gain their companionship.

Claire certainly hadn't meant to feel any such connection with him when she'd come here. Hadn't expected to see anything warm or anything desirable about him.

But now, standing at the window scrubbing her hair dry with one of his thick and velvety white towels, with all trace of the evening's whipped cream dessert itinerary washed safely down the drain, she frowned at the worsening storm and forced herself to face the truth.

I never meant to feel anything for him but contempt. But I do. And I don't want to know what it is.

Moving suddenly, she crossed to the door. Opened it, and peered out into the hallway with its narrow strip of deep blue carpet at its center. Only the rooms on the second floor were carpeted. Just one more strange peculiarity in a house that more and more seemed to overflow with peculiarities.

No one was in sight. The house lay silent, as brilliantly lighted as if a ball would soon take place even though it was almost five o'clock in the morning and she doubted that a ball ever had or ever would enliven this house that felt more and more like a mausoleum.

She was alone. It was one of the few times she thought she would be alone here. So she hurried back to the bed and retrieved the cell phone. Dialed quickly, already apologizing mentally to her mother for the indecency of the hour. Hoping her mother hadn't been sleeping but had been sitting up reading or maybe watching one of her hopelessly romantic and outdated movies the way she did most nights, whether Claire was at home or not.

Her mother picked up almost before the second ring had finished. "Claire?" she asked, sounding both eager and apprehensive. "Is that you?"

"How did you guess?"

"Who else would call in the middle of the night?"

"I didn't wake you?"

Her mother laughed softly, the sound as infectious and spirit-lifting as always. "You know better than that, dear. I was reading."

"Are you having snow there, Mum?"

"Not a flake. Not since earlier this evening."

"That's good. I've been worried about you having to walk to the market if the streets get slippery."

"I haven't seen a need to go out," her mother replied. "You left me with everything I could possibly need until you get back." Then, after a long and somewhat wistful pause, "When *are* you coming back, Claire?"

"I already told you, Mum. The twenty-sixth. I get paid on the twenty-sixth, and then I'm free to leave."

"I hope this job is worth it."

Grim faced, Claire turned to look at the snow-clotted world beyond the window. "It will be."

"How's the house party going?"

For a second, only a second but long enough to create a noticeable gap in the conversation, Claire reeled, confused. Then she remembered the lie she'd told because she'd known that any hint of the truth, any discussion of the real reasons for her coming here and the real job duties she'd agreed to perform, would not only have had her mother instantly outraged and forbidding any such activity, but could possibly induce another stroke that might even kill her.

"Claire? Is something wrong?"

"No, Mum," she denied quickly.

"Something's wrong."

"I'm just tired. The guests…there's been a lot of activity. A lot of running around, arranging activities and…"

"What special thing did you do tonight?" her mother prodded, always eager for details, always looking for something real and exciting to brighten days spent mostly with her movies or between the covers of her books.

"We had a...dessert party," Claire replied, grimacing at herself in the glass. *Well, at least that much is the truth.* Sort of. And maybe, just maybe, it meant she wouldn't go to her final reward someday knowing she'd been a total liar. A total shame to her mother and everything good and decent her mother had always stood for.

"I see. And what about your Mr. Eden? Has he been hard to work for? Hard to please?"

He's certainly been hard. The words trembled on the tip of Claire's tongue, and it was only with enormous difficulty that she managed to stop herself from saying them. Or from braying with sudden and uncharacteristically harsh laughter that would have her mother demanding details she would never, in all her life, ever reveal.

"Mr. Eden is fine," she said quietly. "Though I don't begin to understand him. There's something about him that keeps me totally off guard. He can be so rude, so brusque and demanding in one breath, and then in the next he turns so kind. So considerate..." Staring at herself in the window glass again, Claire shivered.

Now, wait a minute. Is that what I really think of him? That he's kind? Considerate?

Yes. Basically. Deep down inside, she'd sensed a truly kind man. One who would never deliberately hurt anyone unless he'd been pushed to some kind of limit. Backed into some kind of corner he thought he couldn't escape in any other way. She'd picked that up in her brief encounters with him, especially in the one where they'd talked openly and with no weird role-playing to cloud the issue. He was a truly decent man. A truly honorable one. Though for the life of her she hadn't been able to figure out, probably because she hadn't been given much time to figure out anything, how the bizarre sexual games fit into the picture or what they could possibly have to do with Eli Eden being backed into some kind of corner.

Then she realized her mother was talking. She'd been saying something and Claire had missed half of it. "...only a vague memory, mind you," she said. "But it's there, and I wish I could..."

"I'm sorry, Mum," Claire broke in. "Someone came to my door for a minute. What was that you were saying?"

"I hope you're getting enough sleep."

That wasn't what she'd been saying, and Claire knew it. "I'm getting plenty of sleep. It's just that tonight...what were you saying before? About something you were trying to remember?"

Her mother sighed. "Well, as long as you're sure. About the sleep, I mean. I was saying that I keep trying to remember where I've heard that name before. Eli Eden. It's such a distinctive name, such a hard one to forget."

"He's a software designer, Mum." Turning away from the window, Claire climbed up into the gold and white bed, a frown creasing her face. "He's designed all kinds of software for accounting and banking. I imagine everyone's heard of him."

"Well, of course, Claire. I know about that. I may not be any good with a computer, but I'd have to be deaf, dumb and blind not to...no, this wasn't about the computer business. This was something else, something about..."

"It doesn't really matter anyway." Suddenly, Claire did feel tired. Almost numb with exhaustion and eager to just collapse against her soft, soft pillows and sleep the rest of this nerve-wracking week away. Though, of course, she knew Eli Eden had no intention of letting her sleep anything away.

"It seems to me there was some kind of tragedy," her mother had gone on, rambling the way she often did when she was lonely. And that sent an all-new dart of guilt, sharp edged and pervasive, through Claire.

I've got no business leaving Mother alone this way. At Christmas, when she... when neither of us... has anybody else to share the holiday with.

There had to be another way to get the money they needed. Even though she'd looked and looked for over a year until the unemployment insurance ran out and then the savings nearly ran out, there had to be a way. If she'd only looked a little harder, surely she would have found a job. Surely she could have...

"Something to do with baseball," her mother reminisced into her ear, oblivious to everything else now that the memories had started. "I don't remember...or, no. Yes, I do remember! Your Eli Eden was known as quite a ball player, Claire."

"Mum, he's not *my* Eli Eden." Though if she was to be completely honest and completely aboveboard, something in Claire had started to think of him that way herself.

It was shocking. But it was true.

"All I know, dear, is that he was a ball player. A very good one, too. Major league, I think, until..."

"How do you know so much about baseball all of a sudden?" This time Claire did allow herself to laugh, and to her relief it came out sounding perfectly natural. Sounding just like the self she'd feared she was going to lose somewhere during the course of this long and life altering week.

"Well, of course I don't know a thing. But your Uncle Milton did. He used to follow the game like it was a…a religion, or something. And I remember quite distinctly him talking about a fellow by the name of Eli Eden. There can't have been more than one, not with a name like that! I remember Milt saying how it was such a shame, that this Eden boy had been one of the best to move up to the starting roster in years. That he surely would have been a star in another season or two. Only there was this terrible tragedy. Something to do with Eden's father…"

Claire sighed. Yawned. "Mum, I really do have to get to bed. El…Mr. Eden is sure to want me on my toes tomorrow to entertain his…guests."

"Of course, dear." Her mother sounded abashed, and that made Claire feel even more guilty. "You get a good night's rest."

"I will, Mum. You do the same. And I'll call you the very next chance I get."

Then, without waiting for her mother to launch herself onto another tangent that would carry them back through the sports oriented and slightly tedious world of her late Uncle Milton, or the even more tedious world of baseball, a game that had completely baffled and mystified her for as long as she could remember, Claire turned the phone off. Rolling over, she inserted it back into the ripped place beneath the box springs.

Eli Eden. A baseball player.

That didn't seem right, she thought as she punched her unfamiliar pillow viciously, trying to mold it into a shape she could deal with.

Or did it?

Turning out the lamp next to the bed, she lay on her back in the darkness, staring up at the dim glow of light from the pole outside, watching the hazy, swirling patterns of snowflakes driven by a rising wind dance in the dim gold reflection.

Somehow, the idea of Eli being a baseball player, being some sort of accomplished athlete, did have a certain rightness to it, after all. There was something in the way he moved, something in the easy grace of the broad shoulders that always seemed to tower over her as she sat or lay or crouched in some less than dignified position or other that said yes, he hadn't always been a world-renowned and filthy rich software designer. He'd been something else once, not so terribly long ago. He'd been something completely different.

Briefly, her eyes beginning to slide shut even though she hadn't finished thinking this through, Claire had a vision of him as he'd been yesterday when she'd been admitted to the sitting room of his private sanctuary on the ground floor. A vision of him lounging, indolent and sure of himself, on the buttery-colored suede loveseat. A feeling that he'd been tightly coiled and ready to spring. A feeling that when he did, it would be with all the power and lithe ease, all the grace and superb confidence of movement she'd sensed when at one point he'd raised an arm to point at her, his every muscle rippling with pent up energy just waiting to explode into motion.

He was a strange and intriguing man, she thought with a little smile as she sank deeper toward the blissful darkness of sleep.

Some kind of awful tragedy, her mother's voice reiterated through the rising fog that filled her mind. *Something about his father...*

Maybe that would explain the look Claire had seen in his eyes, and the vague expression that sometimes softened his face with regret for an instant. Maybe she should watch him and try to figure out what drove him. Maybe...

And with that, with a small and blissful sigh, she gave up completely to the fog that reached out to envelop her.

Chapter Eleven

He WAS HAVING AN UNCOMMONLY DIFFICULT TIME GETTING HIMSELF SITUATED tonight. An uncommonly tough time making himself comfortable.

It's Claire, he thought, turning his head to watch snow hiss and tap at the windows of his bedroom. He'd let Claire in. Against all better judgment, he'd started to get to know her. Started to let himself have feelings for her. And now he was going to have to pay for his stupidity. He was going to be made to suffer, just as he'd predicted he would suffer if he ever allowed himself to care for one of the women he'd ordered Burton to send to him from the moment he'd taken up residence in this house. This great and infernal prison dedicated to every last, damned one of the things his bastard of a father had thrown away so carelessly and without so much as a second thought. Here he'd begun serving his life sentence.

He'd about worn himself out earlier. Twice in one day was something he didn't usually do, *couldn't* usually do. But, then, this was Claire. And she was something else. Something unique and special. She'd wormed her way under his skin and into his heart, going beyond what she'd been paid to do. Going beyond granting sexual gratification and a few hours release from the never-ending and unremitting pain of the life he'd been forced to endure. Somehow, she'd touched his mind as well as his body, and now that she'd done it…

Sighing, he lowered a hand to himself. Touched himself gingerly, with fingers that wondered just how much more of this he could stand.

God almighty. She wasn't going to be banished. Not easily anyway.

Already, just at the thought of her, his tired, aching, worn out cock had started to harden.

He really had it bad. And that wasn't good.

Not for him and not for the woman.

There. That's better. If he just forced himself to think of her as the woman, the way he'd thought of all of them before, never allowing them to have names or personalities, never allowing them to have faces…

Maybe that was the problem. He'd allowed Claire to have a face. And that had made a difference. All the difference? Automatically, he shook his head. No, that didn't account for it, the idea that just because she had a face…

She had a personality, too. A strong one. She'd stood up to him in ways he couldn't remember anyone had ever stood up to him before, at any time. Except his bastard of an old man. Claire was strong. She was beautiful. She smelled wonderful, better than he'd known or imagined a woman could smell.

I should send her away. Get rid of her. Right now.

But not this exact moment. Because his hand had begun to move. Without conscious thought his fingertips had begun to smooth the tired and defeated, yet suddenly and miraculously responsive length of his cock.

Was this what they meant by recovery? By getting back to normal, even if at the moment normal seemed about the most unlikely adjective to describe what had become of his life and his future? If it was, you'd think someone might have warned him. You'd think someone might have taken at least a second to give him some advice about how to *be* normal again. How to survive and get along in an ass-over-teakettle world in which he'd been knocked down and was never again going to get up. Not completely anyway. Not so much that he'd ever…

But still. Even so.

What had his old man always said? What was that saying that had grated on Eli's nerves every time the old bastard used it against him, used it to control him or to get out of him some damned thing he'd never had any intention of giving?

Never look a gift horse in the mouth.

That was it. Though Claire was hardly a horse, he thought, watching the dim and shadowed ceiling intently as his hand drifted where it would, coming and going in ways that probably wouldn't take him to the brink. Not tonight and maybe not, regretfully, for a day or two to come. Maybe not until his time had run out with the precious, the incomparable Cla…woman.

He smiled up at the dancing, whirling snow shadows.

What was Claire doing?

Was she curled up in the wide, soft bed with the cherub carved headboard that he'd seen only in the decorator's photos of the room he'd had created especially for his guests? Was she asleep with the rich brown crescents of her lashes brushed like perfect, dark ink strokes against the pale curves of her cheekbones?

She had wonderful cheekbones, he thought, curling his fingers all the way around his hot, throbbing shaft.

He'd meant not to arouse but to soothe. Not to reach a climax like the ones he'd achieved earlier...explosive, ecstatic climaxes...but only to ease the pressure that had started to grow and expand more in his mind, he devoutly hoped, than anywhere else. More than anything, he just wanted to rub himself in this quiet, private and snow-swirled darkness. Because that was a way to ease himself to sleep and keep his mind off other things. Any other things. *All* other things.

Only it wasn't working. Because he'd grown hard again. Hard and surging and ready.

So maybe Claire had been a gift. From some God who'd finally, almost too late and when it didn't matter anymore, gotten around to noticing an injustice had been done. An undeserved punishment had been inflicted on a son who'd only been trying to please a grumpy and dissatisfied old man who'd never been pleased in all his miserable life. Maybe she'd been a gift meant to prove Eli was still strong enough to...

Slowly, as sleep drifted over him, he allowed his thoughts to roam as freely as the hand that would, in another minute or two, finally grant the release he so desperately needed. His mind drifted to other thoughts, to the snow beyond the window. To the way it had been coming down a little while ago, when he'd peered between the curtains one last time before getting himself ready for the night.

The snow had been deeper out there than the last time he'd been out, earlier in the evening. For that stupendous and unbelievable sleigh ride that had set the tone for what promised to be one hell of a stupendous and unbelievable week. The snow had passed two feet deep, he'd guessed, using the large concrete urns at the edge of the steps that led down to the wide and forbidden terraces at the edge of the lawn as his guide. And the wind had been howling. Shrieking around the corners of his marble prison in the same way he imagined it always would. The same way he remembered it always had shrieked and wailed around the eaves of the other house. The older one he'd so carefully hidden from himself even while he'd kept it there on purpose, just so he could torture himself with the knowledge that it was still there.

The wind had a human sound tonight. Like a woman or a man in enormous distress. A woman or a man moaning out in terminal agony, unable to find enough strength and courage to die, yet unable to find a way to go on living with the hand it had been dealt. Unable to find a way to cope with the circumstances it had been forced to accept. It had driven great and billowing waves of snow before it, a fury of thick white flakes already dropped from the obliterated sky only to be lifted again and tossed around against their will, no more able than Eli to find peace and comfort. And always there had been more flakes, more of them dropping every minute in swirling clouds of white, adding their weight to the layers upon layers of cold and frozen anonymity they'd already deposited. It was that very cold and frozen numbness Eli wanted more than anything else, more than any stroking or release of the pent up and red hot unmet physical needs he'd come to regard as just one more way his old man reached out from the grave to punish him and make his life a living and unbearable hell.

Numbness and forgetfulness. That was all he wanted. All he asked for. All he demanded the women give him during their brief stays beneath his roof and in his company.

Eyes closed, frowning now, Eli stopped the motion of his hand for a moment.

Was that why he'd sent them away? The women? All of them except Claire? Was that why, invariably up until now, he'd fired them after only one encounter? Why he'd fucked them to the best of his ability. Or to be more accurate, why he'd had them fuck him only to proclaim them *completely unsatisfactory* and let them go without paying them one single, goddamned, solitary cent? Why he hadn't ever dared let the episodes turn into anything other than mindless, soulless *fucking* of the first degree? Why he'd refused to let them be what they should have been...beautiful moments that, even if the women had been paid, could have been shared? Could at least have held some semblance of love?

Had he treated them that way because they *had* numbed him, and in reality, that was the last thing he wanted?

He felt his face burn. Knew it turned red enough almost to light up the seething darkness in his lonely bedroom.

He'd done that.

He'd used them. Shamelessly. Without ever, he realized in one of the first honest moments of the last five years, intending to pay them a cent.

He'd been a jackass. A monster. Had been just like his old man...an unfeeling, uncaring worm concerned only with himself, so wrapped up in himself and what he wanted that he'd completely failed to realize that anyone else, anyone he'd subjected to his disgusting attentions, might have feelings, too.

It was an awakening. A rude one. A not entirely welcome one.

Shivering, shuddering, Eli pulled his hands away from the cock that did not deserve to, if he had one single solitary thing to say about it, have the release it craved. Locking his fingers together behind his head, he lay naked and erect, his body uncovered to the hips, all the undamaged and functioning parts of him exposed to the chill that crept through the window glass like it was tissue paper. Finding even the tiniest cracks so that it could invade his sanctuary in the same way glacial ice had invaded his heart. He lay on his back and punished himself by ignoring the cock that stood painfully erect in defiance of everything he'd believed about his own capabilities.

Erect, because he'd made one mistake.

With a woman named Claire.

One *more* mistake, he amended. In a lifetime full of the most pitiful, the most laughably tragic and stupendously stupid mistakes any one man could ever make.

Chapter Twelve

SHE'D TOLD HER MOTHER THAT *MR. EDEN* WOULD WANT HER ON HER TOES IN THE morning, even though she suspected he'd be more likely to want her on her back. Or on her knees or her backside, as that seemed to be the way he preferred to have her do things. And she'd been half truthful about that. Even if she *had* wanted to end a conversation that had seemed to be heading straight into subjects that could not be discussed with her mother, Claire really had been concerned about getting some rest.

If the first part of her stay in Eli Eden's peculiar mansion had been difficult and exhausting, she could only expect the rest of it to be more of the same. She could only expect she'd need the sleep she'd found so hard to get.

And then, this morning, this gray-skied and snow-buried day that seemed like merely a break between waves of the same immense and overbearing storm...

Nothing.

Standing in what had become her favorite place next to the window, clutching the shimmering brocade of the curtains close to her cheek, she stared out at the dismal, monochrome twilight. Stared at the dreary brown wooden house that was the only spot of color in an otherwise lifeless landscape.

She'd dreaded the next encounter with Eli Eden. Yet at the same time she'd been terribly disappointed, almost bereft, when the expected summons hadn't come. When Estella had brought a breakfast tray with a delicious, steaming breakfast Claire had barely been able to touch, but no word about him. No word about when he would expect her or how he would expect her.

During the night, tomorrow had become today. And then this morning had become this afternoon, only to be quickly followed by the encroaching this evening. And still she remained alone in her gold and crystal tomb. Now this evening had nearly faded into tonight, and she was about to go out of her mind.

Moving suddenly, she flung herself away from the window. She *was* about to go stark raving mad if she didn't find something to do, and find it quickly. Forbidden to leave the room or not, she had to find some way to entertain herself and occupy her mind. Had to find something to read at the very least, before she snapped under the sheer and unrelieved stress of sitting alone, waiting and wondering why in the *hell* Eli Eden didn't call for her.

Hurrying to the private bathroom that adjoined her bedroom, Claire grabbed the golden silk robe that hung on the back of the door. She stuffed her feet into a pair of open toed, open backed golden mules with impractical spindly heels and even more impractical marabou trim, and headed back into the bedroom.

Flimsy garments, thin and clinging things, they offered no protection from the creeping chill of this terrible, high-ceilinged and hard-surfaced mansion that no longer seemed glittering as much as it seemed frozen. But they covered her nakedness and gave a good illusion of modesty even if the very idea of modesty seemed unutterably silly, what with Estella and Eli the only other people who seemed to inhabit this place. What with both of them having already seen her at her most naked and most humiliated already.

She could get dressed. She actually took a step or two toward the wide armoire and the jeans and sweatshirt she'd hung neatly inside. She could pull them on, and... but that was silly. That was senseless.

The mansion stood empty and echoing. And she was only heading downstairs for a minute. Only long enough to locate a magazine, a newspaper, a milk carton, *anything* readable.

Her slippers clattered on the silvery marble of the hallway floor, the racket they raised enough to surely wake the dead. Or, at the very least, to bring Eli Eden or one of his no doubt hidden and spying henchmen running before she reached the strip of carpeting that would deaden the sound. Running to force her back inside the unbearable prison of her elegant but dead bedroom.

Thinking she'd rather die than go back in there just yet, she pulled the slippers off and tucked them into the pockets of her robe, then crept down the magnificent, pale swirl of the grand staircase.

Like the upper levels, the lower floor lay silent. No sound of voices raised in discussion or laughter echoed through deserted rooms or along the hallways. And had she really expected them to? Of course there wouldn't be life or laughter, at any rate. No sound of music, of a radio or a television, rising from even the most distant corner to break the heavy and sparkling silence.

Stepping up to the first of the rooms she encountered, a wide and gold embossed double door at the left hand side of the hallway, Claire shivered.

It's like I'm the only person alive here. Like all the rest of it, the maid Estella, and Eli Eden, and the strangely peculiar and intoxicating sexual escapades she'd endured, had been nothing more than parts of a crazy and besotted dream.

Except she knew she hadn't been dreaming. Knew she wasn't dreaming now. Laying a hand on the cold brass handle of the double doors, she turned it and peered into the room beyond.

It was vast. A music room, dark green and vaguely masculine in contrast to the feminine golden whiteness that seemed so prevalent everywhere else, dominated by the massive blackness of the grand piano at its far end. But deeper color notwithstanding, the room only had the potential to be cozy and welcoming. Because it was every bit as cold and uninviting as all the other rooms, with the one exception of Eli's sitting room, that she'd seen.

Backing out of the green room, she pulled the doors shut quietly, and began to work her way along the hallway that led toward the back of the house. Room after room loomed on either side, each one silent and shrouded in shadow, each one so lifeless it might have been constructed and decorated in the interest of numbers rather than purpose. All of the rooms seemed the same. All of them seemed nothing more than glamorous shells of rooms, placed there to be deliberately uninhabited for some peculiar and completely inexplicable reason.

The house was enormous. Bigger, even, than it had looked from the outside or felt when it seemed to press down upon her and try to suffocate her with its weight.

And then, suddenly, opening one more in that long series of doors, Claire found something else.

This double door, lying just beyond a sudden bend in the wide corridor, led not to a purposeless room but to the outside. It led, across a very short, level and clean-shoveled stretch of concrete sidewalk, to the front door of the other house.

Claire hesitated, shivering. Intrigued yet uncertain. Beckoned yet hesitant.

What would Eli say if he knew she'd even considered it?

That, more than anything else, goaded her to do what she hadn't been going to do at all.

Stepping forward into ice-laden wind, she tested the double carved doors to make sure they wouldn't lock behind her and leave her outside to freeze in her whipping silken robe. Once she'd determined there *was* no lock, she stopped for a second to glance nervously back and forth along the length of the deserted hallway while she pulled her slippers from her pockets and put them on. Then she stepped outside, pulling the doors shut behind her.

Shivering harder, wrapping her arms around herself in search of whatever feeble and fleeting protection they had to offer, she scurried across the short stretch of concrete that lay perfectly straight and perfectly flat, seeming deliberately positioned so that visitors could access the porch of the older house, set lower on the slightly rolling hillside, without stepping up or stepping down. Too cold after even such short exposure to a wind that had risen again and brought with it a fresh flurry of heavy white flakes, she hurried to the massive door she knew she'd find locked.

But when she grasped the knob and turned, the door swung open.

Into another world. A dark and gloomy one, its light scarce and dim, falling through a series of small and oft times stained glass windows, its rooms devoid of any furnishing save the occasional broken and forgotten straight chair or wooden table. This house might be abandoned and dusty, but it was still breathtakingly elegant in its own way, in a way the marble mansion, for all its polished sheen and rich furnishings, would never be elegant.

This house had what her mother would call character. It was inherent in the inlaid wooden paneling, the smaller proportion of rooms that seemed to have been designed for living and not just for looking, in the odd twists and turns that prevented any path from room to room or hallway to hallway from being straight, and in the strange ups and downs of its terrain. In rooms that stood, inexplicably but charmingly up a step or down two steps, so that before she traveled very far in any direction, she came upon the very steps that seemed to have been so purposefully obliterated from the entrance.

Stepping down two of them, she paused inside a small room to glance around. The empty fireplace called out for a cheery blaze, for warmth to shine out upon deep leather furnishings and books and age-mellowed portraits on dignified walls. She reached up to stroke an antique wall fixture alive with cherubs and curlicues and trailing vines. A bulb, apparently not that old, remained, and after a second she reached down and groped along the paneled wall until she found an equally antique switch.

She flipped it up, and the light came on. For a moment it shone on golden oak paneling and still-radiant hardwood flooring. For a moment it cast a warming gleam on a handsome mantel over a dark tiled fireplace, and some pale object that stood at the very center of that mantel, propped against the wall where an unfaded square hinted a larger painting had once hung. Then the light dimmed with a strange and ominous humming Claire almost thought she could feel.

Bad wiring, she thought, and immediately returned the switch to the *off* position. *That would explain why the place had been abandoned.* If the wiring was bad, how could anyone live there?

That was all well and good. That might be true. But it didn't explain why the house had been left here, so close to the new one, with access between them made so easy and so unimpeded.

Drawn by the pale object propped on the mantel, Claire crossed to the fireplace.

It was a black and white photograph of Eli. A fairly recent one. His face looked nearly the same in the fading light, barely younger beneath glass that had shattered and spider webbed as if it had been thrown violently across some great distance. But it wasn't the same face at all. Because in the picture, Eli smiled. Lit by the sun, his hair gleamed softly beneath a dark baseball cap with a lighter colored *A* on the front. And in a lower corner, atop a glimpse of dark striped white shirt with dark sleeves below his elbows, he'd signed his name in bold, broad strokes, followed by the scrawled word *Diamondbacks.* His photographed face had a feeling of incredible youth, of lightness and vitality and energy she realized for the first time was strangely missing in the face she'd seen every day since her arrival.

This was the Eli she knew. But it wasn't the same Eli at all.

It has to be that smile, she thought, running a yearning and careful finger across the uneven surface of the ruined glass. Such a broad smile, hinting he'd been about to erupt into an explosion of laughter in the instant the shutter clicked.

Some tragedy, her mother had said. *Involving Eli Eden's father.* Suddenly, shivering, Claire glanced around the dusty and deserted room.

The old house was unheated. And she was cold. Even colder than the weather outside, as if this place was haunted by something so powerful, so terrible and irreversible that...she could no longer control her shivering. No matter how hard she tried.

Placing the shattered photograph back on the mantel, taking great care to position it precisely where she'd found it, she wrapped her robe as tight around her as it could wrap and turned to flee from the haunted and haunting photograph.

She would have fled, except that the instant her gaze swung around to the large bay window that faced the marble house, her heart leaped into her throat and froze solid there. Her entire body froze into a useless and unresponsive block of stone.

Someone stood there. Just inside the windows. Cloaked in deep shadow, he was squat and hulking, abnormally wide and misshapen in a way that only suggested...

Claire's scream, as she regained the ability to move with a sudden hot stroke as of lightning, was thin. Watery. Mindless of her clumsy slippers, she ran from the haunted room. Ran back across the smooth surfaced and now snow dusted concrete walk, the slippers making racket enough to hide the sound of the watcher following, if that was what he...or she...meant to do. Fleeing back to the marble mansion, she didn't stop until she exploded into her bedroom, shaking all over.

And came face to face with a stern and scowling Estella, who radiated dislike and disapproval from every line of her face and her body.

"Mr. Eden is highly displeased," the maid hissed.

Oh, great. I was summoned. And not only wasn't I in the room where I was supposed to be, I got caught not being here.

Claire shuddered again. And suddenly, in that one horrible instant, visions of pursuit by some strange and otherworldly being were replaced by other visions. Sobering ones of the fifty thousand dollars she'd been promised and stood to lose if she wasn't careful.

She'd humiliated herself. And for what?

She would be sent away now. So that the worst, the truly unthinkable, could happen to her mother. So that she and Claire, though Claire really didn't matter so much in this scenario, would be thrown out into the street for nonpayment of rent. Thrown out with the coldest part of the winter still to come with nowhere to go, nowhere to be warm.

But Estella was tugging at the silken cord of her robe. Opening it and starting to ease the golden fabric down over her bare shoulders. "You need to hurry," she declared. "Mr. Eden doesn't like to be kept waiting."

"H...he isn't going to..."

Estella had produced a costume. This time it was some kind of wire cage, something so enormous Claire feared she might not be able to pass through the bedroom doorway or any doorway while wearing it.

"I don't know what he's liable to do." Estella snapped the thing around Claire's waist. "He wasn't happy to learn you'd defied his explicit orders."

"You told him?" Without being instructed, Claire lifted her arms so that Estella could tighten the corset, of violet velvet this time, its completely sheer whisper of skirt covering the enormous hoop with...nothing. Literally nothing that would conceal anything.

"Of course I told him. The moment I couldn't find you, I had a duty to tell him you'd disobeyed."

"And what did he say?" Sucking in her breath as she'd been taught, Claire closed her eyes while Estella tugged at the corset strings with a viciousness that didn't seem warranted or necessary. Not even in light of her disobedience.

"He told me to wait for you. To dress you and send you to him the moment you appeared, and to be quick about it. He told me he would deal with you himself. In his own way."

That did nothing to ease the dread in Claire's heart. If anything, it only helped it grow into a hideous and savage thing that seemed to sneer at her, predicting only the worst of all possible outcomes.

Reaching into a basket on the brocade loveseat, Estella produced a flower. An orchid that appeared freshly picked.

Claire caught her breath. "How beautiful!" And caught it again when she glanced down into the basket to see it was filled with orchids in every imaginable shade of pink and rose and white-tipped lavender.

"Mr. Eden wishes you to meet him in the conservatory." Reaching up, Estella began to fasten the flower in Claire's hair.

"Wait! What about the..." Claire looked around, scanning the rest of her costume, the long violet satin gloves, the shimmering orchid-colored crystal necklace, the net stockings and high heeled silk slippers. And found what she'd been looking for. "You forgot the mask," she said, reaching for it.

"Mr. Eden says you are to dispense with that."

For a second, her head spinning and confused blood roaring in her ears, Claire couldn't believe what she'd heard. He'd said something about that before. When he'd dismissed her the last time, at the end of their *dessert party*. But she hadn't believed him.

This was a new development. A completely unexpected and highly interesting one.

A signal that something had changed, maybe?

Or maybe, in his infinitely devious and diabolical way, Eli had simply decided to add a new wrinkle to the game and obtain some new power with which to shame her.

"I want to wear it." She could scarcely believe the words had come out of her own mouth. But apparently they had because Estella stopped, the orchid poised in midair, to stare at her.

Picking up the mask, Claire put it in the maid's hand and took the orchid from her.

"Mr. Eden won't be happy," Estella protested. "He ordered me to cut the orchids especially for you and put them in your hair. He doesn't like to waste. Especially not something as valuable as..."

Reaching for a box of pins on a nearby table, Claire fastened the blossom to the side of her barely there topless gown. "They won't go to waste," she murmured, only just beginning to see the enormous possibilities this new turn of events had opened.

While the maid pulled the mask down over her head and fastened it in place, Claire worked with the flowers.

If Eli Eden wanted orchids, Eli Eden would have orchids. He would find them fastened to her skirt, tucked into the low-cut, breast-baring top of her gown, and even on the mask. She handed one of them, an especially mind-boggling deep rose bloom liberally mottled with purple and maroon and pure, snowy white, to Estella. "Fasten this one on the mask."

After a moment's hesitation, apparently hearing the note of steely determination that had crept into Claire's voice, the maid obeyed.

"This is most unusual," she protested, accepting a second orchid to fasten beside the first. "Mr. Eden is always so explicit in his wants. His instructions are always so..."

"The hell with his instructions," Claire muttered, and almost laughed at the look of outraged disbelief that swept across Estella's face. "This has gone way beyond *his* instructions. This has gone beyond anyone's instructions. It's gone all the way to..."

She wasn't exactly sure *what* it had gone all the way to. Only that, by attempting to turn the tables on her, Eli Eden had given her the power she'd lacked up until the moment Estella tried to dispense with the hated mask. By ordering Claire not to wear it he'd given her the ultimate power, for the first time, to turn the tables on him.

And she was prepared to use that power. In any way she could.

A quick look into the basket on the loveseat revealed still more orchids. She'd hardly made a dent in the supply, even though she'd used all her imagination and all her creativity to fasten them to some very inventive places on her clothing and her person. Even onto the toes of her shoes.

"What did El...Mr. Eden expect?" she asked with a touch of amusement. "Did he want me to *drown* in the blasted things?"

"I'm sorry?" Estella looked slightly confused. And more than slightly dazed.

Which only seemed natural, since Claire felt much the same way...confused, dazed, dazzled, and suddenly giddy with anticipation at what was about to happen. The assignation she was about to take into her own hands and twist to her own needs and purposes.

Let Eli Eden indulge in his fantasies and his costumes, she thought as she grabbed up the basket and tucked it beneath her arm. Tonight, things were going to be different. Tonight, she was going to have what she wanted for a change. Safe behind the anonymity of the tight satin mask, an anonymity she'd failed completely to appreciate until it had so nearly been taken from her, she was going to see her own wishes fulfilled for once. Her own fantasies met.

Chapter Thirteen

As she might have expected, the conservatory was decorated in crystal and gold. Tinkling chandeliers swayed on impossibly long chains from a vaulted glass ceiling and arrangements of the same delicate and formal furniture that filled the rest of the house clustered gracefully beneath…stuff that looked impractical and not meant for real human use. But that was as far as the similarity to the rest of the house went. That was where the semblance of a 'normal' room ended, and what gave the scene spread out before her disbelieving eyes the quality of the ultimate fantasy. Of something she'd not seen before, or ever thought to see.

Below the chandeliers, most of them dark except directly above the stage Eli had set behind spindly gold brocade chairs and elegant, pale tables, stood a jungle. Giant palms dripped with vines. Heavily split and curled leaves twice as big around as Claire's head drooped over and among blossoms in every shade and hue. And the perfume! Scent swirled in air that seemed suddenly thick, and so far removed from the snow covered Pennsylvania mountainside just beyond the windows that it made her head spin. Made her stumble a little, suddenly disoriented, and catch the back of the nearest chair to keep from toppling into a violet-gowned heap. The jungle was cleverly lighted from within by a magical, greenish light from dozens of carefully placed and invisible bulbs, and intertwined with smooth marble paths that twisted off the central stage only to disappear immediately into a spectacular sea of greenery. And everywhere Claire saw orchids.

If Eli had worried about wasting a single blossom in the basket she clung to as if it was the last bit of reality in a scene that could not possibly be real or of this earth, he needn't have. There were thousands of them. Orchids in every color imaginable, some that singed the eye and suspended disbelief, stood in solitary splendor in isolated pots, dropped in fantastic sprays from mountings on trees and poles, draped themselves elegantly in tiny-blossomed fury across walkways and chair seats.

Stunned, she turned slowly, sniffing the wave of perfume that swept over her with even the faintest and most imperceptible stirring of warm, tropic air. Air that whispered seductively across her skin, light and penetrating, and incredibly sweet with the breath of eternal summer beneath snow-frosted glass.

"Plumeria," Eli said softly and for a minute, struggling to re-focus her gaze, Claire couldn't see him. "From Hawaii. That's what you smell. The most wonderful scent in the world. And gardenias. Tuberoses. Everything that has a scent, every scent you could ever want. It's here, Claire."

"It's..." She squinted. Blinked rapidly, then finally managed to focus on him.

He lay on the floor on a wide and barely rose-colored satin pallet spread across pale marble. Dressed this time in a white shirt, immaculate, impeccable, perfect, and jeans that gave him a newly casual and even more enticing air, he lay on his hip, propped up against a pile of satin pillows, a glass of champagne in his hand.

When she didn't move, he lifted the glass to her.

"I hear you've been exploring," he murmured, his voice deep, dusky, and thoroughly unreadable.

Slowly, Claire advanced toward him.

"A person can only stay cooped up in one room for so long," she countered, suddenly wondering if her show of bravado and her take-control attitude had been such good ideas, after all. "Without going crazy, that is."

"I could lock you in the next time."

Unaccountably, her heart soared. Despite his words, she felt no threat from him. Indeed, they'd been murmured in the most delectable, most softly inviting, downright seductive tone she'd heard him use. He seemed genuinely glad to see her. As much as, she'd only just realized, she was glad to see him.

"You could," she agreed, her voice trembling a little at the thought and all the ramifications she wasn't able to consider objectively just yet. "But you'd have to put a lock on the door first."

He nodded slightly, just once. "I would be entirely within my rights." Sweeping up and down her body, his gaze took on a strange and sparkling gleam. Of appreciation, no doubt, for her new and barely-there Southern Belle getup.

"I thought I told Estella to forget about the mask?"

"It was my choice." Claire's voice continued to shake. Harder than before. As did her hands, which threatened to drop the basket and spill orchids everywhere.

"I see. Disobedient to the bitter end, aren't you?"

Bitter end? Is that what this is? There seemed to be nothing Claire could say in response. And since Eli didn't seem to expect anything, still didn't seem to be angry as much as confused, bemused, amused, she held her ground and said nothing at all.

"Come here." He gestured, lifting his glass of champagne again.

Slowly, hands tightening convulsively around her basket, she went.

"I was going to offer champagne," he said quietly. "Something I've never...don't usually do. Since I don't usually invite my guests here. But seeing that it won't be possible for you to drink..." Lifting the glass again, he saluted her for a second time and took a long, slow swallow.

"What would you..." As nervous as a bride, Claire plucked an orchid, an enormous and stunningly striped pink and white one, from the basket and offered it to him. "What is it that you want me to do?"

Smiling, he set his glass on a table behind the pallet, accepted the flower, and stroked the stiff, waxy-dewy petals across his cheek.

"Come here," he said again, rolling onto his back at the precise center of the pallet.

When she did, when she looked at something other than his face and his eyes for the first time, Claire saw that he'd exposed himself. Like before, he remained clothed, his body hidden and off limits except for the erect and thrusting shaft she would soon be required to service.

"Crouch," he ordered, not unkindly this time, and opened his arms to her.

"Crouch?"

He nodded. "Over me."

For a moment Claire hesitated. Drinking in the dreamlike setting one last time, drinking in the soothing, scented air. Then she lifted the basket. Lifted it above her head, turned it on its side, and swung it in a slow and deliberate arc above the rosy satin bed he'd made for them on the floor of the jungle.

SWEET GOD IN HEAVEN. Eli thought he would die for sure when the night suddenly rained orchids. When blossoms fell onto him and around him in a silken cloud. One of them struck his enormously distended and needful cock, struck it with dewy fire that made him twitch and made his balls respond instantly. Making him think he would come in enormous and leaping white ropes before she ever touched him. Before he ever had the chance to live through what he wanted to make her do to him. But somehow he held on. Somehow, counseling patience, he convinced his cock that it was better to wait, better to see if tonight, like last night, Claire would surprise it, and him.

She came to him. Straight to him. Came that last step or two, and without seeming to need further direction lifted the enormous and sweeping canopy of her skirt that covered nothing at all and dropped it over him. Dropped it so that it covered him and left him alone with her. With the half of her that, on all occasions previous to this one, had been all he'd wanted of her.

He could see her through the sheer netting that separated them. See her quite clearly, see her hidden face and purple-gloved hands as they began to find the strewn orchids and lift them as if to revere each as the ultimate treasure for a bare fraction of a second before she flung it back up.

Some of them caught in low hanging branches of the plumeria tree that towered over their bed, to dangle there like strange ornaments perfectly placed upon some wildly exotic tropical Christmas tree. Others landed atop gardenia shrubs and gleamed there, purple-pink-white against creamy blooms. And still others dropped to the gleaming marble floor or gold upholstered seats, Christmas presents wrapped as no presents had ever, in the history of Christmas, been wrapped. Containing secret delights no Christmas gift had ever contained.

Eli saw everything though the gown that cut him off completely from her even as it revealed her…the *real* her. And he regretted the separation. Regretted anything and everything that stood between him and the smell of her hair, the sight of her eyes, the caress of her firm yet soft breasts against hands and lips and flesh that wanted to feel that caress.

He regretted, but he felt powerless to change anything. Because for some unknown reason, in some unknown but very, very tantalizing way, Claire had once again telegraphed to him that she'd taken charge. This had begun as his fantasy, but now it was hers. And she was calling the shots, so that all he needed to do…

Without warning, in one long and sweeping, gliding movement that wrenched a cry of amazement from his throat and another, more violent, lurch of astonished recognition from his cock as well as his heart, she took him in. She just simply descended over his cock and onto it without looking, without moving her hidden gaze away from his face, and slipped herself onto him.

And God, the touch of her! The taut and wet shudder of flesh meeting heated flesh, the caress of her as she parted to accept him and then closed again, tightening in a clear-cut attempt to kill by smothering.

This was what he'd dreamed. Everything he'd ever dreamed and more. Caught in her sweetly clinging satin-velvet vise of flesh gripping flesh, he felt young again. Felt sought after. Desirable. *Desired.*

"My God, Claire." His heart nearly stopped in mid beat, and he could only whimper in the weak and thready voice of a very old man. Of a man about to die in the throes of ecstasy. "Don't..." His back stiffened as she flexed her legs, her good, long, strong legs, and lifted herself. Reaching with a satin-gloved hand, she stroked the side of his face until he wanted to cry. *Did* cry, he realized with a burst of astonishment as tears sprang to his eyes and slipped down his face unabashed, uninhibited, unstoppable.

He wanted to touch her. Wanted it so badly that the inability to do it would surely kill him. He wanted her, without satin or the silken mist of invisible fabric or the crisp cotton of his shirt to separate them. He wanted to feel the gentle caress of her fingertips stroking fire through his skin wherever she touched. Whenever she touched.

But that wasn't to be. That couldn't be. And so...

"Don't stop."

"I wouldn't dream of it." Swiftly, easily, gliding on the moisture that flowed from him and from her to smooth her way, she lowered herself again. But this time when the firm flesh of her thighs met his hips, she stayed. Leaned forward a little so that he flexed inside her and then, just as suddenly as she'd done any other amazing, damned thing in the amazing, damned time he'd known her, she leaned back again.

Flex. Beyond torment, his cock cried out.

Move. Flex. There could be no doubt now. She was trying to kill him. The gentle rocking of her body, the insistent and persistent adjusting and readjusting of his cock inside the tightness of her every time she moved, was designed specifically to kill him.

Her hips seemed to move impossibly with each forward and backward gyration. Seemed to move in ways that no normal hips should be able to move, until finally she rolled herself forward. Still on him, still clutching him with flesh that clung to his, she lowered herself almost flat onto his chest.

Her face was very close to his now. And God, how he wished he could see it, see her eyes. Wished he could bring her to him and kiss her.

It was a shock to realize he had never kissed her. A shock to realize he wanted to, even more than he wanted to...

"That thing's got to go," he muttered, reaching for the mask. But he never made it. Because in the next instant, his hands falling back limp and useless against the satin pallet, he felt, heard, with stunned and disbelieving ears, his lungs empty in a long and low shriek of sheer agony.

Claire placed her hands on his shoulders, and her touch seemed to burn like acid, straight through the two or three layers of fabric that separated his skin from hers.

Eli shrieked because the slight movement as she bent forward over him did something to him, did something to her position atop him, that made it impossible for him to remain silent any longer. Eli heard himself shriek, and then shriek again, the cries of a man in the final stages of his life.

Claire slowly pushed herself upright, moving his shaft with every supple muscle available to her. Tilting her satin-encased head back into a posture of sheer glee, she came upright again, with him buried inside her. With him thrusting and thrashing wildly inside her, engaged in an all out fight for relief.

Eli reached for her breasts. Thrust out above the shimmering top of her gown, they'd poised themselves so close above him, so ripe for the plucking. And he couldn't reach them.

She'd imprisoned him with that enormous damned skirt. Brought it right down over him so that, with her firmly mounted on his shaft and holding it prisoner within the deepest parts of her, she'd also imprisoned the rest of him. The layer of fabric, so sheer and seemingly so flimsy, was in reality a superbly engineered device of restraint, designed to effect maximum suffering from anyone subjected to its embrace.

Arms pinned, barely able to move, he couldn't penetrate what he could barely see. Couldn't raise his hands more than a few inches above his face. Couldn't tear the stuff that separated him from the sweet and warm flesh he desired in ways he felt sure no living man had ever desired sweet and warm flesh before. His hands shook so badly that he found it all but impossible to grip the faintly violet wall of his prison. And even when he finally managed, he couldn't find an opening, couldn't find a ripple or a wrinkle on that smooth and taut surface. Couldn't find a place or a way to tear, or poke through, or force the damned, infernal, devil-spun stuff to give way.

"Please." He heard the word. Knew he said it because the voice that said it, hoarse and rasping, seemed to vaguely resemble his own. But he couldn't believe it.

He'd never begged a woman for anything.

He'd never allowed one to gain such complete control that he'd been *forced* to beg. As he sensed himself getting ready to beg now for mercy. For just one, just a single, touch of that wonderful, incredibly white and swelling skin above the top of her gown, for one fleeting taste of the nipple that floated rosy and tantalizing, and so far beyond his reach that it might as well have been on the moon and not on Earth at all. For one fleeting taste of the lips she'd hidden deliberately. Hidden sadistically.

For another second, or maybe half of a half of a second, Eli retained enough presence of mind to wonder how in the holy, living, screaming hell things had gotten this far out of hand.

Claire had gone exploring this afternoon. She'd apparently gone where, while not specifically forbidden to go, common sense should have told her she had no business going. Over there. To the other house. He didn't know what she'd seen over there, what she could have seen or what she might have concluded if she'd seen anything. But he knew it couldn't happen again. So he'd meant to pay her off. He even had the check for twice the amount they'd agreed upon inside his shirt pocket right now. He'd meant to bring her here, meant to have a last moment of satisfaction or two, and then he'd planned to be rid of her, and the threat she represented to the stability of his life and the peace, miserable though it was, of his heart.

But then...somehow...

"Christ almighty!" While he hadn't been paying attention, she'd slipped backward. Or she'd leaned, or...something. Sitting on his thighs, balancing herself atop them, she'd begun to use her arms and the knees she'd buried deep in the pallet at either side of him to maneuver herself. Completely beyond his ability to touch, bent backward in a position that looked like it should have been awkward and implausible, but turned out to be anything but, she was...

A sob broke from his throat. A genuine sob, when she pushed forward and downward with those long, long legs and forced him into her. When she used muscles he'd never dreamed a woman possessed to close herself around him and draw him in, tugging at him at the same time that she slid herself along the length of him and used herself to sheath him.

Something seemed to break inside Eli's mind and inside his body. Something too long forgotten, too long ignored and neglected. He felt a burst of white light searing him to a crisp from the inside out. And he went weak. Not just the parts of his body that had lost so much of their strength and their stamina a long time ago, but the fit and agile parts, too. His arms shook, and he knew he couldn't have lifted them now to save his life. Couldn't have lifted them even if he'd been granted sudden, miraculous access to the swelling breasts that had passed so far beyond his reach that he didn't stand a chance of having them. His gut quivered, too, with a strange and subtle rhythm that perfectly matched the deeper, more feral and primal vibration that had started inside his balls. The quiver that said the explosion, when it came, was going to be one he would never forget. One that would mark him for life. And maybe mark her, too.

Moving like a belly dancer, her body swaying in sinuous rhythms, back and forth at the same time that it undulated up and down, muscles tightening and loosening in rhythms that generally matched, yet sometimes didn't match at all her shimmering sway, Claire moistened.

At first, at the beginning of her conquest of him, it had been nothing more than a hint of moisture. Something on the order of the grudging mist she'd managed to achieve on their first encounter, when he'd thought she was better than most and he might keep her around for a while. But this…now…

"Oh my God." Tilting his head back, Eli dug into the pillows and thrust…*tried* to thrust with remembered strength, using all the power in his shoulders to force the lower part of his body to rise and plunge into her the way he longed to plunge. But she was indisputably in charge. And she was too much for him.

"No," she murmured, leaning forward again.

The shifting of her weight, combined with the pressure she exerted on a cock just about to go insane with need, ripped the breath from his lungs and the will to move, make that the will to *live*, from his mind. Placing a small hand, an utterly controlling hand, on each of his shoulders, she moved her masked face close to his. "Don't," she hissed. "This one is *mine*."

Another tear slipped down Eli's cheek. One to begin with, but then quickly followed by another and another as, grappling with the infernal layer of spun air that separated them as effectively as a concrete wall and iron bars, he began to cry openly. Cry with despair and desire and anticipation.

Despair that she'd, at some point, decided to give him the kind of lovemaking he'd only dreamed about. Lovemaking he knew was going to end, had to end, before she learned the truth, and he saw revulsion in her eyes and heard it in her voice.

Desire, because he'd never expected it to go this far and couldn't help but want it to go even farther. Didn't want to live one more moment of his life without her, and the possibility she might do this to him again. And again and again and again.

And anticipation, because she hadn't finished. Not yet.

She'd changed her position again.

She sat him now, riding him as easily, as casually and gracefully as if she sat astride one of his dad's cursed, misbegotten horses. She'd found a rhythm, rise and fall, sway and anticipate, lean and control, not unlike the one used by a superb rider with full confidence in her mount and her ability to make it do whatever she wanted.

God in heaven, he wondered as a shudder of deepest, most incendiary and still building desire, the prelude to the climax she seemed to have designed specifically to drive him beyond any limit of human endurance, wound its torturous way through him. *What the hell am I feeling?*

Hurt? Oh, yes. Hurt. From needing her. From having always needed her, even in the long years and months and days of his life that had been completely empty, completely without substance until he'd finally found her.

Deep inside, the soothing, scintillating hurt gathered strength. Gathered momentum. And he was glad he'd kept the damned check in his pocket. Glad he hadn't given it to her and told her she could leave any time because she had no further obligation to him.

This had gone beyond the standard arrangement. This wasn't even an arrangement any more. This lithe and willowy woman, her face hidden from him even as it hovered directly above him, its expression and her intentions hidden as effectively as if she'd worn a mask of solid iron instead of gleaming satin, this body that began to torture his in all the right ways. With meandering movements that carried his stunned cock along for the ride of its life. This was something else. This was more than he'd ever bargained for.

Lifting his hand to his throat, he tugged at the collar of his shirt to keep it from strangling him. Finding it already loose and unbuttoned, he realized the garroting pressure on his throat couldn't be eased. If anything, reacting to a fresh round of tears he couldn't stop and didn't *want* to stop, the pressure was destined only to increase. Was destined, soon, to reach fatal levels, from which there could be no return.

Claire…dear, sweet, beautiful Claire…was pleasuring herself as well as him. She was making soft and guttural, half groaning and half purring sounds in her throat and her chest, taking all the relief from him that she'd been expected only to give. She was taking what he hadn't, until just a moment or two ago, in the plumeria-scented dimness of this very special room where he'd never before allowed any woman to attend him, realized he had to give.

And that scared the hell out of him. Scared the shit out of him.

Because he didn't have that much to give. Didn't, if he came right down to it, have anything to give that a woman like Claire would want. And still he was trying to give it. His body, poor, tortured and disadvantaged thing that it was, was still straining. Still trying to lift itself so that it could take what it wanted, could insert itself all the way into the soft and teasing warmth that flirted with him, played games with him and promised miracles only to string him along.

He wanted to take her. Wanted to turn her over onto her back. Wanted to free his arms of the infernal cage contraption of the gown with which she'd entrapped him, and press her down into the satin sheets. Wanted to feel the sheer urgency, the utter comfort and rightness of his body sliding into hers and claiming it, instead of the other way around.

"Cl...aire." The word came out a shuddery wheeze. Almost a plea for breath.

"What?" Her face was so close to his now, her body pressed down onto his chest, her greedy and searching muscles still holding his cock tight and locking it into a grip from which he suspected no man would ever be able to escape. The brush of sheer netting rasped against his cheek, and her breath seemed to burn his skin even through so many infernal and interfering layers. And this time when he fought to raise his arms, he succeeded.

Fabric ripped.

Sheer, violet-mist netting parted and he reached up. Not for her breasts, as he'd wanted to do at the beginning of this encounter, when he'd still felt vaguely like himself and still vaguely in control of himself.

Now he reached for all of her. Catching her shoulders, he pulled her close with arms that locked around her. Using the power that remained in his upper body, he moved her along the length of him. Used her to stroke him and stoke the fire within. Used her to strike sparks that once ignited would never be extinguished. Sparks that offered him hope like none he'd expected to know again in this life. Hope for the future. For life, and the possibility of life, and all the infinity of possibilities each of the possibilities raised in its turn.

Eli used her. He stroked more and more sparks from his body and hers until finally, fumbling with the satin that encased her head and kept him from the full, unrestricted and uninhibited joy of her, he managed to tear that away, too.

Chapter Fourteen

"LET ME SHOW YOU," ELI SAID IN A THICK AND TREMBLING VOICE THAT SOUNDED NOTHING LIKE his own, his lips near hers, but not touching hers. Not yet. Not in the ways she'd only just discovered she wanted them to.

She didn't know what he wanted to show her. At the moment, crushed to his chest amidst the ruins of the orchids and the violet gown he'd sent for her to wear, surrounded by superheated air that nonetheless felt cool and misty with flower scent whispering across her bared face, Claire didn't much care what he wanted to show her.

She was willing to learn. Ready to learn.

Rolling her onto her back, he grappled for a moment with the waistband of the hooped cage. Finding the fastening, he released it, and when the thing collapsed around her, he tore away with impatient hands all remnants of the sheer and floating fabric. He didn't stop until he'd ripped everything away so that he could fling it, hoops and all, aside to a place where it would never again be a hindrance to either of them.

"Let me show you how it was for me," he murmured and his eyes, when he bent his head over her, shimmered with a depth of feeling she'd never imagined possible. From somewhere he'd produced a strawberry. From an enormous pot just behind their pallet, she realized. A pot that dripped with deep red and glistening berries. Dipping it in his glass of champagne, he pressed it to her lips. Crushed it against them until she opened her mouth and then closed it again, sealing her lips tight around long and strong and talented fingers that had barely released the fruit.

She heard him gasp. Heard him draw in one sharp and shaky breath, and then another.

Heard him and *wanted* him.

For himself. Not for any reason of duty, or obligation, or need for the money he'd offered. She wanted him simply because she wanted him. For himself, and because she loved him.

The realization came to her through a dazed and sparkling haze, and she wondered why the idea that she did love him came as no surprise at all.

Slowly, reading what might very well be an answering and responding glow in his dark and secretive eyes, Claire closed her mouth around his fingers. And felt his entire body tense next to hers as she began to draw the lingering remains of juice from them.

"Claire, I never expected..." With a suddenness that startled and a genuineness that stole her breath away, Eli smiled. Like she'd only known him to smile once before, and only then in the shattered photograph she'd found deliberately displayed in the deserted and echoing wooden house.

A display that suddenly, rightly, seemed symbolic. Seemed to have great and unfathomable meanings.

As if he'd abandoned the young and smiling man in the photograph. Abandoned him completely and forever in a single second of incomprehensible violence. As if he'd put that young man, that baseball star on the fast track to the top, away from him forever.

Claire thought about asking him. Would very likely, in the glow and the security of this moment when he held her close, have asked. But then he smiled again. And her heart felt like it ground to a stop.

"This is..." He tried to extract his fingers from her mouth. But she wouldn't let him. Closing her teeth down gently, but in a way that communicated clearly her intention, she held them where they were and ran her tongue over them, exploring the gently rounded tips of them, the firm and prominent knuckles, the sturdy joints at the place where they joined his hand. His pitching hand.

She didn't know that he'd been a pitcher. Didn't know the first thing about what he'd been or the game he'd played. But she thought he must have pitched. Because once again it just felt...right. Tasting those long and strong fingers, she liked what she tasted. They were musky. Slightly salty. A touch tart from the fruit he'd handled.

Gasping again, sharply, Eli twitched on the pallet next to her.

"What?" Reaching for his hair, she twined satin-covered fingers among its ruby-highlighted chestnut waves and stared down into his eyes, her own now open to him, her emotions and her love there for him to see. If he chose to see.

"I..." He jerked a little again. "Nothing."

"We can..." Too late, she realized she'd allowed him to withdraw his fingers from her mouth. Too late, she wondered if she could think of a way to entice them back, because she hadn't meant to release them at all. "We can do whatever you want, Eli."

She'd never said his name before. Not out loud, not to him. But she liked the sound of it and the way it felt as it brushed across her lips, her tongue tapping the back of her teeth once, very gently, in the process.

"I never..." He stared up at her, a slight frown creeping in to darken the look of pure and unabashed joy that had filled his face and his eyes only seconds before.

"What?"

"What?" He seemed to snap out of some kind of trance. Not an entirely pleasant one, from the sudden look of caution tinted heavily with fear that swept briefly through his expression.

"You started to say you'd *never*. Never what, Eli?"

She wondered if he liked hearing her say his name even half as much as she liked saying it.

"Never knew anyone like you?" he murmured, seeming almost to question.

"But was that what you wanted to say?" she whispered. "Was that..."

His fingers, forgotten in the strange tension of the moment, found her again. Found their way between her legs and began to stroke the flesh at her entrance experimentally, as if he'd never been there before. As if he had no idea what to do now that he'd made his way there.

Shuddering as her hand found the length of his shaft and merely touched at first, until she wrapped her fingers firmly around him, Claire opened herself wide. Expecting him to enter.

He didn't. He only continued to make lazy, stroking motions with the tips of his fingers, inciting already aroused flesh and drawing forth a new and headier rush of moisture from a body she'd thought couldn't possibly moisten more.

"Make love to me?" she whispered, beginning to stroke the beautiful, sculpted and carved shaft with the palm of her gloved hand.

"You're something new," he replied without replying at all. "You're different. Not like anything I ever expected."

"But that's a good thing." Turning her hand, she grazed his long and engorged shaft with the back of it, wondering if and hoping that the satin felt smooth and enticing against such hot tightness. "Isn't it?"

A look of immeasurable sadness and longing passed through his eyes.

"I'm not what you expected either, Claire."

"No," she agreed, wrapping her fingers tightly around the shaft once again so that she could begin to massage it in earnest. The way experience had taught her he liked to be massaged. "You're so much better than anything I expected."

Closing his eyes, he lay back against pale rose satin, very still, the hand with which he'd been toying at her opening falling away to leave her bereft.

"Shouldn't I say you're better?" she murmured, confusion coming through clearly in every word she spoke, though the hand at his shaft never ceased its caressing motion.

"You shouldn't say anything at all." When he smiled this time it was only an attempt at a smile. Because she saw none of the joy, none of the spark of wild abandon and sheer pleasure that had lighted him from within before.

"If I've said something to upset you...if I've done something..."

Catching her hand, he pulled it away. Catching the back of her neck with his other hand, he pulled her toward him. "You talk too damned much," he declared. "*That's* what's upsetting me."

"Make love to me and I'll stop."

His laughter, low and suggestive, made it extremely doubtful she'd last long enough for him to do anything more than what he was doing right now, just by being close to her. Just by pulling her down and forward, so that his probing and swollen shaft met her lips and brushed them with supernatural heat, unbelievable heat. Just by exerting subtle pressure with his hands at the back of her head, he gave her no choice but to part her lips. No choice but to allow him to slip inside. No choice but to taste the maddened and crazed flesh. No choice but to take him as far into her mouth as she could manage and then stroke with her tongue, feeling his every single, twitching leap echoed in the equally maddened and even more crazed nub inside herself. The one that was just about to explode out of her body in its quest for relief, relief, instant relief and unadulterated gratification. Rocking against him softly, she tasted and sampled, gently at first but then with mounting urgency and determination as the need inside her welled and built, all too swiftly reaching the flashover point.

"You started this," he murmured, his fingers straying dangerously close to her opening to blaze astonishing, burning trails across every centimeter of skin they encountered. "Don't you think it should be up to you to finish?"

For a moment Claire paused, going very still around the shaft that leaped anxiously in her grip, as if begging her not to give up on it now. Never to give up, please, until she'd done what she'd set out to do. Which was…

Tilting her head a little to the side, stroking her tongue along the slight ridge near its very top, the one that made him jump and strain with even the briefest of contacts, she thought about that.

She had no idea what she'd set out to do. *Seduce him?* Maybe. *Pay me back for what I did to her in the past? Humiliate him as he humiliated me?* Certainly.

But along the way, something had happened.

Along the way she'd conjured this…desperation was the only way she could think to describe it. This shivering-hot and hard edged fury of need that was just about to consume her from the inside out and that, she thought as she grazed the thrusting and pulsing shaft with just the edges of her teeth, was about to do the same to him.

"You don't want to make love to me?" she whispered, never moving her mouth away from the delight it had found, and delighting even more in the sensation of her lips skimming across him.

He shuddered. His entire body convulsed as his shaft gave a single, deep and demanding throb against the tip of her tongue.

"Not that I don't want to," he whispered, a sob rising in his throat to choke off the last word. "It's that I…"

Suddenly it didn't matter. Not a hoot in a hailstorm. Suddenly Claire didn't care *who* did what to whom. Only that someone do it, and do it quickly.

Pulling her mouth away from his probing and demanding length before he could make a single move to stop her, before he could even think about making such a move, she slipped her body up along the muscled and waiting length of him, and then she took him again. Without any preamble. Without any pretext. Without anything but the sheer force of what she felt welling inside her to be her guide, without anything at all but the need to have him and feel him. To accept with unbridled, undisguised, unashamed joy and pleasure everything Eli Eden had to offer. To enjoy it fully, and without reservation.

It was all she could do, but she managed to slip herself onto him slowly. To insert him without either of them being on the top or either on the bottom. Without either of them being in any position of clear-cut control, in case he changed his mind and decided he really did want to make love to her, after all.

His smooth and unyielding hardness penetrated a little deeper with each motion. Her body slipped up and down along him with incredible ease as delicious warmth spread inside her, and the pressure of wanting reached serious levels. Her body felt like it expanded for a fraction of a second just before it closed around him, so tight she felt certain he'd gasped with pain or terror rather than the satisfaction she sought to give.

But his face, when she looked at him from what seemed a suddenly great and unbridgeable void of distance, had tensed with something else. Something entirely different. She scarcely had time to think about what it might be before his body spasmed once, in a shivery sort of way.

And then he came. Crying out, his face contorting with the effort of emptying himself into her, he jerked repeatedly, as if he'd been shot with a succession of tiny bullets that had just enough strength and striking power to make themselves felt without the possibility of inflicting serious damage. He jerked repeatedly, and with each of those involuntary movements, his fingers clenched around her upper arms to pull her closer. So close, and then closer still. Making her a part of him. Making him a part of her.

The finale, when it struck, left Claire breathless. It struck her speechless, left her an idiot, babbling wordlessly, her every attempt to speak lost in a stammered moan that made no sense whatsoever and yet made perfect sense when considered as a part of the whole.

The soft misting of desire within her, a steady and not always entirely welcome presence whenever she'd been with Eli, expanded suddenly. Quickly, immediately, gaining in both force and volume, the misting became a flow. The flow became a current. And the current became a torrent.

A raging, seething torrent that swept outward from the center of her onto the shaft she had buried so deep inside her that there could never be any chance of retrieving it whole and undamaged. The swelling tide of climax burst from her body, rushed across his, and the swirling eddies of it seemed only to entice her onward. To even greater thrusts. Even greater throbbings and searchings that ultimately, inevitably, led to one terrifyingly final and cataclysmic pulsing of the shaft buried within her. And then his essence joined hers. Blended with it.

WEAK, DIZZY, ON THE verge of complete and total mental collapse from the toll she'd taken, Eli lay limp atop the rosy satin spread across snow-white marble and struggled to take a breath.

Just one that would allow life to continue a nanosecond longer. Just one that would give his overworked, stuttering and hammering heart a final chance to correct its lurching and resume its regular rhythm. Just one breath, so that he could look over at Claire and tell her he loved her. *Loved...*

Eli forced the thought back. Forced it away.

That was not possible, and he knew it. Was never possible, and he'd best not forget it. Best not even go there.

"Eli." She lay beside him, a heap of tumbled bronze-brown hair, motionless except for the quivering that shook every inch of her. "That was...Eli, my God. I don't know how to...I really need to...you know I never meant for this to happen, but I..."

Knowing full well what she was about to say, dreading it as much as he wanted to hear it, aware that he'd never dare say it in return and that that would hurt her, really and truly hurt her for all time and all eternity, Eli reached out. He touched an unsteady finger to her lips and stopped her before she said what she would never be able to take back.

"Shhh," he urged. "It's time for you to go back upstairs now. Time for you to climb into bed and get some sleep."

"Won't you..." she hesitated, shivered, and twisted hands still clad in shimmering purple gloves together, looking inexplicably shy. "I was kind of hoping you would...you know..."

"That wasn't part of our agreement," he replied, deliberately making his voice hard again. Hard and harsh. Deliberately, even when it damned well tore his heart in half to do it.

Claire's face sagged. Shaken visibly, she got to her feet. Lowered her gloved hands and spread them across herself to protect herself and shield herself, though no two small hands would ever be enough to cover her nakedness or restore her dignity. Wordless, chin held so high that his heart really did break this time with admiration for her courage and her grace under the most crushing rejection he suspected she'd ever been forced to bear, she turned away from him and strode to the door. Pulled it open, and left the conservatory. And took with her most of its color and light and sweetly island-scented softness.

Groaning, hating himself for what he'd had to do to her out of his all-consuming need for self-preservation, Eli dropped his head to the pillows and stared at the conservatory roof. Tiny, interlocked squares of black lay so far distant that he could scarcely make out the swirlings of snow, driven by the harsh winter wind that skated and skittered across their surfaces.

He'd have to do something. Though there was no way he could ever make up to her for what he'd done just now, no way he could ever retract the pain he'd inflicted, he'd have to think of something he could give her that might soothe the hurt of loneliness and disillusionment he'd seen in her eyes.

Reaching for his cock, deflated now and as worn out as an old man's, he tucked it away carefully. Put it where it belonged, where he was starting to believe he should have left it in the first place.

A Christmas tree.

Remembering what Estella had told him, he managed a halfhearted and, he suspected, a thoroughly tragic smile.

The afternoon she'd arrived, barely two minutes after she'd walked into the icy marble prison he'd erected for himself, Claire had looked at Estella and asked where the Christmas tree was. Where were the decorations?

A Christmas tree.

Hell. He hadn't had one of the things in years. Not since his old man died and his mother had started to slip away, down the long and steadily narrowing corridor of Alzheimer's that had finally shut the door on her memories and then on her life. Not since...

Not since.

A Christmas tree.

It wasn't much. But it was the least he could do. To thank Claire for giving him so much more than she was destined ever to know she'd given.

Chapter Fifteen

A SHRIEK ROUSED CLAIRE FROM HER SLEEP. FROM DREAMS OF ENORMOUS, GLITTERING and questionably intentioned orchids that had buried her to the throat and hinted they'd like to smother her. A shriek, and a lurid glow that flared outside her window in the instant when her eyes flew open…flared with jagged shards of orange and gold so bright they blurred her vision.

Pushing herself upright in the bed, her heart going from full rest to a mad and horror-driven conga rhythm in less than the time it took to draw a breath, she didn't take time to rub her eyes or try to figure out exactly what had gone wrong or how it had gone wrong. She simply bolted from the bed in a leap that landed her halfway across the room, barely awake and staggering like a drunk at the conclusion of a wild night of partying. Stunned, she shook her head and tried to focus, tried to think.

A shriek. Someone had shrieked. Like this was the end of the world. And maybe it was. Maybe…

The room shone with light, the square of window beside the bed not midnight black as it should be, tinted only with a faint radiance of gold from the light on the pole between the houses, but a brilliant square tinted with demonic shades of orange shot through with streaks of red, and gold, and searing white, an ominous light that set alarm bells to clanging wildly inside her head. Though for a few seconds, still not completely awake, she could only gape, unable to understand why the alarm bells were sounding, or why…

"Fire?" The word, not exactly a question and not exactly an exclamation, broke from her throat on an enormous rush of air. In the same instant, reacting at last, she staggered again, and lunged for the door.

The house was on fire!

Flames licked at her window. That explained the light…that…

The voice of reason cut through her escalating panic just in the nick of time. Just as she was about to grab the door handle and fling herself out into the glittering marble hallway.

I'm naked. And it's cold outside. Fiercely cold, with a bitter wind howling down from the mountaintops. Wind that carried with it the snow-laden breath of another storm, a bigger storm, a quite possibly record breaking storm. Wind that would only whip the flames higher and urge them to greater ferocity that would…must…

There wasn't a minute to lose. Not a second. Turning back into the center of the room, she was just in time to see the small wooden railing outside the window, meant to simulate a balcony where none existed, flare into light for a second before it disintegrated almost magically into a blaze of searing and spiraling sparks.

The railing was gone. But flames still lapped at the window, more hungrily than before, flames that soared not from this house but from the older one next door. But she was still in danger.

The alarm bells inside her head clanged again, more urgently. More insistently, screeching that marble houses might be impervious to flame. That they almost certainly were. But the flames were at the window and if the window broke…

A scream welled up in Claire's throat. Unable to escape, it died there twitching and twisting. Died painfully.

If that window breaks, I don't want to be here. Or anywhere near here. Because even though marble houses were impervious to fire and flames, their contents were not. Their contents were very flammable.

She was very flammable. And she had to get out.

Circling the room in an aimless and increasingly frantic whirlwind of agitation, her breath keening frantically in the back of her throat, she searched for something, anything, with which to cover herself so she *could* escape.

The bed sheet.

There should be something else. But in her panic, the bed sheet was the first thing she saw. And once she'd fixed her mind on it she couldn't think what that something else might be or where she would find it.

"The sheet will do." Snatching the wide swath of satin from the bed, she wrapped it around herself hurriedly, toga-style, and bolted for the door again. Struggling, she barely managed to bite back the bitter taste of bile when it surged in her throat. Barely managed to stifle a scream as mindless and soulless as the one that had wakened her. Somehow she summoned enough presence of mind to close the bedroom door behind her, and then she was running again. Barefoot and stumbling, her breath coming in increasingly hard and strangling gasps, she flew to the stairs and down.

The household was in an uproar. Half a dozen people dashed back and forth in the front hallway, some of them in a concerted effort to escape while others seemed only to sprint madly in one direction and then another, much as Claire had done seconds before. Directly across from the bottom of the stairs the door stood wide open, admitting a swirl of snowflakes as a man halfway dressed in what appeared to be chef's whites alternately peered into the snowbound darkness, dashed forward into it, and then just as mindlessly dashed back into the warmth and questionable safety of the house.

The one comforting bit of the scene, the only comforting bit, was the warble of sirens, still far off but drawing closer with every motionless and time consuming fraction of a second that dragged past.

Fire engines. Thank God! Clutching her sheet still closer, Claire plunged down the last few steps into the hallway, her feet turning instantly to blocks of ice when they touched the bare marble floor.

In another minute, I'm going to join whoever is shrieking. I'm going to…

It was a terrible sound. An ungodly, inhuman and thoroughly nerve shattering one, as if someone was caught up in the throes of a horrible death.

But it was only Estella, and she appeared to be all right. Physically, at least. The housekeeper stood near the little bend in the hallway where double doors led outside to the other house and the heart of the fire. Shrieking, doing the same bizarre and skittering backward, forward dance as the chef in the front doorway, she clutched her head between hands that seemed to want to rip clumps of hair from her skull. And directly in front of her, his hand on her arm as he tried to coax her toward the front door and escape…

Claire's breath turned to stone in her throat. A split second later her heart did the same.

Directly in front of Estella, his hair rumpled and his face ashen as he tried his best to convince the housekeeper to *move*, sat Eli Eden.

In a wheelchair.

"What the hell?"

At the sound of Claire's voice, all activity in the hallway seemed to pause for one shivering and eternal second. Even the flames, visible now only as a distant flickering through the windows of rooms along one side of the hallway, seemed to hesitate and lose their momentum. But only for a second. Only for a fraction of a second before they flared again, brighter. And with that flaring, with that hellish orange soaring and fluttering to new and even more deadly heights, reason and the rapidly approaching wail of sirens resumed again.

At last, Estella seemed to run out of breath. She crumpled a little, first her face and then her knees. Swaying forward, then backward, then forward again, she went pale and limp, in the first stage of inevitable collapse.

Eli made a quick move to catch her arm before she could strike the cold and unforgiving marble. But it wasn't enough, and if it hadn't been for another man...the chauffeur who'd picked Claire up in Pittsburgh and driven her to the mansion, she thought...rushing forward to sweep Estella off her feet, the housekeeper would have fallen. Because Eli's attention, his gaze, had fixed on Claire, his eyes wide and horror struck. "Shit," he said forcefully. "Damn. Hell."

"I couldn't have said it better myself." Woozy, Claire thought for a minute she would be the next to topple. Swaying, her vision blurring, she reached for the banister and clung tight. As tightly as she could.

"Don't you dare." Eli made a small move as if to reach for her, but the distance between them was too great, and his movement too hampered in a way Claire had noticed before, without really noticing. Because all of their encounters had been carefully staged. Expertly orchestrated to hide all kinds of truths.

"What the hell?" she breathed again, realizing that for the first time she'd come face to face with the real Eli Eden. The man *behind* the façade and the fantasies. "Is *this* why you thought you had to buy me?"

His expression hardened into the same smooth and impervious blankness, as marble-cold and uncaring as his glittering house, that he'd worn when she'd first met him. The expression that had frightened her more than a little on the first night they'd been together, during that damned, despicable sleigh ride. The expression, she realized with another lightning bolt of shock, she hadn't seen *since* that night in the sleigh.

"In case you hadn't noticed," he said, maneuvering his wheelchair around her with a quick, but expert flick of his wrists that said he'd had a lot of practice at such maneuverings, "there's a house on fire here." And with that, he rolled away. Toward the front door, where the chef had apparently made up his mind to flee into the night. He went, silent on the marble floor, and Claire went after him, just as silent in her pursuit.

DAMN. SHIT.

Eli could *feel* her behind him. He'd have felt her gaze, astonished and slightly accusing, burning holes in his back even if he hadn't known she was there. *There, dammit,* even after he'd made it clear he expected her to stay...but what the holy, fucking hell did he think she should do anyway?

Stay inside and *burn*?

Damn it to hell.

He was the one who should burn. For letting her learn the truth this way. For hiding so much from her, when all he'd had to do was...

What? *Tell* her?

Shit. Damn. Hell. Fuck. He hadn't wanted to tell her a damned thing. If he was to be honest with himself for one of the very few times in all his misbegotten life, he hadn't wanted her to find out anything.

This was supposed to be his problem. He wasn't supposed to fall in love with the women and hadn't ever set out to do it. Now that he'd been stupid enough to commit that ultimate sin, that was supposed to be his problem, too. It was supposed to be his responsibility to figure out a way to handle it so he'd avoid having to expose the woman of the moment to...

And just who the hell did he think he was kidding? It was time to come in out of the dream world and admit it. Right up front. He hadn't wanted to expose *himself.* That was it. That was the truth. The whole, God almighty, unvarnished, awful truth. He hadn't wanted to expose himself. And it hadn't had one solitary, blessed thing to do with any of the women. Including Claire.

She dodged past him as he headed for the well-concealed ramp at the end of the front terrace. She dodged past him and leaped into his path, and it was just one of God's green wonders he didn't mow her flat and run right over her.

"You have some explaining to do," she declared, scowling.

He knew he did. But...

"Right now?" he demanded, glad to hear only impatience come through rather than that other dreaded and dreadful emotion, that chicken livered, self centered fear of what she was going to say now, and how she was going to look at him.

When Claire shot a glance back over her shoulder at the soft glow of windows along the front of the marble house, so did he.

Everything seemed so normal there. So serene in spite of the screeching of sirens and blowing of horns and throbbing of red and blue emergency lights that had chased away any trace of normalcy *or* serenity, that he almost thought about grabbing Claire's elbow and turning her around. Almost shoved her back into sanctuary that, no matter how it looked, was no sanctuary at all.

But she was right. They had some talking to do. *He* had some talking to do. Backing up a little, he maneuvered around her again and swept on down the ramp to bare concrete beneath the porte-cochere. And once again, shivering in her wrapping of sheet and obviously nothing else, her eyes still shooting daggers his way, Claire followed.

"You're going to catch your death," he declared as the Rolls swept around the side of the house and under the overhang. "Can somebody get a blanket for this lady?" he shouted at the night.

Michael, the chef, was on top of it. Right there as if he'd anticipated the request all along, he grabbed the lap robe from the back of the limo as soon as the chauffeur opened the door and draped it around Claire's shoulders. Then he shoved her into the car, almost catapulting her face first across the backseat.

At least that was one thing off Eli's mind. He'd been worried about Michael there for a minute. Really, really worried, when he'd started to dance in the front door, his face just about the exact color and consistency of one of his own fantastically-rendered ice sculptures. This one of a distraught gargoyle with features twisted out of all recognition by some strange and powerful spell.

It was good to see Michael back to normal. Casting a last look over his shoulder in the direction of the firelight that barely reached around to the front of the house, Eli shuddered. Then he heaved himself into the back of the car and dropped his head back against the top of the seat, eyes closed, chest heaving and breath hitching as if he'd just finished batting one out of the park and running the bases in record time.

"What happened?" Claire demanded, struggling to right herself from a welter of golden silk and dark plaid wool at the other end of the seat.

He didn't answer. Not knowing exactly which *what* she'd been referring to, it seemed safer not to answer. Not to involve himself or incriminate himself until he had a better idea what she was talking about.

"How did the house catch fire?" she wheezed, and when he opened his eyes and rolled his head to the side to see if *she* was all right, he realized she'd let the sheet and blanket fall open. And just as he'd thought, just as he'd suspected, she was naked. Completely, gloriously, desirably and deliciously naked, right here in the backseat of the Rolls, with half of western

Pennsylvania, or maybe *all* of western Pennsylvania, milling around, running and shouting and carrying on no more than fifteen feet from the car.

"God almighty, Claire!" His cock leaped. Mercifully…or unmercifully, depending on the situation and his frame of mind at the time…unaffected by the spinal injury that had made walking all but impossible, it gave one mighty, irrepressible lunge of recognition and greed before settling back. Settling down to a dull and throbbing complaint. "Cover yourself before…"

She twitched the sheet a little. Twitched it higher, though she didn't manage to cover herself completely. Not enough to…it was all Eli could do to not grab his cock and massage it. Not think only about trying to tell it everything was going to be all right, everything was going to be fine, when he'd already looked into Claire's eyes and seen how wide they were. How scared and how worried. And that made it possible to control the impulse.

Let the damn thing suffer. He had a feeling there was a hell of a lot more suffering to come before the night was out, and he sure as hell didn't want to be completely alone when it started.

"I don't know how the fire started," he replied, amazed that he could sound completely calm and in control when his heart felt ready to beat itself to death against his ribs. Or maybe it was about to just explode, and be done with it in one last brutal but spectacular blaze of glory. But then, explosion would be too easy. Death would be too easy. Because that would mean the end of misery. And life had taught him, in the last five years or so, that there *was* no end to the misery that could be dumped on one human being. No end to the misery, and no end to the humiliation either. "The wiring in that house was old," he said in the same cool and collected tone. "That was one of the reasons I moved out." *That, and those damned, uneven floors and the steps all over the place. That, and the damned chair that stymied any attempt to get from one place to another in the old firetrap.* "The place was condemned a few years ago. That's why I built the new house."

That wasn't strictly the truth. The place *should* have been condemned. Probably would have been, if the authorities had had any idea just how bad it really was. But that had been another of his little secrets. Another thing he'd kept well hidden. For a while, at least.

"Eli, I think…" Sitting up straighter, Claire leaned toward him.

And so did his cock. Sat up straight and leaned toward *her*.

"Cover yourself up," he ordered again. "You'll catch your death."

Once again fumbling with the slipping and sliding sheet and blanket, she managed to pull them around herself, though one breast, one rosy, inviting, warm and obstinate nipple, continued to peer out at him as if to sneer at him. *You had me once. But you're a lousy cripple, and you're never going to have me again.*

Amazingly, when he had that thought his cock didn't shrivel away to a limp and useless nothing the way it usually did when he came out of his fantasy world long enough to realize that was exactly what he was…a lousy cripple.

This time it only leaped higher. Only stood stronger, and insisted it wasn't going to be pushed around anymore. Not by anybody.

Because this was Claire?

Because, damn my soul to eternal hell, I've started to want her? To need her the way I have no right, none at all, to want and need anybody?

And to think he'd believed he could make up for all the hurts he'd inflicted on her with a Christmas tree. As if a damned, sawed-off chunk of dead Scotch pine could ever, possibly…

"I think I might have c…c…caused it," she said through teeth that chattered so violently he barely understood her. *And would that be the chattering of cold, or of revulsion?*

He had no way of knowing, and reluctantly, very, very reluctantly, he turned his head to look at her again.

In the pale gold gleam of the exterior lighting that still shone so placidly on the front of his marble house, Claire's face was white. Tense, pinched, deathly white.

"What the hell are you talking about? How the devil do you think you could have…"

She touched his arm. Not with revulsion at all, but easily. Naturally. As if she'd forgotten all about, or maybe never even noticed, that he wasn't quite the man he'd painted himself to be. Which was a whole new wrinkle on the problem. One he hadn't encountered before. Not that he'd ever given himself, or any of the women he'd hired and had hauled up here, a chance to encounter it.

"I was in that house," she breathed, her voice shaking definitely with fear. "This afternoon."

"When you went missing," he finished for her as understanding began to dawn.

In the gleam of reflected light, her face turned red. "I was so bored," she declared. "I was just about out of my mind with boredom, being cooped up in that bedroom for hours on end without even a book or a newspaper to…"

"Look. Claire. I ought to apologize for that."

"I knew I wasn't supposed to be wandering around. You'd made that absolutely clear. And Estella. She'd made it pretty clear, too. But I did. And then I opened the doors in the hall and saw the front of that house, and I couldn't..."

"I should have torn the old dump down years ago," he muttered, no longer sure if he was talking to her or only to himself.

Impatient, Claire shook his arm. "Eli, will you stop babbling, or whatever you're doing? Will you listen to me for a minute?"

"I am listening. You said you started the fire, but I don't see how you could think you did."

"Well, I didn't start it deliberately. I didn't actually take a match, and kindling, and...but oh, Eli, I did it all the same! I know I did, and..."

"Now who's babbling?"

She stopped. Gulped in a deep breath of air. Straightened her shoulders, shivered, and after one heart stopping moment in which he thought he wasn't going to be able to resist the temptation a second longer, yanked the blanket shut around herself and hid that one enticing, rosy nipple.

"I was in the house," she said again, her tone making it clear she was working hard, working with almost superhuman determination to control both her voice and the random and skittering direction of her thoughts. "I went in to...explore. And, Eli, I turned on the lights. I...they flickered and started to dim in this horrible way, so I turned them off again. Right away. But you don't suppose..."

"No." Relief shuddered in the syllable. *Apparently she's forgotten. What she saw of me. Apparently in her preoccupation with everything else that's happened, I'm going to get away with this. I don't deserve to get away with it. But I am, all the same.* "I do not suppose anything of the kind. The place was a mess. My father built it, and God knows he never paid much attention to anything that really mattered. He was all for appearances, and the hell with anything else. The hell with the substance of a thing. Or a house. This was not your fault, Claire. It was absolutely, unequivocally not your fault."

"Wh...while I was in there..." It looked like her thoughts had started to wander again. Her expression had turned wild, the way it had been when she'd first come blasting down the stairs at about a hundred miles an hour, hell bent on...well, he still didn't know what she'd been hell bent on doing. But she'd sure as hell been hell bent.

On escaping, probably.

"Eli, while I was in that house something frightened me half to death."

Despite a desperate and all-consuming need to stay on the alert, be on the lookout for danger before it approached so he could head it off before he had to look it straight in the face, Eli felt himself begin to relax.

"What was that?" he asked, actually chuckling a little because he thought he knew what she was about to say.

"Someone was watching me. From right beside the windows. And it was someone..."

"Not someo*ne*," he interrupted with more of that strange but entirely welcome lightness in his heart. "Some*thing*."

"He or she was watching me, not making a sound, and...huh?"

It felt good to laugh, if only a little. Really, really good.

He'd have to make it a point to try laughing a little more often.

"What you saw was my grandfather's Indian."

Her jaw dropped a little. "His *what*?"

"His Indian. He owned a cigar and candy store down in Latrobe years ago. When I was a kid. The Indian stood in the store, and there was supposed to be a secret about it."

"A secret." Now Claire looked as relieved as Eli felt, though definitely more, very charmingly much more embarrassed.

"The man who sold it to my grandfather said there was a secret, but Granddad never knew what it was. Or if he did, he never said." Eli paused. Smiled a little at the memory of one of his favorite activities when he'd been twenty years younger and a thousand years more innocent. "I crawled all over the hideous thing, and I couldn't find anything either."

"What's it doing over there? In that house? Isn't it..."

"Valuable?" He sighed. Groaned. Lifted a suddenly tired, completely exhausted and unsteady hand, and dragged it back through his hair. "Probably. It's been there for years. Ever since Granddad retired and closed up shop for good. I've thought I should have it hauled over to the new house, but...well, it looks like it's too late now. The thing's about to be burned to a crisp, and where the hell would I have put a thing like that in my house anyway? Where the hell would it have fit?"

Claire looked thoughtful. For a second, opening her mouth and pausing to frown a little, he thought she was going to offer a suggestion. And not a very polite one either, he imagined with a little twitching inside. But she surprised him. Horrified him, and sent him zooming straight back to the reddest red alert possible.

"That's not all, Eli. While I was there, before I saw the..." She blushed a little, as if realizing she'd been in absolute terror of nothing more than an overgrown tree stump. "Before I met up with your grandfather's Indian, I saw something else. I saw a picture."

Shit. He felt the ice form around his heart again. *Here it came. Right out of the blue, right after you let your guard down and thought you were safe. Here it comes to get you. The way you always knew it was going to get you.*

"It was on the mantel, in the...I don't know. One of the rooms."

She might not know. But I do. It's one of the too many rooms I could never reach in this goddamned chair. The room just to the left of the entryway. He remembered it well, and remembered the publicity still. Remembered the day he'd smashed it to smithereens in a fit of frustrated rage, then ordered one of the household staff to prop it up there where he could see it and never get to it. Where he could torment himself with the sight of it.

How could he have forgotten the damned thing was still there? How could he have neglected to order one of the staff to remove it? Or better yet, to bring it over to the new house so he could continue to torture himself?

"It was a picture of you," Claire murmured, giving his arm another of those little squeezes that had the power to surprise and scare the hell out of him now that he had no idea what or where they might be taking him.

Swallowing back a groan, he rolled his head back to neutral position against the top of the seat and stared at the roof of the car.

"It's true, isn't it?" she asked. "What my mother told me my Uncle Milton said?"

"Depends what Uncle Milton did say." Eli still didn't look at her, and she squeezed his arm again. Harder. More insistently.

"That you were a ball player."

At last, screwing up every bit of courage he could summon, and that wasn't a hell of a lot, Eli looked at her. Looked her right in the eyes and said, in a flat and toneless voice that sounded like he'd died about five years ago, right about when he should have died, "I was."

"Uncle Milton thought you were one of the best, until...until..."

Christ. Shit. Damn. Hell. Gut clenching into one solid, iron hard mass of pure damned, evil sickness, Eli wished he knew a few more, a few better, swear words. *Here it comes. Oh, God, here it comes, and I'm not ready for this. I'm never going to be ready for this.*

"Eli, we have to talk."

"I know." And the knowledge made him sicker. Made him sick enough to die.

Chapter Sixteen

THE SNOW OUTSIDE THE WINDOW WASN'T AS BLINDING WHITE, WASN'T AS PRISTINE OR as sparkling as it had been before. *But isn't that appropriate?* Eli thought gloomily, barely able to touch much less enjoy the mushroom and asparagus omelet Michael had set before him a few minutes earlier. Because his mood, his outlook, wasn't all that pristine or sparkling either.

He'd hardly slept a wink. Not surprising, considering all the activity of the night before, or the fact that they'd been kept out of the house, the relatively undamaged and completely safe marble house, until long after dawn, when the fire had burned itself out and the danger been declared over. But it wasn't the activity and the excitement of it that had kept him awake. It was that other thing. That…

From across the table, he felt Claire's gaze riveted on him.

He had to give her credit. She *had* been able to eat. And probably to sleep, too. She hadn't said a hell of a lot since he'd wheeled himself into the breakfast room ten minutes ago—or had it been more like twenty?—not meeting her eyes and barely speaking to her. She'd been staring at him ever since. Staring nonstop. But she'd been packing away the groceries like they were going out of style.

And why the hell shouldn't she? She wasn't the one with the guilty conscience, the one who'd kept secrets that should never have been kept. *She wasn't a goddamned cripple who'd made a habit out of playing the entire rest of the world, at least the female majority of it, for a bunch of witless fools.*

He put his fork down. Carefully, deliberately. Still not looking at her, he grabbed his cup and took a long gulp of coffee.

"So," she said, apparently taking that first real movement since he'd slipped into his place opposite her as an invitation to proceed. "Are we going to talk about it, or aren't we?"

He put his cup down as carefully as he had his fork. Picked up his napkin and blotted his mouth with it, more to hide the sudden quivering of his lips than out of any need to wipe away the remains of what he hadn't eaten.

"We can't keep ignoring each other forever."

Damn, she's persistent.

On the other hand, she hadn't grabbed her things and checked out first thing this morning when he'd told her he'd have the car take her home and mail her the check just as soon as they'd let him back into the house. She'd said it was late and she was tired. And if someone would point her to another bedroom, one where there hadn't been any fire and smoke damage, she'd prefer to go to sleep. If he didn't mind.

"I don't know what you want me to say," he mumbled at last, feeling an overwhelming need to say *something.*

"Well, you might start by looking at me instead of acting like I've just grown a second head or something."

He didn't. He just stared out the window again, at the layer of snow, smooth over rolling lawns and softly mounded over shrubs and steps and retaining walls. It was soot darkened now, filmed with an ugly coating of ash. But new snow had begun to fall in the last half hour, fresh, fat flakes that dropped from a sky the color of lead. A sky that promised another foot, or six inches at least, before the day was done. Fresh, fat flakes to cover the dingy layer with the new and sparkling promise of a second chance. To start over, and...

The thought had him looking at her at last. Peering at her across the breakfast table, no longer nervous or defensive or self-conscious about the wheelchair, which he'd seen no point in trying to hide now that it was all out in the open anyway.

Was that what she was doing?

Either consciously or unconsciously, was that what she'd done when she hadn't run away at the first opportunity?

Was she giving him another chance? To start over with a clean slate, an *honest* one?

He found it hard to believe. Impossible to believe.

But could it be happening? *Was* it happening?

He had no clue. He'd shut himself away so completely and so effectively since the day his old man had goaded him into the accident that had damned near killed him that he had no way of knowing what was happening. No way of knowing how he was supposed to interact with the world in this still new and terrifying as shit altered reality into which he'd been thrust. He didn't even know how the world was supposed to function any more.

The break with outside contact had been that complete. That thorough.

And Claire was still looking at him.

Reluctantly, he lifted his gaze. He met hers and hoped to God he didn't flinch or flush or look scared to death. Though he felt pretty damned sure he'd done at least one of them when she bit her lip and furrowed her brow, looking like for once in her life she didn't have the first thing to say about anything.

"You want to talk," he growled, sounding fierce even to himself. "What about? What's there to say?"

Her mouth dropped open and she looked astonished. Amazed.

"Why don't you start by telling me why you thought you had to put on this...charade?" she demanded.

"Isn't that obvious?"

Slowly, she shook her head. "Maybe to you. But not to me."

"Be honest with me, Claire." Lifting his chin, he tried to look as fierce as he hoped he sounded. "Would you have had the first thing to do with me? If you'd met me somewhere? If you hadn't been paid to come up here, and if we'd been just two strangers in a bar or at a party? Would you have..."

Her lips quirked a little in the damndest way. In the most kissable way. And he had to order his cock to stay still, stay out of this, because he had no time and no patience for any of its interference right now.

"Probably not," she said and flashed him a tiny, apologetic smile.

"There!" Automatically, his hands dropped to the wheels of his chair, getting ready for flight. Full out, hell or high water, no-holds-barred flight away from her and what she was about to say.

"For God's sake, Eli, you were my *boss*!" she declared in the next breath, startling the crap out of him.

"What?" His hands returned to the table. One of them found the coffee cup, grabbed it, lifted it. The cup was empty. And he needed coffee. Dragging in an enormous breath, he prepared to bellow. To *demand* more coffee, demand it now, demand to know why the hell he didn't have it and who the hell he should fire first because he didn't have it.

Shaking her head slightly, Claire lifted the pot and filled the cup for him.

Shit.

He was really rattled. So rattled that coffee began to slosh over the rim the instant he picked the cup up, and he had to set it down again without tasting it. Either that, or risk new injuries from third degree burns.

"You owned the company I worked for," she declared, her smile vanishing as quickly as it had come. "At least, I worked there until I was let go a year ago for…what was it? Oh, yes. For *downsizing*. Which meant you thought you'd keep your profits from deteriorating to the point that you might lose a nickel. Or two."

"Claire, if you think you were deliberately let go…"

"Of course I do." Now she scowled. "Your companies make an obscene amount of money, Eli. An obscenely obscene amount. What the hell do you think people think when they're laid off without warning from jobs that barely pay a survivable wage? Jobs that aren't going to make a dent in the amount of money you earn every single day?"

He didn't have an answer for that. Squirming a little, for real this time and not just internally, he wished he could look away from her hard and accusing gaze.

"I was told I was being laid off because the company needed to tighten its belt," she persisted. "Which translates into *we don't care about you and your family. All we care about is our disgustingly enormous profit margin.*"

"Claire, I don't see how…aren't we getting a little off track?" Now, that was strange. Really, really strange. Ten minutes ago, five minutes, he'd been looking for any way out of having to talk about himself and the reasons he'd had for all the stupid things he'd done in his life. Now all he could think about was getting the conversation *back* to his life.

"Not at all." She didn't miss a beat. Not even half a beat. "You asked me if I would have had the first thing to do with you if we'd met in a bar somewhere, and the God's honest truth is, I wouldn't. Unless it was to spit in your face and call you a name or two." Another smile, the barest ghost of one, flitted across her face. "I was angry with you. With your whole self-centered organization and its damned profit margin. I resented being laid off, still resent it. Just like I resent being put in a position where I had to come up here and have *sex* with you just to make sure my mother, my sick and frail mother, didn't get put out into the street because we hadn't been able to pay the rent on our miserable little one-room efficiency apartment." Pausing, she glanced around at the brocaded eggshell elegance of the small dining room. "An apartment I'm sure *you* couldn't imagine in even your worst nightmare."

Lady, you don't have a clue about nightmares until you wake up in a hospital bed with some doctor telling you you're never going to walk again and your own old man telling you that the shame of it is going to ruin his position in the world.

It was a brief thought, and Eli didn't say it. He only sat still in his damned wheelchair and stared at Claire Hardistique with his mouth open, astonished into silence.

"So you have some nerve demanding to know if I would have had anything to do with you," she finished, and sneered. Literally lifted her upper lip and *sneered* at him.

"Then why the hell did you come here? Why the hell did you—"

"Because I needed the *money*!" she shouted, and threw the piece of buttered toast she'd been playing with at his head.

Eli ducked, but the slice of bread caught him on the ear and careened off. Plopping against the window, it slid down the glass, leaving a long and streaky smudge.

"I came here because I didn't know how else I was going to survive," she said, and her anger seemed to have spent itself with the hurling of food. "And I guess I came because I thought this was going to be my chance to confront you and maybe give you a little bit of hell."

"Which you did," he pointed out.

Her face turned red. Dull, ominous red.

"Not half as much as I wanted to."

"Well, then, go ahead. Because I'm here now to tell you I deserve it. I deserve whatever kind of hell you want to throw at me...food hell, or otherwise. I behaved like a real scumbag..."

"You'll get no argument from me on that."

"...so just go ahead. Let me have it. With both barrels."

"I can't."

"Let me have...what?" His heart missed a beat. It jumped, lurched, and finally settled back into a rhythm he'd never felt before. Because he'd never in his life, in his *entire* life, both the good and the bad, the healthy and the hopelessly inadequate, ever let himself get into a position like this, where it was just about to break.

Shit.

She was about to dump him. His heart was about to shatter, and he had no clue how he'd gotten here, what he'd done to think he deserved anything else.

Claire took a deep breath. A ragged, jagged, whistling one, and looked him square in the eye.

"I can't let you have it and I haven't been able to let you have it for quite a while now, Eli. Because I'm in…"

She hesitated.

He hesitated.

His heart hesitated, stuck between beats, and he thought he was about to puke.

"I'm in love with you."

The words hung in the middle of the breakfast room. They swirled around and around like a tornado trying to rip off his head and beat him to death with it. They careened, rocketed, soared. They crashed into walls and bounced off, crashed into him and bounced off, and still he sat there, unable to move at all now, staring at her with his mouth all the way open, his hands clenched on the arms of his wheelchair until the knuckles felt ready to break. Felt like they *had* broken, and the pain just hadn't started yet.

"What?" It was all he could say. Was damned near more than he could say.

"You heard me."

"You're in…" He couldn't say the word. Thought if he said it he'd break some kind of grand, cosmic rule and she'd snap out of it. Come to her senses, and…

Dump me.

She stared at him.

"I'm in love with you. And I think I deserve an answer or two, if I'm ever to trust you again."

"What, Claire? What do you want to know?"

"Why."

"Why?"

She nodded. "Why did you lie to me?"

Spreading his hands, he resisted the urge to look down at his own ruined body. "Then we go right back to where we started. Look at me. And tell me you would have had a thing to do with me if I'd approached you somewhere and asked you for a date. Tell me, and don't get wrapped up in all that you-were-the-boss crap, because that's a whole other issue and though it needs to be addressed—"

"Shut up, Eli."

Now, at last, too late, he found the strength to glare at her.

"Just shut up and listen before you make an even bigger fool of yourself than you've done already."

He clamped his jaw shut. Clenched his teeth so tight he thought in another minute they would break. And for once in his life, he did just what he'd been told to do.

He shut up.

"I can't believe you'd think I was so…shallow." She looked wounded. Sounded it, too. And he felt like a bigger creep than ever, even if he did also feel compelled to defend himself.

"Some women are."

"Some men are, too." She scowled at him, and there went the guilt. Jumping again. Jumping higher. Jumping up and down and up and down, as if it thought it didn't have his complete and undivided attention.

Lord in heaven, she means me! She meant he'd been shallow, and he opened his mouth to argue the point as long and as hard as he could. The trouble was, he couldn't do anything of the kind. Because Claire was absolutely right.

Looking down at his hands, folded on the table now, the untasted and congealing omelet shoved to the side, he sighed. Shivered. Groaned a little to himself. And hoped like hell he was about to do the right thing.

"It all started with my father," he said. "With those goddamned horses."

"Horses?" Claire shook her head. "Weren't we talking about being in a bar somewhere?"

"Well, okay. It didn't start with the horses either. It started with the baseball. Because the old man hated it."

"I don't see why. I mean, my mother said Uncle Milton said you were a real talent. That you…"

Lifting his head, Eli scowled.

"That's right. I meant to say something about that. How the hell have you been talking to your mother about me anyway? Didn't I specifically say you weren't to have access to a phone while you were here?"

"Are you going to start with your stupid orders again?" She scowled right back at him and incredibly, unbelievably, Eli felt his heart soar. Felt it take flight. Like it hadn't ever taken flight since…never.

Shit, I'm in over my head. And getting deeper by the second.

"Okay. I'll let it pass. But I'd like to know exactly how the hell you did it, when there's not a phone…"

"Cell phone." God, she looked smug. And Eli wanted to kiss her. Wanted to try, except that he had no good idea how to go about doing it. He wasn't even sure he should do anything until he'd gotten a few things off his chest. Before Claire decided maybe she really didn't want to hear them after all, and maybe wanted the car to take her back to Pittsburgh right now.

"I suppose you could say I had a talent," he said, and felt himself flush. "At least that's what my coaches always told the old man. From Little League on up. But of course the old man didn't want to hear it. He didn't want me to have anything to do with it. Because baseball wasn't good enough."

Claire shook her head.

"And the horses? Where do they fit in?"

"Be patient." Deciding he did want something in his stomach after all, Eli took a gulp of the coffee. It was cold, but strong. Just what he needed. "I'm getting to that. My old man had delusions of grandeur, Claire. He built that damned house out there in a fit of one of them." Eli waved a hand in the direction of the burned shell of the firetrap. "He had to have this estate, up here in the mountains, and he had to make himself out to be some kind of goddamned country squire."

"If you feel that way about the place, why the devil don't you leave?"

Eli flashed her a look that was meant to silence, and did.

"Sometimes leaving's not so easy," he replied, glancing down at his legs. "Sometimes it's just a hell of a lot easier to hide. And punish yourself."

"Now, see, that's the part I don't get. Why you would want to punish yourself."

"Because I didn't tell the old man 'no'. I didn't tell him to kiss my ball-playing ass, and refuse to get on the horse."

"So. We're back to that again."

"Hell yes, we're back to that. How do you think I ended up like this?" Eli spread his hands wide, then dropped them onto the arms of his chair. "It was the goddamned foxhunting. The old man thought it made him gentry. Thought...hell, I don't know. I think he thought he could become some kind of English earl or something. He bought a dozen horses, built a fancy stable...I *did* tear that down, by the way. Got rid of the whole mess about five minutes after the old man died. But while he was alive, he had this...thing...about foxhunting. Insisted it was the only proper sport. Made everybody's lives miserable until they went along."

"Which you did."

Eli could see understanding starting to dawn in her eyes.

"Oh, hell, yes. I went along. I no more belonged on the back of a horse than I belong in a beauty pageant right now. I hate the damned beasts. Always have. But that summer the old man was at his worst. He was starting to get a little older and a lot crankier, and he just kept picking at me. I was supposed to move up...the Diamondbacks are a farm team. I was going to go up to the Rockies in a couple of weeks, have my shot at the real big time. But the old man wouldn't leave me alone. He kept picking at me, about how I thought I was some kind of big shot when I was nothing but a low class...well, let's just say that if it wasn't done on the back of a horse, the old geezer thought it wasn't good enough for him. So just to shut him up, I went on the foxhunt. And he decided it was time to teach me a lesson. He did something...I don't know what. Spooked my horse, and I wasn't ready for it. I got thrown and cracked my back on a boulder field, and the rest is history."

Pausing, he realized he'd started to breathe hard. Started to sweat, too, and quit looking at Claire or at the snow falling beyond the window. Quit looking anywhere but at his two hands, the fingers clenched tightly together, white-knuckled, and at one of her hands that had somehow come down on top of them and started to rub the strained and aching knuckles.

"And you blamed yourself," she murmured softly, understanding a hell of a lot more than he'd ever expected her to understand. "For not saying *no*."

Eli laughed, and it was an unhappy sound. A genuinely bitter one.

"Hell of a thing, isn't it? The old man always said I was a spineless coward. And that's just exactly what he made me. A *real* spineless coward."

"You're not a coward, Eli."

"No?" he demanded. "I hire women to have sex with me. And then I abuse them. Because I'm afraid to face them openly. Afraid to have them look at me and react honestly to me. If that isn't being a coward, then maybe you could tell me what the hell is?"

At some point, Claire had ducked her head so that he could see nothing, but the top of her short and gleaming bronzy-brown hair. As the silence ticked on and on and on, as the only sound in the room became the soft and scratchy tapping of snowflakes fluttering against windowpanes, he thought he had his answer.

Chapter Seventeen

CLAIRE WANTED TO BE ANGRY. SHE TOLD HERSELF SHE SHOULD BE ANGRY. SHE'D BEEN used, hadn't she? Really, sadly used and misused. The problem was, she couldn't hate Eli for any of it.

Not now and, she thought, probably not from the very first time she'd set eyes on him and he'd been so abrupt with her.

It just wasn't possible to be angry with him. Or maybe not to hang on to the flickering of anger when it tried to sprout into something more serious, something more long lasting. Because she'd seen something good in him, something kind that had been wounded almost beyond repair and might never be completely healed now that it had had so long to hurt. She thought she'd seen it right from the beginning, long before she'd had a clue there was any kind of mystery about him, or any idea what the answer to that mystery might be.

"So now you know," he said slowly, his voice tired and heavy. "The whole stinking story. You know everything about me, that I'm a cripple and a—"

"I thought that word wasn't politically correct?" she countered quickly, hating the note of resignation that had crept into his tone, hating it so much more than she'd ever hated the superiority, the barking of orders, or the demands.

"It's only politically incorrect when the person saying it isn't the cripple in question."

"Maybe. But I don't much like it."

"Fine. Dandy. What the hell do you want me to call myself?"

"I don't know why you think you have to call yourself anything, Eli."

Biting his lip, really biting down on it, he turned away from her again to stare at the snowstorm that was reviving itself beyond the windows. "Look," he said after a silence so long and so profound she feared it would turn out to be the final silence between them, the one that usually came just before parting. And she didn't want to be parted from him. Ever.

"I've got no right to keep you here," he said after a very long while. "I've realized that for a long time now. Your check is in my study and I'll…"

Feeling suddenly, strangely insulted even though the money was exactly what she'd come here for and even though she still knew she couldn't afford to leave without it, Claire started to tell him he could keep it. That money was the last thing, the absolute, very last thing, she ever wanted from him. But she never had a chance.

"Mr. Eden?" Quiet and pale, just as she'd been ever since her panic attack during the fire, Estella appeared in the doorway. She didn't look at Claire, didn't even glance at her.

Eli looked up, a sudden gleam of eagerness and anticipation filling his eyes and chasing away the anguished look of pain.

"Is everything ready?"

Estella nodded wordlessly, still without looking at Claire, and left as quickly and quietly as she'd come.

"Eli?" Instantly, Claire went on guard. *What now?* she wondered. Sweet stars above, a second or two ago he'd been trying to dismiss her, send her home a full three days early, and now he was… *what?*

"You aren't…this isn't another of your strange fantasies, is it?"

"No." Smiling, looking a little sheepish, he held out a hand to her. "I've told you. You can have your money and go any time you want. But there *is* something I wanted to show you. And I was hoping that when you see it, you might agree to…"

"Because I just don't think I'm up for any more fantasies. I think if we're going to go anywhere from here…"

"It's not a fantasy, Claire. Not like you're talking about anyway."

"What, then?"

Slowly, carefully, looking like he had a hard time believing she wouldn't bolt at any moment, as if he thought she was going to be so repelled by even a glimpse of the wheelchair that she would indeed grab her money and run, Eli backed away from the table and rolled around it, toward her. "You have to come and see," he replied, motioning toward the door.

Reluctantly, she got to her feet. "I don't much like that look in your eyes, Eli Eden. I've seen that look before, and it always spells trouble. For me."

"Like I said…" He motioned toward the door again.

"I don't know whether to trust you." Stepping into the wide hallway, Claire heard him behind her, heard the faint whisper of rubber against the sparkling-hard, uncarpeted marble floor that in that instant made perfect sense.

"It's up to you," he said. "I can call the car and have you out of here and on your way home in ten minutes. But then you'll always wonder. For the rest of your life, you'll wonder what I was talking about. What I had up my sleeve."

"I don't even know where we're going." She hated the peevishness that crept into her voice when she realized he was right. About everything. She could go home right now, probably *should* go home, if she only had her wits about her. And then she would indeed end up torturing herself as effectively as Eli had ever tortured himself. With too many questions. Like...what surprise had he had for her? What was that sudden, small and indecipherable twinkle in his eyes? And why did he look so eager, so anxious and so scared, all at the same time?

"Just keep going the way you're going." He didn't pull up beside her and she didn't hesitate or try to force him to. She sensed he felt more than a little self-conscious about the wheelchair, and that if she looked at him for too long or in the wrong way, he'd be likely to vanish into some part of the house where she'd never find him. And the next thing you know, she'd be escorted to the car forcibly and that would be that. That would be the end of everything.

Before it had ever, really, had a chance to have a beginning.

So, she walked. Calmly, with her head up and her shoulders straight in spite of the inner quivering that kept urging her to run and hide. She walked almost to the end of the hallway and probably would have kept on going right out into the wind and the blinding snow if Eli hadn't suddenly caught her wrist. If he hadn't wrapped long, strong fingers around it and pulled her to a stop. And if the touch, even through her bulky sweatshirt, hadn't transmitted his almost electrical excitement and anticipation into her and all through her.

"Here," he said, his voice low and suddenly shaky. As low and shaky as it had ever been in any of the moments when he'd been just about to...

Claire felt herself blush at the memory of some of the things he'd done. Some of the things *she'd* done before she'd known the first thing about who Eli Eden was, or what he really wanted and needed. And she couldn't look at him. Couldn't ever look at him again, not even if he offered to pay her five times...*ten* times...the exorbitant amount they'd already agreed upon.

"This is far enough," he said in that same low, enticing, downright sexy voice. Moving past her, he reached the double doors and glanced back at her, glanced up at her. "Close your eyes."

"Eli..."

"Close them, or before God, I'll barricade this door and refuse to let you through until Easter. Or the Fourth of July. And that would ruin everything, Claire. Trust me."

Sighing, she did as he told her. Closed her eyes tightly and waited, listening to the doors sigh open with a soft swishing of air. Kept them shut even when Eli's fingers closed around her wrist again and gave a silent order to step forward.

Unlike the rest of the mansion. which except for the wildly fragrant conservatory was the very essence of odorless cleanliness and sterile anonymity, this room smelled different. It smelled warm. Redolent of cinnamon and spice and pine.

Redolent of Christmas.

She began to quiver. Inexplicably. All over. Inside as well as outside. Everywhere. Because she had the strangest notion that…

"Okay," Eli said, his tone turning breathless. "You can open them."

She did, and though she'd half expected to see it, the sight before her left her speechless. Completely, hopelessly, maybe even permanently speechless.

A Christmas tree.

Not just any tree, but an enormous, towering, glittering column covered with thousands of lights in every color of the rainbow and so loaded with ornaments that the branches sagged, seeming literally to groan beneath their fantastic, heart-stoppingly fragile and beautiful burden.

The tree stood in a far corner of the room. And it was perfect. It soared magnificently, eleven feet, twelve feet, maybe more, all the way from the lowest branches that hugged close to the gray marble floor up to the white carved ceiling.

"My God." Claire took a step forward. Three steps. Four. "I can't believe…how did you… *why* did you?"

Eli rolled up next to her.

"I decided you were right. You said the place was…what did you call it? Sterile, I think?"

"Cold and heartless," she corrected absently, not really listening and not really seeing anything except that tree. That gorgeous tree. That wondrous, spectacular, shining and sparkling tree that reflected in the polished floor to send back scattered shards of light, of tens of thousands more lights than actually existed, onto walls and ceilings and furnishings. Onto Eli's slightly frowning, slightly hopeful, slightly fearful face.

"I decided you were right," he said, still breathless and with a deep and inexplicable quivering in his voice. "I decided a little Christmas might not be such a bad idea after all."

Without warning, without even suspecting she was about to do it, Claire burst into tears. Multicolored lights swam before her eyes and solidified into one massive, unbroken blur of color. And she dropped to her knees. The crack of bone striking marble had to be painful, probably was painful. But she barely felt it. She barely felt anything beyond a sudden and wrenching twist of her heart when she thought about her mother. Alone today, alone tomorrow. Alone on Christmas Eve and on Christmas Day, too. Alone in the grim and dreary little efficiency apartment with the tiny plastic and paper tree Claire had set up before she'd left, and the three or four small gifts from the dollar store that they'd agreed not to open until Claire came home.

For Marie Hardistique, Christmas would be just another day. One more dreary, lonely day with nothing to look forward to and nothing to do. Suddenly, staring at the magnificence of the Christmas tree that had been given to her, Claire wanted to go home. She wanted to see that plastic and paper tree. To see her mother and hold her. To hug her, and see the delight that would sparkle in her mother's weary eyes when she saw the knit hat and earrings Claire had bought for her. Even if they had only cost a couple of dollars, the gifts would mean so much. Would mean...

"Claire?" Eli's voice reached her dimly, as if from a great distance. A very enormous and very foggy distance.

Lifting her hands to cover her face, she closed her eyes against the spectacular blur of lights and bent almost double over the knot of anguish in her stomach, her forehead nearly touching the floor. *What the hell was I doing? What the hell was I thinking, coming here? What the hell was I*

"Claire?" Eli was right beside her. Moving as soundlessly as ever, he'd swept in close enough to drop a hand onto her shoulder. And now he began to massage, working his way around to the second knot, the larger and tighter one at the back of her neck. "Please don't. What is it? What did I do wrong?"

For a moment Claire couldn't answer. Couldn't do anything but work to get her sobs under control.

"I didn't mean to upset you."

"I kn...know."

"Then what?" Leaving the back of her neck, Eli's hand found her shoulder, then her arm. And once there it tugged gently, urging her to sit up again. To look at him.

But she kept her face turned away. She'd resolved to be so strong about this. So strong about everything, to never let on that anything bothered her or that she needed so terribly to be with her mother on Christmas day. She was twenty-six years old, for heaven's sake. She shouldn't need to be with her mother. And the fact that she did made hot embarrassment burn in her cheeks.

"Claire?" Eli was still tugging at her. Still trying to get her to turn to him.

"I'm sorry," she gulped, wiping at her eyes. "I don't know why the sight of a Christmas tree...I mean, it *is* only a tree after all, and...I was just being stupid." Unable to resist his continued pressure on her shoulder, she looked at him at last.

Their gazes met, just about on the correct level with her staring up at him slightly, and him chewing at the corner of his lower lip as he gazed back down at her, his brows wrinkled together and a look of mixed devastation and concern on his face.

"You're not being stupid," he said. "Something's bothering you, and I wish you would tell me what it is. I wish you'd let me try to fix it."

"It's nothing. Nothing you'd be interested in fixing anyway."

His frown deepened.

"Why don't you let me be the judge of that?"

Shrugging off his touch, Claire got all the way to her feet and turned to the tree again. Squaring her shoulders, she faced it as if it was some horrible entity to be dreaded, as if it was the horrible and hulking monster she'd thought she'd seen in the deserted house next door rather than the most beautiful Christmas tree in the world.

"It's Christmas, isn't it?" Eli moved closer to her and caught her hand this time. "That's what's bothering you."

Slowly, against all better judgment but unable to control the impulse, Claire nodded.

"I guess it was easy to forget about Christmas while the house was so...lifeless. But this...how am I supposed to think about anything else with this?"

Eli remained silent for a minute. For such a long minute that Claire almost forgot he was there. That she let the tears well up again, and begin to spill silently down her cheeks.

Her mother was so frail. So ill. This could be her last Christmas. Though neither of them had ever put that possibility into words. Neither of them had dared. And yet here was Claire, in this beautiful place where she'd almost forgotten...

Her tears had started in silence. But now a sob escaped. One, wrenched up from the very depths of her soul, to shake her violently.

The pressure of Eli's hand on hers increased. He gave another little tug and suddenly, again without really intending to do anything of the kind, she was in his lap. Seated atop him, wondering with a short and fleeting burst of horror if she might be about to damage him in some way. And then her arms just naturally found their way around his neck. Her face found its way into the small hollow of his shoulder, and when his arms closed around her to hold her there, she gave way to tears again.

"You have somewhere else you'd rather be," he said, his breath warm against her hair, his lips tracing barely felt paths across the scalp beneath. "I've been such a jerk, thinking you wouldn't."

"I d...d...don't..."

"God, I could kick myself. *Wish* I could kick myself. Might actually figure out a way to kick myself."

"It's not your fault." Now that she'd found this place next to him, in the circle of arms that felt as strong and steady as any arms could ever be, she was reluctant to leave. Reluctant to be cold again, or alone.

"I should have known you wouldn't want to be away from home on Christmas." This time something new came through in Eli's voice. Something that stopped Claire's thoughts of her own need in their tracks, and nearly stopped her heart. He'd sounded bereft. A sad loneliness echoed in every word he spoke, and she sat up. Sat away from him, to look into dark eyes that shone so close to hers.

"You don't have anybody," she said, not questioning because she already knew. Somehow, just *knew*. "Do you?"

Anguish flickered briefly in those dark depths.

"This isn't about me."

"The hell it isn't."

"I don't want you to worry about me, Claire."

Tightening the arms that still wrapped around his neck, she caught the hair at its nape between her fingers and pulled, none too gently.

"Answer me."

He smiled, and it was a brave look. Almost a convincing one. But it carried the same emptiness she'd seen in his eyes moments before, the same longing and loss and loneliness.

"You don't have anyone."

"It's okay. Really."

"No, it's not."

"Claire, it's no big deal. I'm used to spending the holidays alone. It's kind of…a choice…I made for myself. And I guess I'm just going to have to live with it. Because I did make it." He glanced at the tree. Lights and sparkling ornaments, every kind of glittery, silvery, shimmery bauble imaginable to man or woman, reflected in his eyes. But the brilliance, the glow, wasn't enough to hide the depth of the longing that flickered all too briefly in them again.

"It is a big deal. I made an agreement with you and damn it, I'm going to keep it. I'm not going to run out on you, when…" Clumsily, awkwardly, Claire staggered to her feet and backed away from him, seeking safety nearer the tree. "I'm sorry if I…what I mean is, I didn't mean to…I won't get so carried away again. I won't do anything to damage…"

"You didn't hurt me." He looked slightly amused. "I'm strong as an ox. Just not quite as agile as one. And I think you should run out. I think you should go back to your mother before it's too late. Before Christmas comes and goes, and…"

Her mouth opened. "How did you know I was thinking about my mother?"

"Well, it wasn't that hard. You mentioned her. You said you'd talked to her. About your uncle Morton."

"Milton."

"Whatever. Your uncle, the baseball nut. You said you'd smuggled a cell phone into my house, and talked to her against my specific orders."

"Please. Don't start on that again."

Eli barely cracked a smile.

"I just think I should send you home right this minute." Flicking his wrist, he glanced at his watch. "I could have you there before midnight, if you leave right now."

Send her away? Unable to believe the pang the idea sent through her heart, Claire shook her head vigorously. Impatiently. "I won't go. You'll have to hog tie me and throw me into the car forcibly."

Eli's eyes took on a wicked gleam. "Hog tie? Now that's a fantasy that might bear some looking into."

Backing away a little more, she scowled at him. "Don't start that again either."

Eli rolled forward. His gaze never leaving hers, he closed in on her slowly. Determinedly. And she kept backing away until she wondered how much farther she could go before she stumbled into the tree and began knocking off fragile and expensive ornaments, making a real mess of things.

"Another step," he said as if he'd read her mind, "and you're going to impale yourself on a branch. Of course it might be a sweet idea to find a real angel on my Christmas tree, so maybe I should just let you..."

Real angel?

Stars and heavens above.

Claire couldn't believe the sudden flaming of heat that sprang to life in her cheeks. And elsewhere. In places where...

"It seems we've reached an impasse." Moving deftly, in that unnerving way he had, Eli positioned his wheelchair in front of her so that she really was nearly impaled on the tree, with nowhere to run but straight ahead and into the arms instinct told her waited for just the right moment to sweep her up again. Sweep her, literally as well as figuratively, off her feet.

"There's no impasse." Lifting her chin, she tried to look like the idea of being swept off her feet had never entered her mind. Never changed the hot and flaming shards of embarrassment into equally hot and even more fiery fingers of desire that found their way right to the one place where fingers of desire could wreak the worst, the most irreparable and irreversible, kind of havoc. "I'm staying until the end of our agreement. Until the day after Christmas. And that's that."

"Then I have no choice." Eli grabbed the wheels of his chair, and Claire took one more instinctive step back. Right into the tree.

Ornaments jingled softly, glass bumping against fragile glass. But none of them fell. And for some weird reason, a branch dropped across her shoulder. A branch that bore an enormous ornament, bigger than her hand. An ornament shaped like a heart molded with cupids and flowers and hand painted in the most tenderly romantic shades of pink and lavender and pastel green. Claire stared at it, shivering. Shuddering against a surge of sudden and unparalleled delight that seemed to say, seemed to hint...

"If you won't go, I'll have to take drastic measures," Eli threatened. "I'll have to—"

"If you're talking about hog tying me again, Eli Eden..." Dear God, was that her voice? And if it was, why was it so shaky? So breathless, as if she'd like nothing more than to tumble to the floor right now, beneath that Christmas tree? With him?

"Maybe later," he said and laughed softly. "The idea of hog tying you still has its charms. But for right now, I was thinking...the car runs both ways, Claire."

"Huh?" That wasn't what she'd expected and she cocked her head a little, eyeing him suspiciously.

"If you won't go, and I don't really want you to go, I guess I'll just have to send the car to Pittsburgh. To gather up your mother and..."

Claire gasped. She heard herself gasp, though she'd gone suddenly numb, unable to feel much besides the sudden and painful jerking of her heart. "Eli?"

"I can have her here before midnight as easily as I can have you home before midnight," he murmured, reaching out to capture her wrist with a hand that instantly began to caress. "And in the meantime..."

"You would do that? For me?"

Very slowly, never breaking the eye contact that had turned in these last few, incredible seconds into something that felt like it would never be broken again, he nodded.

And then it was time. For Claire to take that step forward. For her to leave the painted glass heart behind and bend forward. To press a soft yet urgent kiss against his waiting mouth. "I can't believe you would really do that."

"Call it a Christmas gift. One of a couple I'd like to give you. If you don't mind."

Chapter Eighteen

A CHRISTMAS GIFT.

He'd meant to give one to Claire. A real one. And there was still time. But of course she'd turned everything around on him. Had turned it all upside down and topsy-turvy with her insistence that this time things were going to be done her way. That this time there would be no hanky panky, no fantasies or strange goings on, no bowls of whipped cream... *damn it all to hell, anyway! I'm going to miss that whipped cream.* Eyeing the strings of colored lights that now furnished the only illumination around the bedroom, the ones Claire had draped over tables, and windowsills, and even over the low headboard of his bed, Eli wondered where in the hell she'd found them. And he thought no lights, no matter how soft and muted the glow they cast and no matter how magical they made these plain and everyday surroundings, would ever be a replacement for the whipped cream. Because that had been... his cock leaped at the memory of how delicious Claire had tasted, how sizzling sultry hot she'd been beneath that cool white coating of the ultimate sweetness.

Christ, his cock was hard.

Staring at the closed door, lying flat on his back and motionless between blue and white cotton sheets, Eli wondered if the cursed thing was up to another second of this waiting, this torture. And that was exactly what it was. Torture. Claire's way of paying him back for all the things he'd done to her. Really paying him back, in the one way that was *guaranteed* to hurt.

Paying him back, by doing it *her* way.

Groaning, he resisted the urge to massage the aching, overextended and erect thing. If he touched it, it was going to blow. Literally launch sperm all the way to the ceiling, where it wasn't going to do anyone a goddamned bit of good. And then, when she finally did come through that door, when she finally did come to him...

Hell. He probably didn't need to worry. There'd been no shortage of sperm since she'd arrived on the scene. He'd become a regular sperm factory, and he doubted that was going to change any time soon. But even so...groaning again, he clenched his hands behind his neck and tried not to concentrate on the hot, hard suffering between his legs.

Her way? What the hell did that mean, anyway? What in the sweet, living, unimaginable hell does she have in store for me?

He'd just about reached the point of screaming, or maybe of just bellowing for her to get in here now, dammit, and put him out of his misery. And then the door to the study swung open.

The study was dark. A midnight backdrop of unrelieved black that showcased her, her smooth and silken curved and perfect body illuminated only by the soft glow from the strewn and scattered strings of Christmas lights.

Beautiful. The word didn't begin to describe her. But it was the only one Eli, in his shell shocked stupor, could think that even came close. *Simply, incredibly, unbelievably beautiful in a dark lace negligee. Lace that gleamed softly blue, then velvety black when the light touched it from different angles.*

Blue or black or whatever, the sight of that lace against creamy, almost translucent alabaster skin was enough to make him cry out for real. His voice hoarse with need, his body surging with desperation, it was a cry of mingled invitation and agony.

She'd removed his wheelchair before she'd left the room to change out of her jeans and sweatshirt. Left him stranded naked on the bed, unable to get up and go to her. *Though if I really try, I might...*but he wasn't going to try any such thing, and he knew it. Even if he'd had a pair of perfectly healthy, perfectly responsive and steady legs, he doubted he could have stood upright and taken a step on them anyway. Because the sight of her, the thought of being with her, of the promise that waited for him in the silken body glimpsed beneath even more silken lace, it just left him weak. Unable to concentrate on anything beyond this second. Or maybe beyond the second when she'd do things her way.

Whatever the hell that is.

"My God," he moaned, beckoning urgently with a fluttery hand.

Claire advanced toward the bed. Slowly. Almost floating, with the most damned incredibly seductive sway in her hips and that body she'd hidden yet not hidden at all beneath the lace that was nothing but a whisper of a covering.

"Claire, you..."

"So." Stopping a few feet from the bed, four feet, just beyond reach when he managed, struggling against the strange and debilitating tremor that had seized him, to swing his arm over the side and extend it toward her, she lifted her hands to the scrap of dark ribbon that held her lacy robe closed at the throat. "Isn't this better than any old fantasy?"

"It is." He choked on the words. His arm dropped, too heavy to be held up, his fingers trailing uselessly over the edge of the bed. And his cock surged. She had to *see* it surge, had to feel it surge in the superheated air. But if she did, if she noticed at all, she gave no hint. She just stood there for a moment longer, a lifetime longer, and smiled at him.

She's the fantasy.

She might not know it, but those other times...in the sleigh, the dining room, the conservatory...those had been the realities. *His* realities, the only ones he'd been able to imagine since the morning he'd first sat in the wheelchair and stared at the rest of his life from that humbling and devastating vantage point. But now this, she...

This *was* the fantasy. The most incredible fantasy of all. The one he'd believed he'd never be able to create for himself, and so hadn't even tried. The one that had been destined not to come true, never to come true only...what? A day ago? An hour? A few minutes?

"My God," he said again, his voice every bit as strained and unnerved as his poor, defenseless and thundering cock. "Claire, you've got to...you can't keep on..."

Slowly, with deliberate and taunting care, she untied the small bow in the ribbon. Even more slowly, she shrugged her shoulders so that blue-black lace fell away. The robe had wide sleeves. Billowing, enormous whimsies of sleeves that started at her shoulders and ended at her elbows and for a minute, too dazzled to hang onto a coherent train of thought, Eli found himself musing on those sleeves. On the miracle of construction that kept them from just drooping all the way to her wrists and losing their cloudlike splendor.

The lace fell away more. Bared, her shoulders gleamed softest ivory turned opalescent by the soft brush of color from the scattered strands of lights.

Lace. Dropping first past the points of her shoulders, then to her elbows and wrists, lace finally floating free to reveal her more than before yet still leave her covered by a filmy and intoxicating gown made of sheerest, flowery nothing.

Lace.

Catching the floating robe by the neck before it fell to the floor, Claire swung it around like a bullfighter wielding a cape. She swung it over the bed, over him. Over his face, his eyes, over the arms that had begun to try desperately, still barely able to overcome their palsy enough to move, to reach for her. Flung it over his cock, which had gone beyond the point of reason and seemed about to begin to thrash its way toward her on its own, dragging him helpless but certain as hell not resisting along for the ride.

"Claire." When he tried to speak, no sound came out. Nothing intelligible anyway. Merely a dry and croaking rasp, the sound of a dying man.

And he was going to die. For sure.

The bed shifted when she placed a knee on its edge. Shifted more as she transferred her weight from her foot to the knee. Shifted still more as she leaned forward, her hands at either side of his shoulders, to kiss him.

He made a sound. Not a human one. Rubbery fingers groped, anxious to find his cock and touch it, to reassure it that it could survive this. Could, if only...

"I want you," she murmured between short, nipping, seductive bites.

I want you, too. He wanted to say it. Scream it. Shout it. Wanted to tell her so many things. But he'd been rendered mute. Tasting the pearly sweetness of her, feeling the lace that was the softest, the most incredibly female and drifting thing that had ever tortured him, teased him, tantalized him, he found himself too breathless to speak. Too powerless to breathe.

"I want you to make love to me, Eli Eden."

"What?" His head swam.

"You heard me." Transferring her attention to his nipple, his left, straining, agonized nipple, she caught it and a layer of the intoxicating lace between her lips and tugged, very slightly.

Something ripped through him. Ripped him right, straight in half, so that he shrieked.

"I want you to make love to me this time. I want you to..."

"Claire..." He dredged up the strength to protest from some deep, never before tapped well of self control that he'd been holding in reserve without ever knowing it for a crisis, a dream moment, just like this one. "I..."

Now she was grazing the nipple with her teeth. Was grazing both of them, alternating back and forth from one to the other, catching at them and pulling at them, biting at them and licking them, sending those fiery and all-devouring thrills of complete and helpless weakness through him again. "I want you to make love to me. I want you to show me that you..."

"I can't, Claire."

"You can."

"No. I...my legs. Won't support me enough to..."

Nip. Tickle. Lick. Bite.

The woman was about to drive him mad. *Had* driven him mad, and he didn't much care. Didn't give one holy hoot in a hailstorm if she drove him completely and permanently out of his mind, so that in addition to being a cripple and pretty much useless, he would be a babbling, slobbering, idiot cripple.

"Anything's possible," she murmured, transferring her attentions away from the nipples that, abandoned and not liking it one damned little bit, immediately cried out for more. But then she trailed her tongue slowly upward, to his Adam's apple. And once she reached it, she began her soft and devastating licking again.

His cock thrust. Jumped. Twisted and strained and pleaded for mercy, unable to locate anything in the world but the lace that had gone in an instant from delightful enticement to the most savage instrument of torture ever devised.

"That..." He gasped, barely able to swallow when she nipped at his throat and then continued upward, blazing a trail straight toward his mouth. "Isn't. Not possible, Claire. I..." He had to stop when her mouth found his. When her tongue brushed across lips that hurt every bit as much as his cock. Had to stop when his mouth fell open, desiring to penetrate and be penetrated. And now somehow she'd moved the sheer barrier of lace up. Moved it over his mouth, too, repeating the suffering she'd first inflicted in the conservatory with her damned, her unconscionable...

"God *damn* this thing!" he shrieked, vaguely hoping the household staff had taken themselves off to their quarters, or at least to some far distant corner of the mansion for the night. Raising his arms in a single, convulsive thrust, he shoved the curtain of lace aside. Unknowing and uncaring whether it tore to shreds or whether he escaped it yet somehow managed to leave it whole and undamaged, he flung it away and reached for her. Caught Claire by the shoulders and pulled her down, one hand grappling with the hem of the sheer lace gown that matched the robe. Pulling it up, he urged her to roll over. Roll onto him so...

She stiffened. Became suddenly resistant and entirely immovable. "No."

"What?" Rage welled up inside him. Cold, and black, and killing. "What the hell, woman? Did you think you could just come in here and play cock tease and I was going to let you get *away* with it? Because there's no damned way in hell..." *Well, okay. Yes, there is.* He was unable to move more than a few feet from the bed, unable to take more than one or two feeble and tottering steps without help before his legs would give out beneath him. He knew it, and she knew it, and he knew she knew it. So that left them…

"Damn, damn, damn!" His voice rose on a howl of outrage. "Claire, I demand you…"

"No demands." Rolling onto the bed next to him, turning onto her side, she urged him to turn onto his and face her. "Not from you. Not tonight. It's my turn to make the demands. And I *demand* you make love to me." With that, she moved in close to him. Moved right up against him, her skin bare now beneath the lifted hem of the gown, bare and open and free for the taking if only he had the slightest idea how he was supposed to take. Then she lifted her leg. The one on top. She swung it over his hips. Inched herself closer, so that he felt her opening press against the tip of him. Felt her, and suddenly understood. Suddenly, thrusting once, penetrated her as easily as if he'd had all the strength and all the agility in the world.

"Damn!"

She sighed a little. Swung her leg a little higher so that she opened even more for him.

"Claire, how in the hell did you ever…" He'd begun a slow rhythm. An almost forgotten one, rolling his body gently back and forth, thrusting his cock deeply, effortlessly, into her and then slipping back with the same ease that confounded. With a delight that befuddled and a growing need that incinerated. "Where did you learn to do this?"

"Kama…" she gasped as a particularly deep and exceptionally well timed plunge stroked him all the way into her, all the way against the sweetest and most sensitive part of her. "Sutra."

"Huh?" He barely heard. Didn't hear much of anything now except the stuttering beat of blood in his ears, driven by the explosive pressure building in his balls.

"Kama Sutra. Oh, Eli, I *like* that!"

"This?" He thrust again, adding a slight sideways twist to the forward motion. Cupping her ass with the palms of his hands, he pulled her forward at the same time so that they met halfway…met, and went all the way.

"Yesssss! Oh, don't *stop*."

He laughed. Softly. "The thought never entered my mind." He pressed a kiss to her forehead, then caught a stray lock of her hair between his lips as he push-pulled her onto him again in one long and exquisitely slow slide. Then they lay motionless. Clasped together. Joined.

"You were saying," he murmured, exerting tight pressure on her ass and feeling her opening compress around him as he did. "About the Kama Sutra?"

"I looked it…up. On the In…ternet." She barely got the last word out, gasping and shuddering and groaning as he began to pull away from her. Degree by torturous degree. Until they clung together by no more than a thread, no more than the tiniest millimeter of the flesh that still, remarkably and impossibly, joined them.

"Why?"

"Bec…cause…Eli, please…*please*?"

He held her there. Positioned barely on him, not completely free of him but scarcely a part of him either. "Tell me why first. Tell me everything. And then you can have your…" To illustrate his point, to make his promise all the more promising, he shoved into her a little. A quarter of an inch. Only enough to make her open to admit him and stretch to accommodate him. And then, when she'd been opened to her widest, when the need to have him finish what he'd started had to be at its most killing, he stopped. "If you tell me like a good little girl, I'll give you your reward."

Shuddering, tears pooling at the corners of her eyes and streaming down the side of her face, Claire clutched at his shoulders. Dug her fingers in and hung on as if she meant to kill him should he decide to renege.

As if there's a chance in hell of him reneging now!

"Tell me, Claire. Why did you consult the Kama Sutra before you came here?"

"Bec…cause I didn't…know anything. Ab…booooout…" she tried to force herself onto him. And he held her tight, refusing her the release either of withdrawal or of penetration. "I didn't know anything ab…bout…sexxx."

He gave her another quarter of an inch. Eased her suffering a little. "You could have fooled me."

"But I…did…n't." She tried that sneak tactic again. Tried to steal home. But he was too strong for her. Amazingly, he was in control now, and it was such a mind-boggling experience, such a mind-boggling idea, that he hated to let it go just yet. Hated to let it go *ever*. "I didn't know anything at all, Eli. I'd only…and I'd never…I had no idea there was…anything like…please?"

He allowed her another quarter of an inch, marveling at the sheer, panicked desperation this freeze frame method of entry seemed to set up in her.

I'll have to remember this. Have to use it again in the future. On her. Whenever…

Whenever?

Shit. Hell. He was assuming an awful lot. A hell of an awful lot, if he was starting to assume there was going to be a *whenever.* He was so startled he almost relaxed his guard and in that instant he felt her flex around him. Felt her muscles begin to tighten in that greedy way of hers, and knew she was about to take him. So he firmed his grip and once again held her off.

She screamed, literally screamed, in frustration. And he bit back a laugh. "Not yet, you don't," he said. "Not until you finish what you started to say."

"I knew," she cried, her voice rising on a wail of unbearable anguish. "That I didn't know anything. About sex. I knew that's what you wanted. Expected. And I...so I looked it up."

"In the Kama Sutra."

She tensed around him. Readied herself for another try at him. And he tensed, too. Readying himself to hold her exactly where he wanted her. Exactly where she was until he decided it was time.

"Yes," she finally whispered, her tone implying she'd accepted defeat even as her body loosened momentarily, preparing for the next grab.

God, she was strong. Stronger inside than he'd known a woman could be.

"To please me."

"I thought. Th...th..." He moved into her a little more, just to see what she would do. And the result was...phenomenal.

She came.

Oh, dear, sweet Lord in heaven and all the angels at the right hand side of His throne. She came! In great and glistening waves. Trembling inside, tight muscles convulsing to even greater tightness around his cock as it slid forward carefully, experimentally, she came with a tremor that shook her entire body and, by connection, shook his as well.

Great God in heaven, the things she'd done to him. For him.

She'd *studied.*

He hadn't thought it was possible, but she had. Studied. He found the idea so endearing, so heart-wrenchingly sweet and thoughtful and just plain old *sexy* that he started to tremble, too. Releasing the tight and controlling grip he'd held on her ass, he maneuvered himself into her as though he'd never had a doubt about his ability. As though he'd never struggled with the doubt. He reached the farthest limits of her with that same easy precision and then he tipped his head forward to nuzzle the sweet and soft skin of her neck as she came around him, her body arching and thrusting, tightening again in a way that said this was what she'd wanted all along. *He* was what she'd wanted.

Chapter Nineteen

OH, HOW SHE'D WANTED HIM.

As her body emptied itself onto him, around him, for him, that was all Claire could think. That she'd wanted him from the first instant she'd ever seen him, so handsome and yet so icy, so remote in the snow-swirled darkness of that sleigh.

She'd wanted him, surely, from the first instant she'd lowered herself onto his shaft and felt the throbbing of his pulse inside her. Wanted him for certain from the instant she'd first realized the coldness and harshness was nothing but an act, and a very poor one at that. Wanted him in the instant when she'd sensed so much pain beneath the harshness and when she'd determined, without even knowing she'd done it, to find out what it was and how she could ease it.

Well, she'd found out. In some ways it had been worse than what she'd imagined. But in so many ways it hadn't been nearly so bad at all. But she had found out. And she'd convinced him his physical limitation didn't matter…thought she'd convinced him, as she felt the unyielding pressure of his shaft pressing into her and her own body yielding up to him, even more pliant now that the first tensing wave of climax had passed.

It was the first time they'd been naked together. The first time they'd pressed skin against skin for the entire length of their joined bodies. And it was intoxicating. His shoulders, gripped tight with clawed hands that sought some immovable and unshakable center to a universe in which instinct insisted there was no such thing as immovable or unshakable, were smooth. Like silk or satin or the petals of the orchids with which she'd decked herself the night they'd met in the conservatory. His skin felt softer than petals, a dewy and indescribable substance stretched taut over the muscles he used every day, muscles that had grown hard and rippling with constant use and in compensation for other muscles that had failed.

She ran her hands across his shoulders, moving her leg up a little more so that it found a better grip on his hips. Ran her hands down his arms as she tightened the leg, smiling a little as he made a soft and moaning sound that might have been protest or might have been acquiescence. Purring softly as her hands slipped from his arms to his hips, she pulled him into her. Pushed herself onto him.

She'd had an orgasm. Not the last of the evening, she suspected, though she found it hard to imagine there could be one greater. But Eli hadn't. Even as she'd released with a single and epochal convulsion that had drenched her, drenched him, drenched the bunched and wilted lace that almost but not quite intruded between them, she'd felt him holding back. Felt a deep down internal tightening in the male body that even at this moment incited hers to complete and unconditional surrender.

He'd egged her on. While he'd held back. And that was a situation she couldn't tolerate. Couldn't ever be *expected* to tolerate.

Tightening around him in every way she could, using the power of her leg and her hands and her abdomen, of all those internal muscles for which she had no immediate or specific names, she pulled herself onto him. Pulled him into her.

"Your turn," she murmured around the glimmer of a laugh.

"You think?" He resisted her pressure. But not by much. And she sensed that with a little more urging, a little more convincing, she might have the result she wanted. The one she demanded.

"Absolutely." Flex. She clung to his shaft. Tried to pull it deeper into herself with every muscle that surrounded it.

Eli gasped. Close to hers, his face took on a dewy sheen of sweat that shimmered on his brow, his cheeks, his upper lip. His eyes glowed in the soft radiance of the Christmas lights she'd found in the hallway, the leftover ones the decorating company had forgotten to take along with them once they'd finished with the tree.

Christmas lights.

Perfect.

There is redemption, she thought. *For all of us.* Redemption in the fact that Eli Eden had become her Christmas gift, had been meant to be her gift right from the start, her chance to end the desolation and monotony and lonely fear of a life that hadn't worked out all that well so far. He was a gift, and she'd never sold herself to him at all, never *had* to sell herself. Because some tiny, golden and gleaming Christmas angel had brought her to him and him to her.

And what better light in which to receive such a wondrous and impossibly perfect gift than the soft and rosy glow of strings and strands and streamers of pinpoint, sparkling lights meant only for, especially for, Christmas?

Christmas lights.

"Eli," she murmured as she felt his body begin to slide beyond the edge of control. "I lo..."

She said...oh, dear God. She almost said his name.

ELI WAS A DEAD man, and he knew it. He was a goner, a hopeless cause, a completely vanquished and eager prisoner in the sweetest war any man had ever fought and lost. And he didn't deserve what she'd given him tonight. The freedom. The realization that he wasn't nearly, wasn't even half, as disgusting or repulsive or powerless as he'd believed for so long. He didn't deserve it, and it had nothing to do with being a cripple either. It had never, now that she'd forced him into a kind of honesty he'd become all too adept at avoiding, been about that at all. He hadn't deserved for good things, people like Claire, to happen to him because he'd behaved like an idiot. A complete and childish idiot, bent upon using his own hurt to inflict hurt upon everyone else. To inflict hurt upon innocent and already wounded women who'd never done a single thing to him, women he'd only imagined *might* do something terrible if he gave them the chance.

I've been an idiot. And in return some great, merciful, kind and understanding God had sent him his Claire.

His Claire. He didn't even pause at the thought. Didn't hesitate or miss a beat in the rhythm of his body meeting hers and making it a part of his. Didn't even think about hesitating, because the end was near now. The unequivocal end of one part of his life.

And the beginning of the next? The beginning of the rest?

He didn't dare think it. Didn't dare believe it. But his body did. His body knew. Gathering its strength, his shaft searching deep inside her one last time, reaching out for the home and the belonging it...he...craved, he felt a long and rolling rumble start deep down at the center of himself. Felt it begin, and gain strength, and sweep effortlessly and swiftly toward the surface. Felt a tightening and a tensing, and then...

Release.

He emptied himself into her. Thrust his hips as hard as he could, shoving himself deep inside her so that he could give her all that he had, all that he would ever have. All that he had to offer.

Next to him, clutching him as if she feared he might force her away, he heard Claire's soft and shuddered breath. "Your turn," she breathed again, her eyes closed, the faint tracing of a blue vein pulsing beneath the skin of her temple, a bead of sweat gathering at the fragile and tender indentation in her upper lip.

"My turn," he agreed, the desperate pounding in his cock easing at last as the jagged and jerky thrusting of his body slowed to a stop. Once again he held her motionless, delightfully this time, on his full length. "We're going to have to make another arrangement, you know."

"Arrangement?" Eyes opening, she frowned. Or maybe even scowled.

With her joined to him so completely, Eli didn't much care which it was.

"Did you ever," she demanded, "even once, give any woman a chance?"

"Chance?" Dumbfounded, he could only stare at her, still taking the greatest care not to release her. "What the devil is that supposed to mean?"

"You and your damned *arrangements* anyway! Why do you think it's always necessary to try to buy people...women...try to buy what should be given freely, and with no strings attached?" Obviously miffed, she tried to pull away from him. Tried to pull off him.

But he had enough erection left, enough determination, to make sure that didn't happen. "I'm not trying to buy anything, Claire. I was merely trying to suggest..."

"Oh, I know all about your *suggestions*."

"The hell you do."

"Did you ever consider, Eli...did you ever once think that all those women you hired might be *people*? Real people, with problems that drove them to desperation, to doing things they never wanted..."

"So now you're saying you never wanted to be here. You never wanted what just happened?"

"I never said anything of the kind! Because... "

"Damn it, Claire. I wish you'd make up your mind. I wish you'd..."

"What?" she demanded after a few taut and uncomfortable seconds of silence. "You wish what?"

"Damn it all anyway. This isn't the way I wanted to do this."

"Do what?" She squirmed around him. Almost got away from him. But he caught her just in time, because no matter how angry she was with him, no matter how much she deserved to be angry and to let him feel the full force of it, he wasn't going to let her go. Not Claire. Not when she meant everything to him and he really and truly would be reduced to nothing if he ever let her get away.

"Oh, God. Claire." Her name came out a low sob. And that was enough to end her struggle for freedom. Enough to still her in his arms and send a half questioning, half understanding and completely wondering look to her face. "I've tried to tell you. Wanted to tell you. So many times. If you knew…if I thought you'd ever even dreamed…"

"What? Tell me what?"

He'd begun to fall out of her. Begun to lose the hardness, the last lingering remnants of the erection he'd maintained more out of wishing to maintain it than out of any real, physical reason to maintain it. He had only seconds left. Fractions of seconds, at best.

"I love you, Claire."

An expression flickered on her face. Was it astonishment? Surprise? Horror?

Please, God, don't let it be horror.

"I love you, Claire. I promise you I do. With whatever I've got in my heart, whatever is left of my heart after I tried to kill it and came so damned close to succeeding. I love you. And I was hoping…"

"Yes?"

"Or maybe I was wishing…"

CLAIRE KNEW WHAT HE wanted. She knew what he needed to say. But she needed to hear him say it. Because this was an important moment. As important as the one just moments ago in which she'd felt redeemed, and relieved of the burden of believing she'd sold herself to him. It was too important by far to be made light of or to be allowed to pass unnoticed.

She needed to hear him say it, if only to validate the importance of the moment.

Then he did, but what he said wasn't what she'd thought he was about to say.

"I want you to marry me."

She stiffened. Knew she had when she felt him stiffen, too, the arms that held her turning almost to bands of iron.

"Claire?"

For a moment, struggling to stay calm, she looked straight, deep, into dark eyes that did indeed, now that it had been pointed out to her in a way she could no longer mistake or deny, gleam with the low and burning light of real and genuine love. She looked at him, and wondered if he could see what she felt on her face.

The thrill of what hadn't seemed conceivable just a few days before.

The thrill of hearing her own sweetest longing put into words.

The thrill of the slight stirring she felt in the arms that held her, pulling her closer and then still closer.

"Yes," she whispered.

"Yes?" He sounded like he didn't believe it. Didn't believe he'd heard correctly. And why should he? As much as it was the right answer, the only answer, to a question like that, she couldn't believe she'd said it. Might never believe until the ring actually slipped onto her finger. Might not believe even then.

"Yes," she said, and snuggled tighter against the dear and cherished warmth of him. "I can't imagine any other arrangement that would be suitable."

"Then..." He'd begun to stir now in other places. Other ways, that only boded well for the future.

"My mother," she murmured, only half protesting. "She'll be here in a little while."

"That's long enough." Hands sliding down across her body, caressing every curve, every swell of flesh and every valley between those swells, Eli nuzzled her neck with lips that left sparking and shimmering trails wherever they ventured.

"L...long enough for wh...what?"

"You know."

"I do?"

His laughter burned low and soft in her ear. Against the side of her face. Against her mouth as he moved in closer still, preparing to kiss. And kiss, and kiss, and kiss. "I think that comes a little later. The *I dos*. But first we have to..."

Shivering as he began to probe gently with the shaft that had already begun to bounce back, eager for more, Claire slipped her leg up and over his hips again. "We have to what?"

"You know."

"I don't."

More probing. Harder this time. More determined. "We have to consummate."

"I thought that was supposed to come after the *I dos*?"

"Claire." He thrust. Found the opening, and penetrated with the same long and silken stroke that had finished her off the first time...the last time.

"What?"

"Be still now."

"Or what?"

"By God." Cupping her backside, he settled her onto him for an instant, then immediately released. "Are we going to seal this *arrangement*, or aren't we?"

Laughing lightly because she had him where she wanted him at last, she had him at her mercy, Claire pulled away before he had a chance to think twice or react. She turned her back on him, not necessarily to reject or to tease, but only to...

"Hey!" Like clockwork, just as she'd hoped and expected, he snuggled up next to her and behind her. He pressed himself against her like a couple of old spoons in a drawer. Which, according to the Kama Sutra, was the whole idea. The whole purpose of an exercise promised to give the most bang for the buck, the most sizzle for the steak, the most reward for the effort.

"Try it," she said back over her shoulder.

He hesitated. "Kama Sutra again?"

"They say it gives maximum shared contact."

He moved in closer. Feeling the tip of him begin to probe, she adjusted her position the tiniest bit, tilting her hips a little and propping a leg up to allow maximum entry to go along with maximum contact. And after a second he slipped into her. His body pressed tight against hers and she felt a surge of heat, white hot and delectable, as one of his arms wrapped around her, pulling her back against him.

It was a posture of complete submission for her, of unquestioned dominance for him. Propping his head on his free hand, he pressed his mouth close to her ear and whispered, "I like this."

Shuddering as the liquid silver feeling of her body about to turn entirely to steaming fluid rippled through her again, much more quickly than it had the last time he'd lingered inside her, she laughed huskily. "I thought you might."

Slowly, he began to move. Obviously relishing the gift of mastery she'd given him. Obviously reluctant to let it go. She could feel him straining, could almost feel him *aching*, to maintain his self-control. To not give up, not give in, but to go faster.

Claire shuddered inside. Felt the glow start, felt it build and become more urgent with each long, languorous and powerful entry. Felt the first faint, but undeniable ripplings of orgasm sweep through her body. Felt the tingling begin, and then the deep, hot throbbing. Felt the sensation of floating and the dizzy disorientation that came with it as…

"Nice," he murmured as the wave broke. As the next one swept forward a little higher and a little faster. And the next and the next while he seemed utterly undaunted, completely unaffected. "So nice." But his voice gave him away. His unsteady, suddenly thick and needful voice, and the arm that tightened around her waist and locked her onto the shaft that went ominously still inside her for a moment. He'd pressed himself into her at an angle she'd never expected to experience, but one she meant to demand again and again, because it was wonderful. Spectacular. The most spectacular thing she'd ever…

When the next wave crested and broke inside her, she cried out. Just his name, quavered in a tone that made it clear what he'd done to her. What he was continuing to do with each and every swift and certain stroke of his shaft skimming past her entrance in its search for the deepest depths of her. What he did to her with each and every brush of flesh that whispered against quivering flesh, arousing soft and hidden tissues that began again, in the same second that he jerked, to mist with soft and eager moisture.

Flesh that shared its moisture and mixed it with what flowed from him with such enormous, warm and penetrating force that she realized for the first time exactly how completely she'd been joined to him. And he to her. How momentously, inextricably, unbelievably joined in both soul and spirit.

Eli gasped, continuing his rough and slightly desperate assault for another moment. Half a moment. Then, groaning, he fell still, buried inside her and clinging to her, the arm around her waist clutching at her as she deliberately tightened herself around the deflating shaft and wrenched another moan from him. "Claire, I don't think I can…"

"I don't think I can either. But…"

"But what?"

"I hope you know I'm never going to let you go. Not unless I'm forced to by something that's bigger than me. Stronger than me. Bigger and stronger than both of us."

His laugh was shaky. Riddled with an undertone of delirium. Maybe even hysteria. "I was counting on that."

Silence fell. A long and thoughtful silence in which his shaft left her at last, unable to maintain its firmness or its position. Silence in which he rolled back and let her go. A silence in which she turned and snuggled into him, into the scintillatingly musky curve of his shoulder and the arm that came around her to hold her there.

"Are you going to teach me what else you learned in your Kama Sutra?" he asked after a while, his breath and his voice barely more controlled than they'd been when he'd still been inside her.

"Tonight?" Automatically, she shook her head. "I thought you said you didn't have it in you."

He chuckled. More normal, but still not normal. The way she suspected he was never going to be completely normal, whatever that meant, again. "Give me some time, and I might just surp…"

Time!

Claire struggled to sit up, and when he wouldn't let her she struggled to turn enough to see the clock on the nightstand. "Oh, Eli, look at the time! Mum will be here in…"

She wasn't sure. She didn't know what time the car had left, didn't know how long it would take her mother to get ready for such an impromptu trip, didn't know how long she, the least spontaneous and impromptu of people, would spend protesting before she finally gave in.

He sighed. "You're right. Another time."

Sitting up, Claire pulled the twisted and snarled sheet around herself to cover herself. Then she leaned forward, leaned over him, and planted the smallest, most suggestive kiss she could manage on lips that opened immediately to make it something more. Something deeper.

"We will be together again," she promised. "We'll be together for a lifetime."

Return to Eden

By

Evelyn Starr

Chapter One

"CLAIRE?" ELI REACHED FOR HER, HIS FOREHEAD WRINKLED IN A FROWN. "IS something wrong? You seem...distracted."

Shivering a little, shoving aside an overpowering desire to check the clock the way she'd already checked it at least a million times today, Claire tried to smile.

She was pinning everything on the precious cargo in the back of that truck. Had been ever since she'd tracked the thing down in Connecticut and started making all the arrangements necessary to bring it home. Where it belonged.

"Are you all right?" He truly did look concerned, and her heart reached out in search of his.

He loved her that much. *Still.* And that was something precious. Something she couldn't afford to lose.

"I was just thinking," she improvised, only to wonder immediately what she would say when he inevitably wanted to know *what* she'd been thinking.

"What?" he asked, lips quirking in a half-smile that made her heart instantly roar. Made it instantly throb harder and fill with renewed determination to make things right between them. To make them as they'd once been.

"I was thinking of new ways to please you."

Eli's eyes sparked. They glittered hotter, glittered almost fantastically with a new, brandy-colored light. "And?"

His question hung in midair, more challenge than question. More request than rejection. More laughing, loving, warm and caring Eli as he'd been once they'd gotten past the trials of first knowing each other and realized they were head over heels, madly and incomprehensibly in love with each other. Eli as he'd been when all things had still seemed possible.

Looking down at him as she knelt astride his thighs, seeing the fevered flush that lit his face and the low, steady glow simmering at the back of brown eyes that couldn't seem to get enough of her, she wondered what could have gone wrong between them.

The sex was good. It always had been, right from the start. But that other thing...this terrible distance that had been allowed to creep in...how had that *happened*?

Three and a half years, the entire span of their marriage, wasn't an eternity. It wasn't even a fleeting *moment* in the longer scheme of eternity. And yet it *was* an eternity to one who felt she'd somehow managed to lose the only man she could ever love. Not physically. Not yet. But she felt she'd lost him all the same. Lost him in some indefinable, uneasy, psychological way.

Staring down at him through a long and quivering moment when they both seemed to be waiting for something that might not yet happen, Claire laughed. Suddenly. Unexpectedly, the sound of it bubbling from her lips the way it had in other days, better days. The kind of spontaneous laughter she knew had been hers before, because her heart kept telling her it had.

"Show me," Eli whispered, his eyes glittering more feverishly...glittering indescribable brandy-rich as plain deep brown faded from their depths and fire crept in to claim them.

"Show you?"

When he laughed along with her, his teeth shone perfectly white and deliciously perfect.

Pale morning light infused their bedroom with a soft-blue stillness flung like a veil over the warmer gold of walls and curtains and satin-smooth polished floor. A stillness so real Claire felt she could hold it in her hand should such become necessary. And in the midst of it, his eyes dared her to go on.

Dared her to *do* it.

Whatever he thought she might be about to do.

Moving smoothly as if she'd practiced for years and years, Claire rose off the thighs she'd held captive beneath hers. Leaning toward him, she fell to hands and knees, her breasts dangling free within easy reach of hands he didn't immediately lift from the pillows upon which he'd propped himself. Her breasts were fuller now, rounder since she'd had the twins, as was her entire body. Fuller, rounder, more lush and, she knew just from the way he looked up at her, more desirable.

Taking her time, she moved toward him. Slinking like the lovely cat she sometimes imagined herself to be, she moved slowly. She'd fixed her gaze upon him in the same way that hungry beast might regard a delicious morsel. And she never let it waver.

Still motionless, seeming almost mesmerized, Eli stared back.

He wanted to lift his hands. Claire could *feel* the want hovering in heated summer morning air between them. She could feel the ache of it in her own hands. The hardened, burning ache of hands that needed to lift. Needed to graze her breasts with peaked knuckles, to lift their weight with sweat-slicked palms. Hands that needed to…

A fevered wind swept through the open window a few feet from the bed, bringing with it inspiration that seized her in the same instant Eli's hands managed a feeble twitching.

I should deny him.

He'd finally found strength and mobility. In another instant he would be able to seize what his eyes said he wanted.

But sometimes denial was the best part of it. Sometimes the torture of denial was the only part of it that made any sense.

Acting quickly before he could get the jump on her, spurred on by that lightning flash of inspiration that came from somewhere out in the still and heat waved morning beyond the windows, she sagged away from him. Sagged deliberately, allowing her arms to collapse so that her face dropped close to his chest. A chest that began to heave visibly, perfectly in tune with a sudden rasping as his breathing became labored. As every intake, every outflow, became suddenly, more torturously than she'd ever planned, difficult.

"Jesus, Claire." His lifted hands met only thin air. Met only the hair at the very top of her head as he grasped and strained in search of what had been there a split second before.

What he wanted now. Immediately. With the kind of insatiable impatience only he could be capable of.

"What the hell—"

Before he could complete the thought, it ended in another intake of breath. A sharper one. One that rose to the ceiling and quivered there alongside the heat waves that had already gathered in a thick and smothering cloud even so early in the day.

"My God," he said when the first contact of her flesh to his, when her first experimental brush of the inside of a thigh against the parched head of his shaft set a sizzling arc of heat and light to flashing between them…an arcing that began even before the contact was complete. Even before she'd done more than simply whisper against the erect and waiting length that leaped eagerly at her touch and forced another gasp from his throat. "Claire!"

The single syllable sounded in that instant like a thousand. Beginning as little more than a shimmering whisper, it grew immediately, grew exponentially and without hesitation to an agonized groan of delight.

"God." Eli groaned again. Louder.

In response Claire stroked scalloped arcs against him, carefully avoiding the contact she knew he wanted. The contact that would put her most secret, most female and most vulnerable flesh against that which wanted only to plunder. Only to penetrate and have its instant, its full and unbounded gratification.

"Where do you *learn* these things?" Coming up, his hands captured her hips as they'd been unable to capture her breasts. And in the capturing, they guided her. Pulled her closer even though she tried to resist, pulled her close enough that the tip of his engorged, agonized shaft found the secret flesh it sought. Found the place between her legs that she'd revealed to him and dangled before him, thinking to entice him and then deny him. Thinking to toy with him for as long as she wanted, in any way she wanted.

But Eli would have none of it. A short and tearing sound erupted from his throat, a sound of unmitigated agony, as he pulled her almost onto the long and searching length. As he stroked a series of slow and deliberate, steaming paths across taut and eager flesh that could no more resist the scoring and scalding or the long and sleek paths of sheer, wanton need than tides could resist the moon. He coaxed from her a long and shivery series of gasps that matched, that at times exceeded, every one of his own.

Gasping repeatedly, seeming at times to have to fight for every breath, his eyes closed now and his face a study in pure, burgeoning rapture, Eli whispered her name over and over. He tantalized with the touch of himself, the promise of himself, the sheer and utter irresistibility of himself. Until without warning he laughed. Just as Claire had laughed precipitously and unexpectedly before.

It was a sound she heard too seldom these days. One that brought with it another old and all but forgotten sensation as Eli began to guide her again. Guide her expertly, with hands that would not be refused or shrugged away. As he held her upright with hands that would not be resisted, guiding her to the place where he could slide into her with an ease that startled. An ease that refused to give so much as an instant's respite or an instant's chance to adjust to this new fullness.

This new sense that she'd just been completed as only Eli had ever been capable of completing her. Pulling her down, slipping her down, he laughed softly, laughed promisingly and tantalizingly as he seated her upon him. Firmly, so that any movement by either of them, no matter how slight, would automatically invite the kind of sinuous torment that had brought them together so precipitously time and again in the past. And precipitously, too, this morning. Precipitously, the way it always did.

Shivering, Claire dared to move. Experimentally. Instantly aware of the swollen length that had already penetrated as far as it could into her. And just as instantly aware of the barely contained delight the throbbing length held for her. In abeyance. Just waiting for her to...

Damn it all.

She'd nearly forgotten about the truck.

But the truck would wait. And even if it didn't, Hannah would meet it. Hannah would take care of everything because that was what good housekeepers did. Because Hannah knew the cargo was meant to be a surprise, and she knew to be discreet.

So screw the truck anyway!

She had more important things on her mind. Much, much more important.

"What now?" Eli's voice turned sharp. It took on some of its old and commanding ferocity. From times *before* before.

Staring into his eyes, anxious to read their expression and yet thoroughly unable, Claire realized she hadn't even *begun* to feel the torment he was capable of inflicting.

"My God." It was her turn to murmur in a jagged, ragged voice as he moved her again with those irresistible guiding hands. As he changed the angle at which she sat upon him, and thereby changed and somehow, magically enhanced the way his engorged and hardened length met the inner limits of her.

Eli was laughing again. He was laughing harder, laughing with a shimmering rumble of sound that translated into even more aggravating delight as the force of it moved his shaft inside her. As every movement coaxed every centimeter of her to adjust in accommodation, only to have to readjust again, immediately since his movements against the inside of her, the variations on his movements inside her, were never-ending.

Claire sighed first. Then she cried out, and then finally she had nothing left but another long and sharp series of gasps, each one beginning almost before the previous one ended.

His shaft burned with its every touch against inner, unprotected flesh. It shot long and sunset-red rays of churning heat into the deepest and most hidden places inside her in less than...no more than...the single instant it took to draw in breath. And in the next instant, when she found herself forced to hold that breath as if her very life depended upon holding it, the heat came back. Came out, ricocheting off something deep inside her so that it was retransmitted, rejuvenated, returned to the outer layers of her. To outer layers that instantly, explicitly, blossomed with a fine misting and beading of internally driven sweat that made even the sultry summer morning air seem tame and chill by comparison.

The movement of his shaft was unlike any she'd felt before. It struck at oddly unpredictable angles even Eli, in all his enormous and never-ending sexual creativity had never thought to try before. And even Eli seemed to realize it.

Catching her hips again, tightening the grip he'd allowed to loosen for a moment, he growled softly. Deep in his throat. Long and supple, his fingers wrapped into her flesh and dug deep as he prepared to take them to the next...the unimaginable...stage.

Tensing in preparation, feeling a slight internal tugging and tightening where she'd been just about to grow soft and pliant a moment before, Claire didn't try to resist.

"Sweet Claire," he murmured, urging her with his strong hands to do what he wanted. To give in and give way, to take up the slight circular motion he'd dictated without rising away from him. Without separating from him by even the slightest degree. "Take your time. There's no rush." He murmured this around an even more seductive rumble of felt-inside laughter...a rumble that left her chilled and trembling inside even as she burned on the outside with fire that instinct...experience...declared would not be easily quenched now that it had been ignited. Fire that would never be completely quenched by any means.

"You don't have anything better to do this morning," he murmured. "Do you?"

The image of the truck with its treasure...it would be a large truck, Claire imagined with the half of her mind that remained capable of thought beyond this moment and this heated, swirling, mist-shadowed room, a great and rattling behemoth of a thing...flickered though her mind. And then was gone.

"No."

The searing, sweet and still sweetening hardness of the length he'd buried inside her had claimed her. And the even sweeter, the deliciously arousing sweetness that surged through her body and from her body as it went along with his had already long since sealed her fate.

Screw the truck. Screw everything except him. Except this man. The one she loved, and would continue to love until the day...the nanosecond...she died.

Swaying softly, her body taking on the slow and repetitious, slow and arousing motions of the most accomplished of lap dancers, she remained upright above him, stiffened and strengthened by a sweltering resolve to still find her way with him. Still do what she wanted with him...to make love to him any way she could and every way she could. But she remained upright for less than a moment. Because a sudden swirling of sensation sprang from every part and parcel and fiber of her as he adjusted his position again. As he pulled her harder down, forcing himself even deeper into her, into places where she was even less strong and much, much less able to resist.

The new penetration...the unprecedented depth of it...left her weak. Trembling with a luscious agony few had ever known and fewer still had survived. Softening abruptly, both inside and out, she collapsed. Simply collapsed, sagging forward in a way that folded her nearly double and tucked her body into a new, a more acutely aware and receptive position.

Bracing the flats of her hands against crumpled golden sheets at either side of Eli's thighs, she fought to find steadiness in a world that increasingly began to whirl and swirl out from beneath her.

Pulling her back, his hands firm and increasingly unyielding upon her hips, he allowed her to slump only a little. Only enough that she reached a new level, a new and startlingly searing angle of penetration that allowed him, incredible as the notion might seem, to find an even deeper depth of her.

"Lovely," he murmured, keeping her firmly anchored where he so clearly wanted her. A fresh suggestion of laughter from deep inside made him sound not at all like a man in fear of sustaining some kind of grievous and tragic injury. It made him sound...

Anticipating now, quivering both inside and out with the force of anticipation, Claire held herself with more controlled determination and more fiercely exerted pressure against sheets she'd caught in her fists and begun to crumple with all the strength left to her. Steeling herself, she took a second or two more to gather her scattered strength in preparation.

For feeling her way.

For rapidly spiraling exhilaration inherent in everything Eli had set in motion...every sensation he'd set to ricocheting madly and without end inside her.

She steeled herself to resist crying and quite possibly shrieking mindlessly in the face of the rich and convulsing warmth that was completely different from anything she'd felt or known before. It was a softer warmth. A more soothing and yet more unnerving warmth, a whole river of warmth, always punctuated and perfected by the heated length that filled her so well. A curling warmth that quickly infiltrated every part of her, that softened her even more than she'd been soft at the first indication Eli wanted her. And now that she'd softened, her body knew the way. It knew to moisten. Repeatedly. Deliciously, in preparation.

Warmth.

Hadn't that always encompassed the feelings Eli set in motion whenever he touched her?

Didn't *warmth* describe perfectly all the murmuring bursts of desire, and need, and eagerness that always and forever caused her to leap inside? That incited her to such heights of joy that…

"Eli!" It came out a jagged shard of sound…a white collection of sparkling and dissociated shards, expressed in about eighteen singing, barely distinguishable syllables.

"I don't…" He'd begun to gasp as well as the speed of her movements increased. As the round and round component he'd started and she'd continued began to fade quickly, replaced and then almost immediately overshadowed by an eager up and down and up and down that took his body, pulling him into hers and using him to fuel the myriad of dissociated sparks that hadn't yet coalesced…not quite…into true flame. Intoxicating, never to be duplicated brews of sparks in red and blue and greens, and the most vivid, most dazzling and bedazzling bewitchment of backlit violet any woman…or man…had ever been privileged to feel.

"You don't…" Claire could barely make a sound.

"What?" Eli seemed to have the same difficulty.

"You don't what?"

"Don't know…"

A rigid grimace overtook his face. It was a tight and straining urgency, accompanied by a beading of sweat on his forehead and a tightening of his fingers upon her hips…a bone-deep digging in that would have been, might have been, painful if she'd had wit enough left to understand the meaning of pain.

But in this new state of existence, this silken-steaming one in which Eli lifted and lifted, insisting she rise now where he'd stopped her before, insisting she rise to the point her knees felt in danger of completely leaving the bed, there was no pain. No knowledge or hint of pain. In the resulting series of plunges, when Eli lifted her higher than she'd ever wanted to go and then released her, allowing the endless and stroking plummet that needed to follow as surely as the moon followed the sun and the stars the moon, she knew only pleasure. A shrieking torture of pleasure that built and built, all the while allowing nothing to hint there might be an end to this glory. This utter and chaotic torment.

Thrumming now, her body more than ready for the kind of depredations history taught Eli was capable of inflicting, Claire strummed him with greedy female folds that had no choice but to seek their reward.

"You said you didn't," Claire persisted, when it became obvious that in silence lay utter, raving madness. "A while ago. You said—"

"I know."

This time when he lifted, she did dangle. Completely aloft and almost entirely free of his shaft, with only the heated tip of it pulsating against the drenched and nearly bereft outer folds of her. Only the tip of it to remind her in heartbreaking terms what she'd almost lost.

"So." Uttering a small and strangled cry, Claire struggled against his strength when he gave no sign of allowing her to descend again. "What did you..." She struggled harder. But just like before, it was no use. In his face, in the laughter and the gleam of his taunting brandy-colored eyes, she saw no hint, not even a clue, to what he was really thinking. "What did you mean? When you s...sssssssssssssssssaid..."

The last word drew itself out in a long and undulating scream.

Eli began to lower her. At last. Controlling her, forcing her to move with tragic slowness that could only have equally tragic consequences, he began to allow her to slide down and ever, unendingly down the shaft that seemed suddenly to have no limit. No finishing point.

"Claire." Eli's voice still carried a tremor of laughter, but Claire heard something else there now, too. A warning. Clear and unmistakable, ringing with unspoken instruction to forget what he'd said earlier. Forget everything but what was happening now and what might happen in the next moment. If she did as he asked and did as he wanted.

As if to illustrate that point, Eli allowed her to descend again, a very little more. A precious millimeter more, before his hands re-tightened, caught and held her trapped, suspended in the midst of incipient, swirling satisfaction.

"God." She breathed the word. Begged the word. Pleaded with him for her release. For her finish.

And still she hung. Suspended, waiting and pulsing for what was so close. What seemed likely never to come.

Slowly, her movements no longer quite connecting, no longer quite a part of any reality or any present time, her movements seeming rather to be fragmented reminders of some half-realized dream, Claire slipped her hands between them. Between the hard, taut plane of Eli's abdomen and the rippling, saturated folds he'd stretched tight with his first entry into her. Folds held that way with the part of him that remained embedded there.

Claire held his shaft in the circle of her fingers. She marveled at its girth. Its arcing heat, its rising pulse and matchless strength. As if this was the first time she'd encountered them. Hanging breathless on the very verge of poignant, enchanting discovery.

Eli might be steadfast in his refusal to grant her the release she needed now more desperately than ever.

But Claire had her ways.

She had her methods.

Like the fingertips with which she began to stroke herself and stroke him at the same time.

Chapter Two

HER FINGERS WERE LIKE FLAMES COME TO LIFE ALONG THE LENGTH OF HIS COCK. Her fingers, so small and yet so incredibly, inarguably powerful, were like balm to a soul in desperate anticipation of wounding. Possibly fatal and irreparable wounding. Her fingers, the feel of them as she took up the diabolical, delightful stroking she'd done almost as an afterthought in the midst of what promised to be one of the steamiest moments they'd ever shared, were the greatest relief of Eli's life.

He'd been worried about her. About them.

Really and truly, seriously worried. To the point he'd at times been barely able to function, even in his own deprived and severely limited way. To the point he'd felt himself sinking repeatedly, lower and lower into a depression from which, one of these soon to come days, he knew he would never be strong enough or courageous enough to recover.

Lately she'd been so…Eli didn't know what.

Distracted?

That might be it.

She certainly hadn't been the Claire he'd fallen head over heels in love with not so very long ago. There had been a gap between them. A growing one, a pervasive one he'd never understood and thought now he never would.

He didn't know who'd started it, who'd fostered it, who'd allowed it to grow unabated and unchallenged until it had damned near overcome them both and silenced them both.

It made his head ache even to *want* to know. With all the difficulties he had already, all the problems Claire had once found it possible for reasons God didn't even understand to overlook, the last thing Eli Eden needed was a terrible, irreconcilable distance holding her away. Holding her heart hostage.

But now the blessed heat had risen inside him. Was still rising, close to being out of control and beyond any human boundaries.

Claire was the only woman in the world who'd ever brought him to that point. She was the only one capable now of bringing him…his heart and his mind in addition to his damaged wreck of a body...back from the dismal kind of death in life to which he'd so recently thought himself re-condemned.

Looking at the long and sloping curve of her neck, watching the rippling fall and play of morning light on drifts of hair that had turned unexpectedly curly as it grew longer and longer, Eli wondered how he'd ever imagined she could be rejecting him. The way he'd expected and feared ever since that first night they'd spent together...that very first instant he'd set eyes on her, striding unwillingly but purposefully toward a horse-drawn sleigh on a cold and snowy Allegheny Mountain night, wearing nothing but a skimpy costume he'd chosen without her input or consent beneath a fur-lined velvet cape.

God, she'd been a vision then.

And sweet God, she was still a vision. Was more than a vision hovering close to him. Was an angel of grace. Of mercy. Of...

He'd feared her rejection so much. But she'd only been playing with him. Toying with him, teasing him into an uproar of uncertainty in much the same way she'd always teased his cock and balls, tormenting them until they didn't know left from right or up from down. Her strange distraction had vanished as she'd come to him a little while earlier, maybe only another part of a game designed to drive him to distraction...drive him to the brink and then unceremoniously push him over, into an abyss of absolute, neglected insanity. Now she was touching him. Still playing with him, in ways that now gave him hope that whatever he'd thought lost might not be lost after all.

She was lovely. The loveliest woman alive, a vision in creamy, naked skin and glossy brown hair, a vision seen through a mist of fevered passion all set to consume, all set to change everything. For all the rest of time. Settling herself to her business with him...and what business it was...she was lovelier even than he'd dared remember in his desperate dreams on all the nights when she'd slept soundly next to him, yet separated inexplicably from him by something he could neither touch nor breach.

"Jesus!" He didn't know if she heard. It didn't matter if she did. He hadn't really meant for her to hear. He'd said it...*exploded* it...more for his own benefit. More to ease the suddenly escalated pressure of a body overtaxed in less than an instant to something well beyond its limit than to get her attention.

His body was doing that well enough all by itself.

There was no way Claire could *not* be aware of his response when she sank down onto, not quite onto but very near, what strained aching and hardened beyond all endurance between his legs. What roared and thundered, demanding attention and reaching incredible heights in the instant she made her first steaming and testing pass across it. Teasing it. Teasing him, coaxing him, setting him instantly to an eager fever of waiting. The way he always seemed to have to wait ever since she'd walked into his life that snowy-frozen night and changed everything forever.

She'd taken him prisoner that first night and held him ever since. Held him body and mind and soul.

The caressing didn't last long. Delightful as it was, sinfully delicious and demonically enjoyable as it was, he wasn't able to let it last for very long. He had to do something. Had to take action before she killed him with her caresses, had to place her atop him and slide her onto him.

And now…

God, now!

She all but took over. Lifting and dropping, repetitiously though anything but monotonously, she slid down the length of him time and time again. Always endlessly, always effortlessly. Allowing the weight of her body to drive her, allowing it to do all the work, she took him in repeatedly. Took all of him in.

God in heaven. How could a woman as sweetly-small as Claire take in so much? Without doing some terrible, irreparable damage to herself?

How the secret and living hell could he endure it without worry his heart might explode inside his chest?

"Jesus," he groaned again. Groaned louder. This time wanting her to hear. Needing her to hear.

She didn't respond.

Not with words anyway.

Because she *did* respond in her own inimitable way.

She responded with a deep-sweet flowing. With a burst…just one, just for now…of inner essence that scalded upon the instant of contact. A burst that branded him, as if he hadn't been branded already, as her very, exclusive own.

She responded the way women in his dreams had responded in the time before he'd met her and discovered dreams could sometimes…very rarely…come true. She responded completely. Profusely. Instantly, effervescently.

Somehow his hands found her hips.

Somehow they managed to grasp. Eli could see them grasping, see them clutching convulsively at the twin rounds of satin-silk flesh under laid with perfectly formed bone, though he could feel nothing of them or with them.

There wasn't room in his life, wasn't capacity any more in his nervous system, for anything except what had overtaken his beleaguered shaft and placed it completely, adoringly in thrall. Surrounded by the dewy-foggy heat of her, lost in the depths of a calescent mist from which instinct told him there would be no lasting escape, the engorged and aching length of his cock now represented all of his universe. All of him.

He had no need of anything else.

He never would again.

Holding tight to him with imprisoning flesh, Claire moved her hips a very little. She swayed them from side to side just enough that their movement could be *called* movement. And then quickly, long before he was prepared for it or expected it, she added a new element. She added something lovely, something so intrinsically engaging it made him whimper aloud, too unnerved and too disoriented to put what he felt and wanted into words.

She added a slight circling motion. It was no more than a hint of rotation that might, if he could manage to contain himself and manage to be silently patient, become something even greater. Something that just might, if he could only live that long, become a whirling, clinging steam of Claire wrapping herself around him. Of Claire making herself an integral and vitally important part of him.

Never leaving him, not even to lift herself completely away from him and grant him the moment's relief he craved yet at the same time dreaded, she twisted her body gently. Twisted it in ways he'd never thought a woman's body could twist. And all the time twisted him inside her. Twisted him in ways that stopped just short of injuring him, just short of leaving him truly incapacitated, incapacitated in ways that really mattered and would really make his life the living death he'd once considered it to be.

She didn't leave him. Ever. And that was good.

That was better than good.

Because leaving implied being alone. It implied bereft suffering, and coldness of the heart. Coldness that must inevitably, that could only, spread to his spirit and lodge there, infectious and incurable.

"C-Claire."

His voice worked little better than the hands that remained semi-deadened stumps or the legs that long ago, from times before he'd known Claire, times when he'd lost his hope, had ceased to have meaningful function. His voice uttering that one small but sweet word, uttering her name, was reduced to a torn tatter that, lost in overheated air, drowned there. Before it ever had its chance to be noticed.

Claire quivered a little. Laughing, the vibrancy of it transmitting itself into him as a glimmer of additional tightening of female flesh around his, she dug her knees into the bed. Seeking a firm base. So she could start the agonizing process of removing herself. Permanently, he feared.

Slowly…oh, so haltingly, she lifted off him. Befogged flesh wept soft and sinuous moisture with every millimeter of her retreat. Clinging, tenacious, her body seemed reluctant to continue the retreat even as it did. Even as it dragged gently along his length, giving him up without apparent struggle. With the merest promise that she *would* return. That she would do it soon.

Christ.

Eli didn't think he could stand the agony if she did. If she didn't. When she did or didn't.

Responding quickly, so quickly with benumbed hands that had previously fumbled and felt useless that it startled him, Eli tightened his grip upon her hips before she could leave him. Cupping fingers and palms around them required all the agility he possessed. And holding her required something else again.

Arms locked, hands and fingers straining to the point they ached with the effort, holding her required almost more strength than he possessed.

It amounted nearly to a life and death struggle.

Claire's body wanted to descend. Her every muscle tensed…*every* one…as she tried to force herself down. As she shoved hard with legs so strong, so hard and muscular and *alive* he couldn't quite believe they could belong to any human…couldn't believe they could be flesh and blood at all, and not steel as he sometimes, often, suspected.

She shoved down.

Hard.

And Eli held her where she was. His fingertips gouged tender flesh with necessary force he could only hope wouldn't be too brutal. Wouldn't leave marks on the creamy-soft perfection of her skin that would make him feel guilty. Make him feel like the worst kind of ravishing beast. One who scarcely deserved to live.

"Claire," he murmured, meaning to tell her to take it easy and give him a chance. Just a moment to pull himself together so he wouldn't end up a raving, screaming, wasted shell of whatever small amount of man he'd been before she'd started upon him. But no more would come out. And she paid him no attention anyway. As he'd known she wouldn't.

Claire aroused, Claire on a mission to kill with the pleasure only she knew how to inflict, was a force to be reckoned with. She was as elemental as a virulent force of nature unleashed, and no easier to stop or subvert.

Claire started along this path she'd started almost without his realizing it was the best kind of destruction imaginable. Was perfect destruction looking for the perfect place to strike.

She made a sound. Something indefinable that expressed to the utmost her mingled pleasure and frustration. And, making it, she tried again to thrust herself down as hard as she could.

Greed flowed off her in virtual waves.

Greed for him...the kind of greed he'd thought long dead, long forgotten as the initial heat of her fascination with him had seemed to subside over time.

This was new greed. Even more insatiable greed than he'd known before, greed that made his heart pound so hard and so heavily it threatened to rip itself free, never to be restored or repaired.

Or was it the way her flesh pulsed around his that lifted him to such new heights? Was it the way she tightened herself around what little bit of his cock she'd managed to retain that set him to thrumming with an insistent urgency she had to hear?

The air all around them quaked with the feel of it. The sound of it.

The air virtually shook with the low and pulsating hum of Eli's unmet arousal and need.

Claire shivered. He saw the fine line of it, verging on a shudder, trace a swift track along the sweat-gleamed planes of her face. And at that point, driven beyond any human limit of endurance, he gave up his struggle.

Just gave up, arms collapsing, his hands no longer clenched around her hips, no longer capable of anything but following as, freed at last, she made her lightning-quick downward stroke.

And God, it felt like lightning! Felt like deadly lightning, searing inexorably through his system.

Claire slammed down onto him. Her flesh parted before him like a rippling wave of steam as through no effort of his own Eli sliced upward and inward. Through her. Into her.

She slammed down with such exuberant force and violence that she drove the air from his lungs and a cry of absolute victory from his throat.

"God!" he screamed, not caring if Hannah, the housekeeper she'd hired immediately after dismissing his own hand-picked Estella, who she'd called furtive and menacing, heard. Not caring even if Claire's mother or the Nanny, occupied with their concerns far away on the second floor, heard. Not caring if they knew what the hell was going on here.

Because he and Claire were *married*, for Christ's sake!

Because this marble mausoleum that Claire had made over into something infinitely warmer and softer, infinitely more inviting and comfortable, was their home, and most of all because they were two consenting adults. Because they always had been, even in the days when he'd enticed her here for the strictly business proposition of sex for money.

Because it was nobody's business what they did here, in the privacy of it. Nobody's business how they did it, or how often they did it.

Which hadn't been all that often recently.

Hannah knew that, Eli felt certain. As did Claire's mother, who'd have a hard time hearing anyway even if they decided to do it in the next room, separated from her from nothing more than a flimsy and floating curtain.

Claire made another sound.

He thought it was one of pleasure. Prayed it was one of pleasure, then immediately had his confirmation when her body turned to a pillar of seething steam around him. When moisture began to flow profusely from her in sinuous rivulets that immediately reached out to inundate him. Reached out to eradicate him with their force and power.

Claire came upon him. In the old way. Without hesitation, without any visible reservation or difficulty. And she came completely, devoting herself to it heart and soul now that she'd managed to shove her earlier distraction, whatever the hell it had been, aside.

She came and came.

But not Eli.

He wasn't ready yet.

The same events...the same accident of time and place and his old man's overpowering determination to have things his own way and to hell with the cost to anyone else...that had taken so much away from him had compensated with a certain lag in response. A lag he'd once, before he'd met Claire and been subjected to her unique and special kind of arousing torture, thought a terrible thing. A lag he'd once thought a curse upon his life and something he'd never be able to tolerate without losing his sanity...never be able to tolerate and endure without becoming the kind of embittered, self-involved and heartless monster he'd been well on his way to becoming the night Claire had first appeared on the scene.

Now he saw it as something else entirely. As a singular ability to resist easy satisfaction, easy completion. An ability to withstand things that would have brought other men, most men, to their knees in tears of anguish. An ability to prolong the sex act by exerting very little real effort of his own in a way that experience had taught could very easily have his partners on *their* knees. Crying in *their* anguish.

But not Claire.

Never Claire.

He'd never been able to bring her to anything but even greater arousal with this little trick. No matter how many times he'd used it, or how many variations he'd thought up for its use.

Insatiable now, growing hungry for more and then hungrier still with every second of delay in his response, every instant he forced himself to hold back even once he'd reached the saturation point and passed it, Claire always had the ability to take more than he could give. She had a singular ability to last longer than he ever could. To demand everything he had and relish the victory of draining him down to a dry and empty husk that shivered in its release, believing there could never be another because he would never again have anything to give.

Insatiable and hungry, Claire came on top of him. And in the coming, in every freshet and scorching stream and river of moist heat that burst from her body to lubricate its risings and fallings, Eli felt an unspoken demand.

The old demand. Her demand that he give it up for her. Give it all up, give it up now.

Only it wasn't time.

Even if his body had reached that point and even gone beyond it, his mind wasn't there yet. His mind wasn't ready for the turbulence of release. It wasn't ready for the debilitating sacrifice of pride and dignity that was only inherent in the kind of release he knew Claire expected. The kind he knew she deserved, the kind that would revive and revitalize the both of them. The kind of absolute release he could attain only with the one right, the one perfect and beloved partner.

So he waited.

Eager to see what Claire would do and eager, too, to see what new heights she might drive him to with her continued stream of sultry heat, her continuous and ever more rigorous thrusting onto and ripping away from a cock that felt ready to burst from the pressure she exerted as well as the pressure building within. With each and every one of her low and almost sinister sounds that told him she expected him to satisfy her. That *demanded* he satisfy her and promised only worse torment, only worse and escalating anguish should he refuse.

Anguish, Eli thought through a deafening roar that had only just begun to crescendo inside his head, *I'll welcome.* Because he'd been anticipating it for far too long. Because its time had come and because he meant to enjoy every last, single and solitary, living instant of it.

Chapter Three

HE'D BEEN GUIDING HER MOVEMENTS WITH INCREASING CERTAINTY. HAD BEEN orchestrating the outcome of this latest in a long, long series of encounters that always seemed to end in much the same way. Encounters that always seemed, for better or for worse, to end with her struggling against exhaustion. With her struggling to keep up the pace she'd set and he'd encouraged without so much as a word or a sigh while he…

Claire didn't know how Eli did it. How he remained so in control of himself even when her movements turned increasingly spasmodic, increasingly chaotic and unclear. When the boundaries between one enormous orgasm and the next even more shimmering, even more breath-taking one blurred sufficiently that there really were no boundaries. Was really nothing to separate one from the other from the next…nothing at all to declare her body hadn't transcended reality and gone right, straight, into an apocalypse of orgasm.

She thought surely she'd given everything she had to give.

Of course she'd thought that before. So many times. And had always been proved wrong when Eli's stoicism, his iron-willed control, proved unbeatable. Incomparable.

Already she felt weary inside. Bone-weary, so weary she could barely maintain her grip on the sheets she'd never released. The ones she'd been wadding and twisting, twisting and tormenting between aching, fevered hands. Barely able to maintain another kind of grip, her much more intimate grip on hard male flesh that seemed still to grow and to pulse now more than ever with a thundering beat, she could feel that he was ready. Past ready.

And still he held back.

Claire had never understood this about him.

If anything, it had infuriated her. Driven her to distraction. Driven her to even greater efforts than she'd planned, efforts so great and so frustrating they had to be superhuman in origin and supernatural in power.

She didn't want to let him have the best of her.

Didn't want to allow him the last laugh…or maybe the last orgasm would be a better way, a more fitting and fiendish way, to think of it.

Always, she'd wanted them to come together.

Always, she'd strained for simultaneous release instead of the constant battle, the strumming of her own weary and worn out flesh against his that remained fresh and strong, fresh and ready.

She supposed, in whatever way she was still able to suppose, that could be because it wasn't Eli who expended all his physical energy on these little sessions. It wasn't Eli who worked his body into hers and back out, worked until he was ragged and drenched with a fine sheen of sweat. It wasn't he who rode vigorously, every muscle called into play and every one required to perform at optimum capacity and with utmost perfection long, long beyond the point when he felt ready to collapse.

Gasping, Claire tightened her grip on the sheets that must in another moment or two tear like finest tissue. She clung to them as a horsewoman clings to the reins when it becomes increasingly difficult to maintain her seat upon her mount, when she's lost too much of the strength and dexterity required for the up and down and up and down of maintaining that seat.

Back and forth.

Side to side.

Breath caught deep in the back of her throat and lodged there so tightly no sound was possible save for the small moaning and pleading cries of a soul in absolute, inconceivable distress, she set up a new rhythm atop Eli.

And he responded at once. With another cry. Not so much of victory now as of concession.

I'm ready.

Name of God, he felt like a rod forged from purest, most unyielding steel inside her. A rod that threatened with every adjustment of its position inside her and her position atop it to puncture her. To puncture something vital and leave her from this day on incapable of performing this act in this way. Incapable of ever feeling the sudden, stirring and startling sensation as Eli moved inside her. As, on another wave of her apparently boundless moisture and essence, he lurched.

Only once.

But it was a sign. A very, very good sign.

A sign that for him too, despite the rigid control he exerted in his diabolical efforts to tease and torment and test her will to succeed, the end was drawing near.

"Cl..." For a moment he seemed able to go no farther. As if he'd lost all track of whatever he'd wanted to say, even if it was something as simple as her name. For a moment, his voice thickening and tearing with a wet and red sound, he could only groan before at last, almost too late, the rest of it came to him. "...laire." And that was it. That was all.

Claire knew it.

She felt it. Just like she felt the sudden, lunging thrust of his shaft as it finally met its match. As finally her determination to reduce him to the same liquid and flowing state to which he'd long since reduced her with his careful machinations bore fruit. As finally, gathering itself with a slight shrinking, an all but indescribable loss of size and definition that in another fraction of a second would rectify itself delightfully, his shaft straightened within her. As it came back stronger than before, larger than before, and oh, so much more potent than before.

In the lengthening, he seemed to reach for some new depth of her.

She didn't imagine there could be one he hadn't already found, one he hadn't explored completely and to his full satisfaction.

But he searched anyway.

Groaning, his hands once again tightening upon the hips he'd all but released in the last few passion-driven, insensate and insensible moments, Eli urged her with gentle shoves and nudges to move again. Move harder, move faster, keep up the rhythm that brought him so vitally to life within her.

Shivering as a thrill of something akin to being burned alive from the inside out coursed through her, Claire struggled to focus her gaze upon his face. She struggled to see, then immediately found enormous delight in the sweet and succulent sheen of sweat that beaded his brow and the droop of thick chestnut hair into eyes of almost the same color. Eyes alight with fever identical to what he'd instigated in her.

He smiled a little, a rapturous expression that was rapidly lost in the extremity of the moment, a delightfully rapturous one that turned as she watched to a grimace. The one that always heralded the end about to begin, the straining, draining pleasure now irrefutably in progress and unstoppable by any will of his or any force of nature. A grimace that announced beyond all doubt that the inevitable had just *become* inevitable.

"My sweet Claire." The hushed and very nearly reverent sound of Eli's voice confirmed what she'd thought.

The end was near. It was *here.*

Called forth, as if the very idea of endings and climaxes and fulfillment of each other was all it took to call it forth, a new surge of moisture burst inside Claire. Burst from her. And with the bursting, Eli laughed.

"My hot Claire." And then there was no time for speech...no room, no breath, for it. Eli's caught in his throat with a tight rasp and a dangerous wheeze that sounded exactly like what Claire felt. And he said no more.

The only sound in the room, the only remotely intelligible one, was the sharp and labored intake of their breaths, combined with and at times almost overshadowed by the low groans that emanated from their throats. Groans Claire found herself powerless to stop, groans she could only imagine Eli was just as powerless to stop or even control.

The seething core of her seemed to fuse itself to his warm yet cooler by far rod. Attaching itself intimately and inextricably, her body seemed to burst amid clouds of radiant blue steam she swore she could see swirling, an evanescent vapor straight out of some smoky-throated Hollywood drama of the 'thirties.

Her hips took on new life now. Eli's hands still clutched them, still attempted to guide them. But she felt no hint of strength in them. No hint of the determined will he'd exerted earlier to bend her movements to his whims and twist her search for self-satisfaction around so that at times it seemed all the satisfaction must be his and all the yearning, longing suffering hers. Now he seemed to hold tight to her in some cosmic struggle to stay afloat. Hold tight as if his life depended upon his grip never faltering. Never failing.

Claire suspected the feeling of those strong fingers digging deep into sweat-slicked flesh, seeking out the bone underneath in their futile but never-ceasing effort to anchor themselves tight to reality might be the only thing keeping *her* grounded in reality.

The blue steam-fog was inside her mind now.

Everything had begun to turn a rich cobalt-sapphire-indigo shade.

Everything. The morning sunlight streaming through ground floor windows, golden and dancing, tinted with the deep green of late summer enjoying its last heated fling before autumn, had turned incandescent blue. The walls of the room and the softly-blond polished wood of the floor, the equally blond though more satiny patina of the long and low dresser across from the foot of the bed and even the painting above it, a new version of the old Monet classics done in palest, dreamlike colors by an artist from the other side of the mountain who was supposed to be the latest, up-and-coming thing in the world of art. All had gone blue. Indescribably blue, deep and rich, saturated blue.

All of them tinted not by any reality but by the dream haze inside Claire's mind. A dream-haze that was as much a part of her mind melting itself down in response to what was happening to and in other parts of her body as a reaction to Eli's part in causing those unprecedented events.

Sighing, weakening, Claire clung as tightly as she could to the rumpled sheets that had been *her* way of maintaining touch with the world of reality and concrete ideas.

One more burst, a monumental one that seemed to elicit from Eli a new pounding, a new stirring of the hips she'd pinned to the bed with her weight, a new stretching and seeking of the already magnificent shaft upon which she'd impaled herself, and his body responded. The way she'd known it had to respond if she would only wait long enough. Wait patiently enough.

He made a softly murmured half whimpering sound. A sound like no other that could be confused with no other. A sound that could never be mistaken for anything but what it really was...the sound of a man in utter extremis. A man teetering on the very edge of some bliss no woman could know and no woman could possibly understand even if it was her power and hers alone to grant it. Hers to call it forth, call it into existence, cause it to exist as if she'd given birth to it from her own body.

Eli cried out in the low and unmistakable tones of impending release. And then, with one last great and shuddering upward lunge, he did release. Into her. He released everything, released molten and smoking streams of pure energy that instantly saturated her, instantly made small and inconsequential the previous paltry offerings of her own body.

He came into her in the same moment when, marshaling some last secret store of herself, Claire climaxed again. For what surely had to be the last time in this existence because when it finished, when they finished together and she lost all muscle tone at last, when she rolled off him onto the sweat-dampened sheets next to him, there was nothing left of her. No way she could move. Not even when Eli found her hand and lifted it. When he began to play with her fingers, tugging at them, tugging them to his lips. Laving them with soft and shivering kisses that, incredible as it seemed, instantly sent a fresh surging of white-hot reply through her. That instantly called forth from the drained well of her another moistening.

Only this moisture shimmered softly. This one didn't burst in wild abandon. This one was no more than a misting. A heat-soaked condensation rather than the flowing river of essence with which she'd favored him minutes—or had it been mere seconds?—before.

"Claire." Eli's lips moved against the top of her hand with silken abandon, almost wanton in their laziness and lack of purpose.

His lips moved, and they sent a shock of recognition through her.

They'd drained each other.

Sucked the very life out of each other with their eternally hungry and never entirely satisfied bodies. And still there was this hint of more. This hint that there could be more if only they would rally themselves. If only they could find it somewhere in themselves to coax sated and exhausted muscles to make one last effort. If only…

"I can't," she replied, almost crying. "I don't have any more, Eli. I don't…" She wasn't sure if she wanted him to contradict her. Would never be sure if she wanted him to plead with her, secretly hoping he'd tell her she could and he would help her. Would always wonder if what she'd really been trying to say was 'come to me, Eli. I don't think I'm finished yet. I don't think I've given you all of myself or enough of myself yet'.

But none of those things happened.

The reality was his lips leaving her.

His lips leaving the hand they'd soothed, the wrist and arm in direct line from that hand, and all the other parts of her that might eventually, one day, whenever her nervous system sorted itself out and remembered what it was supposed to do, feel bereft.

She wanted to cry at the loss.

Summoning strength, she convinced her head to turn. So she could see him. See his eyes, his face, the expression on his face.

He lay with his lips pressed together in the thin and not entirely pleasant yet not unpleasant line that had become so familiar over the past years. The line that said the distance was there again. The inexplicable distance had sprung up automatically between them and wouldn't be easily chased away with sighs, or softly-uttered groans, or half-heard whimpers.

The distance is back.

For a while, an incredible and glittering, magical while, she'd had Eli. Her Eli, the one with whom she'd fallen so madly in love that every instant of her life had been sheer torment when he was quiet or when he was proposing or, even worse, carrying out one of the wildly incredible, wickedly sensual fantasies in which she always, unfailingly, found herself cast in the leading role.

Very slowly, every bit of her body screaming out its protest, Claire righted herself. With incredible slowness and nearly insurmountable difficulty, she unwound her legs and arms from the twisted sheets in which they'd become ensnared. And even more slowly she shoved with still weak, still unsteady and barely responsive arms, levering herself into a seated position next to him on the bed.

Consumed by the slow-motion quality of this moment outside moments, she shook back her hair.

Eli didn't move. Didn't so much as flutter the long and splendid eyelashes that lay in dark curves across the high rounds of his cheeks. Didn't lift a finger to stop her when she leaned over the side of the bed, by necessity leaning away from him and breaking the last, tenuous contact of her flesh to his in order to reach the thin summer wrapper she'd dropped to the floor instantly when she'd walked from the bathroom earlier to find him lying on the bed watching her with the old and familiar heat smoldering in his eyes.

He didn't move, and it was all she could do to not sigh. Was more than she could do to keep from wondering what it had all been for…what had been the sense in it all if it was only going to come down to this in the end.

Them. Apart. Again.

The two of them miles and miles apart with no apparent way to bridge a gap too wide to be bridged even with the most extraordinary of efforts.

What was the sense in it anyway?

Rising from the bed, recognizing that somewhere along the line she'd developed a watchful care of her own in response to, or maybe in defense against, the way he always seemed to be watching her without ever making contact, Claire twisted the satin belt of her robe tight around her waist and stood for a moment. She stood staring down at the motionless figure of her husband upon their sweat-stained bed. Stood lost in some kind of afterglow trance, some kind of milk-white letdown from the cobalt splendor of before, until a soft and insistent rapping at the door roused her.

"I need to see you, Missus," Hannah the housekeeper called softly from beyond the carved panel. "Ben, from down to the gatehouse called and said someone was on the way up the hill now. Someone to see you, and you'd want to know."

Straightening her shoulders, Claire moved toward the door.

Knotting her belt one more time, she went to meet what surely had to be her very last hope of saving what she and Eli had once shared so easily.

Chapter Four

THEY WERE GOING TO HAVE TO TALK SOMETIME.

Watching her flutter around the room in a dither as if she'd lost even the basic amount of concentration needed to find clothes and get herself dressed, that was the one thought that kept running through Eli's mind.

He'd been trying to find a way…a time…to talk to her for quite a while now. About whatever the hell had gone wrong with them. Between them. But the time was never right and that only made the terrible coldness grow more terrible. More…cold. And he could tell this wasn't the right time either. She'd been strangely distracted all morning, her mind focused on something else. Somewhere else.

Sighing, tugging himself upright with his back against the headboard, he felt certain this wasn't a good time either.

There never seemed to *be* a good time, with Claire constantly rushing here and there, too busy to stop or even slow down for the minute or two he'd need to bring the subject up and get her interested.

Part of that was because she was a mom now. And even with all the help he'd all but had to force her to hire, even with Nanny on duty and her mother installed full-time in the bedroom just across the hall from the nursery and all too eager to dote whenever Nanny took a night off or saw fit to allow a little spoiling, twin three-year-olds *were* a distraction.

They were part of what was keeping her away from him. But not all of it.

Even twin three-year-olds couldn't account for the odd wariness he sensed in Claire these days. Thinking back, squinting a little as he watched her every move, Eli thought as hard as he could. And felt almost sure…ninety-nine and then some percent sure…the holding back had started *before* the twins were born. A good while before.

He felt sure he'd once thought it was just the stresses and uncertainties of being pregnant for the first time that had changed her. And then later, after, he'd been just as sure the problem was post-partum depression.

Now, though…

"Claire?"

The time wasn't right.

The time was *never* right.

But he had to try sometime. Had to, because this had gone on long enough. This had gone on for so long it had become like a terribly infectious disease. It had made him almost sick with worry. Had taken him all the way beyond worry, all the way to being just plain old, downright scared.

I'm going to lose her.

Eli didn't know where the thought came from, or if it was a thought at all as much as a sudden, stone-cold certainty.

It was just *there.* Inside his head without any kind of warning, as much a part of his thought processes as if it had been there, accepted fact, for as long as he could remember.

He was going to lose Claire. Was going to lose the light and the one enduring love of his life.

If he didn't do something.

Now.

She acted like she didn't hear him the first time. So he cleared his throat. Reached for his clothes on his chair beside the bed. And tried again.

"Claire!"

He might have made his voice a little sharper than he'd meant...a lot sharper than it needed to be.

Her head came up. Pausing with one leg in her jeans as if she hadn't yet quite decided how she was supposed to get the other leg in, she scowled at him. Really scowled, in a way that probably should make his heart stop. A way that no doubt would if he wasn't so worried already.

"I'm sorry." To his surprise it took a little more work than he expected to gentle his tone. To make it halfway civilized and not the tone of a demanding, insensitive brute who'd been badly miffed because he wasn't the center and focus of all attention now and forever. "I was just...it's so hard to get your attention sometimes."

Damn. That wasn't the way I wanted to start this!

For half a second he almost cringed, expecting a repeat of the scowl. Or worse, to have a strip torn off his hide and be beaten within an inch of his life with it.

Instead, Claire smiled. Radiantly. The way she so often did, no matter what her mood. It was a way that instantly had him befuddled. Had him doubting himself and doubting whether he'd really seen and felt what he knew in his heart he'd seen and felt. Wondering if it hadn't maybe been imagination running away with him.

Again.

"I'm sorry." She glowed with that smile.

And his cock, the same one he'd recently thought so far beyond help it would never recover from its earlier exertions or be even remotely the same again either?

His cock leaped to full, straining attention.

The way only Claire could entice it to leap.

God. I love her.

God, I'll die if I lose her.

And that *wasn't* imagination. That had never been farther from imagination, not from the very start. That was one of those facts of life he couldn't get away from if he tried. Like his use of the wheelchair or the fact that his old man had been the ignorant, self-aggrandizing bastard who'd made that use necessary. It was just something he had to live with...the fact that he loved Claire and the strength of that love...the possibility she might one day fail to return it...was enough to drop him dead. Right here and right now. Right on the spot.

"Did you want something?" She had her jeans on now, but she didn't sound impatient. And that was one more thing he loved about her. She never sounded impatient. Not even when she was, and had every right to be. Still, Eli thought he saw something in her gaze. He thought he saw some small flickering that told him she had something else on her mind. That she was already a million miles away from here in her mind and eager to escape with her body, too...eager to escape him.

His spirits dropped as hard as they'd just soared.

"I just..."

Shit. He wasn't handling this well.

Not well at all.

"I think we need to talk, Claire."

At least that's a little better.

At least he'd brought it out into the open.

But the shadow in her eyes, if that was what it was, darkened. Straightening the hem of the bright pink tee shirt she'd just tugged on over gorgeously rumpled and untamed hair that made him want to catch her up in his arms and sweep her away on another cloud of intense and never-ending passionate delight, she flashed him a look. An especially devastating one that said all too clearly she *did* have something better to do than hang around here, talking about something as mundane and uninteresting as their future together. As unimportant and irrelevant as what was to become of them.

"I wouldn't bring it up," he said, a little haltingly now that he'd seen that look and had all the heart smashed out of him. "But I think we've got to face each other sometime. I think we've got a lot to say to each other. I know I have plenty of things I need to say to you. And I've waited too long to say them. So I thought we might grab a few minutes right now to..."

God.

If nothing before had scared the living shit out of him or mangled his heart until not even a bloody pulp remained, the look he saw in her eyes and on her face now made him want to cry.

Made him worry he *would* cry, and thoroughly disgrace himself in front of the one woman he loved more than he loved his own life. Such as it was.

Claire looked afraid.

His Claire.

Afraid.

Of him?

Was she afraid of what she might say if he pressed too hard and forced her to talk before she felt ready?

Or was she afraid of something else?

Was she afraid she might be about to blurt some terrible truth he'd spotted only from the corner of his eye and only when he'd let his guard down for a minute or two? Something he should never have been stupid enough to come this close to confronting head on?

Claire was stammering.

She wasn't saying anything, really, while all the time she seemed to be trying mightily to say something.

Eli wasn't sure what.

She mumbled something about a truck. Or maybe it wasn't a truck at all. Some of the time she sounded like she was more concerned about waiting for someone. Expecting someone and being afraid she wouldn't be there when he or she arrived, though Eli knew damned well and for certain they weren't expecting anyone other than the kids on the baseball team. And Claire seldom had anything to do with them. With the game she'd long ago confessed she couldn't for the life of her understand.

Not knowing what the hell she was talking about scared him even more. It scared him so bad he suddenly had to piss, in the worst kind of way. The way you only have to piss when you've finally, unavoidably, been put face to face with the one thing in the universe you can't bear to think of. The one and only thing that literally has the power of sanity in its hands, the power of your own existence in the form with which you've become if not comfortable at least familiar.

I'm going to lose her.

She was trying to tell him something, and that was it. That she was going to leave him.

Going to take his two babies, who meant every bit as much to him as did their mother, and go away.

He'd been expecting it, of course. Living every day of the last four and a half blissful dream-years with the dim shadow of it hanging over his head, he could hardly have *not* been expecting it. Could hardly say he hadn't been aware this time had to come and couldn't deny he'd known right from the start she'd grow tired of him. She'd grow disillusioned and realize she'd made a mistake staying with him. A mistake coming to him in the first place, and the biggest mistake it was possible for a young and lovely woman, a woman with all the promise of the world beckoning to her and all the wonderful things in the world just waiting to happen to her, to make.

He glanced at the wheelchair waiting next to the bed.

Scowled at it the way she'd scowled at him…with a heart full of black loathing and impotent fury.

Son of a bitch.

He hadn't felt this way since that first night with her. That night he'd summoned her to the sleigh and ordered her to have sex with him, a man she'd never before set eyes on, a man she didn't know. A man who thought just because he'd made an obscene pile of money giving the computer nerds exactly what they wanted in the way of software and services, he had the right to summon any woman he chose. The right to pay her do anything he chose at any time…in any place and any way. The right to withhold payment he'd always made sure was badly needed if she refused.

He'd been hard that night. His heart had been hard and so had his soul, made that way by his own bitterness at his old man's duplicitous thoughtlessness and the accident it had caused…the one that had changed his life in every way and shape and form forever. He'd been incapable of real feeling, having long since walled himself off against anything that even remotely resembled feeling.

And then he'd allowed…hell, he'd all but begged…Claire to knock the wall down.

Just like that.

"Okay then." Lifting his chin, he said it in the old voice. The voice of the embittered and brutalized man who hadn't cared one damn about the world unless he was in the process of making it...or at least someone in it...suffer as much as he'd believed he had. "I guess you'd better go, then. Hadn't you?"

"Eli..." Claire took a step toward the bed. Several steps. "It's just that now isn't a very good time. In fact, it couldn't be a w—"

"Well, don't mind me." Sliding forward, he lay down again. Lay flat on his back and stared at the ceiling above the bed. "I guess I'll be here whether you stay or not."

Who the hell installed cherubs on my ceiling anyway?

Last time he'd looked, around the time he'd married her, this had been a man's room. A nice, plain, functional and spare man's room. Not some kind of...of...

"The place looks like a goddamned bordello," he observed sourly, not bothering to look up and see the sudden flashing of hurt he knew would be filling her eyes. "But for God's sake, don't let me make you late with all my trivialities. I know whatever you have to do is so vitally important it won't wait. Not even another five minutes while we try to—"

"I promise." When he glanced her way, he saw she'd caught her lip between her teeth...such a succulent, utterly desirable and kissable lip that it made his cock give another sudden, traitorous and undeniably lecherous leap.

Damn it to hell. It was impossible to stay mad at her. He *couldn't* stay mad, not even when he thought he'd be justified staying mad. Not even when he tried to stay mad.

She came all the way to the bed. Folded one long and lovely leg beneath her as she sank down onto the foot of it, her wide and crystalline amber-brown gaze never straying so much as a hair's breadth away from his face.

Double damn. Triple damn.

When the hell had she caught him like this?

How the hell had he allowed this to happen, when he'd been all too damned aware the whole time that she wasn't going to stay...that a man like him, a man who used a wheelchair and had enough difficulties to make a saint wince, had only limited charms? Charms that inevitably had to be depleted, because his stock of them was so sorely limited?

How the hell had he *ever* let himself get so caught up in the moment and in sex that was undeniably, no matter what anyone said, the very best any man had ever had, to let her get under his skin this way? To forget himself, forget his place in the general scheme of things, forget her place and…

How in hell had he ever let himself be inveigled into *marrying* her, for Christ's sake?

"I want to talk to you, too," she was saying slowly, appearing not to notice that he'd made a brief side trip into some other universe, some other state of uneasy existence.

He drew in a deep breath that instantly turned to a shudder. "Maybe it's not such a good idea after all, Claire. Maybe I already know all the things you could say to me. And maybe I don't want to hear them said out loud after all."

A little smile played around the corners of her mouth.

He wanted to kiss that smile.

Wanted to taste those lips.

Had to rein himself in fiercely and harshly just to avoid saying or doing something that would only make him look and feel more a fool than he did already.

"I doubt that," she replied quietly, and levelly enough that she almost made him believe. "I doubt you know any more about what's going on in my mind right now than you've ever known."

Tilting his head to the side a little, sliding his joined hands beneath it to lift it off the pillow so he'd have a better angle from which to glower at her, Eli discovered he couldn't glower.

Damn it, I do love her. Too much.

He was just going to have to learn to deal with it. Though he certain as hell didn't have to *like* it while he watched her slip away.

Still smiling in her delicious, devil-inspired and completely irresistible way, Claire leaned toward him. Her breasts, bigger than they'd been before the twins were born, jiggled appetizingly beneath the thin fabric of her tee shirt.

"That must be some goddamned truck you're so hot to meet," he growled, glowering at her tits the way he hadn't been able to glower into her eyes.

"Who said anything about a truck?" She sounded a little taken aback.

"You did. You muttered something about…"

"You're mistaken, Eli." Laughing a little, laughing in a way that sounded nervous and completely false…a way that instantly had his radar turned all the way to high…she made a move to get to her feet. "Heaven only knows what you thought you heard, but I can promise you I have no interest in trucks or trucking. In any way."

He prayed she wouldn't get to her feet, prayed she'd stay here forever like she'd said she would the day she'd said she'd marry him. And felt gratified when she settled back down, settled onto the foot she'd tucked beneath her, and reached for him. Reached to touch the center of his chest and stroke a long, rose-tipped finger along the most sensitive skin at the very center of it.

"I wouldn't go unless I had to," she said softly. Firmly. Inarguably. "You know that, Eli."

Squinting, he fought off a wave of desire strummed into him by the stroking of that fingertip. "Do I?"

She gave him an absolutely level gaze. "I think you do. But I have to go. There's something I need to do right now. And it's not going to wait."

"Let your mother do it." He wasn't about to give up. Wasn't about to give in, and put himself in a position where she'd have the leverage and the advantage she needed to tear his heart out of his chest and stomp it flat.

The way he'd allowed her to tear and stomp just a few goddamned times too many already.

"Let the goddamned maid do it."

"Hannah's a housekeeper." The smile was back on her lips. Was more firmly entrenched and more sure of itself than ever. "And she wouldn't be happy to hear you refer to her as anything else."

"Whatever." Unable to succeed with Claire, Eli turned his glare back to the ceiling and the goddamned cherubs, who didn't appear ready to tremble in their tracks and be impressed either. "I thought you had something so important to do. So why are you still here, arguing with me?"

"I'm sorry." She got to her feet then. Eli felt the bed shift. He saw the neon-pink flash of her looming over it and over him even though he made every effort not to look at her and even more effort not to notice. "This is something I have to do, because...well, it's just something personal I need to take care of. But I promise, Eli. We'll talk. I know we have to. And I know I'm big enough to hear whatever you have to say. But it has to be a little later. Okay?"

"Okay." He didn't move. Not a muscle. Not even an eyelid.

After a minute, she turned away. He saw her scalding pink shirt move away, watched from the side of his vision as she walked to the door and, after a half-minute's hesitation with her hand on the handle and her back turned to him, saw her open it and step into the hallway beyond.

Saw her open it and winced when she left him. Alone.

Chapter Five

"WHAT TOOK YOU SO LONG?" CLAIRE ALL BUT ATTACKED THE DRIVER AS SOON AS HE stepped down from his truck. Darting down the front steps from the place where she'd been lurking, waiting, in the shadow of the house, she had time only for a quick and surreptitious glance over her shoulder, even though she knew Eli wouldn't come to this part of the house at this time of the day.

The baseball team was already here. She'd seen their minivan parked around the side of the house beneath the porte-cochere where her whole life with Eli Eden had found its strange and unusual start. She'd heard its driver's voice booming at the back of the house as he flirted with Hannah and heard, too, the sound of Eli's voice as he came out of their bedroom hastily dressed with his hair barely combed, telling Hannah to watch out because it seemed there were wolves on the loose today.

It had taken the truck a while to make its way up the mountain. Had taken longer than she'd expected, so that by now Eli had to be safely occupied at the far distant corner of the house where they'd built the baseball diamond the summer before last.

Still, she felt an almost compulsive need to make sure he wasn't watching.

And then she flew straight into action.

"Hell's bells, Lady!" The truck driver dodged aside when she tried to grab his clipboard right out of his hands.

"I've been waiting forever." Another glance around, even more uneasy than the first.

"This ain't no sports car, Lady." Well-launched, the truck driver gestured with his clipboard, pointing to Claire's convertible parked a few feet from the truck. "This ain't one of them fancy-dancy Ferraris or Mutt-zeratties or…"

Claire bit back a smile. "It's a Mustang."

"Whatever." His attention back on his clipboard and what it had to say, riffling through the papers it held as if the fate of the free world rested somewhere amongst them, the driver had already forgotten the car. "Can't be toolin' a big rig like this up and down them windey mountain roads like there ain't no tomorrow," he grumbled barely loud enough for Claire to hear.

She almost pointed out that this was hardly a full-sized eighteen-wheeler. It was just a delivery truck. A little bigger than your average panel truck, maybe, but no big rig by any stretch of the imagination. But she decided against it before she finished opening her mouth.

Insulting his pride and manhood wasn't going to get the Indian out of that truck and into the house. It wasn't going to get the truck out of here either, any quicker than if she just went along and played nice with him.

The driver hadn't quite finished though.

"Damn narrow road you got there, Lady," he went on. "Real treacherous-like."

"I'm sorry."

"It's a wonder how they ever got up here through all them woods t'ever build a place this size t'begin with." Here he stopped and took in the view along the front of the house. A view that made it look every bit the mansion...the cold marble palace, as Eli liked to phrase it...it really was.

But Claire's impatience won out. Finally. "My delivery?" she tried hard to demand without shouting. "Are you ever going to..."

Grunting, he rolled up the back door of his truck. "I gotta say, Lady. It's one helluva thing."

Claire looked over her shoulder again.

The longer they stood here discussing the weather, the condition of the roads, the price of tea in China, the greater the chance Eli would decide to appear and demand to know what the hell was going on.

When she wasn't ready for him to know what was going on. Because that would ruin the surprise.

That would completely ruin what might well be her very last chance to win his heart...the last to save a marriage she didn't have to be told was in deep, deep trouble.

She wondered at the lack of an assistant for the driver. Remembering the sheer bulk of the thing in the back of the truck, waiting inside its nest of heavy and nearly opaque plastic wrapping...a thing that had to be as tall as the tallest man and twice as broad...she wondered how the devil one lone truck driver expected to unload it by himself. Even if he was big and burly and, theoretically at least, strong as a moose and prepared to take on just about anything.

But he had it covered.

He'd already had the monstrosity strapped to an oversized hand-truck. And the delivery truck itself was equipped with a very efficient lift at the back.

In no time at all her one lone truck driver had the Indian on the ground and was maneuvering it around to the concealed wheelchair ramp to which she directed him, pronouncing it *real handy, Lady.*

Claire didn't relax until the thing…the massive, carved cigar store Indian…was safely inside. Until it was ensconced just where she wanted it, in the big music room off the front hall. She didn't dare relax until Hannah took charge, signing the papers the driver presented with that same air of protecting the free world, then hustling him out the way they'd come in, whisking both him and his oversized hand truck safely out of sight in case Eli really did decide to pick this moment to do the unthinkable. To abandon his fledgling baseball players and appear inside the house at an hour when he should be at the ball field. And even then, even with the Indian tucked into the corner she and Hannah had prepared ahead of time and on the sly, a secluded corner where the hulking figure couldn't be seen and wouldn't be seen easily unless a person was actually looking for it and expecting to see it, Claire didn't relax completely.

Too much depended upon what would happen next. So very much depended upon Eli's reaction to her very strange and, no doubt at all about it, decidedly unusual gift.

Peace offering.

She reminded herself it was a peace offering. Something to ease the terrible upset he'd suffered when the monstrous old thing was damaged in the fire that had destroyed his father's house. And the even more distressing upset when the clean-up crew, seeing no apparent value in the charred hunk of wood that had belonged to Eli's grandfather and had stood guard outside his store down in Latrobe for years and years…all the years Eli had been a boy and had climbed all over the Indian in search of the secret his grandfather assured him lay hidden within…had carted the thing away.

The thing had no real value other than the sentimental. Not now anyway, Claire thought as she tore away the heavy plastic wrapping.

It had been ugly before. So ugly and menacing that the first time she'd seen it, cloaked in the gloom of that dreadful old house, it had scared the living hell out of her. Had sent her running in terror. And that had been *before* it was charred and scorched to brooding malevolence in the fire.

Now…

Bundling the plastic together into an untidy ball, Claire sat back on her heels and regarded the Indian with dismay.

Now the thing looked one hell of a lot worse.

It was black, of course. Not so much with soot anymore, since someone at some point had obviously taken great pains to clean much of that away. It was black with char, ruined along one whole side. And age, and visible water damage too, no doubt a result of the fruitless efforts to put out the fire that had nearly consumed it. And other evidence, of all kinds of mishandling and abuse by all kinds of careless people. Claire spotted a pair of great gouges at the sides that she hadn't noticed before...deep and fresh gashes as if the Indian had been shoved through some narrow space that hadn't yielded at all to accommodate its girth. And the towering feathers at the very top of the figure, three of them, had been wrapped around and around repeatedly with a thick layer of silver duct tape.

I'm going to have a hell of a job making this tragedy even remotely presentable again.

And the *smell*!

Maybe because it had been bundled so tightly for God only knew how long in the shipping process, the Indian reeked. Of smoke, and barely-averted rot, and just a general rough and dirty age.

Maybe this wasn't my best idea ever. Maybe...

"Oh, Dios mio." Bustling into the room, Hannah pulled to an abrupt halt four feet inside the door. "Missus, that's..."

"Pretty bad. I know." Claire sounded only about half as gloomy as she felt.

"Dios mio."

Hannah knew only part of the story. Only the part that had Claire setting out in the dead of the previous winter in search of a missing family heirloom. Up until now Hannah had known only that it was a somewhat large and strange heirloom, and that when she'd finally located and taken possession of it in the spring, Claire had hoped to surprise Eli with it. But all the rest...all the part about the distance and coldness it was meant to repair, about the failed or failing marriage...

Well, some things just weren't a housekeeper's concern. They weren't anyone's concern except for the parties directly involved.

And as for the part about Eli being surprised...

"What a surprise this is going to be," Claire muttered heavily, never moving from her huddled crouch on the floor in front of the Indian.

"Dios mio," Hannah replied.

"Open some windows, will you?" Claire couldn't seem to make herself move. She couldn't seem to convince her muscles to flex, her arms or legs to straighten and unfold.

Frozen, she thought dismally. *In shock.*

Luckily Hannah…practical, efficient and unflappable Hannah…had no such difficulty. She'd reached the tall French doors and was progressing along the row of them, flinging them wide to admit a hot late-summer-scented breeze that lifted the white curtains and made them flutter feebly. A breeze that wasn't really a breeze, one that held out little promise of relief from what looked like another sultry and motionless day. A breeze that said even if Claire hung on for another month or two it wasn't going to do one damned thing about driving away that *smell.* Or the atmosphere of incipient horror that surrounded the thing like a hideous cloud and had already dropped like a pall over the entire room.

"Dios mio." Claire hadn't heard Hannah come to her side. But she was there now, standing right over Claire. Wringing her hands together, her gaze fastened fascinated on the spectacle in the corner. "Dios mio," she murmured again almost reverently when Claire looked up at her. And crossed herself. "The mister is going to be…"

"Surprised?" Claire suggested when she didn't finish.

"Dios mio." Very slowly, seeming entranced as well as fascinated, the housekeeper nodded. "That would be a word for it, I guess, Missus."

"This was a mistake."

Dios mio.

Hannah didn't say it this time, though Claire certainly expected her to. Though Claire thought it an entirely appropriate reaction under the circumstances. A reaction with which she wholeheartedly agreed.

"What have I done?" Hearing the mingled tones of disbelief and despair in her voice, Claire shivered.

"Maybe I can fix it up a little," Hannah suggested. She didn't sound or look like she held out much hope for success, but Claire knew she'd give it her best. "You better give me an hour though."

As if the housekeeper's take-charge attitude was exactly what she'd been needing to hear, Claire's muscles released from their horror-stricken paralysis and she shoved herself to her feet.

"On second thought…"

Claire looked at Hannah inquiringly.

"Better make it two hours."

Groaning under her breath, Claire turned away. "I'll be with Mr. Eden," she declared. "Out on the terrace by the baseball field. Whenever you think..."

Hannah's look said even more strongly than any words she might have uttered...any Dios mios...that she didn't think the Indian was ever going to be presentable. Or ready.

"Right." Claire's footsteps dragged as she headed toward the hall and the back of the house. Her hard-soled flip-flops made kind of a hollow *splatting* sound. A half-hearted racket on the polished marble floor as if even they had lost their enthusiasm for the whole undertaking. For *both* undertakings...the return of the Indian and the salvation of her marriage.

She found Eli right where she expected him to be. Right where he spent increasingly more and more of his time as the summer grew longer and the days for baseball more limited. He sat at the edge of the terrace overlooking the ball field that lay just about where the old house had stood. The one that had burnt until only a part of the front and a porch had been left to show it ever existed.

At the moment she stepped through wide double doors onto the awning-shaded terrace, he had the most peculiar...the most intrinsically *Eli*...expression she'd ever seen stamped all over his face.

"For the love of Mike!" he shouted, barely nodding acknowledgment of her arrival. "You can't pass a man between bases, Sammie!"

This instantly brought the pint-sized players...most of them, at least...to the edge of the field at Eli's feet.

"But I can run faster than him," Sammie protested, her voice high and a little shrieky. The way all their voices became whenever Eli tried to insist on something as mundane and practical as rules. The way they got whenever he backed them into a corner bounded by those rules.

"I don't care." Eli's voice was stern. "You can't do that. There are rules in this game and it's my job to teach you to follow them."

Claire's smile broadened. She had to hold herself in check with a hard and brutal hand, had to resist the nearly overpowering urge to bend over and plant a kiss on the side of his face. When she wanted, almost more than she'd ever wanted anything, to whisper a suggestion or two...wholly inappropriate and unacceptable ones...into his ear.

Hot sunlight bounced off every strand of his hair. Finding each strand

Individually, it highlighted them with molten gold, casting them into sharpest relief.

On the level below him, beyond the marble balustrade that separated the terrace from the baseball diamond, Sammie stood with her hands on her hips and her baseball cap skewed at a heart-wrenchingly charming angle. Though at the moment she wasn't using her wide blue angel's eyes to charm anybody.

She was *glaring*. With all the ferocity with which it was possible to glare. Straight at Eli.

He gave a sudden shout of laughter. One that made Claire's heart twist and wrench, because she missed the sound of that laughter so much. Because she'd never forgotten the days…golden days, wonderful days…when more often than not those shouts of laughter had been directed at her. In response to something she'd said or done.

He looks happy.

He always did whenever one of his teams…he had several, and loved coaching them for free…was on the premises.

"If you'll pardon me, Mr. Eden," Sammie declared with a glance around at her teammates in search of support, "that just sucks."

"Sammie…" His voice carried a warning. Started to carry a warning before her opponent, a crusty little tyke named George, sailed into the battle.

"That's because you're a *girl*," George sneered. "And everybody knows girls can't…"

"George!" Eli tried to sound like he was furious…tried to sound like he was ready to shout and lay down the law. But Claire knew him too well. She knew he was just about to laugh again. Harder than before, and twice as loudly.

George, however, seemed oblivious to that.

He fell into an obedient, if unwilling silence.

"Do I have to remind you that Sammie *does* run faster than you?"

George pouted. "Maybe. But she's still a girl and girls don't…"

"And she throws harder and catches better."

"She's a year older." George was running out of arguments. The expression on his face said he was all too aware of it.

"Well, there you go." Eli sounded perfectly reasonable. So reasonable that Claire wondered, not for the first time, where he found the patience for this kind of thing.

She didn't have it, for sure.

Sometimes she didn't even have patience for her own pair. Often she worried she'd never be a good or even an adequate mother. Worried she'd do something wrong to turn her twins against her before they saw their fifth birthday or the start of kindergarten, even though her mother and Nanny and Hannah all reassured her repeatedly that she was doing a good job. That she wasn't feeling anything most first-time mothers of three-year-olds felt and was handling it, in fact, a great deal better than most. But she worried, while Eli...

She smiled again.

He'd been born to be a father. Born to be a coach, born to be a cheerer of victories and a dryer of agonized tears.

He excelled at it.

Down below the terrace Sammie had turned to George, her intent absolutely clear.

She was about to say something that would re-ignite the battle of the sexes right there at the side of the ball field. Something that, unless Claire missed her guess, might be so inflammatory it could ignite World War Three and the very possible apocalypse of man.

"Okay, guys!" she said with a laugh. "Snack time! I just passed by the kitchen and I smelled something delicious. Something that told me Hannah's been baking this morning, and..."

Her words, not really a shout but still loud enough to be heard clearly, drew the rest of the players, the ones who'd remained in their places on the field content to watch the start of the conflict from afar, forward.

"Take forty-five," Eli instructed as they hustled up the stairs, shoving each other and nudging at each other, the debate continuing unabated now that Sammie and George had given it a start. And some of them, a disbelieving and perennial inconvincible few were marveling aloud as they always did that a one-time 'great' baseball player whose record they knew and had memorized...one who awed them all a little with the time and energy he expended upon them and their usually flawed games...had so much time for them and so much apparent, even to nine- and ten-year-olds, love to give them.

Eli wasn't watching them.

He was looking at Claire. Was smiling at her with a look she knew. A look that made her knees tremble and her mouth water.

"So," he said, his voice losing all its coach's gusto and cheeriness as it dropped to a lower register. A deeper, and far more enticingly enticed one. "What are you up to now?"

"U-up to?" Her heart gave a lurch. A guilty one this time. "Whatever do you..."

"You have that smile on your face," he replied, reaching for her with one hand. "That one that says you're about to do something I'm not going to expect. Not in the least."

Chapter Six

SHE WOULDN'T TELL HIM WHAT SHE WAS UP TO. AND THAT WASN'T LIKE CLAIRE AT ALL. Usually she wore her heart on her sleeve, her feelings visible and obvious once you took a little time and got to know her a little better. Once you got a good understanding of where she was coming from.

Mystified by her sudden descent into secrecy and inscrutability, Eli followed her into the house and down the long hallway to the front.

At least she'd said she would show him when they got there. Wherever *there* might be. That was a breakthrough anyway, after so many weeks and months of keeping herself to herself and so separate that sometimes he'd wondered if a pretty stranger hadn't invaded his life and taken his wife's place.

Stopping at the door to the big front room, Claire spun around on one foot with all the grace and drama of a prima ballerina showing off for an appreciative audience. Almost pirouetting, she flashed him an enormous smile.

A genuine one.

At last.

"What is it?" he asked for what surely had to be the millionth time. "What's up, Claire?"

Her eyes all but danced. "I have a surprise for you."

Instantly Eli caught his breath.

She hasn't looked my way, almost exactly this way, since...

"Oh, Claire. You're going to tell me you're pregnant again."

Now she looked astonished. As if the thought had never crossed her mind. "No," she said, the effort of saying it seeming to take a lot of the life, almost all the fantastical glitter, out of her.

"Then what?" So curious now that he knew for the first time exactly what people meant when they talked on and on about cats and curiosity, he wheeled forward. Wheeled closer to her.

Curiosity is about to kill me.

Wordless, she stepped aside to let him enter the room first. And there was nothing different about it. Nothing he could see right off the bat anyway.

"What?" he asked again, looking at her, and not at the room. "Are you sick, then? Claire, you're starting to scare me. Because before God, if something should happen to you I don't know how I could ever..."

His heart lifted...*soared*, all the way to the sky and then some...when he saw a sudden flash deep, deep in her eyes. A flash that said maybe the love she'd felt for him once, way back at the beginning, wasn't dead and maybe wasn't even dying the way he'd thought. A flash that gave him all kinds of *hope*. And all kinds of surging, straining, roaring fever in the parts of himself he'd finally managed to get calmed down after this morning's romp between hot and crumpled sheets.

"There," she said simply, and pointed.

And even the letdown of realizing she'd been flashing that way not because she remembered what they'd done a few hours earlier in the bedroom and was eagerly anticipating doing it again but because she'd been all wrapped up in whatever surprise she'd planned for him wasn't enough to dull the ardor he felt in that part of himself.

Nothing could dull the kind of aroused awareness Claire could spark in him. Awareness that once aroused was likely to stay aroused until he could find a chance to...

Better keep my mind in the present, he told himself sternly.

With her mother and a pair of three-year-olds wandering around the place, they'd lost a certain amount, a large amount, of the freedom they'd enjoyed way back at the beginning...to take a tumble whenever they chose, and wherever. On the spur of the moment, without so much as a thought for anyone being around to see.

But now...

Wheeling around to look where she pointed, at first Eli saw nothing out of the ordinary. Just the green marble fireplace veined in silver and white, in itself an understated masterpiece, and his mother's little gold and crystal dome clock...she'd always called it an 'anniversary clock' for some reason that eluded him...sitting squarely at its middle. But he felt sure Claire wasn't pointing there. A certainty that was quickly confirmed when her arm came down over his shoulder and one long, perfectly manicured finger directed him to look farther to the left. Farther into a corner that wasn't visible from the door.

"Jesus Christ." It was a miracle he could get even that out, considering he'd just felt himself shrink. Literally shrink, all the way to nothing and then even less.

Considering he thought he might be about to have a heart attack.

"It's the Indian." Claire's voice lost its buoyancy and he knew without looking that her face had lost its lovely sheen and sparkle as well.

"I can see that."

God, I sound choked.

Maybe this really was the end of the short, glorious and simultaneously ignominious life of Eli Eden, one-time pro baseball Rookie of the Year and full-time, permanent cripple. He didn't feel the much-publicized crushing pain in his chest and shoulder and jaw. Didn't feel the famed numbness in his arm either. If anything, he thought he'd never felt better. Not even when he'd been in his prime, running the bases like lightning on fire with no force on earth capable of stopping him. Not even when he'd had the singular ability to dance all night and still be ready to go when morning rolled around. But what did he know?

He had no medical training. No experience with the downside of health either. Not really, other than his one horrific brush with long-term hospitalization which, surprisingly, hadn't been all that horrific. All things considered.

For all he knew there could be a euphoria that came along with a fatal attack. The euphoria of making his peace with life and getting ready to see what lay beyond. Euphoria of the body anyway, since his mind felt dizzied and dazed, anything *but* euphoric at the moment.

"It's your…you know." Claire sounded not at all sure of herself now and Eli realized there had been a long silence…a long and *humming* one, relieved only by the gentle ticking of the anniversary clock that seemed somehow to have grown as loud and violent as a series of dynamite blasts…while he'd been trying to decide if he was about to die.

"My granddad's goddamned cigar store Indian," he growled, too shocked and startled even to try to keep his voice even. Or calm. "What I want to know is what the hell it's doing here. And where the hell it came from."

"It's a l…long story. I…" Claire really did sound unsure. Rapidly veering toward crushed and defeated. "Aren't you surprised, Eli?"

"Oh, I'm surprised all right."

I never wanted to set eyes on that misbegotten monstrosity again.

Claire moved around to the front of him. Into his line of sight. She'd gone all white and visibly shaky, looking like she might collapse into a boneless and lifeless heap on the floor at his feet. "I thought you'd be…you know." Her mouth trembled. Not her lip. Claire's lip never did that. It was her whole mouth that lost its crisp definition, her whole mouth that blurred into an unsteady expression of anguished grief.

Already beleaguered almost to the point of giving up, his heart damned near shattered at the sight.

Holding his arms out to her, he tried to smile. But the smile felt as trembly and ready to slip as she looked.

"I thought you would…" She didn't look ready to cry as much as ready to fall completely apart.

"Come here." Eli didn't lower his arms…didn't make even the slightest move that might be construed as lowering them when she didn't rush straight to him.

The way she rushed to me once. Not so long ago.

"I knew it was a mistake," she said. "I told Hannah it was a mistake, but by then it was too late. By then the truck had come and gone, and I was stuck with it." Her mouth trembled again. A little more.

"Claire." His arms were beginning to ache. But he wouldn't let her see it. Wouldn't lower them. "Come here. Now."

She took a step forward. One very hesitant step, then stopped only to start again. "I don't know what I could have been thinking, Eli. I wanted, thought…"

He waved her to silence.

"Here," he insisted.

When she came within arm's reach at last, he caught her wrist and wrapped his fingers around it. He stroked it a very little in the process, to make it clear he wasn't feeling anywhere near as firm or in command of himself as he'd tried to sound. "Sit."

She did.

She sat on his lap, *the way she used to.* And wrapped her arms around his neck. "I thought you'd be…oh, God, Eli. I don't know what I thought."

He held her close. Held her tight. "It's okay, Claire. Really it is. It was just the shock of coming across that damned thing lurking in the corner like some kind of…I'm not getting any younger, you know. And it gave me a…"

Giggling half-tearfully, she pushed herself away from him. Just far enough to meet his gaze and smile a smile that wasn't quite as trembly or off kilter as before, but wasn't exactly anything close to normal either. "You're thirty-four," she said. "That's hardly old."

Looking past her, he scowled at the Indian again, not quite able to look the damned thing in the eyes. "Plenty of people have heart attacks at that age. And die from them."

"Didn't I hear Dr. Stevens say just last week that a man couldn't ask for better health?" She was recovering now. She was getting back her color, getting back control of her mouth and lips, and some of the sparkle in her eyes. Was getting back enough of it to be so damned attractive he'd like to…

"Doesn't matter," he replied, ordering his cock to sit still and behave because it *wasn't* going to get the gratification it suddenly, rampantly demanded and seemed to expect as just a matter of course. "I could still drop dead any time."

"Such a cheerful outlook."

He met her gaze. Delighted in the amber-highlighted depth of the one she directed at him in return, and had once again to order his cock to back down. Back *off.*

"I damn near had a heart attack just a minute ago," he insisted. "I was actually ticking off the symptoms, expecting to meet Jesus any second." Lifting a hand away from her…a grudging and reluctant hand that didn't want to leave the sweet curves of her or the dusky heat that penetrated even the stout fabric of her roses-on-steroids pink tee shirt to burn a swirling, simmering pattern into fingers and palm and wrist…Eli pointed to the Indian. "You shouldn't leave things like that lurking around in corners. You shouldn't leave *that* lurking around in corners. Waiting to pounce on people."

When she giggled this time it was for real. And when she straightened away from him, that was for real, too.

Too goddamned *much* for real.

Putting his hand back on her shoulder to pull her to his chest again and *hold* her there the way he hadn't had the pleasure of holding her in almost as long as he could remember, Eli couldn't help but smile.

She was so goddamned delectable.

So delightful when she smiled, and when she giggled so…

"It's kind of like the first time I caught a glimpse of it." This was accompanied by another giggle, causing another hot leaping of both heart and cock. "Remember that?"

"As a matter of fact, I do." Despite all the liftings and leapings, Eli felt guilty.

She'd been so terrified that night. She'd been utterly demoralized with terror, streaking out of the old house where she'd wandered without his knowledge or approval. Mostly because he'd been such a damned pig's ass, forbidding her the basic freedom to leave her own room between their carefully staged encounters. Keeping her practically naked to make it as difficult and uncomfortable as possible if she did decide to disobey orders.

And even with all that working against her she'd still gone exploring. Only to meet up with that damned, hideous monstrosity in the worst possible place when she least expected it. In that gloomy old house that had been custom made to give a person a good case of nightmares.

"The Indian looks..."

"Bedraggled?" Claire suggested.

"Worse."

Turning her head without lifting it away from the spot she'd found for it next to his neck, she studied the statue with a puckered little frown creasing her face. "How about wrecked?"

Eli couldn't help himself. He laughed. "You're getting closer."

"Then...disgusting?"

"That's it. Disgusting says it all."

They sat, then. Claire on his lap and he in his wheelchair, their arms around each other and the silence between them growing long. Growing warm and easy and companionable. They sat pressed close together, closer than they'd been in a very long time, and stared at the Indian.

"I'd like to know what that thing's been through," Eli said after a while. "I thought it looked like hell *before* the fire. And then after...but just look at it now. Look at the way it...and where the hell did you find the old monstrosity anyway? I'd made up my mind it was lost forever."

"I know." Claire sighed heavily. "That's why I thought..."

"Where the hell *did* you find it?"

"Connecticut." She sighed again. "I saw a story about it in a newspaper. Well, not a real newspaper exactly. It was one of those scandal rags. You know, *Dog With Six Legs Born To Manhattan Socialite.* That kind of newspaper. There was this big story on the cover about a couple of lawyers who were going head to head in court in a big custody battle."

"Over *that*?" Eli's voice cracked a little, rising incredulously toward the end.

Claire nodded. "Hard to imagine, isn't it? But some people will sue other people over anything. There was a picture with the article, too. I took one look and knew it had to be the same Indian. It's kind of..."

"Unmistakable," he finished for her.

"And how."

"Must have been a hell of a trial. The thing looks like it's been drowned. A couple of times."

Claire chuckled. "Some of that has to be from the fire. But according to the papers that came with it, the bills of sale and things, your Indian spent a bad winter in Yellowstone."

"As in National Park?" His voice cracking again, Eli sounded astonished.

This time she nodded. "Apparently there was some kind of disaster involving a blizzard and a grizzly bear. Or maybe it was a moose. I don't know. It doesn't matter. The important thing is that a window got broken and the Indian got a real soaking. The people at Yellowstone weren't too fond of him to start with—"

"Gee, I wonder why?"

Claire gave him a pinch. On the cheek, the way his grandmother's sister used to give him a pinch whenever he did or said anything she considered *precious*. Which was damned near everything he'd ever done or said so that by the time he was ten he'd worried his face would be lopsided for life.

"They said it was not in keeping with the image of the Old Faithful Inn. Something like that. So they sold it. And off it went on its merry way to Connecticut."

"What about the feathers?" Eli was enjoying this more than he'd thought he would. Once the initial heart attack and its aftereffects had worn off, he'd seen how the whole crazy, impossible story brought the sparkle back to Claire's eyes and the lilt back into her voice. And he'd blessed it for doing that. And decided the Indian might be worth putting up with after all. Provided it kept on bringing the life back to Claire and in the end brought Claire back to *him*.

"Did the good puritans in Connecticut try to scalp him?"

"No." Claire was enjoying this, too. Everything about her told him she was. "That happened in Michigan. Or was it Minnesota? It was someplace cold, I know that. There was this house full of Russians who apparently...what are you laughing at?"

He *was* laughing. Harder than he'd laughed in ages. Harder, maybe, than he'd ever laughed. "Indian-scalping Russians?" His shoulders shook with the force of his laughter. "What did they do? Stab him in the sides with one of his own feathers after they ripped them out of his head?"

Claire shook her head. "*That* happened during a drug raid in Santa Fe."

"Damned Indian gets around more than some people I know." Eli tried to say it jokingly, but name of God, a *drug raid*? No longer laughing or even feeling like laughing, he eyed the Indian with growing skepticism and suspicion.

"Somehow the drug dealers got him lodged in a doorway, and—"

"Was this before Yellowstone or after?"

She thought for a second. "I don't really know. Before? In any case, I don't think the drug dealers cared much about the damage they might be doing."

"Drug dealers usually don't, Claire. Care, I mean."

Nodding again, she looked faraway. Looked thoughtful.

"So what are we supposed to do with the nasty old thing?" Eli asked carefully. He didn't want to hurt her feelings, but God in heaven, he couldn't imagine spending the rest of his life sharing a house with the thing either.

"I..." She paused. Shivered. Slipped free of his encircling arms and got to her feet. "I thought," she said, and wasn't looking at him *anymore*. Wasn't looking at the battered and worn-out, absolutely trashed Indian either.

"Sweetheart...Claire...I have to ask. What *were* you thinking?"

She didn't tell him. She just wrapped her arms around herself the way his had been around her a minute or two before. Hugging herself as if she'd just been seized in the throes of that Yellowstone blizzard she'd described, she crossed to one of the wide-open windows to stare out at scorching sunlight on the white concrete terrace just outside and the heat-hazed rim of the Allegheny Mountains across a wide swath of warm-green lawn and meadow. "Do you remember what you said your grandfather told you, Eli?"

He frowned. "That the Indian had some kind of fabulous secret, you mean?"

Nodding again, she still didn't look at him.

"But didn't I also tell you..." Eli felt the old impatience rise. Impatience that his grandfather, an otherwise practical and down-to-earth old gentleman, had given in to tall tales and fantasies when he'd told his stories that had no basis in reality. That he'd done it in what Eli now recognized as a completely transparent effort to keep an overly rambunctious grandson occupied. For hours and hours. And all for nothing.

"There is no secret, Claire."

"But if there was..."

"I'm telling you. I've explored every inch of that statue. Time and time again. And there isn't any secret to it. That was just Granddad's way of keeping me out of his hair so he could conduct his business."

"But what if you missed something?"

"Claire..."

"What if you did?" She came to stand beside him again.

And…

What if?

Despite all his best, his most concerted, efforts to avoid getting caught up in that snare again Eli had to admit it. If only to himself.

He'd always felt bad about his treatment of the Indian…his attitude toward it. The unsavory old thing had been about the only thing his granddad had to leave him after monstrous medical bills in the last years of his life had eaten up everything he'd saved for his golden years. The Indian had meant something to his granddad, and he should be more receptive to it. Should treasure it a little more, should want to look after it a little better.

And what if?

The idea of a secret…some special, wonderful secret that would mean the world to him and hold the key to happiness for him…intrigued him now as much as it ever had when he'd been an impatient, baseball-besotted kid.

It intrigued him one hell of a *lot.*

Chapter Seven

At first Claire thought the ringing was part of her dream.

She'd been getting married all over again in the same little seaside church in California that she'd chosen the first time because Eli had said they could get married anywhere they wanted. Because, as in all things, money was no concern. Because there was no family to speak of…just her mother and a couple of cousins on his side who he'd said wouldn't want to attend and who he hadn't invited.

She'd been feeling nearly as silly in the dream as she had in reality, strolling down the aisle of a tiny, empty church in a glittering taffeta gown with a train nearly as long as the aisle itself.

But it had been the gown for her. The only possible one, once she'd tried it on in the best store in Pittsburgh and realized *this* was exactly how she'd always wanted to look on her wedding day. The only possible one when Eli had insisted she indulge herself because she'd had so little in her life up to that point. Because she'd had nothing at all to compare to totally impractical seven-thousand-dollar gowns encrusted with jewels that burned in sunlight like liquid set on fire. Nothing like a private jet to carry her to the festivities or afterward to the three week honeymoon they'd spent on Waikiki while her mother enjoyed a vacation of her own at one of the best, the most posh and pampering, health spas in the country.

Nothing.

In the dream, the palm-lit sunlight was just as bright on the fantasy of her gown, the limousine just as long, and Eli every bit as breathtakingly handsome. In the dream his eyes shone with just as much open disbelief at what he'd called his unbelievably good luck.

And church bells rang.

Thousands of bells. Millions.

Somehow though, the dream bells were raucous instead of pleasant or joyous. Shrilling, they'd twisted themselves up in some kind of pressing darkness. They'd lost their silvered clarity and turned to a brassy nuisance. A demanding distraction. Like…

Rolling over onto Eli's side of the bed, Claire forced her eyes to open.

He wasn't there.

Through a blur of sleep and the incessant ringing of a phone that was *not* going to stop, she saw it was three a.m.

Three a.m.?

Growling a low and feral sound in the deepest depth of her throat, she punched the lit button for the house phone and reached for the receiver.

House phone.

Another growl.

She'd known nothing like that in her previous life either.

Imagine. A phone in every room of the house so no one ever had to shout in the cool marble halls. So no one ever had to go searching for anyone in the vast rooms or go unsummoned when the time came for summoning.

"Hello?" she groaned, pressing the receiver against her ear.

"Come here," Eli said with a crackling in his tone that instantly, immediately, started a tight and anticipatory tension at the bottom of her belly. "Now."

"H…here?" Still foggy with too-abrupt awakening, her voice reflected the feeling in her stomach. "Where's *here*?"

"My study. And hurry."

"What…"

But he'd already hung up.

Quivering more than shivering because the night *was* warm and rapidly growing hotter, Claire fished around on the floor in the darkness for her summer-weight robe. Then, barefoot, turning on no lights as she went, she hurried toward the study at the back of the house.

She saw a gleam of light the instant she stepped into the long hallway. Dim, red, it glittered. A burning crack beneath the study door.

For an instant Claire froze. Remembering another night she'd seen the red glow of light. A night she'd seen the lurid glare, the hot and a hundred-thousand times more brilliant glare of an old house on fire just beyond her bedroom windows.

There had been terror that night…terror in that hellish and flickering light. Terror that rose up in her right now as if it had been only minutes instead of years since she'd spotted those flames and worried they might be about to consume her as well. It took a fraction of a moment, a very long and fear-paralyzed one, before she regained her power to move and to breathe.

This light was different. This light didn't threaten or frighten. This light...

Stomach tightening again, pleasurably, she hurried forward. Her heart was thumping now. Thumping with a wild and jerky rhythm high inside her chest.

This is like the old days.

The scene before her when she shoved the door open *was* straight from the old days. The days when Eli had paid her handsomely to come here. To indulge him by participating in any and every fantasy he could devise.

She'd hated them in the beginning, of course. Hated the fantasies and the way the desperation of a hard life and a gravely ill mother had backed her into an inescapable corner. The way desperation had forced her to prostitute herself to Eli Eden just to keep her tiny family alive.

She'd resented Eli for what she'd perceived as his easy life...for the millions upon millions of dollars he'd made in a runaway software market, for the glistening marble mansion high on its private mountain. But most of all she'd resented him for the bad-boy lifestyle that made it possible for him to drop fifty thousand dollars without a thought for a week of mindless sex with a perfect stranger.

She'd resented every one of those things and quite possibly a few more. Until she'd learned the truth, of course. Until she'd seen for herself that nothing ever came without a price and Eli's life hadn't been easy or happy. Not in the very longest of long, long times.

And to her complete and utter amazement, she'd found herself head over heels helpless in love with him long before her contracted week ran out.

How I hated those fantasies in the beginning! And how I miss them now.

More, she realized in the completely shocking and debilitating moment when she stood in the doorway to the study and saw what he'd set up for her this time, than she would ever have dreamed possible.

Straight ahead across a room left vague and dusky by a single lamp turned low behind a dark shade, Eli waited.

Eli as he'd been. As chestnut-haired, brandy-brown-eyed irresistible as he'd ever been. As he'd truly been even at the start, no matter how much she'd tried to think otherwise. The way he'd been that night in the sleigh where he'd ordered her to have sex with him and cater to him while he did nothing in return.

He sat on the big circular divan. It was a ridiculous piece of furniture, sand-colored and covered in soft leather, a kind of enormous round half-chair half-bed built for two. Or more. Claire had always thought the thing was some interior designer's dyspeptic way of getting revenge on the human race for some perceived slight or insult. She'd planned a dozen times…make that a hundred…how she was going to get rid of it. But now she saw the possibilities. All *kinds* of possibilities. And they were enough to draw her forward. Draw her in.

He'd spread a lap robe over the pale leather, a heavy woven thing in brilliant colors of the southwest and he sat atop it, his arms spread out along a backrest that curved around a third of the divan. Naked, his flesh gleamed pale against dark jewel colors. His legs were crossed casually at the ankle and all his…charms, for lack of a better word were concealed beneath a long and curling plume he held with both hands.

A brilliant red plume.

As brilliant a red as Claire had ever seen, a red that seemed to glow with some warming internal fire that enticed rather than put off, compelled rather than impelled. A glowing, devilish red that caused all sorts of preliminary softening and private moistening in preparation for…God only knew what.

Hesitating in the doorway, Claire had no idea where he'd gotten that plume. But it wasn't the only one, she saw once her vision cleared and her attention was able to focus on something else, even if only briefly.

He'd gotten many, many plumes. They lay scattered across pale leather and dark spread, lay across the satin-soft polish of the uncarpeted floor like drifts of dreams. Stood in the three enormous brass vases on the table at the back of the divan too, and lay in sculpted patterns around the base of those vases, bits of burning fluff and fancy strewn aimlessly yet purposefully across dark wood and gleaming glass.

Red plumes in all shapes. All sizes. All hues.

Some looked like the curling, fluffy product of mutant oversized ostriches, their tips floating and fluttering softly in a light breeze filtering through dark windows, while others resembled the straighter, stricter plumage of a kind of rubicund pheasant she'd certainly never in her life seen. One she wanted desperately never to have to see.

Eli held one of the mutant ostrich things. And as she approached the divan, feeling the brushing delight of ruby and garnet and blood-colored feathers beneath her bare feet, he moved one arm from the backrest. And in so doing lifted the plume.

Not far. Not enough to reveal himself.

Only enough to use it to stroke himself.

Even at the short distance still separating them, Claire saw him shudder the instant that long and flutter-soft frond touched the flesh he chose to keep hidden. Head falling back against the cushions, his eyes slipped shut. And a low, already intoxicated groan escaped his throat.

Claire's hand was at *her* throat. Forgotten, her silk robe slipped open to reveal the matching gown she wore beneath. A gown in the deepest of ruby shades, she realized, a gown almost purple in the depth of its color. A gown that fit perfectly and blended so perfectly that the choice of it might have been deliberate for precisely the scene Eli had created.

A gown that stroked silken tendrils around her ankles and calves as she moved forward, barely moving at all. A gown that, while floating in gently curved folds all the way to the floor, concealed nothing at all. Because the rest of it...the top of it...had been cut low. Cut simply, gorgeously, on the bias so the fabric clung to every rising swell of her body. Cut to highlight every sweeping concavity with color shadowed nearly to black. Nearly to the midnight-violet shade of the sky beyond the windows, a sky lit only by the smallest sliver of crescent moon. Nearly to the verging-on-black maroon of shadows stacked one upon another in every corner of the barely-lit room.

"Lock the door," Eli ordered before she took more than half a dozen steps across the feathered dream-field. Never lifting his head, he didn't look at her. Didn't cease his soft and stroking motions with the enormous feather with which he'd chosen to pleasure himself.

Turning back, Claire did as she'd been told.

"How did you arrange all this?" she asked once she had. Once she'd returned to the drifts of dream feathers that once again brushed her feet and ankles with titillating promise as she began her journey across them. "Did you get Hannah to..."

Eli laughed.

Dreamily. Softly. As if already detached from earthly existence, his earthly body. As if he'd already ascended into the same dream realm toward which her own body and existence were so rapidly rushing with each and every step.

"No," he murmured, the word a bare quiver of sound riding gently upon columns of heated summer air. "Hannah would have *Dios mioed* me to death if I'd even thought of asking. Which I never did."

"Then how..."

He lifted his head at last. Still using the feather for its incendiary purpose, he fixed his gaze upon her, his eyes burning red-brushed brown fire. Burning an even deeper fire, muted into darkest maroon to match the shadows in the corners by the desire she saw leaping in them. The desire she couldn't help but see in them when she reached the edge of the divan...the edge at his feet...and stopped again.

Stopped, she knew, for the very last time she'd be able to stop in a night filled with pleasure-clotted hours yet to come.

"I have my ways," he replied, his voice simmering lower, too. Simmering deeper and richer in both its shade and texture. "You don't need to know how, Claire. You just need to..."

Never finishing what he'd been about to say, what he'd been about to suggest, Eli lifted his arms. Both of them. He lifted them completely at last, allowing the long scarlet plume to droop forgotten from the fingers of his right hand. He held his arms out to her. In welcome. In command. In demand, and in pleading.

Claire had no attention for his arms though. No attention for the trailing feather either.

She could only look at him...only see him.

He was erect.

Rampantly erect, fully erect and ready for her.

He's been sitting here along for quite some time, she realized. He'd been sitting here while she slept on in their bed upstairs blissfully unaware. Had been sitting with his plumes and his tufts and his floating fronds of all descriptions in the world he'd created for the two of them. He'd been sitting and stroking himself, possibly for hours. Readying himself. Seeking out the private moments she'd come to know he needed before the final one arrived. Before the final act, when he'd summon her to the stage he'd set and show her the role she was supposed to play. The role he'd predetermined for her and scripted for her so that she had only to follow his lead. Only to allow herself to be guided into kinds of sensual torment and torture and delight she'd never be able to imagine for herself. Never be able to experience without his expert, creative, sometimes almost diabolically inspired help.

Eli held out his arms and for a moment Claire could only look at what awaited her.

She could see only the standing golden shaft, lit and enhanced by the dim lighting so that it cast its stark and stabbing shadow across the creamy planes of his abdomen and chest. She could see only the perfection in its shape, the light-distorted enormity of its size that, in the end, would prove not to be so very distorted after all.

She swore she could see the pulsing of it. The red-hot eagerness that made it seem to lift and fall, sway and steady, in time to every beat of Eli's heart.

For the longest time nothing happened.

For the longest time they hung suspended, both of them, in this place between there and here, between then and now, between expectation and completion.

In that time there seemed no possibility of movement. Ever again.

In that time Claire had the clearest picture of herself forced to remain as she was and where she was forever. Forced to linger outside the magic circle the round and now-inviting divan represented. Forced to tremble here, able only to see him and never again to reach him, the softness of plumes tantalizing the bottoms of her feet as she wished…desperately and hopelessly wished…for them to tantalize all the other parts of her, the swirl of silken skirts stroking heated streaks of desire into legs and thighs and the sultry patch of female flesh that lay already simmering near extinction between.

She might have to stay here as punishment for what she'd done…for allowing the distance to come between them and separate them. For almost failing to realize there even *was* a distance until it was nearly too late. Until they'd grown so far apart she'd almost lost the one and only man it would ever be possible for her to love. And what a fitting punishment it would be, this heavy and pressing drenching she felt both inside herself and outside. A punishment going on forever. Lasting forever, stretching into forever, with no permission ever again granted for the easing of it or the…

Eli lifted his feather.

Almost in slow motion, almost as an afterthought, he lifted it and pointed it straight at her.

"I need you," he said, directing the gently curled and floating-soft tip of it toward the very center of her. The very tortured, tantalized, aroused center that had feared it would never again have what it desired.

She moved, then.

She felt awkward. Jerky. Off balance. But she did manage to move.

One knee found its way onto the divan. One knee bent, one knee pressed into soft and pliant leather, trembling so badly that for a moment she feared it would simply slip off again, plunging her painfully to the hard wood floor. Feared it would slip and wreck this moment of eternal, incredible sexual tension that had just sprung up…for her, at least…out of thin and moon-shadowed summer night air.

Leaning forward, bracing herself with both hands against just such an untimely disaster, Claire found her face moving close to him. Moving so terribly, tenuously close to the shaft he left revealed now that he'd pulled its plumed covering away.

Her mouth watered. Eyes fastened upon the shaft and only the shaft, she leaned into the divan a little more. Lifted her other leg, pulled it clear of the floor and the strewn feathers, and placed the knee just as carefully on the firm yet soft surface.

She barely felt the strain and tug of her gown, soft silk resisting for a moment the stresses her movements placed upon it before it gave way and slipped upward. Slipped between the point of her knee and the smoothly-slippery leather surface of the couch in accommodation to her movement.

Eli sighed.

It was the most miniscule of sounds. The most patient, the most heavily expectant.

And it spurred her to action.

Real action, hungry action.

Allowing her arms to collapse, allowing them to deposit her onto the divan between his legs and still woefully short of what her heart desired more, even, than it desired the continuation of its own life or hers, Claire responded with a low and heavy sigh of her own.

So far yet to go.

So far, and Eli…

Gently, moving almost as if seen through a floating and concealing curtain of tissue-transparent gauze, Eli lowered the plume. He lowered it, stroked with it as he had before, strummed the upright length of himself that danced…visibly *danced*…in response. And murmured another sigh of wanting and needing. Of desperation that it was possible to want so much or need so much.

The plume's motions seemed to direct her.

Seemed to urge her forward. Call her forward.

Summon her forward.

Chapter Eight

ELI WONDERED HOW SOMETHING MADE UP MOSTLY OF AIR CONNECTED ONLY TENUOUSLY with filaments of substance so fine it almost didn't exist in the real world could feel this way. Could stir in him such feelings. Ones he'd all but forgotten. Or maybe never truly known to begin with.

The stroking of the feather across his cock, across balls that hung already low and heavy beneath, across the fine and secret skin in the place where his thighs joined and his body experienced its greatest, its most fundamental and earth-shattering sensation, was like fire. Like a maelstrom of fire, driven by high winds into a shrieking, all-consuming frenzy of flame and heat and greedy desperation.

Claire seemed equally affected by her forced stroll across the field of feathers he'd strewn deliberately and so carefully, with considerable difficulty since he'd almost toppled out of his wheelchair several times in the process. But he'd succeeded eventually, and the result was…

Sensational!

He'd always heard the soles of the feet could be a tremendously erogenous zone. He'd always guessed he would have to explore that a little more fully some time…at some point in the future. And right now, the expression on Claire's face, the look in her lovely gold-flecked eyes as she knelt on the edge of the couch and leaned forward over him, proved the point.

She'd been aroused by what he'd left for her.

Fully aroused, calescently aroused. Eagerly and anxiously aroused.

"Eli."

Even the way she said his name, just the two simple and unremarkable syllables, spoke of utter arousal. Of incipient, wanton abandon that would beyond all doubt have enormous consequences, life-altering consequences, for both of them.

He barely had strength to lift his arms. Barely had strength to hold the one that pointed the long and lusciously red plume at her aloft long enough to move it back to its resting place atop the cool leather of the sofa. Leather that already, joining the spirit of the moment and the heat of it, softened and warmed in anticipation of what lay at the end of Claire's journey across its foot.

Leather that anticipated far less patiently than he the feel of her skin, the pliability of it and of all the rest of her. Anticipated too the warmth only he knew. Warmth he felt certain with another surging strengthening of the shaft he'd tortured into full arousal that suddenly didn't seem so entirely full or aroused at all waited for him when she completed her journey. That long and time-consuming, utterly debilitating in its slowness journey across what suddenly seemed to be a vast and unforgiving desert of leather and strewn Mexican blanket.

She paused with a knee on the edge of the couch. Paused to stare at him, an open question glittering in her eyes.

"Come here," he rasped, no longer certain he could or should trust his voice. "Come now," he insisted and beckoned with the feather he'd thought to use only to entice. Only to draw her forward, though he thought he had a better plan now. Thought he had the most fantastic plan it had ever been possible for his mind to hatch.

She kept her eyes on the feather. Watching it, never taking her gaze off it, seeming completely unable to take her gaze off it, she lifted another knee and, her hands down between his legs and seeming eager to separate them even more, she did.

Come to him.

Leaning forward, her breasts quivering enticingly beneath the thin dark silk of her gown, the space between them delectably shadowed with all the possible colors of dusk and darkness, she moved toward him so slowly.

Torturously slowly.

More slowly, he thought, than she'd moved toward him in all their times together before this, her question still burning in her eyes. Her inquiry about what he wanted her to do next. Do now.

"Sit." Transferring the feather from his right hand to his left, still using it to create the softly swaying motions that seemed to captivate her so thoroughly, Eli patted the couch next to him with his free hand. He patted and he watched, the hot blood of desire swirling through his veins and into his cock. Hot blood that swirled and then immediately hardened, making a laughable mockery of any pain he believed he'd felt in the past. Making a mockery of any erection, any desire or resolve or plan he'd known in any past he could remember.

Her eyes still questioned. But they had a long history together, he and she.

At some point, without either of them knowing, she'd learned to trust. Learned to come to him and sit next to him...or lie under him, lie entangled with him, kneel over him if those were the things he chose to ask her to do.

She'd come to recognize his fantasies and, he hoped to God, come to relish her role in them as much as he relished his.

She sat.

Next to him.

Still fascinated by the long and supple, slightly curved and airy red plume he held out toward her, stroking just the tiniest fragment of its very tip across pale and gleaming flesh above the neckline of her gown...pale and gleaming flesh above breasts that promised the very same satin-cream, velvet-perfect delight waited beneath the thin and silken layer of fabric.

Going to him, Claire could barely breathe.

She realized it with a jolt and a shock of recognition so flawless and so complete there could be no room for error. Not even the tiniest and most fragile margin of error.

Her throat had nearly closed.

Her heart had begun to hammer, and when Eli moved...when he turned to her to lavish his attentions upon her, the long and fluttering plume still in his hand and wielded like an instrument created by the devil himself for the most refined kind of torture ever known...he had a look in his eyes. A hazy and subtly shimmering one. A slowly burning, infinitely and inexhaustibly fueled one.

Distracted, Claire shivered again.

Delighted all over as the curled tip of the burning red thing slipped like flame incarnate across her shoulders and down, she scarcely dared *try* to breathe.

The feather...just the tip of it, just the part Eli chose to use in his tenuous and yet very, very real contact with her...dropped.

And dropped.

Across the fully alive, fully aroused and diligently straining peak of her breast. Just once. Just for the time being.

Suddenly impatient, suddenly fearing the promise implicit in that feathered stroking around a nipple covered by a layer of whisper-thin silk that nonetheless in that moment felt like a full and fire-hardened suit of steel armor, Claire shrugged herself out of the gown.

It wasn't difficult.

Constructed and clinging as it appeared at a glance, the gown was designed to give way easily. To be slipped out of easily and be cast aside like so much worthless nothing. As was the frail lace scrap of her panties, which followed a scant second or two later.

And all the while, as she removed the small amounts of her clothing, Eli sat with his lips curved into a slight, almost a porcelain-perfect smile. He sat with his eiderdown weapon poised and describing casual, elusive arcs and circles in thin and steaming air just millimeters from her breasts. He sat until she resumed her place. Until she once again lounged against the cushions of the backrest, her naked breasts thrust forward, their nipples already hardened into desirous peaks that strained to feel again his burning touch. Peaks that strained to feel his touch for the very first time unencumbered by any kind of covering. No matter how slight or insignificant.

He touched her breast again with the tip of the scarlet plume. The same breast as before, in much the same way. And then he touched the other. Leaving nothing at all but wasted char wherever he chose to venture.

"Eli!"

He laughed and the sound of it, like the feather he continued to stroke and drag across hard-peaked nipples that begged for more at the same time they begged for their torment to end, seemed to have been spawned by Satan himself. Or was this the laughter of an angel at work? An only slightly fallen angel bent on the most divinely heavenly work imaginable?

Claire couldn't decide.

Her *body* couldn't decide.

Eli gave her tormented nipples one last incredibly gentle flick almost as an afterthought. And then, even before the final reverberation of the destruction he'd sought to wreak finished coursing and crashing through every sensation-inundated part of her, he moved the feather away.

Took it away. Denied her the insufferable torture upon which she'd come to depend if she was to survive intact. If she was to survive at all.

Before she could cry out, before she could fill her lungs in agonized preparation for a cry that would surely shatter the earth and awaken everyone, even in this sound-proof and enormous house with its vast number of remote and removed rooms where sounds most often went unremarked, he returned the blazing tip of his chosen weapon to her. He returned it in even more diabolical and inspired fashion to the shaking, taut and terrified flesh beneath her breasts. To the flesh around her navel. Flesh that now strained impossibly hard, just as impossibly and hopelessly as her unsatisfied nipples had done before. As her nipples *still* strained, heaving with anxiety and shimmering deadliness in response to the continued whisper of molten flame that had taken to circling her navel.

Once around. Twice around. Three times, gathering speed and momentum.

Only to depart again. Depart, though this time not to abandon her entirely. This time, still trailing its long streamers of havoc and destruction, the tip of Eli's floating, froth-tipped plume made its stroking and curl-tipped way along the flesh *beneath* her navel.

Now she earthquaked beneath its meandering brush.

This time, when Eli laughed in that way he had...that quietly knowing way that promised so many unspecified pleasures, so many intimate and never before experienced or imagined ways he might eventually grant her the release she almost dreaded...she all but convulsed. Convinced that in release, *this* kind of release anyway, lay the sure and remorseless cessation of all existence. All as she'd ever known it.

Eli laughed, and the resulting heat of it slashed a broad and tremorous swath through her.

Claire spread her legs wider as the slashing elicited a long and spiraling stream of moisture...an entire long and glistening, sparking and sparkling series of streams...from the very center of her. From the place where all such miraculous and mind-numbing streams found their origin.

Thighs atremble, quivering so hard in their unmet and no longer humanly meetable need, Claire thought the involuntary and spontaneous motion of her flesh seemed actually visible in dim light that seemed to flicker now that her vision had begun to fail. Light that threatened to fail itself as her breath, rasping savagely above the low mutter of Eli's continued laughter, strove to fan the flames that erupted from her body. Flames that took their ultimate toll and left her powerless to do anything but roll her head back against her neck and the cushions of the divan, groaning her ecstasy aloud as Eli finally...finally...

"Oh, God," she whispered, unable even to groan now that her throat had closed almost entirely. "Oh, God!" She wanted to shriek when the tip of Eli's soaring and searing weapon of mass destruction reached, *finally*, the destination she knew he'd had in mind the entire scalding, torture-riddled time.

All of that.

From a feather!

Wielded by a master, maybe. Wielded by a master, assuredly. Yet a simple feather all the same!

At last Eli allowed the flutter of that silken-tipped whisper of destructive nothing to drop down. And then even farther down. To the places he'd reduced to little more than a seething turmoil of conflicting wishes and desires and impossible wants.

Seeing a strange and in some vague way unsettling flutter of red through the distorted cloud that was all that remained of her vision, Claire realized it was the plume he'd held. It was that long and airy thing she swore with all the vehemence and conviction he always held in carefully guarded reserve for just this kind of swearing. And she swore she could still *feel* its brush against the softer, sensitized and infinitely inflamed area between legs she could no longer hold steady. Not even when she exerted all her strength in the effort to hold them.

She could *feel* the feather yet.

Could feel the extraordinary silk of it still sending plumes of sensory fire into and through the just as extraordinarily raw and aching outer folds of her body.

Swore she could feel it, though…

Her vision cleared once again. Just enough that she could see Eli sitting next to her. Leaning close to her.

She could see with utter and strangely crystalline clarity the look on his face…a look that made it just as crystalline clear he, too, felt the early, incipient stirrings of passion that would not be stopped or averted. And she realized he'd dropped his long and fluttering plume only so he could grab up another. One as different from the one he'd used to entice her forward as was night from day. No longer finding it necessary to intrigue her into initial, explosive and eager response to what he'd offered with every long and wavering, tendril-topped enticement of scarlet-laden, tickling air and nothing, he'd chosen a more compact feather now. One that was infinitely more practical in the close quarters in which he so obviously intended to maneuver and use it.

He'd chosen his new weapon from amidst the scattered drifts of assorted bits of scarlet and vermilion and brightest blood-colored plumage that thronged the table behind the divan. And it was just as vibrantly, just as viscerally colored as the original. It was no less capable of doing exceeding harm to both her body and her mind, Claire felt sure. No less capable of inflicting any and all manner of delirium and insanity when wielded with the kind of expertise she already knew Eli possessed in large and unlimited measures. Even if it was smaller than the first. Even if it was a more businesslike, chillingly and thrillingly businesslike, model with no flyaway and floating tendrils. She had no doubt he could use it to evoke exactly the same kind of runaway reaction he'd invoked before.

And maybe even a few new reactions into the bargain.

Smiling, Eli leaned over her. He leaned forward and applied his new weapon diligently. As diligently, more diligently, far more creatively than he'd ever applied the first.

Concentrating first on the outermost layers of her, concentrating with a ferocity that left her limp, weeping and whimpering for him to stop in the name of a loving God, please *stop* at the same time she kept on begging with eyes, and hands, and the volatile heaving of her entire body for him to do *more*. Give her more!

And Eli, laughing softly in his eternally incomparable way, did exactly that.

He gave her so much more.

Proceeding directly from the tormented outer folds to the even more anguished, moistened beyond human belief or comprehension, flowing and secret folds beneath, he applied the gentle flutter of his demonically inspired device of soft and swishing torment to flesh that had never felt anything like it. Flesh that never, beleaguered by this new and incomparable series of scorching, scoring, scalding sensations felt anything even *remotely* like it.

Chapter Nine

HIS USE OF THE FEATHER...*ALL* THE FEATHERS, ALL THE RED ONES HE'D BEEN ABLE to find at short notice...had been inspired. Like all his sexual fantasies, this one had just seemed to come to him. From out of the blue. And he was glad as hell it had.

One look at Claire lying limp and motionless beside and partially beneath him on the big round couch, and he was more than glad. He was damned, deliriously, dementedly near ecstatic.

It was one of those things that hadn't been supposed to happen to him after his life had taken such a harsh and hurtful turn. After he'd cracked his spine and damned near killed himself trying to be what his old man wanted instead of what he'd known...*known*...in his heart he was and should be content to be.

Claire made some small sound. Not a word. Not anything even close to a word. Seeing the way her eyes widened and glazed, noting the way her mouth fell the tiniest bit open, her lips swollen and blazing as unabashedly scarlet as the oversized plume, he thought he'd toy with her to the point of no return. The point where she would no longer be capable of resisting.

And that was where the wonder of it all came in.

Because Claire never resisted.

Never, in all the time he'd known her. Never in all the sometimes extreme and sometimes crazy but always inventive fantasies he'd ever been able to devise for their delight.

Sighing, her chest heaved visibly as a quick and rapid succession of gasps shook her body. Escaping those lushly full lips with small but harsh rasping sounds, they spoke of so many things. Of need and wanton abandon. Of eager anxiety to remain as she was, quiescent and willing, awaiting whatever might come next. But most of all, most incredibly of all, her expression and the softly keening sound of her breathing spoke of love. All of her love. Love so unconditional and absolute it saw none of the flaws with which he'd been cursed, and not a one of the shortcomings. Love so impossibly more than he'd ever dreamed could exist.

Love.

His heart did a stuttery, worried dance.

Love directed straight at him. Love strong enough and focused enough to pierce right through him. To make his heart first flutter wildly, speeding into its lopsided gallop only to almost immediately, almost fatally, subside so completely it gave every indication of wanting to stop. Just stop dead, stop cold, stop without regard to what he hadn't yet had a chance to accomplish with the lovely woman fate had sent him in repayment for all he'd lost. All he'd *thought* he'd lost.

He'd intended to play with her for much longer.

Had intended to run the feather across the quivering folds she'd exposed by flinging her legs wide for him. Had intended to probe with the airy and inconsequential tip of it to see the kind of reaction, the kind of moistening, misting, mounting agony it could induce if given the chance.

He'd meant to stroke her with it. To stroke those tremulous thighs and that aggravated flesh so near to the hidden entrance of her. The same flesh that yet, when it became the object of his teasing and his attentions, remained so heartlessly far away and beyond his reach.

He'd meant to do all of that.

Meant to do more…to explore so many things he'd never thought to explore before, in so many ways he hadn't until now realized it was even possible or advisable to explore.

But his cock wouldn't let him.

Demanding traitor that it was, infernal and insufferable intruder every time his fantasies seemed to be about to reach the kind of inhuman peak few men saw in their lives and even fewer saw any chance of surviving, it had tightened until the pain was excruciating. Until the throbbing ache, every single throb standing out in complete individuality and insistence from every other throb, threatened literally to rip his cock from his body. To render him useless once and for all if he didn't give it its way. Now.

"Claire." His voice rasped as desperately as hers.

He tried to put the feather away then. He'd been running it back and forth, lightly and tenaciously, the tip of it finding its barest way between her folds. Just deep enough to tickle. Just far enough to enrage and outrage and urge her to new heights. Better heights. Heights even she, sexual goddess that she'd long since proven herself to be, had never scaled.

But *she* wouldn't let him.

When he moved his hand away, trailing scarlet plumage, she caught his wrist with fingers that wrapped around it like molten steel. Fingers that felt liquid when they grasped only to immediately temper and harden into a restraint he couldn't escape. Not without running the all too real danger he'd have to snap a bone or two in order to succeed.

"Don't!" Dragging his hand back, she also dragged the plume it held to the place where it had done its greatest work. Back to the exposed and vulnerable, yet no more vulnerable than a killing man-trap, center of her.

"Claire, I need to…"

"If you stop…" Her breath rasped harder. Rasped insanely as all the rest of her began to pulse. As her own hand dragged the tip of the plume across her most private flesh just once before it lost its grip and failed utterly. Failed visibly. "I'll die."

That last was barely audible. Barely spoken and all too entirely believable.

When he tried to pull his hand away this time, Eli succeeded.

"I have something to show you, Claire."

Leaning his head against the cushions of the couch back, he smiled at her. Smiled directly into eyes that no longer seemed completely focused or even marginally aware of anything beyond the scope and circle of her own suffering. And then, unable to bear the frisson of hurt and abandoned loss he had so deliberately created in her, he looked beyond her. Looked at shadows gathered in waiting masses in all the corners and up high, next to the ceiling. Shadows ready to do their part in making this liaison secret and private. Shadows anxious to conceal with their ripe heaviness what should be concealed, and expose what should be exposed. Shadows with sense enough to leave Claire untouched, to leave her shining and gleaming, his perfect gold-and-rose goddess upon the bed he'd arranged for her. Shadows ready to watch, too. Ready to smile in their own way upon what would happen soon. What couldn't, now, happen soon enough.

"Come closer," he urged. "Let me show you."

And when she did, flesh and skin meeting flesh and skin at last in a silken touch not unlike a collision of worlds…*fiery* worlds…he urged her to sit beside him. Urged her to sit much as he did, with her legs spread and her arms splayed open wide across the back of the cushions.

He urged her to open herself once more to him. Urged her to give herself to him.

She did that, too.

Without a word.

Willingly, with a welcoming smile curving soft lips in a way that warmed his heart and made it seem to pause for a moment in its stride. Wondering at its good fortune, and his.

"So this is your latest fantasy?" she breathed, obviously questioning though he thought there should be no reason at all to question. Leaning close to his ear, she allowed her lips to brush first the surface and then the deeper and more unreachable levels just beneath. All the while leaving dewy trails of molten fire in their wake.

"Keep doing that," he replied around a very unsteady, very out of control laugh, "and you're sure to find out."

Half turning to him, Claire wrapped her arms around his neck and pulled herself closer to him. Or maybe she pulled him closer to her. Either way, the effect was the same. The effect was devastating for every bit of self-control he'd managed to muster and sought to retain. "I was counting on it." This time when her lips made their brushing, stroking, searing, scalding foray across the twists and turns of his ear, she added something new.

She added the tip of a scorching tongue he could imagine as sweetly pink, innocently pink, deceptively pink as it swept across his earlobe in the process of taking him captive. He could imagine the way that sweeping would look. And the effect of the imagining, down in his cock and the balls that had instantly twisted tighter, twisted insufferably and irrevocably tight, was a new surging. A new and more insistent energy, a new aching pulse that seemed to begin way down at the very base of him as a dull hammering only to progress to his tip with ever-mounting virulence until, reaching the tenderest flesh at his head and the sensitive flesh that lay just beneath and just behind his head, it became a shrieking anguish. As if someone had caught that exquisitely vulnerable knob of himself in a red-hot vise and twisted it tight. As if they were still twisting.

And twisting and twisting and...

The sensation was too much for him.

It was too much, he thought, for any man to endure. Too much for any man to be expected to endure.

Shuddering, the sound escaping as a low and halfway-audible vibrato between tightly clenched teeth, Eli shoved Claire back. Shoved her into the sitting position he'd designed for her, her back upright against the cushions, her body held rigidly away from his.

Her *lips!*

Thank God in His merciful heaven, her lips had left him behind now. They were held absolutely away from the ear that even now pleaded with him to allow them to come back. Pleaded for its survival in the form of more, and then even more and ever more delirium inducing heat from her pink, pink, soft and utterly ruthless tongue.

Claire made a sound of protest.

It might be a word of protest.

Eli thought it was, but through the escalating banshee-whine of feedback in his ears, the sound of an overloaded brain just about to implode with all the self-destructive vigor of a universe in the final stages of death, he couldn't be sure. He couldn't hear much beyond the shrilling of a million and one inhuman voices inside his mind. All of them urging him to die now. Die in the utmost pain it was possible to suffer during death throes. And underlying it all, adding a sort of weirdly off-center rock and roll beat that only underscored the desperateness of his situation, he heard the sound of his own heartbeat.

Thump-a-thump and hammer. Twitch and recover. Trip and restore.

It went on and on. Frighteningly on, for no more than a millionth of a second while he held Claire in the place where he wanted her, the place where she would be best prepared and best positioned to participate in all he had in mind. While she struggled to overcome the force of his hands upon her shoulders.

His hands. Holding her immovable against a softly flowing curve of sand-colored leather.

"Wait," he commanded, and decided it was lucky she heard him the first time and saw fit to do as he asked.

He didn't think...knew almost for certain...he would have another chance.

Because there were no more words.

There was no chance, now or quite possibly ever again, to utter even that one simple word.

The touch of her, the wrapping of creamy-satin skin against his and around his as she reached for him and surrounded his neck and his shoulders with arms every bit as dangerous as that deceptively soft and pink tongue, left him too breathless for words. Too insensate and insensible to create words another human being would have a hope of understanding.

"Like..." It was a great effort...a mind-boggling one, one that took almost the last of his strength and left nothing for him to fall back upon...just to say it.

Instead he had to show her.

It was almost more than he could do to leverage himself over her. To move his legs which at the best of times didn't fully cooperate and do what he wanted them to do and told them to do, so that he sat atop her splayed thighs. So that he sat with his legs spread, his forehead pressed to hers and his arms holding her in the same way she'd already long since begun to hold him.

Face to face, thigh to thigh, they sat shivering together. Shivering in mutual, wordless and yet perfectly understood, perfectly synchronized harmony.

Shuddering as hard as Claire…and she was shuddering, was quite literally quaking from head to foot with a long and endless series of shudders that wracked every inch of her body…Eli maneuvered himself the last small bit of the way into position.

This was the easy part. Now that he'd lifted his right leg, the stronger of the two though 'strong' was an extremely over-optimistic way to describe what little was left of it across her, now that he'd pulled himself up to sit between her spread thighs with his legs across hers and outside hers, with them controlling hers and her, it was easy to shim himself forward. Easy, knees bending to tuck themselves snugly and firmly up and into his armpits where they would be firmly under control, to move forward until he touched her.

Until the hammering tip of him, seeking and searching, touched and found the steaming quiver of female flesh that lay between Claire's legs.

"Like this," he managed at last, his voice sounding like nothing human. Like nothing, indeed, from Planet Earth.

His voice had a misty sound. A faraway one, as if heard through the oddly rarefied atmosphere of a world or maybe a dimension humanity had not yet discovered. Or, if discovered, one they'd certainly not mapped and might never map. Because this new existence, created with the single questing strike of the tip of his cock against the place where it had too long longed to be buried, too long dreamed of being buried and despaired of ever being allowed to be buried, defied mapping. It defied logic as humanity knew it. Defied quantifying or calculating.

This was an existence of sheer spirit.

Sheer will, sheer…

Another move forward, only the very slightest one, brought him into firmer and even more deadly contact with what he'd been seeking.

Another slight movement and the tip of him was not only in contact with the warmest and most deeply, dewily desirable flesh of her. It now parted that flesh.

Their voices mingled in a single, sharp catching of collective breath and a single resulting silence as that breath was trapped and held, no longer allowing itself to be released as Eli parted the outermost folds of her. In search of what he knew lay concealed beneath. *Knew*, though no matter how diligently he searched the memories and recollections of his heart, he couldn't imagine how it would be. Couldn't remember how it had ever felt, or any of the things it had ever done to him.

The action of sliding himself forward toward her created a slight rocking motion. An infinitesimal swaying of his hips, side to side and also forward…ever forward. And with each sway his cock, barely beginning to be lost in warm and glistening folds of flesh that instantly, seeming to sigh and cry out themselves in their victory with each of those subtle forward and sideways movements, seemed to tug the tip of him deeper. Seemed to tug it farther into her hot trap with a will of its own. Into a lovely and seductive trap that once it closed around him and once it grasped him with its full and incalculable power, promised never to let him go.

"El…iiiiiiiiiiiiiiii!" Claire's voice rose. Not to a shriek, because there wasn't enough sound there to create a shriek. There was, really, no sound at all. There was nothing but a soft rush of exhaled breath that only suggested the sound of his name while refusing to take on the definite shape of it.

"Like this." As her voice deserted her, as the tight and scorching sound of her gasping increased to a tortured groaning that also lacked the capability of making real sound, Eli eased himself forward again.

He had moved very close now.

With her thighs trapped firmly beneath his bent legs, with her body now snug on his and in the most inescapable control of his, he had moved so close he could feel the heat pouring off her.

Waves of heat.

Sultry heat, moist with the essence of the hot and still night beyond the windows, heat dewed with the essence he felt beginning to trickle from the deepest layers and recesses of her trapped and tormented body, heat that rose and rose ever higher to greet him. Heat that tried to pull him in as her flesh had…tried to entice him deeper than ever before as the folds of her began to quiver. Began to give way in the delightfully indescribable way female flesh had known from the beginning of time how to give way before harder, more insistent, invading male flesh.

He resisted for a last moment. Resisted the temptation she offered, the trap that lay just beyond the silken temptation.

But it was useless.

He might have trapped Claire. Might have brought her onto him with the idea of controlling her, controlling her movements and her responses, controlling the speed of those responses and the degree to which they granted her release at any given moment. But that went both ways.

He controlled her. But only as much as she controlled him.

He could stage-manage everything that happened to her body and everything that happened within her body. To exactly the same degree that she managed the turmoil inside him.

Shuddering again, teeth bared, scalding beads of sweat slipping down his forehead and into his eyes, stinging beads that blinded temporarily and left him wishing he could lift a hand to them, wishing he had the strength or the ability to brush them away, Eli moved into her. He moved all the way in, plunging with an urgency that took him completely by surprise even though he'd known it was coming.

Her body flexed.

The encroaching, entombing, ensnaring folds of her opened. They widened in response to the pressure he placed upon their outer surfaces and he felt them give way all too willingly. All too eagerly.

He felt them mist his own flesh with a sweetly slippery film that made the entry, the long and gliding crescendo of his flesh slicing into hers and claiming hers so much easier. So sweetly, tumultuously easy.

Spurred on by that new mistiness, enticed by it, Eli continued to slip forward upon her legs until their bodies touched full-length. Until his forehead dipped forward again as her head lolled back. The way his had lolled moments before.

God, it was so incredibly easy to enter her. So incredibly easy to reach the farthest, most closely guarded depth of her through cloud-soft layers that rained their slightly effervescent warmth and moisture down and over him to facilitate and encourage the entry.

And then it was so difficult to leave.

When he reached the bottom of her…surely it had to be the bottom because there was no more left of him, no further depth to which he could hope to penetrate…he could do nothing but stay there. Stay where he'd placed himself while he'd still been fool enough and naïve enough to believe he had any control over himself or what he was doing. While he'd still believed she'd actually allow him any kind of control over what she would do once she won her turn.

He could only stay when her flesh tightened around him. When every muscle in the deep inside of her contracted, strong enough to crush, sure enough to maim, determined enough to succeed.

"My G...God." He choked the words. Nearly strangled on the utterance of them, nearly died a thousand deaths before the quavered and whispering old-man sound of them reached his own ears. "Claire..."

"*Is* this your fantasy?" When she spoke, the effort of it seemed to originate from, seemed to derive its very existence and clarity from, the muscles with which she held him.

Impossible, to believe a woman's voice could come from that part of her.

Impossible to believe that part of her could have anything to do with the creation of sound or the formulation of speech.

But it did.

In every possible way, it did.

Eli felt the words as she uttered them. He felt the pressure and the tension upon the part of himself that he'd surrendered and was not going to get back. He felt them flow into him and through him as a small series of tightening and loosening, of contractions and releases. As a small and incendiary series of pulling that urged him to go deeper still, deeper than was even possible.

"Or is it my fantasy?" she whispered, moving her insanely inhuman lips close to, directly against, his ear again.

And Eli thought he was going to faint.

Chapter Ten

RIVERS OF FIRE.

Eli could feel the burning of them. He could feel scorching deluge after scorching deluge of some molten, elemental substance rioting inside him, furious in their passion to reach the surface. More than furious that he'd managed so far to exercise every bit of his most iron-willed control to hold them back. Hold all those punishing rivers in strict abeyance until he could use them later…use them when the time grew right and Claire grew ready. Use them to his best advantage and, he hoped to God, to her advantage too.

But the internal fire roared.

It leaped and crackled, fanned and fueled by every sleek and swift entry Eli made into the heart of her. Unrelieved by any of the much slower, thoroughly grudging and reluctant exits. Unrelieved and without hope of relief as long as he retained his singular, sometimes remarkable, ability to contain and control.

It was a hard-won ability. Not a natural talent. It was one of those results he'd been forced to face, forced to suffer through and at length accept, in the days and months and years following the horseback-riding accident.

It was an ability he was glad as hell he'd won in the end, if only by the sheer force and persistence of inevitability.

Because it was driving…always did drive…Claire over the edge.

He could feel her quake violently. Could feel her loosen around him as his next thrust proceeded uninterrupted.

Her inner muscles, previously so tight and grasping, almost to the point they had a moment ago threatened to mangle him to a shredded and useless pulp, lost their strength. They lost it in the midst of a sudden, startling and sweeping torrent of moisture.

By comparison to what had already begun to happen inside him, the steaming eruption from the deepest reaches of her felt cold. The whisper of air as she gave up everything she'd only just gasped into her lungs felt cold, too. As did the middle-of-the-night air brushing across his shoulders.

All of it, all of them, felt so cold. So incalculably and inexpressibly frozen that Eli shivered though Claire was warm and he knew the night was just as warm. Knew the night had been sultry and heavy even before the heat of their passion had risen to color it the dull, sullen red of a smoldering coal in a vast and overheated furnace.

He felt Claire try to move, too.

Familiar with her responses, able to anticipate almost to the second when they would occur and their intensity in relation to what he had done or what he hadn't done, he knew she was trying to move. Trying to adjust herself and find ease for herself around him.

She was struggling to accommodate him while at the same time satisfying herself.

And he wasn't about to let her succeed. Because that would ruin all the fun. Her fun as well as his.

"Calm," he urged though he felt anything but calm himself. His voice was too tight for calm. His voice was boiling-tight. As were all the parts of his body that mattered at a time like this. "Stay calm, sweet love," he instructed in a tattered whisper as he reached the limit of a particularly long, particularly lush and luxurious, absolutely unnerving plunge into the soft-shimmering pool of her. A pool that, rather than extinguish his fire or appease it in even the most trivial of ways only seemed to ignite it more. Only seemed to fuel it more and, ultimately, to set it to raging beyond control at the smallest, the most inconsequential of contacts.

Bursting into her own kind of insatiable flame, Claire gained power of movement at last. Even with his thighs pressing her to the couch, even with his weight squarely on top of her and supposedly pinning her to soft leather that felt hot beneath his heels and toes...leather that felt like it had begun to burn beneath the hottest sun ever recorded, she began to move.

She regained use of her arms and hands first. Lifting them, she grasped his shoulders with wickedly clawed fingers and used all the force available in her body to tug him toward her. To tug him hard, her trapped thighs flexing with near-superhuman strength and determination as she pulled him in again. Pulled him all the way in not with internal muscles that remained shaken and weakened, rendered all but inflexible by the power of her responses, but with her arms. Pulling and flexing, she tilted her body somehow, in some strange and inexplicable way, so that he lost what balance he'd had. So that, when she pulled again, he had no choice but to tumble forward toward her. And by default, all the way onto her. Just when he'd been about to realize his plan of full dominance and absolute control. Just when he'd been about to begin the infinitely complex and oddly gratifying process of retracing his earlier path...of backing away from her as far as he was willing to go. Which, of course, was not all the way. Because all the way would kill.

And he had no wish to die.

Not now. Not yet.

Not for quite a while. If only Claire would let him...

"Easy," he whispered, his voice jolting as he slammed forward violently and found the very violence of the blow they inflicted upon each other dangerously titillating. Dangerously stimulating. As stimulating and irresistible as anything he could remember her ever doing to him before.

Not that he was in any condition to remember much that had happened before she'd walked into this room tonight. Before he'd taken one look at her and remembered with his mind and every part of his body all the wonderful reasons he'd fallen in love with her. All the incredibly unbelievable reasons he'd remained in love through all of these years, even when familiarity had shown signs of setting in and the ardor had seemed in danger of wearing thin.

The violence of the blow she inflicted was very dangerous. The suddenness of it, the way the move was so cleverly and provocatively executed, the way it was accompanied by another flexing as her deep-down muscles found the strength for one more effort and one more try, the new and different, slightly off-center angle at which he'd been placed, did nothing to help the already incendiary situation in his cock and his balls.

They weren't going to stand for much more. They were, in fact, just about to take charge of the situation. In just another second or so.

A scalding column of all that had been held back for far too long began to rise inside Eli. It began to rise almost unstoppably, like some kind of force of nature.

He felt twisted inside.

Felt flushed and achy, felt hot and miserable, felt like a man in the last, desperate throes of some kind of terrible and fatal, tropic disease.

Has a man ever died from having sex?

He could only wonder.

And Claire...

Oh, Christ in heaven.

Claire moistened again.

He had no idea where such enormous quantities of misty, wanton fog could come from. No idea what deep well he'd tapped within her. He'd thought surely all the wells had long since been tapped and all the reserves long since mapped and drained. All the depths plumbed to the fullest extent possible.

Claire, too, had no idea what he'd done. Though she knew it should never have surprised her.

Clinging to Eli with strength she no longer had, afraid to show him her sudden and overriding weakness for fear he'd see it as an invitation to seize command and take the kinds of wicked and devilish advantages only he knew how to take, she actually felt foolish for having been surprised.

She should have learned by now that there were no limits to what Eli would do. No limits to what he would try, what he could dream up.

She should have long since been immune to the shock value of it all.

But she wasn't.

As some indefinable, surging mass gathered itself together inside her, gathered its strength and its forces for one last and final, one mighty and unforgettable surge of all that she was and all that she would ever be, Claire knew she'd never be immune. Never cease to need the surprises he planned for her, never cease to…

"Eli!"

He'd begun a new kind of thundering inside her.

She could feel the pulse…actually *feel* it. She could mark the time of it by matching it with the rhythm of her own body, could sense the heavy pulsing inside the long and sculpted shaft he plied with such expertise. Such increasing urgency.

He had taken on a new motion.

She didn't even know for sure what it was.

Only that this way of touching her, this way of approaching from the slightest, the most immeasurable of angles, sent a matching thunder of approval through every part of her. A thunder of approval *and* of agreement that this was right. Eli was right. That she'd been a fool…a damned near criminally insane one…to have thought for an instant that what they'd had once could have died. That it could have faded or grown somehow less magnificent. Less important.

She did her damnedest to move, but he held her down.

He pinned her, her legs beneath his and intertwined with his. Hers, so much stronger and so much more useful in almost every respect, were no match for his in this moment. In this time. Maybe because she'd been fighting a losing battle against surging weakness. Against a strange and hot desire to collapse before him and worship him as he finished what he'd begun so many hours and days and weeks before. Maybe because she'd begun to feel that this weakness, this softening and loss of energy that compared to no softening or loss of energy she'd suffered before was right.

As right as *them.*

As right as together.

"Eli."

He didn't respond. At least, not with words.

How could there be time for words, how could there be breath or sensibility for them, when the thing between them, the thing they'd created together here, starting with that infernal, demon-driven and delightful red plume, had grown so enormous?

How, when she could feel the heavy pounding at the inside of his body...the inside of his shaft that was like no other in the world...against the hidden folds inside her?

How, when something had knotted inside her? Knotted tight, knotted as if it would never be released. As if it would remain there, pained and cramped, for as long as she had to live.

It seemed her body would never be capable of unknotting itself. Never be capable again of ease. But Claire knew that wasn't true. Knowing the feelings of which she was capable, knowing them as intimately as ever it was possible to know such things, she knew release would come.

Very soon, if Eli didn't stop...

"Please..." Taking the lobe of his ear in with the opened and accepting part of that greedy-hungry word, Claire sighed softly. Sighed directly into his ear and felt instantly gratified, instantly on the right track when his shaft gave a hard leap. When it seemed to pummel itself against the inside of her, frantic and thrashing for any kind of peace it could find. At any kind of cost it might have to pay. "Don't...stop, Eli. Don't...ever..."

"Who said anything about stopping?" His voice was thick and his laughter as heavily merciless as the thing that had coiled itself so tight inside her.

And he didn't.

Stop.

The rhythm of his movement was hard enough and purposeful enough now to shove the heavy round divan slightly across the polished wood floor. Heavy enough to shove it against the massive Spanish table at its back and rattle the tall brass vases against glass insets in the table's top. Accompanied by the tiny sounds of brass ringing madly against glass, by a series of shivery metallic pings and rings and clatters, the rhythm of his movement continued unabated. Continued growing stronger. Continued to take the slightly different approach she found so indescribably irresistible.

"If you stop," she breathed, wrapping sweat-slicked and still much too weak and pliant arms around him in one last, one supreme and failing effort to hold him tight and hold him close, "I'm going to die."

"I..."

Claire felt the twisting now.

She felt it in both of them. Simultaneously.

Felt the surge of heated effervescence rise inside her, anxious to win the race and beat his to the surface even when common sense and all the knowledge of her heart urged it wasn't wise for either of them to win. That this was one race better concluded in a photo finish. One race that was better concluded together, as all such races should ultimately be concluded.

"Eli..."

"I'm going to..." The muscles in his back and shoulders...heavy muscles, superbly developed and powerful muscles that did all the work for his body, all the work weakened and failed legs no longer could...flexed beneath dampened palms that slid and slipped. Palms unable to find or maintain the purchase they so desperately desired. "Going to die too, C..."

She couldn't extricate her legs from the mass of twisting, writhing and senseless flesh that was all that remained of the two of them.

Couldn't.

But she needed to.

She needed to wrap them around him. Needed to clasp him with them so that when he tried, as she knew he would, he wouldn't be able to retreat. So he wouldn't have any choice but to remain with her and a part of her for as long as it took for the end to come. As long as it took for the inevitable to claim them both.

But of course retreat was an essential part of what he was doing to her and what she needed him to do to her. An indispensable one.

He had to retreat. Had to shimmer backward as he did when her hands failed to grasp him and her inner flesh failed to hold him.

He had to move back in order to move forward.

Had to withdraw in order to conquer.

But he hesitated. With only a millimeter of flesh...maybe less...joined and still creating one where there had a short time ago been two of them, he hesitated.

Claire sensed he was getting ready for the final moment. The final plunge that would spell absolute victory, absolute surrender to victory and absolute concession by both of them. And she couldn't wait any longer.

Could.

Not.

Wait.

"Don't stop!" she gritted through clenched teeth and, as if the exclamation gave her one last, one indisputable though indisputably finite measure of strength to do the job, she tugged again. Tugged, sweat-sheened flesh still slipping across sweat-soaked flesh, though nowhere near as uncontrollably as before.

She tugged him to her. Tugged so that his shaft…the long and delirious, penetrating and stabbing and plundering length of all of him…roared back into her. Only it didn't roar as much as shriek. Didn't shriek as much as thunder. Didn't thunder nearly as much as…

"Don't ever stop!"

The scalding current her body produced was uncontrollable. Utterly.

She felt another rising, this one inside herself for there was now no feeling left, no sensation, for judging what was going on with him and within him.

She'd have to tend to her own desperate state of affairs first. And trust Eli to tend to his. Trust him to do the perfect thing at the perfect, well-timed and most propitious of moments. But in the meantime the heat they generated was intolerable. The heat they passed back and forth so recklessly threatened to kill, more surely than any lack of it had seemed likely to kill in the moment before.

Struggling to *pull*, desperate to have it all this very instant, Claire pressed her face against Eli's shoulder. Teeth bared, not caring what carnage they might create or if they created carnage at all, she tasted the slightly salty tang of his sweat and a hint…just the faintest hint…of the richness of blood from some freshly-incised wound.

"Give…" She could hardly speak through the effort of clenching her teeth. Could hardly breathe for the effort of struggling to breathe. "…it…to…me."

"Gladly, sweet love." With those words one massive temblor rumbled through the body he'd joined so thoroughly with hers. One enormous rumble of nature's thunder, nature's pre-eruption jitters, and he came apart inside her.

The finality of it struck her like a million and one shards from some cosmic, unheard explosion. Stabbing her as if they were sharp and crooked, they at the same time caressed and soothed as if they were perfectly smooth. Above all those shards filled her until it wasn't possible, could never be possible, for her to be filled any more.

They filled her. Satisfied her. Inundated and overwhelmed her.

And then the weakness came back.

Shuddering and slipping, no longer able to maintain a grip upon anything of any importance in a world turned utterly to ruin and void, Claire sagged against him. Allowing him to hold her up for one last instant. One last victory as his shaft emptied itself of what it had guarded so jealously just seconds before. As with one mighty, gathering, lunging, surging and leaping plunge, it took everything she had to give in the same instant it gifted her with all of itself. All of *him.*

Then there was nothing.

Then Claire thought she would faint. Thought she must have already fainted when she opened her eyes to discover they lay side by side on the heat- and passion-ravaged divan, gasping like they were indeed about to die.

Killed by the most profound pleasure ever known.

Chapter Eleven

IF THAT DAMNED INDIAN HAS A SECRET, IT'S NEWS TO ME.

Eli had been over it and over it in his mind about a gazillion times. And the memory searches always came out the same.

He'd climbed all over the monstrous thing when he was a kid. A dozen times. More. He'd never found a sign of anything secret or hidden then, so how in hell was he supposed to do it now, when he couldn't even stand up and look the thing straight in the eye…err, chin?

He'd taken to spending a lot of time in the big front room recently. In the three or four days since Claire had had the monstrosity dragged in there to dirty up the place and devalue the entire property by taking up space that could have been used one hell of a lot better for something else…that could have been used one hell of a lot better just by staying empty.

Now, on a misty-gray rainy late morning when he had no reason and no desire to be outside and no reason to be in the front room either, he couldn't help himself. Fascinated, almost mesmerized, he sat directly in front of the thing with one twin climbing around on his lap…Sophie or Stephie, there were times like now when he had no clue which was which because they were *so* identical…and the other ambling back and forth between him and the Indian, giving the lion's share of her attention to the hideous, hulking statue. She looked like she might be about to start scaling the front of it herself, in dedicated search for what her old man had never stood a chance of finding.

"Better come away from there," he advised the adventuring twin. "Your mom and Nanny will have fits if you get that mess all over you."

They would. But if was up to him, he wouldn't care.

He thought kids should be kids. Their time to be kids was too short as it was. And a little dirt had never hurt any kid.

Eli *liked* to see a kid get filthy dirty every now and then.

The twin ignored him. She'd stopped and was peering up at the statue. Reaching for something she apparently saw that no one else did…something that lay just beyond her grasp even when she stood on tiptoe, precariously stretching herself to her full three-year-old height.

"And what do you think?" he asked the twin in his lap, distracting her when she decided it was time to make a little pre-lunch snack of the buttons on his shirt.

That settled it.

Sophie. Catching her chin to turn her face away from the delicacy of the buttons, Eli chuckled a
little. *This has to be Sophie.*

She'd eat anything. Eli quailed sometimes at the stuff she'd been caught eating. Or trying to eat. He really quailed whenever he got to wondering what the hell she might have succeeded in eating when nobody was looking.

Some things just didn't bear thinking about.

"What do you think?" he asked again, bouncing her a little as he pointed her toward her sister.

Stephie had no time for either of them. Standing firm at the base of the Indian, she'd quit her stretching and straining. Now she'd taken to just staring straight up. At whatever it was that fascinated her. She seemed completely unconcerned that the monstrous old hunk of junk seemed to loom over her with all kinds of menace. Like it was getting ready to gobble her up as part of its nebulous and non-existent secret if he didn't keep a strict eye on it. And her.

"What do I think about what?"

Eli jumped. Enough to startle a brief grunt of protest from Sophie and a not so brief, not nearly so harmless jolt of surprise from his heart. For a second, dumbfounded and befuddled, he looked down at the top of Sophie's dark head. As if the thoroughly adult voice could have come from a food-centered twin whose conversational skills so far appeared non-existent on any subject other than food.

Stephie was the talkative one.

When Stephie wasn't caught up in some overwhelming mystery fantasy the way she was right now, she'd chit-chat your ears off if you gave her half a...

"Think about what?" Claire asked again, stepping into his sight at the same time she pulled Stephie away from a preliminary attempt to climb the Indian. "Come away from there, sweetheart," she said in response to Stephie's fully infuriated wail. "That old thing's nasty and dirty."

"Nasty." Turning toward Eli, Stephie scrubbed blackened hands down the front of her yellow cotton tee shirt. "Dirty," she muttered, and made a face.

"It certainly is," Eli agreed, laughing at the long streaks of black on

Stephie's face, her hands, the front of her shirt that was no longer yellow and no longer even remotely clean.

"Ewwwwwwww!" Sophie pulled back, burying herself flat against Eli's chest when Stephie launched herself headlong at the two of them in obvious, complete unconcern about spreading her filth around.

"No way." Claire caught her by the back of her shirt before she closed the distance. "One dirt bag in the house is enough, young lady. Now here's Nanny and she's all set to give you a nice, hot bath and make you look like a human being again." Turning Stephie around deftly, Claire handed her off to the waiting nanny, then held her hand out to Sophie. "You, too. Time for your lunch."

That caught Sophie's interest.

Of course it would.

Scrambling down from Eli's lap, she ran for the door, as headlong as her twin and twice as focused. She never looked back once she caught sight of the nanny she loved, Eli sometimes thought with a small and poignant aching in the area around his heart, more than she loved either of her parents.

Of course. After all, Nanny's in charge of food.

And food went a long way.

"So," Claire said once they'd gone...once even the sound of their going had died away on the thick blue carpet of the stairs. Standing before him, her hands twisted together a little, she looked unaccountably nervous in the watery, approaching-storm light.

"So." Eli squinted up at her. "What?"

"What you kept asking Sophie. What do *you* think, Eli?"

He looked at her face for another second. Or two. Then he let his gaze slide back to the ill-timed and poorly thought out 'gift' she'd decided to give him, for reasons he still didn't understand or even, necessarily, appreciate.

The damned Indian that lay at the center of it all. Lurking and brooding in its corner like some kind of malevolent, threatening shadow sent specifically to remind him of all the failures and foolish mistakes he'd made in his life. All the ones he'd let himself be talked into making through more fault of his own than he ever wanted to admit.

"I think that thing's a disaster," he declared, dipping his head in its general direction.

When Claire looked at the Indian he knew he'd said the wrong thing.

Her face didn't crumple. Not exactly. But something in it, something in the underlying and hidden layers of her expression rearranged itself a little. Very slightly, something shifted. And it wasn't in a good or a very positive way.

"Come here," he said in the same tone he'd have used with one of the twins in the midst of a major upset, and held his arms out to her.

"We could clean it up." She didn't look at him. Taking a slow step toward the Indian she seemed as unwilling to get close to it as he'd felt ever since he'd had the shock of his life at finding it in the house.

"Claire..."

"It hasn't been taken very good care of." She wasn't just wringing her hands now. She was *really* wringing them. Twisting them together with a harsh motion that looked like it might soon wrench one or both right off her wrists. "That's all it is, Eli. It's just in need of some T.L.C. and a little bit of cleaning up to make it good as new."

He doubted that.

He doubted there was enough soap or T.L.C. in the entire world to make the thing look good as new ever again.

The last thing he wanted in the world was to move closer to it. He worried he might actually freeze solid or turn to stone, or meet some other horrid and unimaginably Biblical fate if he was careless enough to allow the Indian's shadow to fall across him. But Claire wasn't listening to a word he had to say. She wasn't going to do anything he asked...wasn't going to come to him. So he'd have to do it. He'd have to swallow his jitters and go to her.

Lifting his hands to the wheels of his chair, he hesitated one last time. Searched one last time for a little...just a smidgen of...common sense and self-preservation. And then he rolled forward.

Into the shadow.

And breathed a sigh of relief, silly as he knew it was, when he *didn't* turn to stone.

"This didn't do any good." Claire looked at him again. "This whole idea. About finding the Indian and bringing it home. Did it?"

Careful.

Eli suppressed a warning shiver that tried to shake him to his very foundation.

If there's ever been a time in my life when I need to be cautious and carefully as hell, this has to be it.

"The Indian was supposed to bring us together."

"Claire. Sweetheart."

It broke his heart to hear her say it. Even if he'd suspected, very strongly suspected that was what lay behind this strange plan of hers, it damned near killed him to hear her put it into words. Because it showed just how shaky she thought their marriage had become. Just how shaky and unsteady she thought they'd both become in it, if she imagined a goddamned old piece of burnt-up and burnt-out wood could ever…

"The Indian was supposed to make all the difference." She'd turned mournful now. She was grieving openly, her lovely mouth turned down at the corners and her eyes suddenly, ominously glistening with unshed tears. "The Indian was supposed to put everything right that's gone so wrong between us."

Eli felt a headache coming on. A real skull-buster of a headache. Like he hadn't suffered in a very, very long time. "Who ever said anything had gone wrong?"

Eyes widening, she made a little gesture. An utterly futile and heart-wrenching one. "I…" And then she couldn't seem to finish.

"Come here." It wasn't that twin thing anymore. That hyper-patient voice of reason he felt sure wasn't going to fool anyone much over the age of three. This time his voice was gentle. Really and truly gentle in the tenderest of ways, the one that had always used to make her claim she felt so safe. So secure and so far out of harm's way it would never stand a chance of finding her.

She looked at him, but she didn't move. Not a single step. "All I did was upset you and frustrate you," she mourned.

"You did no such thing, Claire. I just…I'm at a loss to understand what you want. What you thought I was going to do with that damn…*thing*."

"It was supposed to…"

"I know." And he did. He thought he knew now exactly what it was supposed to do…supposed to represent. He thought he knew everything, though the knowing sure as hell didn't seem to do any damned good since he still didn't really understand *how* the Indian was supposed to do what it was supposed to do. "But…"

He had to ask. *Had* to, and to hell with consequences. "How is it supposed to do all of that, Claire?"

He thought she was going to shrug. Just simply toss the question aside as undeserving of an answer. But she dropped instead. She simply dropped in her tracks, collapsing in a bundle of limp and lifeless nothing to the floor at his feet. "I don't know." Staring up at the looming and terrible shape above them, she seemed more like the three-year-old now than the adult. "It really is a disaster looking for a place to happen, isn't it?"

"Well." Eli managed to summon a small chuckle. A very careful one. "Like you said. We can clean it up. I guess."

"Eli?" She sat up, but her shoulders still sagged. Really, visibly sagged in a way that got to him like nothing else she could do. "What are we going to do?"

"About the Indian?" It was hard not to smile, but Eli knew he had to try. Knew he had to succeed. He knew they'd reached a big turning point here. A crucial instant. He knew it would be all too painfully easy to screw it up royally. And for good this time, even if he was pretty sure it hadn't been screwed up all that badly as of yet.

The time just wasn't right...was in so many ways terribly, horrifically *wrong*...for anything even resembling amusement. Of any kind.

Claire made a gesture. A half-gesture that ended almost before it started. And she wasn't looking at him again, which wasn't good. Couldn't be good. "About all of it," she said in a voice that mirrored almost exactly the defeat he saw in the droop of her shoulders.

Defeat?

Claire?

That made him shiver as even thoughts of the Indian, thoughts of meeting it head-on some night when the sky was dark and the house was silent had never made him shiver.

He shivered almost uncontrollably because Claire was a survivor. The two words...'Claire' and 'defeat'...didn't belong in the same sentence. Not in any sentence he had ever heard.

"Look at me, Claire."

She didn't move. Not immediately, not until he started to speak again.

"Talk to me." He couldn't keep the wistfulness out of his tone. Didn't want to keep it out, didn't even try.

"I..." Claire spread her hands wide. "What is there to say? I know something's wrong with us. Between us. I just don't know what it is. And if I don't know what it is, how can I have a clue how to go about fixing it?"

"Sweetheart, it's not..."

"I've known something's wrong for the longest time now. Since before the twins were born, I think."

"Even if that was true...and I'm not saying it *is* true. I'm just saying if it was true...how could you ever think that run-over piece of junk in the corner would do the trick?"

Tears shone bright and hot in her eyes. She blinked rapidly, repeatedly, trying to force them back. But all that effort was wasted. Because the great and glittering drops pooled at the corners of her eyes anyway. Though Eli had to give her credit when she managed to control them enough that they didn't actually fall.

Or maybe that broke his heart. Because if she couldn't cry, didn't feel safe enough or trust him enough to cry in front of him, the man who loved her enough to do anything or brave anything for her, then what did life matter? What did *anything* matter?

We need to talk.

We need it badly.

He'd resisted the truth of that for a long time. Probably too long, in the chaos of terror the mere idea of losing her stirred in him. Definitely too long in his pig-headed stubbornness that said if he just refused to face the fact, then it wouldn't *be* a fact. If he just didn't acknowledge something might happen, then it never would.

They needed to talk the way she'd tried a hundred times already to talk to him. And now that he was ready, it was starting to look like he was just a little too late.

"I don't know anymore what's going to work." In Claire's eyes tears still glistened bright. Tears that still didn't fall. As if…

Shit.

Forget not trusting him enough to cry in front of him. It was like she didn't *care* enough to let him see her cry. And that hurt like hell. That hurt more like hell than anything…*anything*…Eli'd had to endure in his life.

"Shit, Claire." He started to speak his thoughts before he took time to think about it. And then it was too late. Almost. Then she was looking at him with those tear-bright eyes, looking at him expectantly as if she hung on his every word. On every one he might say and on the impact the sum total of them might have on her life…both of their lives.

And he couldn't do it.

"I just meant I know we have to do something about the Indian," he said as slowly and cautiously as he'd ever in his life said anything. "I just don't know what. That's all."

"We could look for the s…secret." Now that it was all over, now that the danger had passed, for the moment anyway, it looked like she was finally going to lose it. Sniffling a little, her shoulders taking on a first, warning tremor that a no-holds-barred deluge might be just about to follow, she turned away from him. Turned back to the Indian and fixed her concentration on it the way their daughter's had been fixed a minute or two…surely no more…before.

"It was like Stephie *saw* something," she said over that same small and practically inaudible catch in her voice.

"Maybe we should let her search for the secret then." Eli thought it would be safe to joke this time. Safe to joke about this anyway.

Claire cast a look back over her shoulder. "No way. Did you *see* her after she'd barely touched it?"

"Oh, so it's okay for me...us...to get filthy dirty, but not for the kids? When it's the kids' job to get dirty?" He was laughing openly now, and Claire wasn't doing anything, wasn't saying anything, to try to stop it. She just looked at him. Harder. As if she weighed his words as thoroughly as she'd seemed to hang on them before.

"I think we should clean the thing up before we do anything," she replied after a while. "But I do think we ought to look for whatever's hidden inside."

"I've told you, Claire..."

"I know. You've been over the statue and over it. You've spent hours on it. And there's nothing."

"That's right."

She paused then. For effect, Eli thought. And the result of it, when she tilted her head back a little like she meant to stand there and *stare* the secret out of the Indian's blasted hide, was just bone-chilling. Was just...

"If what you say is true," she murmured. "If you've done as thorough a search as anyone is ever likely to do..."

"You know I have. I said I have."

What the devil is she getting at?

What the devil has turned her so serious? As if this is something that actually matters in the long run?

"I wish I knew what you're thinking." He said it. But his words came out all small and shriveled. Like hearing what she was thinking, knowing what she was thinking, was really the very last thing he wanted.

"I know you've been all over it," she said more slowly and thoughtfully than ever. "But I just keep asking myself...if there's nothing there, then what did Stephie *see*?"

Chapter Twelve

WHY DON'T YOU ASK STEPHIE?

Eli didn't say it. He didn't say a thing. But Claire knew, as surely as anyone had ever known anything, that he wanted to say it. She knew just as surely that he held back from saying it.

There was only one thing she *didn't* know.

Why.

"Don't you want to know if there's a secret?" she asked, turning to face him, turning to look at him closely so he wouldn't stand a chance of putting anything slick and underhanded past her. The way she felt more and more certain he'd put all kinds of slick and underhanded things past her in the recent past.

"I..." Eli took his time about answering.

His eyes, seeing only the Indian and not her at all, looked distant and hazy. Unfocused, even at a distance of several feet. An inconsequential distance that should make such a slight haziness all but undetectable.

Seeing his frustration, seeing it reflected so clearly, so unmistakably in his eyes and every line of an expression that made him look suddenly old and very, very tired...even more tired than he'd looked when she'd first met him and he'd still been working through the bitterness of finding himself disabled and weakened after a lifetime of physical strength and activity...Claire felt helpless.

That was the only way she could describe it.

Just...helpless.

"What do you want?" she asked after a few seconds, the way she should have asked in the very beginning. Should have asked before she lost her head and took all kinds of crazy action she'd only thought would be enough to solve anything. "What would make you happy, Eli?"

He drew in breath to answer. Drew in an audible, rasping and slightly moaning breath.

"What would it take right *now*?"

His breathy moan ended with an even more breathy sigh that carried in its depths all the frustration she'd only seen before. "I don't know what kind of secret that thing could have that could make any difference now," he replied quietly. Very solemnly. "I don't know how it could change anything, or..."

"Well, of course nothing is going to really *change* anything."

Hearing herself say that, Claire felt sadder than ever. Sadder than, surely, was humanly possible.

Is that what I expect?

Some kind of wondrous magic fix for the past and all its hurts? The past and all its heartaches? The past and all its mistakes?

She'd thought she knew him better than that.

She'd thought he was more down to earth, more grounded in reality and fact than that.

"Nothing can change the past," she went on a little stubbornly when he said nothing. "We both know that. As well as we know anything. But what if it was possible to understand the past? What if it was possible to understand things in a way that gave them enough clarity that you could put them to rest and learn to live with them?"

Now he looked amused. "And you think one goddamned...I'm sorry if that hurts you, Claire, but it is a thing damned by God into all eternity...Indian is going to do that? You think one goddamned charred, beaten to death and dragged through hell chunk of wood is going to..."

"Your grandfather *said* it had a secret."

"And I've told you. And told you. Granddad wanted to keep me out of his hair. Wanted to keep me from bothering his customers with my infernal questions, and wanted to stop me from trying to play baseball inside his store. It was an economic move. So I wouldn't shatter everything in sight and drive away all his business. It wasn't..."

"Did you ever know your grandfather to lie?"

That stopped him in mid-protest. As well it should.

Claire had never known the old man. But from what she'd heard, everything she'd heard of Eli's sometimes laughing and sometimes despairing reminiscences, old Barron Eden had been one heck of an upstanding guy. Church-going. Honest to a fault. The kind of old-time gentleman businessman who wouldn't lie about anything. Not even to a hyperactive, sometimes troublesome grandson with more energy and baseballs than one aging shopkeeper could ever hope to cope with.

But Eli wasn't thinking about Barron when he fell silent.

Claire didn't *think* he was thinking about Barron.

Something about Eli's eyes, or maybe about the way he held his shoulders suddenly, the tiniest bit scrunched up into a defensive and combative posture, told her he was thinking about somebody else. About his own father and the way his father had been, from everything Claire had ever heard him say, exactly the opposite of Barron. About how his father had had the rare and infallible ability to damage, very often irreparably, everything he touched.

Surely Eli was thinking again about how his father had damaged him. About his putting on airs by staging those massive, counterfeit foxhunts at what he'd decided in his own mind, in contrast with anything that was real or believable, was his 'estate' in the Alleghenies. About his insistence that Eli learn to ride and learn to ride well even though Eli had no interest in horses or riding. Even though his talents lay elsewhere. And she knew Eli was thinking about those under-appreciated talents, too. About the way his own father had steadfastly refused to approve of Eli's unique ability on the baseball field, or acknowledge it had any kind of worth that would be of interest to anybody. About the old man's mule-headed insistence that Eli had to take more chances than anyone, that he always come out the unquestioned winner in everything the old man chose for him to do.

Eli had had to excel at whatever his father chose for him to do. Always.

And as a dark cloud moved through his eyes and across his face, darkening his gaze from the rich warm brown she loved with all her heart to something all but midnight-black and just as barren as a cold and forgotten midnight, Claire knew for certain he was thinking about the day he hadn't excelled. The day he'd taken one chance too many at his father's insistence, on a horse he hadn't known and hadn't ridden before. The day he'd been thrown head over heels in the middle of one of those ridiculous fox hunts and woke in the hospital with his spine cracked and marginal use of his legs. With marginal hopes he'd ever regain the full use of them again.

He was thinking about his baseball career.

That was where thoughts of his father and what his father had done always led. Right back to that one short and glorious season when he'd been hailed from all sides except the one that really mattered as the savior of the game and its brightest hope for the future.

He was thinking hard. Claire could see him thinking hard. She could see the pain in his expression, and it was unbearable to witness.

"I'm sorry." She took a step toward him, then stopped.

She didn't know how to handle that kind of pain. She never had, and guessed she probably never would.

She didn't know what to do next. And Eli seemed to realize it.

"You don't have anything to be sorry for," he said, and as the words came out his expression brightened. Not much, not without an effort she could see as clearly as she'd been able to see his thought processes played out across his face. An effort she could *feel*, too, emanating from every pore of him.

But his expression did brighten.

Enough to make her halfway believe what he said. Enough to let her off the hook, if only just a little.

"All you did," he said after a long pause to let the first of what he'd said sink in and take root, "was give me a gift." A ghost of a smile played across his taut and strained face, lightening the look of it marginally more. "All you did was try to do something you thought would mean something to me."

"But it doesn't."

It wasn't a question.

It didn't have to be.

Claire didn't even try to make it sound like one.

"That Indian's a part of the past," Eli replied, sinking back a little into the thoughtfulness he'd only barely begun to shed. "A past that doesn't matter anyway. Because it never mattered."

"I don't think that's true." Despite the overwhelming sadness that still echoed in the faraway timbre of his voice and shimmered faintly in the equally faraway look of a gaze he'd set upon nothing in particular, Claire's heart lifted. Despite everything that told her she was being foolish and premature in allowing it, her heart leaped and actually seemed to take flight.

Are we going to talk now?

Was this the opening for which she'd sought for almost as long as she could remember? The one that would bring things out into the open where they should be? The one that would expose everything…all their problems, all their differences, all their hesitations and holdings back…to the light of a day that…

Here she cast a glance at the tall windows on the other side of the room. Almost a furtive one, as if there was something about looking at them that she should feel ashamed of.

Not a day that would illuminate them, certainly.

Though a version of sunlight had been attempting all morning to peer through low-hanging layers of mist-gray clouds, it wasn't strong sunlight. Wasn't brilliant enough or penetrating enough to reach even through the windows, much less into the darker and more hidden recesses of all the things she and Eli had to talk about.

It was watery sunlight. Good for shedding a little light, and not much else.

Claire sighed.

Still, we are about to talk.

Still, that had to be good. She *prayed* for it to be good.

Eli was looking at the Indian again. Looking at it as hard and not from all that different an angle than Stephie had looked at it. He'd seemed to scrunch down a little, sitting lower in his chair. And he'd moved forward. Moved right up next to the front of it.

"What?" she asked.

"You were right about one thing." Now that he had something else to focus on, something else to think about, there seemed no time for the incipient discussion of just a second ago. "It did seem like Stephie was looking at something. But I'm damned if I..."

Claire hunkered down next to him. Squatting first, she quickly dropped to her knees and tried to lower herself to the approximate level of Stephie's gaze. "If anyone saw us like this," she said softly, never actually meaning to finish the sentence because some sentences just didn't need to be finished.

"They'd think we'd lost our minds," Eli finished for her. "I know. The thing is..."

"I don't see anything."

"Me either." His laughter was short. More like a bark than a laugh, and not very amused. "Nothing except a piece of junk."

She turned her head. Looked at him.

"Sorry, Claire. I know you were doing your damnedest to...but you have to admit, this thing's not worth anything. Not anymore. Not if it ever was."

She sat all the way down. Sat on her heels and then slid sideways onto the polished marble floor that felt cool on a sultry-humid morning. Sat, and still kept looking up at the towering monolith that more and more was beginning to look like evidence of the greatest hoax of Eli's life. "So what are we going to do with it?"

"I don't suppose that truck driver would come back and take it away?"

She shook her head. "Probably not even if we paid him."

"Well, then, we'll just have to find somebody else to do it."

"If that's what you really want." Sitting there, afraid to look at him and afraid to look at the Indian, Claire felt the last of her hope crumble. She felt it fail completely and disintegrate into a cloud of dust that could never be repaired, never be put back into even a semblance of what it had been before.

So this is it.

This was the end.

Of everything.

She'd tried her best. She'd done whatever she could think to do, done whatever she'd thought had to be done. It wasn't much, that was true. Wasn't anything. But it still *was* her best.

And where had it gotten her? What had it amounted to?

She sighed, and Eli's hand touched her shoulder. Lightly, at first. Tentatively, as if he thought she'd reject him completely when nothing could have been farther from the truth. When the truth, if she ever managed to gather together enough courage to admit it in so many words, was that he'd rejected her. He'd been the one to pull away first, for some still unknown reason. He'd been the one to pull into himself and refuse to share the most important parts of his thoughts just when it had seemed they might forge a real connection. Just when it had seemed they were about to make it together, about to make something real and lasting out of the future.

His fingertips brushed her shoulder. They hovered there for an instant, then moved down a little to the bare and exposed cap of her arm beneath her sleeveless summer shirt. "I think…" he said.

"You think what?" The gesture of affection, if that was what it truly was, seemed too little. And much, much too late.

But he didn't give up on it. "I think we should wait," he said after a little while, his fingers continuing to caress her shoulder and upper arm, continuing to draw little electric trails across skin and underlying flesh that even after all the disappointment and all the acknowledgment of impending loss as black as any loss could ever be, tingled wherever he touched. Flesh that still came alive at his touch as if it didn't know or maybe just hadn't yet admitted the truths she'd only recently begun to accept as immutable fact.

"You do?" Finally she managed to look at him. And felt an odd leaping inside, a leaping almost as though this was the first time she'd ever looked at him. The first time she'd ever really seen him.

"I do." He smiled. A little. Not quite comfortably and not quite with all the self-assurance he usually wore in his expression.

"Okay." She didn't want to let herself trust that smile. Didn't want to let herself believe what she saw in his eyes…a glimmer of a shine replacing the earlier sadness and faraway regretfulness. A sparkling shine that said maybe all wasn't lost after all. Maybe her hope had died prematurely and maybe, just maybe, it could still be revived. Maybe she should do something more about reviving it and resuscitating it before it really did get to be too late. "I have to ask." She tried hard not to let any burgeoning ray of eagerness come through in her voice. "Why?"

"Because..." Tilting his head back again, pulling down lower into his chair in the same experimental and peering-up way he had before, Eli all but glared the Indian. "What if Stephie did see something?"

"Something we didn't see. Don't see."

He nodded.

"Do you really think that's possible?"

He hesitated. Cocked his head to the side and seemed to think a while before nodding again.

"So what are we going to do about it?" Which seemed to be the one question they always came around to in the end.

What are we going to do?

No matter where else their conversations or their thoughts led.

"I'm not sure. I just...I guess you've got me to thinking again."

Well, okay.

So they weren't talking about the things she'd hoped to talk about. The things they needed to talk about.

At least they *were* talking. And that was a start. *Isn't it?*

"Are you going to tell me what you're thinking, Eli?" Twisting around, she looked up at him. A state of affairs she knew he enjoyed because usually...almost always...it was the other way around. Almost always he who had to look up at her.

"What if there really is a secret to that blasted old monstrosity?"

She couldn't believe it. Her ears rang...actually *rang*...at the impossibility of what she'd just heard. "So now you think there *is* a secret?"

She wondered when the day had grown so hot. When it had grown so oppressive, with humid iron-colored clouds seeming to press down too close to her. As if they wanted to press her all the way into the earth. As if they wanted to press every bit of life from her.

She wondered when she'd begun to sweat so terribly. Like she'd just been caught up and nearly drowned in the greatest and most desolate anxiety of her life.

She wondered when the day, never all that auspicious or promising even at its best, had turned so suddenly ominous.

"You just put it all in a new light, that's all." Eli said it easily. Almost naturally. But there was a hint in what he said, or maybe in the way he said it, that he'd felt the malevolence too. That he was aware of it and responding to it with the same instinctive drawing-back and drawing-in that made her shoulders tighten. That made her stomach tighten, and her jaw. That made her want to shiver even though shivering was now totally impossible with her body locked so tight and herself sealed so deep within herself. "And you got me to thinking. What if there really is something to it? What if there really is something to all this secret mumbo-jumbo, and what if I'm on the brink of throwing away my very last chance to find it?"

Chapter Thirteen

ALONE FOR THE TIME BEING IN THE SUMMERHOUSE HE'D HAD BUILT FOR CLAIRE'S amusement and enjoyment, Eli eyed the sky with a worried eye.

It had been threatening to rain all day. The air had been thick with gathered humidity...the kind of airborne moisture only the east coast could produce. Thick and suffocating moisture that made skin turn to water at the slightest touch of other skin. Moisture so heavy it seemed actually to impede movement, dragging at limbs and body as if a person was caught up in a life or death struggle to swim through a vat of clinging glue.

Pennsylvania, even the cool and mountainous regions, had a way of being insufferable on summer days like this. But there were times...like now...when insufferable, sticky-hot was preferable to the alternative.

The air had turned cooler in the last half hour. A front had driven waves of cooler air down from the higher mountaintops all around.

Normally Eli would have welcomed it. Normally he would have breathed easier, considering it and the incipient rain it carried with it a blessing. But not now.

God in a sweet and bountiful heaven, not *now*!

Not when he'd finally managed to entice Claire away from the house. Not when he'd finally, after more than a few false starts and several hours of staring at that goddamned Indian and dithering in his mind over what the hell she expected him to do next, worked up the courage to lay down the law to her for one of the few times in their married life. Not when he'd told her in a way she couldn't ignore and couldn't shrug off that he had to talk to her. That she had to talk to him, and they had to do it before even another day passed.

She'd been skittish.

He'd seen it in her eyes.

But she'd agreed to come. She'd agreed when he'd changed his tactic and hinted it might become an assignation with very little effort from either of them. When he'd suggested he meet her here, in this most special of places he'd had built for them. As a place where they could escape when they needed. A place where they could be alone together, away from telephones and twins and all the rest of life's pressures. A place where they'd be free to have honest to goodness and for real assignations if that was what they chose to have.

The pavilion…in reality a large, glass-enclosed summerhouse offering all the shelter they could ever want from all but the most severe elements…sat deep in the woods. It sat at the end of a long and gently sculpted paved path that swept up the flank of the mountain at an angle that posed no difficulty for a man maneuvering alone in a wheelchair. It sat in the very most secluded part of Eli's heavily-secured estate where they could be…had very often and not so long ago been…certain of absolute privacy.

This was *their* place.

Lost in a carefully-hewn clearing filled with a just as carefully orchestrated chaos of the trailing and climbing heaven-scented roses Claire loved.

Once she'd loved to come here.

Once there would have been no need for pleas, no need for desperate arguments and convincing. There would have been no cautious-eyed hesitation on her part when he asked her to meet him here in the middle of the day.

Once.

Glancing around, Eli took in streaked windows, accumulated dust beneath wide benches that circled the space, the slight but noticeable fading and fraying of several of the deep cushions atop those benches.

This looked like a place where no one came any longer.

And how the hell long *had* it been?

How long since he and Claire had really used the summerhouse? For its intended, its openly stated and freely accepted purpose?

Too long, he answered himself, and felt another sinking inside his heart as he again remembered the wariness in Claire's eyes.

She still hadn't come.

And now it was raining. Or promising to rain very soon.

The air, laden with its heavy silver mist throughout the morning and early afternoon, had begun almost imperceptibly to condense into fine droplets that weren't quite ready to fall. Droplets that nonetheless *felt* like rain when he rolled to the glass-paned door he'd left open in anticipation of her arrival and lifted his face toward the outside.

In that precise instant he saw motion. Over among the forest's deepest rainy-day shadows, just beyond the edge of the clearing.

A soft and floating swirl of rose-mist billowed, and pale flesh gleamed in shades of polished rose quartz and alabaster. And Claire emerged from the darkest part of the pathway through the woods, her face gleaming like brightest sunlight in the midst of the silver-gray day. As dearly welcome as that sunlight, and every bit as necessary for the maintenance of his life.

Sighing a little, Eli retreated so she'd have an unobstructed path through the door. A clear chance at escape from rain that really did turn to rain the instant she dart-floated across the clearing between massed boughs of mist-laden, drooping roses.

She was a rose herself.

In her palest of pink dresses that drifted with every movement and floated like a fragrant fall of petals, she was the loveliest rose by far, laughing as she flew the last few feet to the summerhouse in a way that both lightened his heart and simultaneously, inexplicably, shattered it to bits of sad nothing.

She came.

Just as he'd dreamed she would, Claire had come. Laughing her way between droplets that began to pelt the depths of the rose garden. Laughing and shaking her lovely dark hair back from her face with a lithe and graceful sway of shoulders and head as she swept and swirled in from the outside world.

"It's going to rain!" she cried. Needlessly, since the threat of it had been clear from the very start. And even more needlessly now, since the mist had finally finished its condensation. Since the scattered diamond droplets of a second or two before had been eradicated. Swept out of existence by truly enormous drops that already hurled themselves to oblivion against the glass panes of the summerhouse.

Eli reached past her to swing the door…glass-paned like all the rest of the summerhouse…shut behind her. "You think?"

His only answer was a crashing of thunder directly overhead. And a thicker pelting of drops heavy enough, surely, to do real damage should they actually strike a person. Rain that almost immediately removed the very last traces of silvery light from the day.

Still laughing, running her hands through tossed waves of dark hair glistening with and spangled by diamond-droplets, she flung herself onto the pale cushions of the bench seat nearest him.

"So." Now that he'd convinced her to come…now that she had, looking like a man's loveliest dream in a fluttering drift of a dress that looked like she'd just spent her entire day getting ready for the most long-anticipated party of her life...Eli didn't quite remember what he'd wanted to do. What he'd wanted to say.

"It's beautiful here." Looking around, Claire tossed her hair again. As if she'd never before seen the place. As if she'd never spent a single delightfully entertaining and satisfying hour or minute here. With him. "We should come here more often, Eli."

We used to.

He didn't think he could say it. Didn't think he could trust himself to say it without running the risk of dissolving into tears when his heart heard all the loss and loneliness that once small sentence would imply.

He felt nervous. When he reached for Claire's hand he felt like he'd never seen *her* before. He felt like some kind of wild eyed, hormone driven kid who didn't have a clue about anything. "Since when do you float around the woods like a demented housewife in an old-time furniture polish commercial?" he asked when nothing else, nothing remotely intelligent or sensible, came to mind.

Damn. That didn't come out right.

It hadn't come out right at *all.*

Claire looked at him with blank eyes. Making him feel more stupid...more criminally and unforgivably stupid...than ever.

"You know." His tone said he knew all too well how lame his joke had been. "The dress," he finished awkwardly, with a feeble motion.

"Oh." Claire looked down at herself. "Didn't I tell you? I felt sure I told you."

"Tell me what?" Eli didn't want to get his hopes up over what was probably nothing. But a man couldn't help but hope. Could he?

"Mindy Stevens' bridal shower is this evening. At the country club."

"Right." Even though he'd known it was coming and halfway resigned himself to its coming, Eli had to fight a wave of disappointment so strong, so soul-consuming it nearly toppled him to the floor. Nearly finished him off for once and for all, a victim of his own hopeless and hapless hopefulness.

Here he'd been thinking she'd dressed up for him. The way she used to dress up. He'd been thinking she'd gone to such an incredible amount of trouble to make herself look beautiful when he'd asked her to make a trek through the deepest, darkest woods in Pennsylvania. *Because* he'd asked her to make the trek.

"You didn't ask me to hike all the way up here on the muggiest afternoon of the summer just to talk about furniture polish and cocktail dresses?" Claire was smiling.

And he wished like hell he could reciprocate. Only his face felt frozen...permanently, idiotically frozen...in some kind of half-grimace, half-blank stare that would do nothing, he knew in his heart of hearts, to help the situation. "Is that what you call it?"

"Furniture polish?" She started to shake her head.

"A cocktail dress."

Leaning forward, the skirt of the dress a fluffy, foaming dream of pale rose atop sun-faded yellow...softest color of living, rain-washed roses intermingled with golden highlights of the most perfect sunlit roses of a cloudless summer afternoon...Claire did what he couldn't seem to bring himself to do. She took his hand. Slipping her fingers first beneath it and then around it, she lifted it away from his knee and clasped it between hers. Surrounding and surprising it with an even greater tide of shimmering, simmering warmth, leaning close to him to look straight, deep into his eyes.

And that was one more thing he hadn't been able to make himself do.

Look straight at her.

Straight *into* her.

"You didn't ask me to come up all the way up here to talk about my new dress." Her eyes took on the unexpected sparkle of her laughter.

Suddenly Eli relaxed. Very suddenly he felt sure of himself and sure of what he had to do. In all kinds of ways he hadn't felt really sure of anything in years and years and years. Since long before he'd met her or even suspected women like her could exist in a world that all too often seemed harsh and unforgiving.

"No," he said, lingering over the word like it was his very last chance to avoid facing the truth. Which was utterly preposterous, because he'd faced that truth a long time ago even if he hadn't wanted to admit it to Claire or, more importantly, to his own deluded, deranged, denying self. "It's like I said when I asked you here. We need to talk."

A look of resignation flashed across her face. It was there for a second. A second and a half. No more. But Eli saw it quite clearly before it vanished, washed away by a more subtle look that spoke of some lingering amount of surprise along with a new and steel-willed kind of determination that said he wasn't going to get out of anything now. Not since he'd said those words.

"You've been wanting to talk for a long time..."

Her hands tightened around his. "How do you figure that, Eli?"

"How could I not figure it out?" It took all his strength to not back away from her. Every last ounce and iota of it to not jerk his gaze away from hers and fasten it on the floor, the rain-blurred window beyond her tantalizingly bare and opalescent shoulder, on anything that wouldn't hurt him more than he'd already hurt himself by ignoring her for too long. "How many times have you told me you wanted to talk…needed to talk? And even if you hadn't…I know you, Claire. I know you think I don't, but I do. Know you."

"Whatever gave you a silly idea like that?" Her hands tightened again. Tightened more, around both of his now. Commanding him to look up at her. Her hands tightened in a way that warned she might smash his fingers to a bloody pulp if he didn't look, and soon.

"I just…"

Silence fell.

Brooding silence, futile silence. Silence broken only by the steady drumbeat of raindrops upon the summerhouse's tiled roof and the drizzle of water from its gutters. Silence made up of so many kinds of wanting and needing and desperate wishing that Eli couldn't even name most of them. Couldn't think how to describe most of them in terms anybody would ever be able to understand. Least of all himself.

"What went wrong with us?"

He'd looked up at some point. Looked into her eyes. He didn't remember doing it, but their gazes had already locked together. Already fastened to each other in a way that was weirdly reminiscent of their first few months together, those mid-winter months just after their first Christmas, when they'd been unable to tear themselves away from each other. When he'd realized that for better or worse and whether or not it was the smartest or safest thing he'd done in what was left of his life after his old man had finished with it, he'd fallen so far in love there would be no backing out. No escaping in any direction, not with any amount of trying.

No desire to escape.

It was almost the same now. But it was different too.

Different because in Claire's eyes he saw naked loneliness. Haunted longing that said she missed whatever they'd had together back in those beginning days…the closeness of spirit and thought and laughter as well as of body.

That was a lot to digest. For a man in his situation, a man who'd done everything he could except wall himself away in a concrete tower with no exit, it was almost too much to digest.

That she loved him that much.

That she loved him enough to miss him. That she *still* loved him that much and that way, even after…

All of it.

"Nothing went wrong with us." Eli managed to look away then. He managed to take up his study of rain washing across streaked glass again as if he'd never left it.

"Something had to go wrong." She dropped his hands. Let go of them, released them from the infinitely soothing warmth he hadn't realized he'd been depending upon to see him through until it vanished. Getting to her feet, she strolled to the far side of the summerhouse.

He turned his wheelchair, fumbling a little, awkwardly, the way he never fumbled any more, to make it go where he wanted. To make it face where he wanted. Toward her, so he could watch her cross the dusty floor to the door opposite the one she'd used for her laughing, swirling entry. The door he'd already discovered had swollen and jammed, sagging on uncared-for hinges so that it could open no more than a crack. And even that could be accomplished only with the greatest difficulty.

"I'll have to get someone to fix that door," he said quietly when she stopped in front of it, close to it, close enough to lean her forehead against the unkempt glass and stare out at rain-blackened woodland beyond.

"Something went wrong," she said again, as if she didn't hear. Or if she did, as if his words didn't register. "Somewhere along the way. I know it did. Only I never…" Her voice broke on the 'never'. It split right in two, right down the middle, and she stopped for a minute, her head tilted slightly to listen to the gush of rain as the storm refreshed itself and renewed itself. "I never knew how," she said after a while, her voice again in complete, almost icy control. "I never knew what I did to make you leave me, Eli."

"I never left. How can you even insinuate…"

"With your heart, you did." When she faced him again, her hands doing that twisting and anxious thing he only now realized had become a constant, maybe even a permanent part of her body language, her expression was wide and open. Filled with fear. With anguish. With angry hurt and suffering futility. "You left me somewhere along the way. Don't try to tell me you didn't. You left me when you stopped sharing yourself with me."

I did that.

One thing his granddad…his old man, too, in the old man's kind of sideways and haphazard approach to such things…had taught him was to be honest. With others. With himself.

Eli had let honesty slip by the wayside a little down through the years since his life had tried to go straight down the tubes. There had been moments, of course. Moments like the one when he'd married Claire and promised her the world on a silver platter. Like the one when the twins were born and he'd sat next to the bed bedazzled with wonderment looking into Claire's strained and tired, proud face. By and large though, he'd let the basic honesty of his early years slip. And never more than when he'd been dealing with his life in the last couple of years.

"It's..." Folding his hands, squeezing them together then releasing them so he could lift one to wipe a film of sweat from his brow, Eli bit his lip. "I didn't mean to. I swear. I never meant to make you feel that way."

"Fine." She swung around then, a rose-petal flutter of softly fragrant skirts against a dim and dingy, neglected gray background. Spun around and faced him head on. "I can accept that. I can deal with that. You didn't mean it, and I don't believe I ever thought you did. Not in my heart of hearts, I didn't. So the only question is...what now?"

"What now?" Eli knew he sounded obtuse. Hell, he *felt* obtuse. But he'd been thinking so much, feeling so much, suffering so much in the minutes since she'd floated like a dream back into his life that he was having a hard time accepting it all. An impossible time trying to consider it all.

She nodded. Took a step toward him, tall and lithe in her rose-dress, the most beautiful vision he'd ever seen in the misty rain-light, and then stopped. "What are we going to do now?" she asked again, so quietly he almost couldn't hear the rise and fall of her words above a fresh round of thunder and a heightened pounding of rain on the roof so close overhead. "What are we going to do to fix this, Eli? How are we going to make absolutely sure it never happens again?"

Chapter Fourteen

"WHAT HAPPENED?" THE INSTANT THE WORDS LEFT HER LIPS, CLAIRE FELT THE worst kind of sinking inside. Like she might for the rest of her life regret ever saying them.

Already Eli looked thoughtful...already he looked like he was searching his mind, trying to put together an answer. Maybe not a straightforward one, but an answer all the same.

She'd pushed him into it. And now she was going to have to live with the results. Unless...

"It doesn't matter." She said it with a total lack of conviction that was as transparent as the curtains of rain falling beyond the windows.

"It does matter." Somehow he'd moved in close to her. Silently, the way he could move so easily in his wheelchair. Now it was his turn to take hold of her hand, and he did. Reaching out, he enfolded it in the warmth and security of his. The warmth and security she'd lacked so long that she no longer completely remembered a time when she *hadn't* felt shut out and denied. "You were right all along," he said softly, after a moment's pause to let the promise of that new and burgeoning warmth sink in. "You were right about everything. And I was an idiot. I was a fool."

"Oh, Eli. I don't think..."

"You were right when you said we needed to talk. You were so right, and I think I knew it all along. Only I was too stupid or too stubborn to listen. Or too both."

"So that's why you wanted me to come up here?" Moving very carefully, so she wouldn't shatter the contact he'd made between them, Claire sank onto the end of the curved bench next to the door.

She wanted to cry. Just, literally, fall to the floor and wail out her anguish.

Somehow she'd had an idea he was summoning her here to romance her. Somewhere she'd gotten the notion that it would be romance that saved them, romance and the kind of wondrous connection romance could give them that would eventually lead to a permanent reunion.

She'd been counting on it when she'd slipped into the lovely new dress, only half-intending to appear at Mindy Stevens' bridal shower later.

She didn't like Mindy Stevens and had never intended to go. But when Eli had made his proposal, his quietly-worded request that she'd taken as an invitation to the kind of sexual encounter she craved from him, the shower had become a very convenient excuse. A reason for appearing before him dressed like this, a reason in case he hadn't been serious.

As it now appeared he hadn't.

"Don't look so disappointed." Taking his hand back, Eli clasped it tight inside his other one, watching her with something that might have been amusement. Or despair.

Sometimes she couldn't quite tell the difference.

Sometimes like now.

"Most women would turn back flips if they heard a man tell them they were so unequivocally right," Eli said in a wry tone. "Most women would mark the day a man admitted he'd been a complete and stupid jackass."

"I'm not most women."

Something sparked in his eyes. Something that set hope to flaring in her heart again. Something that much more practically and altogether more positively set it to flaring in the patch of aching, yearning flesh between her thighs as well.

"I realized that a long time ago, Claire."

"So we're really going to just talk?"

Even though it was what she'd wanted...what she'd *thought* she wanted and what she'd so often begged for and prayed for and hoped for, the disappointment of the realization now, in this setting and at this moment, was bitter. Terribly, vilely bitter.

"About what's gone wrong with us?" he asked.

Hesitant now that they'd drawn perilously close to the one subject that could drive them apart forever just as quickly and easily as it could bring them together and unite them, Claire nodded. "That's what we need to do, isn't it?"

I'm afraid.

Of what might come next.

She was almost deathly afraid of what Eli...her dearly beloved and cherished Eli, the only real light she'd ever had in her life...was going to say. Deathly afraid he'd say everything she didn't want to hear. Everything she halfway expected to hear. Terrified she'd be left alone again the way she'd been alone before she'd met him...alone and unable to pay her bills. Alone and watching her mother's frail health accelerate on its long and terrible slide toward death because there was no way to pay for even the most basic medical care.

Alone.

Afraid.

A chill ran through her and, without meaning to, she shivered.

Eli saw and his answering smile was bleak. About as wintry as she'd feared. "You want an honest-to-God honest answer to that, Claire? To the age-old question of what the hell went wrong, and why?"

"Yes."

No!

Resolutely she shoved the small but screaming voice of protest right out of her mind. "I'd appreciate it, Eli. I think I deserve a little honesty after...after all this time."

"The absolute honest truth, then. I don't know."

Claire felt her shoulders slump. And no matter that she tried to hold them straight and firm, no matter that she tried her damnedest to keep from humiliating herself by appearing vulnerable. "I thought it was me," she almost whispered. "All this time I was so sure I'd done something or said something. Or maybe there was something I *didn't* do or say that drove you away from me and made it so impossible to...to..."

"Nothing drove me away."

"Then, *what*?" Tears threatened, burning like acid in her eyes. She barely managed to hold them back. "What happened?"

Lifting his hands. Eli scrubbed them across his face and dragged them backward through his hair, crumpling it into a million and one softly rain-lit peaks that Claire immediately wanted to touch. That she wanted to crumple for herself exactly as he had. Peaks she wanted to reacquaint herself with. So she'd again have the freedom to explore at will every last deep, dark, crisply-curled depth of it.

She actually had to tuck her hands beneath her legs to stop them from reaching out automatically. From reaching hungrily. Eagerly.

"You didn't do anything. I need you to understand that, Claire. I need you to..."

"Then what *didn't* I..."

"Claire!" Eli's voice rose on a note of aggravated frustration that stopped her cold. Stopped her in shocked silence because she couldn't remember he'd ever spoken to her that way before.

To underlings, yes. Those who failed in their jobs at one of his companies, those who didn't act fairly or honorably, those who aligned themselves with some other, opposing side after he'd paid them handsomely to work on his side.

But not her.

Never, before, her.

"You didn't do anything." He made an obvious effort to gentle his tone. An effort met with only marginal success. "You didn't *not* do anything either. I keep trying to tell you that, keep trying to convince you...so why won't you believe me when I say this isn't about you? It's never been about you. Not for a minute. This has always been about me. This has always been my problem, and I don't for a minute want you to ever think otherwise."

Claire's eyes widened. She felt them widen all the way to the point of horror. "So help me God, Eli Eden. If you're about to tell me there's another woman and that's why you..."

"Name of God!" His astonishment couldn't be fake. Couldn't possibly be anything but exactly what it appeared to be...what it was. The real and genuine astonishment of a man who'd just heard something so amazing he didn't know whether to laugh, cry, or sail into battle with every flag flying and defend himself indignantly against all accusations.

She stayed silent. Feeling a little bit the fool and more confused than ever. Silent, since that was what he seemed to want. What he seemed to expect.

"Sometimes," he mused quietly after a very long time, "I think there's something wrong inside me. Something broken. Something that's been broken, maybe, right from the beginning. Sometimes I think it's something that can't be fixed because nobody's ever known how to fix it. No matter hard how hard they...we try. And then there are other times..."

We.

Claire's mind seized on that one small word. It repeated the word over and over like some sort of magical mantra designed to repel evil and protect from indignity. Her mind *shouted* that word, in a sort of wild and frenzied, shrilling and exulting chorus of catcalls and cheers.

Eli had said 'we'. And that meant this couldn't possibly be the end. That meant they couldn't have run out of hope...couldn't have run out of future.

Not if that word still applied to them. Not as long as he uttered it with his own tongue and lips and throat.

We.

"You're depressed," she guessed, because that was a safe thing to guess.

That was a safe thing to imagine, a safe thing to try to solve.

They'd lived through occasional bouts of depression before. Occasional times when the world and its troubles, the world and the troubles it had inflicted upon him through no fault of his own, got to be too much for one or the other of them and they'd had to hang on tight. Had to keep the faith and know they could come out the other side and would come out because they were both strong. Because they both knew how to survive when the odds were stacked against them.

Particularly when the odds were stacked against them.

Shrugging, shaking his head then nodding immediately in denial of the shaking, Eli chewed on his lip. He lowered his gaze and once again seemed to focus on nothing specific. He just let his gaze drop away from hers and let it come to rest on thin air a few inches above his knees. And Claire knew he wasn't seeing them either. He wasn't seeing anything but a distant and troubled past that still haunted him. A past that would always haunt him a little even on the good days…would always be there in one form or another, to one degree or another. No matter how long he lived or how diligently they might try to work together to cancel it out.

Some things were just facts.

And they couldn't make the past un-happen. No matter how much they might want to. No matter how hard they might try.

"I guess it's been a hell of a long time since I was *not* depressed," he replied after a while, echoing her thoughts so exactly that it startled her and wrung a small gasp from her. And he still stared at nothing.

"I can understand that, Eli. I think."

That spurred him to action. Lifting his gaze, he smiled at her…a faint twitching around the corners of his mouth that left him looking unutterably sad in dim storm light that was already sad enough in its own right. "I think you do. Understand. I think that's one of the reasons I love you enough to die. I think you're one of the few people who haven't been through what I've been through who does understand."

"And you're still depressed."

"It's not like you think."

She leaned toward him. Leaned in. Leaned closer. "Tell me, then. Whatever it is, we can work through it. It's like you said. I do understand. I try to understand. And I know that together we can…"

His smile widened. It grew brighter. Almost bright enough to light up the day and chase away some of its gray. Almost bright enough to appear genuine.

"You think it's going to be that easy, do you? Just say the magic word and Poof! All the problems in the world will just vanish. Like so much smoke in the wind. And things will just turn themselves right around and be all hunky-dory from this day forward."

Frowning, Claire sat up straight. Perched on the very edge of her seat, she pulled away from him, her feet planting themselves flat and firm as if they'd made the decision to storm away in frustration and fury when the rest of her hadn't had quite enough nerve to make that decision. "That sounds like the old Eli," she murmured tonelessly. "That sounds like the Eli I found when I first came here. That first night. In the snow. That sounds like the Eli who didn't care about much of anything. Not about himself and for sure not about anybody else."

"I'm sorry, Claire. I..."

She felt her forehead furrow. Into the next best thing to a scowl. "I didn't much like that old Eli."

He sighed. Started to say something, then stopped. Started and stopped, started and stopped. Several times. "What do you want me to do?" he asked finally, when nothing else seemed to work for him.

"Talk to me," she suggested immediately. "Talk to me all the time, every day. That's why you dragged me all the way up here today. To talk to me. And you've made a damned good start. So don't stop now. Don't keep bottling everything up inside. Don't keep shutting me out, leaving me to guess with no hope of ever knowing for sure what in God's name I did wrong."

"Talk?"

She nodded.

"That won't be easy to do."

She nodded again. "You've had a lot of practice bottling. You're going to have to re-learn how to let it go. If you ever knew to begin with."

He opened his mouth. To protest, she felt sure.

"You want easy?" she cut him off, "then go and find a cliff. And fall off."

The barest ghost of a smile flickered in his expression. "Anything else you think I should do? While you're at it."

"Isn't that enough?"

He shrugged. "Now that we're having it out and now that you've convinced me I need to either do the impossible or take a long, flying leap, I figured I might as well hear it all. Get it all over in one big, ugly shot."

"Impossible?" Claire knew she looked hurt and she felt powerless to hide it. "To talk to me? To share what's hurting you with me? When we promised each other, the day we were married, we'd share everything for the rest of our lives?"

"See?" he asked, leaning forward to press a light touch to the point of her knee when she wouldn't let him capture either of her hands. "I try to tell you what I'm thinking and feeling and you get all hurt by it. All weepy-eyed and wounded."

"I am not weepy-eyed!" Claire knew before she said it that the protest would make her look foolish. Because anyone with half a brain could see that she *was* weepy-eyed. And getting weepier...potentially weepier...all the time.

Eli didn't say anything. He just looked skeptical.

"We're not doing very well anymore," she mourned. "Are we?"

It took him a minute to maneuver closer to the bench seat. And another half a minute to transfer himself with a quick and agile flexing of arms and shoulders to the spot on it next to her. "We're going to be okay," he said gently, slipping one of those same arms around her shoulders.

"It just seems so...I don't know. So hopeless."

"It's not." The sheltering, surrounding arm tightened. "I promised, didn't I? When I married you, and again just a couple of minutes ago. I promised I'd share everything I think and feel with you. That I won't hold anything back. Ever again. No matter what."

Claire tried to look like she really held out hope that that was going to be true. But even so...

"I still think it might be," she said half under her breath. "Hopeless, I mean."

"Claire, why can't we just give it a chance? I mean, now that we've agreed and everything..."

"We could go on like this all day," she mumbled through a smile suddenly as watery and unstable as the shifting day outside. "It is hopeless and it isn't. And what's it going to solve in the long run?"

Tightening his arm again, this time with a quick and abrupt movement that pulled her tight into the sweet duskiness of his shoulder, Eli laughed softly. "We've made a start at an agreement. A good one. That's nothing to sneeze at, you know...the idea that we might just have found the perfect way to start solving everything that could possibly be wrong."

Claire laughed. A little. Her face mashed against his shoulder, her expression hidden from him on purpose, she felt the welcome relief of it bubble up from deep inside her. Straight from the place she'd feared all laughter would be trapped forever.

Eli had always known how to make her laugh. He'd always had a gift for making things seem better even when it looked like things couldn't possibly get worse. They hadn't lost that one little bit of a connection. And if they'd managed to sustain that much, couldn't it be possible, mightn't it be probable…

"Is it a deal?" Cuddling her in earnest now with both arms around her, he held her to him and against him.

Sighing, shuddering out the very last of her weepiness, Claire lifted her arms to his neck. She wrapped them around it and twined her fingers into lusciously thick hair that waved across the back of his collar, around his temples, behind his ears. Twined them just the way she'd dreamed of twining them earlier. So they could enjoy the loveliness of it.

"You have to promise me." Finding the top of her ear, Eli brushed his lips across its rounded outer shell. "I promised you. So now you have to promise me."

"To share?" Her voice shook. Not with laughter.

"That's right. No more holding back when something's bothering you. From now on."

Claire said nothing. Mostly because nothing seemed necessary or even adequate. Not when his sweet-strong nuzzling continued. Not when it progressed quickly, progressed almost without any intervening stages, from the serenity of nuzzling to the silken uproar of his tongue exploring every awakened roundness of her ear, every taut and quivering concavity beneath those roundnesses.

Claire said nothing for a while. Nothing until the strained sound of her own breath rasping through a throat grown nearly too tight and much too constricted to accommodate breath became too explosive to be endured. Too thunderous to be ignored.

"I th…thought…" She murmured it breathlessly.

Laughing, Eli shifted his focus. Shifted his caressing to stroke the tip of his nose against the places his lips had so recently favored. "You thought what?"

"I thought you wanted to get me up here so you could have sex with me." Her voice was no more than a watery echo in rain-soaked air. "Like in the old days."

"Not so old." Drifting, roaming in softly wandering scallops, seeking the hollow of her cheek, the fullness of her jaw, Eli allowed his mouth to leave her ear at last. "Those days."

"I thought you…"

Growling softly, a gently wild rumble of sound that flowed smoothly from his throat, he moved steadily closer. Smoothly closer. Enticingly close to what it became increasingly clear had been his ultimate objective from the start.

"We could make it happen," he advised in the hair's-breadth of a second before his mouth closed with unshakable certainty over hers.

Chapter Fifteen

WHEN HIS LIPS MET HERS, ELI KNEW HE'D HAD A SECONDARY PURPOSE IN BRINGING HER here. And maybe, quite possibly, very probably, it had been his primary purpose all along. With Claire, always with Claire, the enormous attraction he felt for her seemed to come before and above anything else.

She was endlessly fascinating. Eternally and unquestionably the loveliest, smartest, most down to earth and compassionate woman who'd ever existed. On this or any other planet.

All of them were reasons to love her.

All of them were reasons to want to be with her. Here. Now. Anywhere.

All of them were reasons to do anything in the world…anything legal, illegal, or borderline…to make sure she stayed by his side and was happy there. Forever.

He'd crawl through fire for her. Drag himself with his strong shoulders and upper arms into a den of the wildest animals and face them down for her. Allow them to devour his living heart if that would keep her smiling, if that would keep her safe from harm.

Hell, feeling the thrill of her electricity tingle through him and into every part of him, he thought he might even try to jump out of the goddamned wheelchair and run a marathon or two for her. In this instant, charged by the touch of her and energized by the quivering brush of the tip of her tongue across his lips as it sought entry, he actually thought such a thing might physically be possible. It was a for sure certainty that if anyone could ever magically, miraculously return to him the ability to walk on fire or water or just plain old hard and basic dry land, that someone had to be Claire. Could only be Claire.

Of course right now, with her searching tongue at last finding what it had sought…the way in…and with the resulting thunder of her entry reverberating in parts of him that historically refused to be still or resist reverberating, all of that lay far from the center of his thoughts. Right now Eli had only one thing on his mind. And he thought it might be…just possibly could be...the same thing Claire had on hers.

He opened his mouth. Just a little. Just enough to see how she'd react and if his guess had been true. Enough to see if she'd be as inventive and explosive as ever, or if she'd finally, impossible as the notion might seem, run out of electrifying ideas.

Groaning as the tip of her tongue located with infallible accuracy the opening he'd given her, she gave a short, hard and insistent thrust. One that immediately chased any lingering idea of playing games with her, of making her work hard for everything he'd give up to her and making her suffer as much as he already knew she was going to make him suffer, right out of Eli's mind.

At the first sizzling stroke of her tongue against his, he surrendered. Right away. Opening his mouth, drawing in an enormous draught of air that seemed so much sweeter and so very much more lusciously aswim with rain-on-roses scent than in the moments leading up to this one, he let her have her way.

She can do what she wants with me.

She can ravish me anyway she wants.

He didn't care.

As long as she *did* ravish him.

Groaning again, groaning more deeply and in much more obvious despair, Claire rose to her knees on the thickly padded seat. She was careful, extremely careful, not to allow the contact she'd made...the searing, soaring, mind- and soul-melding contact...to break or in any way diminish. She'd already slipped long and grasping fingers impossibly deep into and among the roots of his hair, and now she twisted. Solidifying her grip she made sure she didn't slip away, made sure he couldn't pull away. She tightened her grip so much it hurt. Or should have hurt, maybe really did hurt. But the pain, if it existed, was immaterial. The pain, if that was what Eli felt lancing through him in a thousand and one ways with the cutting force of the sharpest blade, only made the pleasure so much greater. So much more soaringly intense. So much more potentially unsurvivable.

And she didn't stop with the twisting of hair and the intensifying of each successive, greedily brutalizing thrust of her tongue. Releasing his hair at last so she could shove at his shoulders, shove hard with the flats of small palms that packed far more punch than appearances would indicate, she pushed him to his back. Forced him to lie back along the length of the bench and then, locked to him more tightly and completely than ever with clutching fingers and hungry mouth, she climbed onto him. The skirt of her radiant-as-a-cloud dress floated and swirled around the shimmery-smooth bare skin of her legs as she straddled his thighs. As she almost but not quite, not nearly enough for his satisfaction, straddled his hips and the straining, hardened length that waited there, screaming for her in its agony. Its surely terminal agony.

Billows of fabric met his searching hands. Soft and silken, as much like a drifting cloud to touch as they were to see, those billows defied his best attempts to infiltrate their rosy depths.

"Damn," he murmured when finally, seemingly in violation of all human limits of endurance, she released his mouth so they both could breathe.

"What?" Claire's voice was slurred. As was her expression. Thick with unspent and unmet passion, thicker with the expectation of even more passion, she seemed incapable of focusing on anything other than that expectation.

"I can't..." He couldn't say more. Her lips claimed his again...claimed *him*.

Eli didn't want to rip the deceptively durable stuff the dress was made of. He wanted her to keep this dress forever, wanted her to keep it close at hand always, as a cherished symbol they could pull out on some future cold winter's night to remind them of a steamy summer in the rain. To remind them of moments he knew would live on and on, sharp and clear in his memory for the rest of his life. But in his frustration and increasingly engorged agony, he would. He feared his hands would in their fumbling desperation and eagerness rend those silken drifts into so many useless, unrecognizable tatters.

"Help," he said the next chance he got, the next time Claire gave him the opportunity to breathe.

His hands were hopelessly ensnared now. Irretrievably ensnared amidst clinging-soft folds that, if they'd sought to take him prisoner and bind him in captivity forever, were doing a remarkable job.

Claire laughed softly. The sound of it sent fresh spouting of white-hot energy into every last, single corner of the inside of him. The sound of it made him ache. Made all the pertinent parts of him...cock and balls and surely overburdened brain...writhe with new hunger he worried would never be fulfilled. And when her hands fluttered down and between them, when they began to rearrange first his clothing and then her own, when she set him roaringly free, releasing the naked length of his straining cock into air that seemed to suddenly flame with the force it exuded, when she lifted her skirt away from him...

"Jesus, Claire!" Eli screamed her name with all the force and power left in lungs strained to the very brink of collapse. He screamed it into silent, rain-laden forest air that swallowed his screams up whole, swallowed them up as if they'd never been there at all. He screamed it when she lifted the folds of that marvelous skirt to reveal how well she'd prepared for this little tryst in the summerhouse.

She wore nothing underneath.

The rigid length of his cock found only satin-smooth softness between her thighs. Only the velvet-whisper softness of the sacred area between. And finding them, tried immediately, tried valiantly, to beat itself to death upon them.

"Jesus, Claire." The scream, the desire to scream, died completely as quickly as it had appeared. Now Eli's voice escaped as a wondering whisper. It slipped from his throat and lips into increasingly sultry, ever more rain- and scent-laden air.

She laughed.

Again.

Like before.

And he responded as he had before. With a continued hardening in a cock already hardened beyond the point of horrible, suffering death.

"You're going to miss your bridal shower." He couldn't contain, not at all, the gleeful note of victories won and celebrations planned that crept into his tone.

"Screw the bridal shower." Lifting herself, kneeling tall on knees planted at either side of his hips, Claire positioned herself with exquisite care, with excruciating precision, above him. She positioned herself so that the dream-soft and mist-moist folds of what she'd come so plainly prepared to surrender to him touched him. Barely touched him. Scorchingly touched him.

"I think..." Laughing for real now, laughing from the depths of a heart that soared and told him in no uncertain terms it would gladly be willing to never *stop* soaring, he lifted his hands. To catch her hips. "You're about to screw the life out of *me*. And to hell with screwing any fussy female wing-ding at any fussy, stuffy country club."

Claire slapped his hands away. "This one is mine," she declared, sounding like she meant business.

Eli sighed, then. He tried to relax and let her have the way she so obviously meant to have whether he cooperated or not. But how any even remotely sane and rational man could do such a thing beneath an assault as deadly and accomplished as this one?

Still on her knees, she lowered herself a little. So she could press more disastrously...with so much more debilitating delight...against him. Hips swaying, her head tilted forward and her face hidden behind forward-tumbled masses of glossy dark curls, she lost herself in what she was doing. In the way she was doing it. The way she was rubbing the sinfully velvet folds of herself across the tip of his cock. Rubbing just hard enough and with just enough force that he barely parted her folds. Parted them only slightly, parted them repeatedly. Parted them just enough to give a hint of what lay within...what he was missing every time she teased him only to stroke away from him again, the taunting outer layers of her as yet unbreached.

"Je..." There seemed no other thing he could say. "...sus."

The sound of his voice, the awed reverence in every breath and beat of it, had no discernable effect upon her.

She seemed lost in some kind of trance. One she'd inflicted upon herself and was rapidly, endlessly weaving around him as well.

Her swaying didn't stop. Instead it grew more pronounced. Its torment grew more intense and more centered as she lowered herself a little more. As she lowered herself just enough to...

Hands clenched into tight and aching fists that *needed* to touch, *needed* to guide her into more gratifying movement, Eli lay utterly still beneath her. Teeth gritted as hard as his hands were clenched, he tried to do as Claire wanted. He tried to give in. Tried to submit without making demands upon her. Spoken, or otherwise.

With the new sinking of her body came an even more, incomprehensibly more intense sense of the still-denied innermost reaches of her. Of the dewed mist his cock informed him in all seriousness it had never known and demanded to know now. Instantly. The mist that waited for it there if only he could find his way to it, if only he had the courage to find his way. Much as the rain-splattered roses lay beyond the increasingly fogged glass of the summerhouse, waiting to touch passion-parched skin and bless it with their petaled coolness.

He cried out again. A little.

And Claire replied with a low and not entirely earthly murmuring of her own. A muted humming that seemed not to spring so much from her throat as from every single pore of her eternally rose-gilt body.

This was...exquisite.

No other word Eli knew came even close to expressing the sheer avalanche of delighted agony he felt at the whims of the gently snug flesh still barely encasing his hammering tip. The female flesh that showered magically onto his and around his…a non-stop torrent of blazing liquid sparks that were too brilliant to be seen should they ever consent to reveal themselves in a way or a place where it might be possible for eyes to see them. Sparks too startling in their intensity to be actually endured, except as the slightest intimation of endurance.

"I don't think I can take much more." Eli's voice was thick. Uneven and clotted, as if something had been brutally torn loose inside him.

Claire's response was another lowering. Combined with a slight leaning forward in her shoulders so she could take hold of the edges of his shirt that she'd unbuttoned but never removed. This time he could barely focus on anything other than the progression of her flesh as it slowly, steadily, to all appearances imperceptibly took in his cock. As he and it, the both of them together, disappeared bit by infinitesimal bit from the face of the planet.

Her face was in line with his now. Floating close to his, it nonetheless remained at the very fringe of his rapidly diminishing vision. Seen only as a pale and moonlike blur, little more than a half-recognized remnant of reality, her face had gone slack with enjoyment. Slack with concentration upon her objective, yet at the same time fervent with that very same concentration.

"You're trying to kill me." He said it as a declaration of known fact. Not an issue up for any kind of discussion. "Aren't you?"

Her laughter shimmered.

The gray air had lightened somehow in the last few seconds, had thinned enough and grown normal enough that the sound of her laughter was free to strike straight through to him. Straight to the heart of him. Straight to the place where it stood every chance of doing the most catastrophic damage imaginable. And as she laughed, she continued the long and slow progression that surely marked the end of his existence.

Holding tight to his shirt, the crisp summer-weight fabric reduced to no more than a crumpled mess beneath clawed and grasping fingers, she continued to claim him.

And yet she'd barely moved at all.

He was still less than halfway inside her and more worried than ever that she'd never be finished with him. Never grant him the full and unconditional immersion he craved.

"God, Claire." Again that thickness in his voice. Again the quality of a man badly broken. A man destroyed from within by the strength and futility of his own pulsing desires...his own tormenting, twisting needs and sufferings. "I really...can't..."

He wasn't hammering any more. If any good had come of this torture, that had to be it. For the seconds, minutes, hours and lifetimes he lay still beneath Claire's advance, he felt a new and startling peace. A new and thrilling ease and promise that left him breathless beneath the weight of a dozen or more soft sighs of release. In those same seconds and hours and lifetimes it came as no small shock and surprise to realize the hammering had stopped only because it had gone beyond mere hammering. So far beyond that all of his existence seemed...*was*...centered upon the tides of endless sensation, endless and fiery excitement Claire created with every shuddery, *clinging* downward shrug of her flesh onto his. Her flesh, with which she sought to erase him from all meaningful existence.

"This is my dream, Eli."

He couldn't answer. Again.

He could only ache. From the inside out. Could only strain and struggle, again from within, seeming to gain both length *and* anguish as he reached helplessly for her. As the tip of his cock sought uselessly, endlessly, to find the shelter it craved. Shelter within her. Struggling for her, struggling toward the greater and more sensuous depths of her, he tried to lift his hips away from the bench upon which she'd pinned him.

He couldn't have made the movement anyway. Not with his damaged capabilities to do even the simplest of everyday things...not on his best of days. But his body, pushed beyond all tolerance or ability to reason and remember such things, couldn't seem to accept that. Couldn't seem to accept much of anything, really, except what it wanted in ways it had never wanted anything else.

Her.

Claire.

Every misting and tight, softening and taut, clinging and greedily claiming little fraction of her.

I want Claire.

And nothing else.

Chapter Sixteen

He'd said he didn't think he could take any more. And with that Claire heartily agreed.

She'd just about reached that point herself.

She hadn't realized the sinuous dynamite inherent in what she was about to do. Hadn't, in fact, realized much of anything once she'd made that first contact, once she'd decided to take things as slowly as was humanly possible. And then once she had begun to take them oh, so torturously and sinfully slowly she'd simply…forgotten.

Everything.

Except the single point of flesh she'd made the fulcrum of her entire existence. The single point upon which everything else balanced and depended…the point that met her with such intensely catastrophic, for her mental processes anyway, heat.

Quivering atop him, feeling one of the molten flashes of summer lightning over dark mountain tops that he could always produce within her, it was nearly more than she could do to remain upright and coherent. With each successive stressing of the flesh she'd chosen to rub across that finite point that represented all of what she'd ever wanted and all of which she'd ever dreamed, with each slight stretching that urged her to open in anticipation only to immediately, heartbreakingly close again the instant she moved on, a debilitating wave of energy washed through her. Over her. Around her and, especially, inside her.

Her legs threatened to collapse. She had to take hold of Eli just to stop that from happening. Just to ground herself and reconnect herself with an oddly shifting, strangely shadowed ghost of reality.

His shirt…the one whose edges she clutched in her effort to avoid locking her fingers deep into the matting of crisp dark hair at the center of his chest in a way that could quite possibly do real bodily injury to him…was dark. Gray-blue, like the day beyond the windows. Darker. Like the day would become later, after enough hours passed. It was a twilight-dusk color. A stormy and thunderous one that gave a strange and haunting intensity to his eyes…a gleaming depth to their rich chestnut that couldn't be explained away entirely by the onset of passion. Though passion surely had something to do with the change.

Her descent onto him was agony for her. The slow parting of supple flesh that instantly closed around his as if determined to seal him inside permanently was an unending trial that must be endured.

Claire managed to fend off his first attempt to grasp her hips and take charge of her movements. But not the second.

She'd reached a point just about halfway down the hot and slippery, hard-pulsing shaft that had been so precisely made for her enjoyment when he lifted his hands again. And this time their movement was not unlike that same lightning she'd imagined forking and flickering inside her veins.

So swift she never had a chance to see or sense what they were about to do, Eli's hands rose. So surely that there would without a doubt have been nothing she could do to avoid their grip even if she had seen or sensed.

In less than a flash, his hands were simply there. Were simply grasping her. Pulling her down, yanking her down. The effect was to ram into her the full, incredible length of the shaft she'd so naively believed was hers to torment at will. To ram it all the way in.

The ending of her descent was as rapid as the start had been slow and deliberate. As unexpected as it had been carefully plotted at first, and as violent and out of her control as she'd orchestrated the beginning to be all hers. To be everything *she* wanted it to be…everything she decided to lavish upon him and allow him.

The ending took her breath away. Literally.

Finishing with a gasp that tore all the breath from her lungs and an even sharper and more cutting cry that carried in its wavering depths the quality more of a wild thing running loose in some deep and primeval forest than of a sentient, conscious, human being, it was far more than Claire could ever have expected from a finish. Far more than she had bargained for, certainly, when she'd set out to bend Eli to her will.

For the longest of moments she could do nothing. She could only sit stunned, held aloft by hands that now gripped her irrefutably, her mind reeling as her body adjusted belatedly, almost too late, to the invasion of swollen male flesh.

Eli did nothing.

Having accomplished what he'd set out to accomplish, he'd fallen complacent again. Smiling with what Claire dimly perceived through the lightning-illumined haze that filled the last of her mind and obscured her vision as complete satisfaction with himself, he released his grip at last. Released it so completely that his hands slipped away from her and dropped, all but useless, to his sides.

I'm free.

She could leave him any time. Could resume her slowly self-destructive fondling and stroking if that was what she wanted to do.

She was free and Eli lay waiting beneath her. To see what she would do next. As she was kind of waiting to see that for herself. Because her body, still stunned and reeling at the destruction of all its carefully wrought plans, had no more plans. None to speak of anyway. She...it...was reacting purely on instinct now. On passion-fueled instinct. And she could feel herself beginning to gather.

As she sat there motionless atop him, staring down into his wide and unfocused eyes, she could feel her inner self...that same instinctive and unthinking self that had carried her through so many of the rougher patches in her time with him...getting ready to kick in. Big time. And something else was gathering, too. Deep down inside and lower still, down where her body had its center, around the shaft that more and more, increasingly, formed her only real and reliable point of reference.

It was an old gathering.

A very, very familiar one alight with the simmering excitement of something about to happen. Of all the possibilities and endless varieties of what was about to happen. And yet there was something completely new about this feeling. Something Claire couldn't recognize, but something she thought she should recognize. Because it was an inborn, intrinsic part of who she was. What she was supposed to be.

There should be no need for her to have to consciously try to recognize anything.

And then the storm broke.

The lightning- and thunderstorm that had been building and building. Perhaps forever.

Quite suddenly the storm tore free inside her. Tore painfully, joltingly free with a wild abandon that amazed her because she knew with utter certainty that the flood of searing relief had lurked hidden and unknown inside her all along. She knew it had lurked waiting while she'd never so much as suspected it existed.

Claire tried for a moment to rouse herself. To ease the suffering agony of Eli's presence between her legs by tightening and tensing the long muscles in her legs and arms. By shoving hard with hands that let go of his shirt so they could press themselves tight and flat against the lean, dark-furred center of his chest.

But no matter how hard she tried, nothing would happen.

At first.

No muscles would flex, none would obey. None but the ones that encircled him, gripping with nearly manic delirium, tighter and tighter with her every effort to rise along him.

Eli sighed…a long and slow rippling of sound all but guaranteed to fuel the fires she felt within. Fuel them and fan them, urging them to even brighter leaping, even hotter smoldering. Barely disturbing the rain-dense and newly steamed air inside the summerhouse, the faint and barely discernable sound of his sigh acted like a precipitating agent upon her. First releasing her uncooperative muscles from their frozen state, it immediately infused them with revitalizing shots of lightning-fed determination.

Claire's legs straightened. Almost before she knew it was going to happen her hips lifted. They reversed with their motion the enfolding drag that had placed her upon him such a short time before. They turned the enfolding into a denial. Into sweet-sad, poignant denial as millimeter by desperate millimeter, accompanied by mutual groans of suffering and satisfaction, her body gave up its right to his.

Her face still close to his, hovering very near to his and above his, she kept her hands where she'd planted them. Atop the massed silk of hair upon his chest. She needed the steadiness of him, needed the reliability of him to keep her connected. To keep her on the course she'd set for herself while only half-realizing the potential for self-loss and self-destruction that would come as a natural part of trying to maintain that course to its inevitable outcome.

Gaze to gaze she watched the effect of her retreat quiver across Eli's face…watched what began as the wondering slackness of a man lost in the middle of a soft and reverberating sigh metamorphose magically into a fresh and never before seen tensing of increased wonder. Watched, too a sudden clenching of teeth and jaw as flood tides of emotion ran rampant, riot, without limit or discernable end across features that glowed with new radiance. Hot radiance. The unquenchable radiance of pure, unadulterated *desire*.

"I need…" Stopping, her voice faltering badly before it gave way altogether, Claire knew exactly what she needed. Knew she didn't need to make the effort it would take to express it because she also thought...felt utterly and immutably certain...Eli knew too. She thought, as she paused one last time, poised in her delicate balancing act at the very tip of him, her body screaming at her already to inflict upon him one last instant of well-earned torture and one last round of suffering before what would almost certainly be the end of the world, he knew exactly what she'd been thinking.

She thought he'd been anticipating her thinking those very things. Had been looking forward to it and even planning for what it would do to her. And ultimately, by the sheer force of their association and connection, what it would do to him.

The sound of his next sigh, a much more prolonged and pronounced one, was too much for her.

She dropped.

Not slowly, like she'd tried before.

Allowing her legs to simply relax, simply lose all definition, she allowed herself to drop back onto him. Already connected with his, her body slid down the fully prepared shaft, delighting when it leaped with welcome. When it reacted to the smooth and yet surely unbearably rough drag of her flesh along its smoothness and seemed actually to thunder upward. Seemed to grow immeasurably larger and then even larger in its quest to meet her halfway. Meet her more than halfway and claim for its own what it still had little real power or ability to claim at all.

"Ahhhhh." The sound he made represented no real word. No manner of speaking known to humankind. Rather it was a cry of complete, thoughtless and unreasoning surrender. One that, in its primitive and formless way, nonetheless managed to convey every depth of need Eli felt, every pent-up longing he needed to release, every single thing he found himself incapable of expressing in any other way. "Claire, you've got to...I'm begging you. Now. I'll do anyth...th...thing. Any...thing. If you'll just...please..."

Shoving again with hands that remained pressed to his chest as if they'd rooted themselves there, shoving with knees and legs that had regained at least a part of their earlier strength and purpose, Claire did exactly the opposite of what he asked.

Before she finished her plunge, she rose again.

She rose more, and much more slowly. Rose in a way that carried a clear threat that in another instant, another millimeter, she would leave him behind. Completely. Would leave him behind to fend for himself in this one moment when he could not, absolutely and without question, even hope to fend for himself.

She rose in a way designed to leave every doubt in his reeling mind that she would ever again undertake the next, explosive drop. The slow and deliciously arduous process of re-taking what still was hers to take, hers to use, hers to claim and conquer with a single sighing of her moistness across the rigid and suffering length she'd entranced. The length that even now yearned obviously, openly, visibly for her.

Ignoring the cry of her own flesh, ignoring its needful and wounded pleas as she reached the very last of him and felt herself begin the return to her normal, uninvaded and unplundered state…the one in which she spent most of her existence…Claire rose until she could rise no more. Until she didn't dare rise farther because rising farther would truly break every link they'd forged. Every connection they'd so far fought to maintain.

The skirt of her dress swirled about them. Pulled up, pulled back so that she could ply her craft upon him, it now tumbled from the place where she'd tucked it, high up beneath her arms. And tumbling, it enfolded them both. Hid from them both the true nature of what was happening between and to them.

In Eli's eyes Claire saw the reflection of that tumbling and concealing. She saw too the rising thrill of anticipation that came with the inadvertent covering of themselves.

His hands twitched. Down at his sides, seeming unable to rise, unable to do anything but jerk helplessly and spasmodically, they twitched with a desperation that infused itself into all the air around them as they struggled to do just that. As they struggled to rise. To…

"Dress…" Teeth clenched, face strained as the brilliant sheen of perspiration regenerated itself, forming small beads and droplets at the sides and center of his brow, Eli struggled to speak. To communicate what he wanted, and how he wanted it. "Dress."

Claire had to let go of him then. She had to lift her hands so they could catch up the hem of the pink-and-drifting cloud of chiffon and lift it again. Lift it all the way, her arms straightening themselves into luxurious twin columns of taut muscle and tightened sinew high above her head.

Lifting the skirt, holding it in a way that allowed a layer of chiffon to remain between them, only partially and barely obscuring the sight of them from each other while allowing the opaque and more impenetrable layer of thin silk that lay beneath to fall away and cover the thrusting peaks of her aroused and enraged breasts, Claire smiled at him.

His eyes leaped. As did his shaft.

His eyes burned too, as a whimper of complete defeat rose from his parted lips. Rose into air grown intolerable with the weight of need and urgency spiraling upward from the two of them. Need and urgency that acted quickly, efficiently, to fill every nook and cranny of space, every tiniest suggestion of unoccupied summerhouse, with the heaviness of its demand that she…now…immediately…

Sighing as Eli had sighed a moment or two before, her skirt still raised to cover her face and lend its slightly rosy, filmy and dreamy tint to the scene before her, Claire twisted her torso. Once. Twice. Repeatedly, as her legs began to fold beneath her, with carefully calculated precision this time. Her need to dominate completely and finish him off with absolute grace and absolute finality won out in the end, defeating and erasing the burnt quivering she'd previously suffered in every muscle. Desire congealed. Eager to finish immediately, while she still possessed some small measure of ability to finish.

She twisted back and forth slowly. Her body curved in ways she'd never thought to make it curve before, curved repeatedly in the throes of a sort of slow and sinuous belly dance performed to unheard music played at about a millionth of its intended speed. And the veil she held so far above her head, the thin and translucent film made up of a single layer of her floating and fluttering skirt, only added to the illusion. Only completed the illusion and made it, in the strangely sultry Arabic way of the very belly dance she imitated with such agonizing restraint, that much more intolerable. That much more inexplicably sensual and sexual.

Eli groaned.

Eyes shut now, shut loosely as if he'd lost the will to hold them open for even an instant longer, Eli tried one more time to lift his hands. Extend his arms. He tried with another ineffectual and hopeless twitching to do something, anything, to help himself and save himself.

He needn't have bothered.

It was clear to Claire, clear just in the watching and the observing that his body had quit. Had ceased to have any purpose other than the one that stood between them, had ceased to have any real solidity or strength except in the tireless shaft that even now made a fresh effort. Even now gave another hard and pulsing thrust upward. Inward. Seeking what she still wouldn't allow it to find. What she still hadn't decided to grant to ease its suffering and extinguish, at least for a short space of time, its unmistakable flaming.

"Claire." He struggled to open his eyes. She saw evidence of that, too. Saw it reflect in his face as a constantly changing, ceaseless altering of his expression.

He struggled mightily. And finally succeeded.

Staring up at her with a mute plea in the chestnut-brandy glorious depths of the eyes he finally managed to open, he begged her to end this suffering. This inhumanity, this…

"Claire."

Begging with his voice, too, he told her without actually speaking the words or allowing them to form upon his lips that this was the time. This *had* to be the time. And he tried again to move his arms. Tried again to lift and capture. Tried, as she increased only marginally the speed at which she slipped ever downward and ever closer to the completion and the end for which he'd pleaded so eloquently, to take for himself what she still refused to give.

Chapter Seventeen

I WAS RIGHT.
She's out to kill me.

It wasn't a matter of if. It was, simply put, a matter of when.

And he didn't need to wonder how she was going to do it either. That much was already crystal clear.

She was going to kill him one degree at a time. Was going to murder him for sure, just the way she was trying to murder him right now. She was going to use him up, deplete him, leave him screaming and crying, begging for whatever mercy she might choose to grant him. But she *was* going to kill him. Sooner rather than later, with her slow-moving torture that could have no good end. No survivable end.

God in heaven. He'd thought he felt needs in the past. Believed in the days before Claire came along, the days before he'd first found her and thought she'd be just another of the pliant and eager young women with whom he sought to relieve the built up pressures in those callous and self-centered days, he was miserable. He'd thought he knew what suffering was all about, had thought he'd done plenty of it, both as a result of his sorry physical state and of the fear that had made him paranoid about revealing that state to anyone. He'd thought he knew abject suffering in those lost days when his worst fear had been the sight of pity in the eyes of attractive and desirable women. Or worse yet, the sight of revulsion.

He'd thought he had needs then.

But he'd been wrong as wrong could be.

What he'd felt then in no way compared to what he felt now. This need...this aching, born of too many long nights when they'd been separated if not by actual distance then by the somehow unbridgeable gap that had crept into their thoughts and their hearts...reverberated down into the very depths of his soul. Only a part of it was the thundering throb that overtook his cock, only a very small part of it the bursting desire for release that caused his balls to feel like they'd begun to cramp and condense, ready for one last explosion to end their existence. Like the separation he'd allowed to spring up between himself and the only woman he'd ever loved or ever would love, this thunder was mostly mental. Mostly a part of his mind that ultimately showed up as symptoms in his body.

I need her.

He feared she'd never realize it. Or maybe she would. And maybe it wouldn't suit her to fulfill that need and ease it.

God knew it was only what he deserved after the way he'd acted…after the way he'd made it so hard for her to get close to him. After he'd let his own self-pity and bitterness rear its ugly head long after it should have been put away and laid to rest.

After he'd made all of it…so much of it…about *him* and not about them.

He didn't deserve her. He knew it. But she shimmered atop him anyway, a man's sweetest dream and fondest desire. Lifting her dress to reveal the smooth and slim lines of her, the thrillingly curved yet lean body that had borne his twins and then gone on as before, seemingly unaffected by the startling trauma of birth or its aftermath, the body that had returned almost instantly to the luscious thing it had been before. From the beginning.

Revealed, the flesh of her lower half, of gently curved hips and lush thighs, of long and strong legs and lean calves, glowed softly. Glowed almost incandescently gold in the dim and dusky light.

Lying there, watching the lovely gleam of it as she suspended herself above him with more of that waiting, plotting intensity that drove him out of his mind in ways nothing else ever could, Eli felt a new surging inside. It was as if his body tried to turn itself inside out. As if it almost succeeded. It was a deep and gut-wrenching heaving of all the most inner and important parts of him, a filling and trembling, a twisting and writhing. And most of all a sudden rising of a cock that already felt too long and too hard, already felt much too constricted by the very act of erecting itself to actually be capable of achieving the relief it so desperately sought.

Claire had begun to slip down upon him again. This time the friction of her passage seemed to light him afire. Seemed to scorch already flame-damaged skin straight off the cock she used as her own private toy, seemed to sear straight through to its very center and seal its fate forever. Seal his fate by making relief impossible. Ever.

He made a small sound. A choking, strangling, suffocating one.

Please, he meant to say. But even that word, as simple and singular as it was, would not come out.

Nothing would but a growl of animal need. So he begged her with his eyes. He looked straight up, straight into the eyes of the woman who towered over him, a long and slim column of gold-and-rose flesh-and-floating-cloud promise. He stared straight into eyes the color of the deepest woods at twilight and put all his pleas, all his wishes and wants and desires into the look.

Claire seemed to know what he was thinking. What he was trying to ask.

Slowly and then more slowly, she continued her descent. For another half a second. Another quarter. Until suddenly he felt something break free and burst inside her. Until he felt a shimmering, saturating moisture that could only have come from one place, could only mean one thing.

Her movements became erratic as she slammed herself down upon him with even more force than he'd used to pull her onto him when she hadn't been quite ready. When she hadn't been quite willing. Clutching now at the hairs upon his chest, the hairs she'd avoided before as if afraid she might hurt him in some terrible, terminal way if she used them to balance herself and orient herself, she tore at him.

She inflicted pain. Certainly she did. But it was sweet pain.

Lovely pain.

The dewy-palmed, tugging pain of incipient satisfaction. Incipient...

From within her burst another wave of drenching mist. A larger and more inundating, entirely elemental wave that made it possible for her to skim upward along his length at lightning speed. Even with her innermost flesh tightened to near crushing pressure in its effort to retain him for as long as she possibly could, this new bursting and lubricating made her movements sleek and efficient. Sleeker and lovelier than he would have imagined or anticipated.

Claire exhaled loudly as the first wave of orgasm...he knew it was the first, knew there would be more, knew from long and lush experience she was capable of far more...broke from her and over him. Her breath seemed to tug hard at her throat, ready to rip its way free if that was the only way it could escape, with a dry and softly grating sound that only made his cock throb harder. A sound of pure sex in the making that made his cock thrust on its own again. Made it instantly seek greater depths and more crushing tightness. Made it seek the ultimate lightness that would come if he could just locate the one small and secret place within her...the one place that, more than any other, could grant his fondest desire.

"Re...lease?"

He had no idea where he found the strength to utter the plea.

He'd had no idea he was even going to utter it until suddenly there it was, hanging aquiver and alight with expectation in the steaming air between them.

"Release," he whispered again as Claire lifted rapidly atop him so she could throw herself down again, her legs and arms working in perfect harmony, perfect unison, her thickly misted inner flesh dragging long and lovely trails of rose-essence, pearl-essence, *Claire*-essence across him. Trails that seemed to sink into his overwrought flesh and vanish, already a part of him even before she finished passing along him or across him.

"Release," he groaned as it finally came.

For both of them.

Claire cried out as the final wave crested within her. As the sultry creaminess of it, the terrifying vitality of it exploded from her to cover him with its golden, alabaster, singing and steaming glory.

And he cried out, too.

What rose within him...what reached the very tip of his cock, the very last millimeter before it should expend itself as it had been meant to expend itself into the silken and crimson loveliness of the body that waited for it...was multi-pronged. Sharp edged, like shattered glass and yet molten smooth at the same time as if the glass itself had never been completed. Never been perfected. What rose within him rose to the top of him. And stopped. For a fraction of a second it hung suspended beneath the weight and the wonder of all that poured from Claire. All that anointed him and invited him. All that mystified him and ultimately terrified him as he thought surely no living man had ever been so completely terrified before.

The relief for which he'd begged hung. Taunting. Tormenting. Refusing to complete the very last, the very most vital, part of its mission. Refusing to do what he bid it to do, what he demanded it do, what nature intended it to do.

For a second, caught in the horrific tremors of a cock gone almost too far to finish, Eli suffered as he'd never suffered before. He felt a heated pain like no other, a pain of failure and defeat, of being so close and yet being incapable. A pain of loss so bitter and despair so dark it brought tears to his eyes. Allowing them to escape, he felt them stream hot and thick down his cheeks and into the hair at his temples. Because the tears would not be held back. No amount of masculine pride or trying could possibly hold them back.

Atop him Claire descended again. Her movements, eased now by the liquified fire that poured from her in limitless quantities, took on the quality of a silvered glide.

Eli felt no dragging of flesh upon flesh now. No roughness that titillated, no hesitance that enticed with its almost reluctant promise.

Now there was only smoothness. Only a plundering, plunging, swimming claiming that still did nothing to ease him. Nothing to help him ease himself.

Straining, shoving the way he imagined Claire had shoved in the process of giving birth to their lovely twins, shoving much the way he'd *seen* her shove as he hovered helpless and terrified at her bedside, able to do nothing but allow her to cling to his hand as he watched, he struggled to go the last tiny bit of distance. Struggled with all his strength to expel what, for another of the briefest and most burning of instants his body absolutely, categorically refused to expel.

And then...

On the greatest of cries, the most hoarse and tormented of cries, with his head tilted back and his eyes squeezed shut as tight as it was possible to squeeze them, Eli felt the erupting flow of the trap releasing. Of the too long held and too pressurized column of fluid unburdening itself at last. Straight into her. Straight into the heart of her as she reached the bottom of her next downward stroke. The one his hands, freed from their torpor and lethargy at last, freed to regain their mobility and their purpose, ensured would be the last as they cupped her hips and held them. As they held her firmly in place, seated all the way down upon his pulsing, dancing cock as it emptied itself utterly into the very deepest center of her.

In that moment, when his triumph and his release were at their greatest, when the two of them worked so hard and so completely together that he felt light-headed and barely able to remain conscious, Claire answered his release with another of her own. With her greatest release yet...the most silken, most seductive, most flawlessly, effervescently, evanescently lovely bursting inside herself that he could ever remember. *Ever.*

"Claire," he whispered as the climax seemed to drain everything out of her. Every bit of will and strength and stamina. "My sweet, lovely, incredible Claire," he murmured with a shaking and a shiver in his voice as she sagged suddenly atop him, the draining finally taking its toll. The climax finally having its inevitable result.

"Claire," he whispered into her ear when she collapsed atop him spent and warm, the smell of her the faintly dusky, faintly roses-in-the-rain scent he always associated with her and always remembered in his dreams of moments like this with her.

It was the smell of her inner self.

The smell of everything that made her *her.*

Everything that made him want her the way he still, incredibly, with his cock already going limp inside her as it lost its will to live and fight, wanted her.

Everything that had always made them work and always, he realized with one of those flashes of insight and discovery that were almost too insightful to be grasped, would make them work forever.

We've made it.

Somehow, they had been through a long and dark tunnel riddled with doubts and fears. And they had made it through to the other end. They had made it through intact, still together, still able to create this...this...

Limp now in his arms, limp atop him with her face cuddled soft and warm into the hollow at the base of his throat, limp beneath the cloud of her dress and the just as intoxicating cloud of scent made up partly of rain, partly of perfume, and mostly of longing satisfied for one more instant, one more hour, Claire murmured softly against his exhausted flesh.

"What?" he asked in reply. "What was that, sweet love?"

"I thought," she murmured without rousing herself, murmured while burrowing tighter against him as if she wanted to burrow straight, endlessly, *into* him.

"Thought what?"

She laughed.

The sound of it sent a ripple, or maybe the memory of a ripple, through his depleted cock. The sound of it was almost enough to bring the strength back into the forlorn thing, almost enough to give it what it needed for one more round, one more desperate, delicious, pulsing thrust into its most secret of places, its most cherished of places. Into her.

"What?" he insisted as his arms rose. As they wrapped themselves around her, almost without his knowledge or input, and held her against him. Held her atop him where she lay quietly, seeming to lose even the most elemental will or desire to move.

She murmured again. Just as unintelligibly.

But this time her meaning came through without the benefit of actually being heard. Without the cumbersome vehicle of words that had to be heard and then interpreted, heard and then assigned meaning, heard and then assimilated. This time her meaning lay in the faint tremor of her shoulders, in the warm weight of her body covering his, in the soft stream of her hair across the bare and suddenly too sensitive skin of his shoulder and chest.

Love.

That was what he heard in that elusive sigh of sound.

That was what he felt in the languorous cuddling of her limp and satisfied body to his.

That was what he heard in the sudden silence that filled the summerhouse, the settling of steam that began to dissipate rapidly in the aftermath of its creation.

Love.

Eli knew she loved him. Still. He knew all his worries and fears of the last months and years had been just that. Worries and fears. Unfounded ones, silly ones, self-inflicted and imagined ones.

Smiling at the beamed, white-painted ceiling overhead, staring up into the soaring peak at the center of their sweet-scented bower, watching the slight sway of the graceful wrought-iron chandelier that hung from the very center of that peak, Eli realized it had stopped raining.

The faint rattling of drops he heard on the peak and sides of the towering roof was the sound of moisture dripping from ancient trees that surrounded them. Ancient trees that crowded in close and dark around the small circle of rose-choked loveliness with the summerhouse nestled fast in its heart.

Or was it the rattling of his own heart as the too long shattered pieces of it began at last to put themselves back together?

Chapter Eighteen

"We always seem to come back to this damned thing, don't we?"

Claire looked up. Or to be more accurate, perched at the top of a tall aluminum stepladder, she shifted her gaze away from the Indian and looked down.

Eli sat in the doorway to the music room, and he didn't look especially happy. Didn't look anything but irritated, annoyed, out of sorts.

"Good morning to you, too." Dipping her rag into the bucket of soapy water...the third already this morning...she'd set on the pail rest, she returned to her work. "Would you yell for Hannah for me? Tell her I need some fresh water?"

Eli didn't.

He rolled toward the statue and stopped at the base of it. Stopped and reached out, his expression one of unconcealed disgust when he touched the Indian and his fingertips came back dark with soot and heaven only knew what else. "You don't really think this is going to help?"

Claire peered down at him, scowling. "It couldn't hurt."

"Why are you doing this?" Now he looked dismayed, but he wasn't looking at her. He was looking at the statue.

"I have to do *something*. And the episode with Stephie the other day got me to thinking. Before anybody does anything the first project has to be to clean away at least some of the grime."

Eli didn't answer. He just stared at the Indian.

"Anyway, this is better than staring at the thing. Which is all you've done since it got here."

Slowly, he shook his head. Even more slowly he backed away a few feet. As if he was afraid of contamination or something. "I can't believe it's back in my house."

"Call Hannah, will you?" Claire flashed him a commanding look. "I think I'm putting more dirt on the thing than I'm removing."

Once again, he didn't. "How long have you been at this?" Elbows resting comfortably on the arms of his chair, hands folded twice as comfortably in front of him, he looked prepared to stay where he was all day. Watching, fascinated, all day.

"You have baseball practice at eleven," she said with another look. "With...hell, I don't know which team it's with. If you just keep sitting there and staring and don't do as I ask, you're going to miss..."

"Practice is canceled." He glanced at the windows and the lowering, steely sky beyond. "Parents were worried about rain."

Claire shrugged. "Whatever." And then, after another second or so, when he maintained his settled-in position and showed no sign of either yelling for Hannah as she'd asked or going off to find her, Claire lifted her head and bellowed "Hannah!" at the ceiling.

"Christ A'mighty!" Eli started, only to be interrupted by Hannah bustling through the door, a red pail billowing steam in a rubber-gloved hand.

"I thought you might be ready for this," the housekeeper said, reaching up to replace the old pail on the ladder with the new.

Claire beamed at her.

"Why don't you put some rubber gloves on, Missus?" Hannah asked the way she'd asked a dozen or so times this morning, ever since Claire had announced it was time for a little toxic clean-up on the monstrosity that had dirtied the music room for way too long.

"Clumsy things," Claire replied just as she had each and every one of those times.

"But your hands, Missus. Your beautiful hands! You're going to make a mess of them, and wouldn't that be a crying shame?" Her expression turning imploring, Hannah held out the gloves.

"It's no use," Eli put in. "You know that, don't you?"

Now Hannah gave *him* the imploring look.

"Once Claire gets something into her head, even dynamite isn't going to dislodge it." He held out his hand and the housekeeper dropped the heavy yellow gloves into it.

"Maybe you can talk some sense into her," Hannah muttered.

Eli was still laughing long after she left the room.

"Why *are* you so cranky?" Claire demanded, peering between the Indian's feathers at him.

"Are you kidding? It's a hundred and ten degrees in the shade, and the humidity..." He unclasped his hands long enough to pass one of them, knifelike, through the air in front of his face. "I don't know what the humidity is. But it's got to be about a hundred percent. Like I said, it's got to rain pretty soon. It's got to rain hard."

Claire was struggling with the silver tape someone had cocooned around the broken and wobbling feathers. She was struggling to find a starting point…an end, where there apparently was none. "You were the one who built this mausoleum without air conditioning. If you ask me that ought to be some kind of crime in this day and age."

"Who *did* ask you?"

She peered down at him again. "If you're going to sit there hurling nasty remarks, the least you could do is help a little."

"What the hell do you want me to do, Claire? Oh, wait. I know. Let me just bound out of this wheelchair and fly up that ladder to you. Then maybe together we can…"

"Shut up, Eli."

For a second it looked like he wasn't going to do any such thing. For a second his mouth hung halfway open, halfway in the process of coming up with some other brilliant remark. But then finally he closed it, clenched his hands and watched in more silence while she pried and picked at the tape. While she searched for the end that finally turned up in the most inconvenient place possible. Right between the second and third feathers, way down low in the crack between them. Where it was hard as hell to insert her fingers and harder still to bend them in order to pry the edge of the tape loose.

Fortunately the end had started to curl the tiniest bit. That gave her something to grab.

"Do you really think this is worth it?" he asked again after a while, his fit of inexplicable bad humor apparently dissipated.

"I think." Having a firm grip on the end of the tape at last, Claire tugged. She had to push it back through first, back between the two feathers where it had been lodged in a primitive kind of knot. But then she was home free. Then she could begin the process of unwrapping.

The loose end pulled free of the layer beneath with a long and ripping, long and sticky sound.

"Like I said before, it surely couldn't hurt."

"I guess." Eli sounded like he didn't agree. But once again he sounded like he'd lost his irritation. "What do you expect to do when you're finished there?"

The tape was coming off just fine now. It was unraveling into a big, sticky ball in Claire's hands and the roots of the three feathers were becoming visible. Marginally visible, their deep-carved lines beginning to show through the diminishing layers of tape. "I thought we'd look for the secret."

"I thought I told you before. About a thousand times. I..."

"I know." The feathers were almost free now. Another layer or two, another circle around them or two, and... "You've looked and looked. You've spent your entire life, every waking minute, searching and doing nothing else." It was Claire's turn for a little sarcasm and she gave it completely.

"Not my entire life," he said through a sudden burst of laughter. "But a good part of my childhood. A lot of long summer afternoons anyway. And there is no..."

"Secret?" Reaching the end of the wrappings at last, Claire shot him a look of unconcealed triumph. "We'll see about that, won't we?"

"Better get Stephie, then," he advised. "She's the only one who's ever looked like she might be on to something. She's the only one who might be able to believe it's possible to find something."

Claire's wadded up ball of duct tape hit the floor with a hideous plop. It landed a foot or two from Eli's feet and for a second he stared down at it, more thoughtful now than irritated, though Claire thought she could see traces of both in the set of his shoulders and the way he held his head.

"That's got to be a sticky mess," he pointed out when he finally lifted his head again to see what she was doing.

"That's why I have this." Claire pulled the bottle of orange oil cleaner from the back pocket of her overalls. "This stuff is supposed to remove any kind of goo or grime or garbage you can get on a thing."

"I guess."

Retrieving a clean rag from her other back pocket, she went to work with the citrus-smelling stuff. "Like I said before..."

"It couldn't hurt." Eli moved closer. "I know."

"But I have to say, you're right about the mess."

The goo was harder to remove than she'd first thought. So hard that she had to redouble her effort. Had to really scrub, applying no small amount of strength as she went to work on the tallest feather, the wobbly one in the center that looked like it might have been broken off and clumsily repaired at some time or another. "Whoever taped this thing up must have..."

"Claire?"

"...searched everywhere to come up with the gluiest duct tape they could find." Scrubbing harder, she bit her lip.

"Claire."

"This is just about the worst…"

"Claire!"

Realizing he'd been saying her name over and over again, in tones of increasing urgency and increasing something else that wasn't immediately identifiable, she looked up.

Looked down.

Looked at him.

An expression almost of awe had stolen across his face. It was lodged there firmly, unmistakably, in the sudden wideness of his eyes, the sudden sparkling brandy highlights of their color, in the way his mouth hung open again. Not in the process of forming speech this time, but in the process of being…well, awed. By whatever the devil had decided at this late stage of the game to awe him about an Indian he'd seen hundreds of times…make that *thousands* of times…over the course of his life.

"What are you doing there?" he asked when he glanced up and saw her watching him.

"Are we going to start that again?" Now it was her voice that crackled with irritation, her expression that mirrored, she felt absolutely sure, impatience and annoyance. "I told you. I'm cleaning up the statue so maybe we can find out once and for all…"

"No. I know that." His voice turned sharp, too. Notching up a little in volume, it drowned hers out. "I meant, what were you doing just a second ago? You were rubbing at something, cleaning it. What was it?"

Mystified, she looked down. Her hands were no longer on the Indian. They were poised in midair, the rag held in one and the bottle of orange oil tipped partially in the other, just about to pour out more. "I don't know," she confessed. "I was just…"

"Do it again."

Watching him, her brow crinkled with the sudden thought, maybe not such an unreasonable one, that the heat and horrible humidity really *had* gotten to him and he might be about to lose his mind, Claire touched her rag to one of the feathers and began to rub the orange oil in. Slowly. Cautiously.

"No," he said instantly. "Not there. I think you were lower somehow."

Obediently, never taking her gaze off him, she stroked the rag lower along the feather and began to rub again. A little harder, now that it looked like maybe he wasn't going so crazy after all.

"That's not it either." He looked thoughtful for a second. Half a second. "Try another feather."

Claire moved her hand to the middle feather. The one that wobbled alarmingly beneath her touch. Afraid she might snap it off, afraid the feather might be rotten and the damage to it irreparable if she wasn't careful, she began to rub again, more gently than before. "You're right," she said. "I *was* working on this feather. It's the only one that's..."

"Rub harder."

She did.

And he wheeled closer to the statue. He wheeled right up against it and stared up, as rapt and fascinated as Stephie had stared a day or two before. He was hunching down in his chair, too. Leaning forward a little and lowering his head, his face still upturned and wearing that strangely stunned look.

The reason seemed fairly obvious once Claire got over her surprise.

He was trying to get his face down to Stephie's level. He was trying to see things from her perspective. As if she might really have...

"Did Stephie actually see something?" Claire asked, her rag stopped in mid-stroke.

"Keep rubbing," he ordered, peering at what looked to Claire like the same place Stephie had peered. Although from this angle, from above, it was hard to be sure.

Automatically her hand resumed its pressure.

The middle feather started to wobble for sure. It started to wobble like there was no tomorrow, like it had come completely loose and was just about ready to snap. "Eli, I'm afraid..."

"Well, I'll be damned." He didn't even glance at her.

Leaning forward a little more, precariously, already knowing she couldn't possibly see what he was seeing, but needing to try anyway, Claire released the feather and peered down at him.

"Don't stop now!"

"Eli, I'm really afraid I'm going to break something. This middle feather's awfully wobbly and weak whenever I touch it."

"Break it then." Knees pressed up against the Indian, he was still peering at what seemed to Claire to be nothing.

He seemed to have forgotten she was there.

"The damned thing's not worth a plug nickel," he declared. "I'm going to have it hauled out of here one of these days anyway, so just go ahead and break whatever the hell's about to break. Because I think we're on to something here. I think we're really on to something."

"Would you mind telling me what?" Claire's hands had gone to her hips.

The bandanna she'd tied over her hair before starting her project had come loose, and a few strands had escaped to trail into her face and eyes. To torment her.

Impatient, she pursed her mouth and tried to blow them back.

"If you just do what you were doing a second ago, I'll be glad to." Eli was sitting up straight again. And now he was reaching up. Was straining and stretching, trying to touch some part of the Indian that hovered tantalizingly just beyond his reach. "Damn it all anyway," he muttered. "You'd think a man could…"

Thoroughly impatient, Claire grabbed the middle feather with her rag-covered hand. Ready to give it the most vicious scrubbing it had ever known, she leaned back on her ladder, and in the process felt something happen beneath her hand. Felt something new happen, something that wasn't a wobble and wasn't something rotten getting ready to break and shatter into a million smithereens.

The loose feather no longer stood quite straight in its socket. It looked like it had started to turn. Like some kind of weird and outlandish…

"Do it again!" Eli shouted, almost startling her from her perch. "Name of Christ, Claire! Whatever you just did, do it again!"

Frowning, biting her lip, she did.

She grabbed the feather with both hands and gave the most vicious twist she could manage from such a precarious perch. She threw all her weight into it. And then some.

The feather turned.

It clicked once, clicked again. Seemed to drop a little into some kind of slot that couldn't be seen, and that was followed by a raspy and ancient sliding sound.

This time when Eli yelled his delight and astonishment, she was ready.

This time she had a firm hold on the ladder and didn't almost topple off.

Chapter Nineteen

"NAME OF CHRIST!" ELI WAS SHOUTING IT OVER AND OVER LONG BEFORE SHE reached the bottom of the ladder. "Name of Christ, Claire!" He'd started to hyperventilate and his heart felt like it was going to explode. Like it *had* to explode, the way it was putting up a monumental struggle inside his chest. The way it felt like it was just about to split into a hundred and one separate, small pieces and like every one of those small pieces was ready, willing and able to take on a beating frenzy of its own. His chest actually ached from the cacophony he felt starting up inside, and his vision was beginning to turn red. The most awfully, bloody, fatally red a man could see and still expect to live to see tomorrow. Or the next second. "Stephie was right!"

Hand over hand and one foot after another with a speed and agility that left him bemused and wondering if he'd ever had that kind of coordination, if his body had ever, in its glory and its unfettered prime, known how to move with such unthinking ease and unstumbling accuracy, Claire scrambled down her ladder.

Reaching the bottom without the mishap that had seemed all but certain, she turned to him gaping, saying something he really couldn't make out since the world had gone all out of kilter. Since the only thing he could really hear above the shattered chorus of the beating pieces of his disintegrated heart was a sort of low, growling whine.

"Whaaaaaaaaaaaaaaaaaaa..." Came from her mouth. Lower than her voice, slower than her voice, the sound seemed to have a terrible time finding its way from her throat and her mouth. "Theeeeeeeeee helllllllllllllllllll, Elllllllllllllllllll..."

"You have to see this."

And that *was* weird.

His own voice was okay. It was a voice. His voice. While Claire's...

"Youuuuuuu'rrrrrrrrrrrre scarrrrrrrrrrrrrring mmmmmeeeeeeeeeeee."

She'd reached the floor now, and her movements were starting to return to normal speed. Slowly but noticeably, they were starting to lose that awful slo-mo quality that seemed like something out of a science fiction movie scripted specifically to scare the shit right out of him. Nothing about her was returning fast enough for his liking, but she was returning. Starting to return.

"Eli?" Things became normal...Claire became normal...with an audible pop that had him shaking his head in confusion for a minute before he found the wits to look at her.

She stood over him. *Loomed* over him as if he'd shrunk in reality down to the twins' size. Peering down at him, reaching out to put a hand on his shoulder and shake him the tiniest bit, she looked worried. More worried, he thought, than he'd seen her look before. About anything.

"Up there." He pointed, or thought he did, toward the amazing thing her fiddling with the feather had revealed. But if he did, she must not have seen. Or maybe she really was so worried she chose not to notice.

"You're pale as a ghost." She bent over him, her attention all for him. All *on* him.

"I...had a surprise." His hand still hung where he'd left it. In midair. Kind of foolishly in midair, the index finger still extended in the act of pointing where she wasn't looking. "That's all."

"Surprise." Taking his face between her hands...cool, cool hands and sweet hands that had the power to soothe even the turbulence and tumults he felt inside right about now...Claire bent closer. She stared straight and deep into his eyes.

"Uh-huh." Eli waved his hand a little. "*That* surprise."

Almost as slowly as she'd moved before, Claire turned. Eli swore he heard the squealing flex and stretch of every one of her muscles as she did, and the gentle whoosh of dark brown curls slicing a wide and fragrant arc through air turned suddenly, heavily expectant with whatever the hell was going to happen next.

It seemed to take forever for her head to reach an angle where she'd be able to see what he'd seen from the start. What had quite literally been right in front of his nose through all the years he'd known the Indian...what had taken place right in front of it just a second or two ago. And when she finally did reach that vantage point, her gasp was long and slow. Her gasp was still caught in the weird time warp kind of thing that had slowed her movements and altered her voice before.

Thankfully the distortion didn't last long this time. A second or two. No more.

"What the hell?" Claire was already straightening away from him. Already looking up at the Indian's mouth. Or, rather, she was staring stupefied at the place where the frowning, carved mouth had *been.*

"My thoughts exactly."

Standing, Claire was able to reach easily what Eli hadn't been able to manage. With no trouble at all she dipped her hand into the sagging drawer that had opened in the lower half of the Indian's face when she'd done whatever the hell she'd done with that ridiculous feather. "There's something in here," she said, scrabbling around a little since the drawer lay just a bit higher than her eye level.

"What the hell did you *do*, Claire?" Suddenly that seemed more important, seemed much safer, to contemplate than whatever might be hidden inside that drawer. "How the hell did you…"

She was concentrating on getting hold of whatever was in there. Not on him. "I just wiggled the top feather a little. It was loose anyway, and I thought at first I'd broken something. But then it kind of…slipped. Down. Into a notch inside the Indian. Or something. And that was when you started to…"

"Amazing." Eli didn't know if he wanted to know his grandfather's secret now that the moment had finally arrived. But Claire was already lifting something dark and oddly shaped, something not quite soft but not exactly rigid either, out of the drawer. And he guessed he wasn't going to have much choice in another minute or two. "I climbed all over that thing when I was a kid. How the hell could I have missed that?" Steeling himself, tensing his gut and his back and his shoulders, he knotted his hands together in anticipation at the same time that he shook his head a little. "How could I have not even suspected?"

"Not even a little bit?" Mercifully she paused with the dark object…it was a kind of drawstring bag made out of some soft and dark cloth, he saw now…in her hand. Mercifully she didn't make any move to reveal what lay within. All those old things and even older memories that couldn't make one good goddamned bit of difference now.

She'd taken some time out of her busy schedule of shaking up and rearranging all the parts of his life that he'd finally put in some kind of flimsy, false order, and was inspecting the place where the Indian's broad and boxy jaw had miraculously turned into a secret drawer.

"There must have been a crack here," she murmured, running her fingers over the disjointed edges to see how they'd been joined.

"No." Though she wasn't looking at him, Eli shook his head again. "I'm absolutely sure I never saw a crack. Anywhere."

"Did you look?" Now *she* looked. At him.

Sighing again, trying against all odds to do something about the tight ball of agitated nerves and twisted muscles that had once been his stomach, Eli unclenched one hand from the other and lifted it to drag it back through his hair. It was a tell-tale sign, he knew. One Claire and a large handful of others who knew him well had told him down through the years he exhibited whenever something made him really, really nervous.

Like he sure as hell was starting to feel really, really nervous right about now.

"Why would I have ever thought to look for cracks in the Indian's face, Claire?"

Now she looked exasperated. "Well, if you knew there was a secret and you'd set out to find it…"

He fought off a smile and felt it defeat him anyway. "I was a kid. Remember?"

"Seems to me a secret drawer in a scary old carved Indian would be right up any ordinary kid's alley."

"You're just full of answers, aren't you?"

Never missing a beat, she nodded.

"Well, then. How about if I tell you I was never a very ordinary kid? By any stretch of the imagination." Frowning a little, Eli reflected that that might be the single most absolutely true statement he'd ever made.

Baseball.

Even when he'd been tiny, a doddering toddler with a plastic bat twice as big as himself, Eli Eden had thought and dreamed of little else but baseball. *Playing* baseball. He'd never been the kind of kid who'd gone for the Saturday afternoon horror flicks at the movie house in town, and had certainly never been the kind of kid to give much thought to things like creepy old wooden Indians. Not even when creepy old wooden Indians were shoved right into his face. And hidden, mysterious drawers full of some kind of unnamed treasure?

He found himself shaking his head. That just hadn't been up his alley. He'd never been a bit ordinary in that regard.

"Don't you want to see what your grandfather left for you?" Claire was holding up the dark-fabric bag now. Holding it out in some kind of effort to entice him into the game.

And just that quickly the moment arrived.

The end of the saga.

The moment of truth.

The day when he'd have no further excuse to sidestep the past...*his* past...and avoid looking it straight in the eyes.

Already, before he had a chance to answer with a defensive *yea* or the even more likely desperate *nay*, she was opening the bag. Was pulling out the largest, the bulkiest and most peculiarly shaped item it contained.

"What's this?" she muttered. "Some kind of toy?"

Before he could tell it not to, Eli's hand lifted, palm turned up. Ready to receive whatever she was about to give him.

"Some kind of action figure, I think," she said. And did give it to him.

"Well, I'll be damned." Relived that it hadn't been anything that terrible or gut-wrenching after all, Eli burst into laughter.

"What?" Claire peered at the thing he held, still clean and perfect after so many years in its protective plastic bubble.

"Bob The Baserunner." Turning the package over, he studied the back with a critical eye. "I can't tell you how badly I wanted one of these when I was about ten." He turned the package over again. Smiled a little at the memory, and thought he might be in imminent danger of turning misty. "I wanted this at just about the time Granddad starting spinning his tales about secrets inside the Indian. So that's what the old guy was up to." He turned the package over again. "This thing must be worth a small fortune by now. All sealed up and never touched, and all."

"Right. Like you need another fortune, Eli."

He cocked his head, still trying to avoid the dreaded mistiness. "A fortune of the heart then," he said softly. "How's that?"

"There's a box here, too." Too quickly, without giving him time or the chance to adjust, Claire thrust a tiny leather-covered cube at him. And just as he'd known he would, he reached out and took it.

"A ring?" Claire guessed, leaning in again.

"One way to find out." Eli touched the miniscule switch on the front of the cube, and it sprang open. Dazzling even him. The man who could easily and without a second thought buy all the diamonds he or Claire could ever want, without regard for size or cost or any kind of real-world practicality. "Whoa," he said. It was all he could *manage* to say. "This has got to be..."

"Antique," Claire finished for him.

"Treasures of the heart," he murmured, knowing he'd seen the glittering solitaire before, and knowing where. "That's what I meant. Treasures of the heart, Claire. This was my grandmother's ring. I remember seeing it on her hand. I remember it from as far back as I can remember anything." He laughed. Again. His spirits began to soar just as his grandfather had no doubt intended when he'd put the ring into the drawer, surely long after the childhood treasure of Bob The Baserunner had been deposited there. "My uncle Lew's daughters used to fight like a couple of scalded cats over who would get this when Gran died."

"Uncle? Eli, I didn't know you had an unc—"

"We were never all that close." Taking the ring from its bed of slightly frayed, aged purple velvet, Eli reached for her hand. "My old man saw to that. Now, come over here, Claire," he ordered as he slipped the lovely thing onto Claire's finger. Where it unquestionably belonged, because it fit as if it had been made for her and no other. "This is yours. By all that's right."

"But your cousins..." She stared down at the small but lovely diamond, turning her hand this way and that way to catch whatever light it might be possible to catch on an overcast and rain-laden day, "Your uncle's daughters. Shouldn't one of them..."

He laughed again. A little more shortly this time. "Lew's girls fought almost to the death over that ring. And after Gran died...well, that was just disgusting, Claire. The funeral was barely over when they started looking for the ring. Only it had mysteriously disappeared. It hadn't been on Gran's hand at the funeral parlor, and nobody seemed to have it. And that didn't do a damned thing to promote family unity, let me tell you. So, yes. Obviously Granddad didn't want either of the golddiggers to have it. Obviously he meant it to be mine. And I mean it to be yours. So that's it."

Eli knew he was bright-eyed...very dangerously, alarmingly bright-eyed, when he looked up at her. "That's Granddad's secret treasure. The one thing I wanted in my childhood but could never have because my stiff-necked old man wouldn't hear of it. Because he said no son of his would ever play with dolls. And because baseball dolls were doubly heinous. And the one thing Granddad had to give that meant more than anything in the world to him."

"There's something else." Claire had her hand in the bag again. She had it way, way down inside, and was frowning as she worked to grab and pull out that *something else*. A slim square of stiff cardboard.

Right away, Eli knew what it was.

What it had to be.

Right away he tried to warn her off.

"Don't," he said in a cracked voice, closing his eyes tight for half a second against tears that threatened for real now. And that was all that would come out. Just that one word. Just that pathetically inadequate, almost laughably naïve word.

Because of course Claire already had.

Because she *didn't* know. Couldn't possibly know.

He opened his eyes just in time to watch her pull that fatally horrible piece of cardboard out of the bag. To see her look at it with wide eyes. Astonished eyes. Disbelieving eyes that in another second, two at the most, lifted to stare at him.

"Eli! It's...you."

She stood motionless, with the baseball card cradled carefully between her palm and her slender, silken fingers.

Of course it was him.

Who else could it be? Who else *would* it be?

Eli guessed he'd known all along he'd be retrieving that particular piece of his past from the hiding place inside the Indian. He guessed it had only been inevitable and it was the reason...the most important one anyway ...why he'd been so damned reluctant to watch Claire open that bag. To watch her pull out the items one at a time, the sick anticipation twisting tighter around the pit of his gut with every second it took her to pull them out and every second it took him to realize that one by one they'd been revealed as harmless. Little things. Pleasantly nostalgic things.

But this...

This is something different.

This is...

"Eli, this is one of your baseball cards!"

"One?" His smile felt tight. Unnatural. A horrid, cartoon grimace instead of a smile. "I only played a single season, Claire. I only had one card."

"A rookie card?" She sounded like she wasn't quite sure of the term...wasn't quite sure she was calling it by its right, its proper, name.

Unable to resist no matter how much he thought he wanted to resist, Eli reached out and touched the card. With just a fingertip. As if the touch would be enough to kill. "There weren't very many of these made," he said with a wistfulness that made his heart ache.

"Another treasure of the heart?"

Absently, no longer completely with her or completely hearing her, Eli nodded.

He looked so *young* in that picture.

Had he ever really been that young? Ever really posed for that picture with hot sun sparkling on his hair and in eyes that had never, in that moment of supreme joy and triumph at realizing his greatest dream, known defeat? Or disappointment? Or limitation?

"It seems…" Eli had to stop then. Had to clear his throat with an embarrassingly loud noise and shift his gaze a little to the side. So he wouldn't be looking at his own carefree, laughing-at-the-moon face any longer.

"Seems what?" Very tenderly, Claire reached for his hand and enfolded it with both of her own.

Only then did he realize he'd taken the baseball card from her.

He was holding it the way she had…holding it reverently in the palm of one cupped hand, as if it was intrinsically fragile and to drop it would be to shatter it and all the memories it represented forever.

Much as his life, like it or not, want to face the truth of it or not, had been shattered to smithereens in the foolish pursuit of his old man's self-centered, unrealistic whims.

Chapter Twenty

D*AMN.*

Claire wished she didn't have to show him the letter.

Seeing his face as he looked down at the baseball card bearing his picture, watching as he turned his face away from her with no logical purpose except to hide his expression, she thought maybe the smartest thing to do would be to just shove the letter back into the secret drawer. Shove it all the way to the back, where Eli would never see it because he wasn't physically capable of putting himself into a position where he could see it.

Claire didn't recognize the sharp-edged handwriting on the envelope. But she knew a bad thing when she saw one. And this one gave her the worst feeling…a downright horrible, skin-crawling feeling.

"Eli…"

For a second it didn't seem he heard.

He just kept his face turned away. Just kept staring at nothing, somewhere off to the side.

Gingerly she touched his shoulder. "Eli?"

This time he did turn his head and lift it. And Claire thought she spotted a telltale glimmer around his eyes, a warning of iridescent moisture that had her wanting to turn *her* gaze away before she could embarrass him. But she didn't do that. Couldn't, because it somehow didn't seem right.

"Talk to me, Eli."

"I'm sorry." He sniffed once, and that was that. In the very next second he returned to the appearance of normal. Returned to the coolly practical and always self-possessed Eli who'd become the only real, maybe even the very first, stable force she'd known in her life. "Seeing this thing…" He flicked the underside of the baseball card once with the fingers of his free hand, then dropped it onto a small table at his side. "That shook me up a little, I guess. I don't understand why Granddad would put the thing in there. He had to know seeing it wouldn't be the most welcome…"

I can't make her wait any longer.

She's waited too long already.

"Maybe this will explain." She'd retrieved the letter from the bag after the card, and had been holding it behind her back, out of his sight until the time was right.

But there wasn't going to be a time any better than this one. So she shoved the envelope at him the same way she'd shoved the box containing the ring just a minute before.

"What's this?" He didn't immediately touch it. As if he'd gotten that bad, bad, *bad* vibe from it too.

"It was clipped to the baseball card."

Eli didn't move. He only stared at the envelope. Suspiciously.

"It might be something you need to..."

"Shit." When his eyes finally looked like they focused, it was immediately clear he wasn't happy with what he saw.

"Eli?"

"That's my father's handwriting."

"Oh."

Claire wished she could die. She wished she could find a place to hide. Wished like anything she'd had the plain common sense to listen to better judgment when it squalled and squawked at her, trying to tell her there were some things Eli just didn't need to see. Some he *really* didn't need to know.

"I can't stand it." What he said seemed to be a denial of the letter. A refusal to have anything to do with it. So it came as a real surprise when he took it, almost tearing it out of her hands. "No time like the present, is there?" Inserting his thumb beneath a corner of the flap, he smiled. An openly bitter, undeniably unnatural smile. "Isn't that what they always say is the best way to live your life?"

"Depends who *they* are," Claire replied cautiously. "Eli, are you sure you want to do this?"

"Hell, no." He was tearing vigorously at the heavy white paper anyway. Tearing as if there might very well be no tomorrow. "There's no part of me that wants to do this."

"Then why..."

"Because." His smile turned even more brittle. Even more unnatural, and even more desperately strained. "A person can't go around all his life avoiding things just because they might be a little unpleasant. Because sometimes...a *lot* of the time...it's better all the way around to just face up to the unpleasant things so you can get on with the rest of your life."

The envelope contained a single sheet of paper. Folded twice, into a long oblong, it was covered with the same jagged, overly slanted writing.

Eli's hands were shaking by the time he finished the ripping and the unfolding and the smoothing out of creases. His movements became increasingly abrupt and hurried as he tried very obviously to hide from her how nervous he'd grown.

Claire wanted to say something. Wanted in some way, if only a very small and pathetically inadequate one, to let him know it was okay and he really didn't need to be nervous. Because she was here beside him. Where she'd always be. And because he really *didn't* need to do this if it wasn't something he wanted to do.

She wished there was something she could say, some way she could say it. But there wasn't, so in the end she just waited with her heart in her throat, watching in silence until he finished ripping and unfolding and smoothing. Waiting until he was ready to go on.

"You know what?" he asked, looking up at her with surprised eyes.

She didn't speak.

Mostly because she didn't have anything adequate to say.

"I can't do this."

Claire blinked.

For a moment she didn't understand, and when he shoved the paper into her hands and for a moment after that she didn't think her mind *wanted* to understand.

"Read it."

"R...read?"

He nodded. "Read it to me."

"Are you sure, Eli? I wouldn't want to intrude on anything that might be private."

I'd do anything to avoid having to intrude into this something that might be private.

"Private?" He looked stunned. "Name of God, Claire. Didn't we just agree to share things? Share everything? Didn't we agree to stop bottling them up inside and...I know it was mostly me making those promises. That's because I had the most promises to make. But it's got to work both ways if it's going to work at all."

Shivering, Claire pulled an ottoman over next to his wheelchair and then she sat, lifting the letter.

"*Pop,*" she read, then paused to glance inquiringly at Eli.

"What my father called my grandfather," Eli explained, waving a hand at the letter. "Go on. Get to the good stuff. I know there has to be some in there."

"*I know what you're telling me is right,*" she read on, stumbling here and there over the unfamiliar handwriting. "*I know I have to do what you say. But how? Eli is my son. My only child. And I've never known how to talk to him.*" She looked at Eli. "That's a surprise. Considering what I've heard about your father."

"You haven't heard that much, Claire."

Reluctant to go back to the letter now that she'd found a convenient way out, she shrugged. "I've heard enough to know I can't imagine him writing this."

"He did though." Eli's voice turned wry. Maybe even a little sour. "Keep on reading."

Sighing heavily, she lifted the letter and picked up where she'd left off. *"I've never known what makes Eli tick or how to get through to him. How to know what has meaning to him."*

"The old goat." The sound of Eli's voice made her jump this time.

In all the time she'd known him, through all the ups and downs and sadness and depression that came along with every life and his in particular, she'd never heard him speak in a voice like that. One so bitter. So horribly bitter, and uncommonly sharp. "All he had to do was shut his goddamned mouth once in a while and listen. But of course he never thought of that. Did he?"

Claire lowered the letter to her lap. "I knew this wasn't a good idea."

"No." Eli waved her into silence. "I want to know. I want to hear the rest of it. Whatever it is. It's about time I knew what kind of sense Granddad tried to talk into the old fart."

Are you sure?

Eli looked so fierce, so flat-out stubborn and set that Claire didn't want to ask again. Didn't think she *dared* ask again.

After a few seconds, shifting to a more comfortable position on the ottoman, she resumed. "*There's no way I can tell Eli how much I've always loved him. Or that—*"

"Love?"

When Claire lowered the letter this time, Eli looked like he was about to start the bitterness again. And maybe let it devolve all the way into open anger of the kind he hadn't displayed in a long, long time.

"See?" she countered. "I knew it was a bad idea. I knew I should have..."

"What? Hidden the letter from me? Never let me know you'd found it in the first place?"

Biting her lip, she nodded.

"Whatever happened to sharing everything and being open about everything?"

"I'm reading the letter to you right now, aren't I?" Claire shot him a reproachful look.

He smiled. A little weakly. But it was a smile all the same.

"*Or that I was proud of him,*" Claire read on. "Proud?" Looking up at Eli, she felt her hopes rise a little. "I never heard you tell me that! That your father was proud of you."

Eli shrugged. "That's because this is the first time I've heard about it. And I'm not too sure I believe it now that I have. So is that it? Is that all?"

Claire gave him a long look. A considering one. "There's a little more." Bowing her head over the sheet of paper, she read on. "*He's always been so defensive, Pop. About everything that matters to him. How could I tell him anything? How can I tell him now, when I've ruined everything beyond the point it can ever be fixed? Beyond the point where I'm afraid even to try to talk to him? I don't know how I can tell him how much I love him or how sorry I am for the terrible thing I've done to him.*"

Claire let her breath out in a long and uneven sigh. "That's all there is, Eli. That's the end of it."

He didn't answer right away.

In the silence Claire studied his face. Very, very intently. She searched it for signs of the consuming anger she feared and half-expected...the anger that always seemed to go along with discussions of Eli's father. Or thoughts of him.

Finding none...no apparent sign of fury about to explode, she relaxed a little. As much as she thought it was wise to relax.

"It sounds genuine," Eli mused. "The letter." Even without anger his tone remained dubious. Thoughtfully skeptical. "The apology. Sounds like the old man might actually have believed what he was saying. For once." At last Eli met her gaze. "Doesn't it?"

"You should be asking yourself if *you* believe it."

His expression turned even more thoughtful. More sad, too, and more dubious. "I don't know what to believe any more, Claire. I just can't understand why the old man couldn't have said those things to my face. Just come out and *said* them when I really needed to hear them. Instead of...of...I don't know. Hiding them away in some goddamned wooden Indian where I'd most likely never find them."

"I think your grandfather was the one who hid this, Eli. The letter was addressed to him. He had to be the one who...and anyway. You weren't very..." Claire felt like she was picking her way through some extremely dangerous territory suddenly. She felt like she had to take it really, really slowly. Had to choose her every word with utmost caution. "I don't know how you were in the beginning. When your father was still around and you were mad as hell at him. And rightly so. I only know how you were when I arrived on the scene. And you weren't very approachable. Not on a human level anyway." She only said this after a while. After she'd tried out at least a dozen different words in her mind and rejected every one of them as likely to do nothing but set him off again. Set him off worse than he'd ever been set off before.

Eli didn't say a word. He just blinked at her. Blinked, and looked blank.

"You know you weren't approachable." Dropping the letter to the floor, she moved her ottoman closer. Close enough to touch him easily...to touch gentle fingertips to his shoulder and run them down his arm, across the crisp fabric of his blue-striped summer shirt and finally, after what seemed like an incredibly long and arduous journey, trail them lightly across the bare and sun-gilt skin between his elbow and his wrist. "The first time I ever met you, Eli, you were just..." Here she did run out of steam. And words. And, really, ideas for words.

"Scary?" he suggested with a smile that wasn't a smile at all as much as an uneasy quirking at the corners of his mouth.

After the slightest hesitation, Claire nodded. "That's as good a word as any, I guess."

"God." Lifting a hand he covered hers. "I've been a monster. Haven't I?"

"I wouldn't go that far." Claire tried to laugh but it sounded strange and forced. Uneasy, verging on just slightly hysterical. "I figure you've had some pretty good reasons for the things you've done. After all, from everything I've heard, your father wasn't exactly a sweetheart either."

"Good reasons?" Wide-eyed, Eli shook his head. "For treating you...and all the women before you...like you didn't matter? Like you weren't really human, and I wouldn't be harming anyone by hiring you to come up here and have sex with me because I didn't know how else to get sex? For bribing you with money and treating you like a common pr...pros..." He couldn't seem to choke the word out.

"Well, okay. I'll admit that was a bit extreme. And not all that flattering. But look at it this way, Eli. If you hadn't thought you could buy me, if you hadn't thought that was the only way you could meet and interest women, and if I hadn't been genuinely at the end of my rope and desperate for the money, where would we have ever met?"

He continued to stare at her. Wide-eyed, his expression rife with failure to understand. "So you're telling me..."

"You're a millionaire," she said as a small and now completely genuine laugh bubbled from her lips. "Numerous times over. And I'm... *was* nobody. I was an unemployed secretary with no more unemployment, a sick mother, and a stack of bills I couldn't even hope to pay. I was in over my head and going down fast. With no hope of ever seeing my way out of the trap I was in."

"The ends justify the means, then? Is that what you're saying?"

She smiled again. Squeezed his arm and saw a responding sparkle light up the far, inner depths of his eyes. "In this case I'd say that's a big 'yes'."

"Because it worked out right."

Again, she nodded.

"Not that you're excusing my behavior?" Eli was beginning to look confused, and Claire guessed she couldn't really blame him.

She was getting a little confused herself.

"There's no need to excuse anything," she said softly. "Like I said before, what's past is past. There's no use dwelling on it other than to see our mistakes and say we sure as hell aren't going to make any of them again. It's no use beating ourselves up over it if we've used those mistakes to change in some way. For the better."

"And you're saying I have? Changed? For the better?"

More enthusiastic than she'd felt in months, and more hopeful too, Claire felt her smile broaden. "Of course you have, Eli. I'm still here, aren't I?"

Chapter Twenty-One

"I DON'T KNOW WHAT I DID TO DESERVE YOU."

Claire blushed.

Delightfully blushed.

But he was the one who should have blushed…who should be turning red as a fire truck right this minute, embarrassed by all the attention she lavished on him and undeserving of a bit of it.

Her love was a constant wonder to him. It was one of the most enduring wonders…really the *only* enduring wonder…of his life. The only wonder he'd never been able to explain or rationalize to his own satisfaction.

He'd done enough things, screwed up enough times and in enough ways of his own making that he should have driven her away a thousand times. A million…as many millions, he suspected, as he had dollars tucked away in the bank down in Latrobe. And still she kept coming back. Still she was here beside him right this instant. And still he had trouble getting around the astonishment in his heart to believe it could true. To understand *how* it could be true.

She didn't answer. Didn't say a word to try to address his question. And then he realized he hadn't asked it.

"Why do you love me so much, Claire?"

She looked surprised. Like she'd never thought about it before. Like she'd always accepted what she felt on faith, and faith alone. "Because you're you," she said at last, her voice dropping into a new, husky and chill-inducing register. "Because I love you and I can't stop myself. Because I've never been able to stop myself."

Eli knew his eyes lit up. He felt the flames start to burn in them, knew they burned in his expression too. "We're going to make it, aren't we?" he asked, hardly daring to hope he'd hear the answer he hoped like hell he was about to hear.

Smiling, Claire leaned closer.

He could smell her perfume. It was that same delectable something. That intoxicating fragrance made up in good part of the kind of roses-in-the-rain duskiness that had driven him all the way to distraction and beyond just the afternoon before in the storm-misted summerhouse. And then there was that other part. The one that was a complete mystery to him even now. Even after so much time with her and even after he'd gotten to know her better than he'd known anyone…any woman…before.

It was a whiff of somnolent stillness. Of mingled angel's scent and flower nectar he couldn't identify because he wasn't all that fluent in the ways and scents of flowers. Though angels might be a different story.

In any case, he knew what he liked, and wasn't that all that really mattered anyway?

He like Claire. *Loved* her, in all the ways it was possible to love. And then some.

He loved the way she was looking at him right now. With all the love she'd ever declared she felt shining in her spectacular eyes for all the world to see. With all that amount of unbelievable love coloring her face to the exact shade of a rose. With all that blushing, blooming, sweet and delirious color making her appear lovelier by far in this moment than she'd been lovely in any moment before.

Christ, I can't breathe.

I think I've forgotten how to breathe!

"I never thought we weren't going to make it," she murmured close to his ear.

And Eli knew that wasn't right.

He'd seen the look on her face in times past. In times when she *had* been worried about that very thing. Times when her worry had been the clearest thing in the world to him. He knew she'd worried terribly, suspected she'd never been able to admit to herself exactly how worried she'd been. So habitually worried that even now, even after they'd put to rest all the reasons they'd had for thinking they should worry, the worry continued to linger. He continued to see it in some guarded depth of shimmering brown eyes that remained closed to him. Protectively closed, defensively closed.

"You could have fooled me," he replied.

She looked embarrassed. "Well, okay. Maybe I was a little bit worried."

Eli fought off a smile. Or at least he fought off *part* of one, because the joy and the sheer delirious relief he'd begun to feel inside were things he wasn't going to be able to contain. Not by any means known to him. "You were worried a lot more than a little, Claire. You were worried within an inch of your life or I've missed the entire point of everything you've done. Everything you've said. Everything that led up to you dragging that damned, filthy wreck of an Indian into this house in the first place."

"Why are you doing this now?" Her smile and much of her sparkle turned wistful as she raised her hands to his face. As she cupped the sides of it and caressed tenderly. As the softness of those hands, the loveliness of their silken delight, brushed life-sustaining fire into him. Brushed the fire he needed if he was to continue all through him.

God, the fire was intense. So intense, so enveloping and all-consuming it nearly choked the voice out of him. Intense enough to dim all but the most basic thoughts right out of existence.

"Why are you saying things like this now?" she asked. "When we're finally about to move beyond them?"

"Because…" His voice really *was* a choked whisper. A strangled memory of itself. "Whatever happened to us over the last couple of years, I don't want it to happen again."

Her expression softened. Her mouth curved into a gentle dreaminess that really did take his breath away, really did set his heart to hammering and stuttering, wildly out of any semblance of control.

"It won't happen again," she promised, fixing her gaze on him in a way that had the power to unnerve completely. Unswervingly. Inescapably. "Because I don't intend to let it happen again. You have to know I'll do everything in my power to make sure it never happens again. So this is your warning, Eli Eden."

She'd been drawing closer and ever closer throughout her speech. By the end of it, by the last word or two and the half-whispered uttering of his name with lips that seemed the only center, the only possible or acceptable focus of his entire world, she drew so enticingly close that her mouth did everything but meet his. Her lips did everything but fondle his with the same kind of inexhaustible fire her hands streamed into his body.

In response, Eli shook.

Not a shiver, not a tremor, not a mere unsteadiness, this was a genuine quaking. Like some kind of terrible neurological malfunction that had taken him over in his entirety and threatened never to let him go, this started from someplace inside him. It started in some far and unreachable inner place and then flowed outward. Erupting as an unstoppable tremor in hands, and lips, and gut, and every other part of him.

And there were plenty of other things going on inside him too. Things that had their own ways of incapacitating him. Things that if he wasn't careful and Claire didn't stop could conceivably and logically become far more incapacitating than any mere shaking or tremor.

Deep inside Eli felt the rising tension Claire always instigated…the sudden and burgeoning *desire* to have her in all the ways it would ever be possible to have her. Only this time it was the strongest tension he'd ever felt. The most demanding. And right alongside it, as a result of it or maybe as an integral part of it…

He groaned when her lips moved that startling scintilla closer.

When they made their long-promised contact with his.

He groaned aloud, first in anticipation and then again almost immediately in absolute distraction. He groaned when she gave up her sweet and all but intolerable whispering with her lips pressed right up against his…whispering that allowed him to *feel* her words more than he heard them. Could feel them reverberating into the tensed and waiting inner places she'd already rendered all but helpless simply by being here. Simply by touching him.

Most of all he groaned at the sudden, ripe and heavy tightening in his cock. "Claire…"

"Be warned," she repeated, her lips now pressed as close to his as it was possible to press without engaging fully. Without sealing his fate altogether by destroying the very last reserves of his ability to think, and reason.

"About what?" Somehow his hands found her shoulders. He managed to convince them to clasp tightly, with all the brute force his desperation had loaned him and his love allowed him. And once he clasped, he urged her with touches instead of words to rise from her perch on the big footstool.

Responding, she did. But only a little. She rose only the barest minimum required to come to him. To come into his lap and into the circle of arms that had waited, suffering untold silent agonies for far too long already.

"Be warned that I don't intend to let you get away from me again," she said softly. Soothingly. Disruptively. "Be warned that I won't ever allow you to pull away from me again. Or hold yourself apart from me. Not for any reason, Eli."

As if I'd ever want to do such a thing.

As if I haven't learned my lesson. The hard way.

As if I'd ever be stupid enough to repeat the mistakes I've made. Or the…

"And if I try?" Holding her, feeling the warm wriggle of her as she enticed him, Eli was enjoying this. Just the way he intended to very soon enjoy much more of her warmth. And much, *much* more of the sinuous, sensuous, stirring excitement of her body against his. "If I do my damnedest to pull away?"

Laughing, Claire leaned in again. Laughing harder, she touched her lips to his. Tight at first, the touch quickly turned torrid. Quickly turned to the type of touch designed for invasion. The type that by its very existence sought new and interesting depths always, new and ever more delicious depths everywhere. Depths she might have missed before. Ones she might somehow have overlooked during her previous excursions into these same quivering and shivering territories. And she held his face again too. She pressed a searingly cool hand firmly against the side of his jaw, making it impossible for him to turn away.

Once again his cock leaped.

More. Wildly.

"Claire?"

"Hmmm?" She didn't stop what she was doing. Didn't give it a break, and certain as hell didn't give *him* a break. Twining an arm hard and tight around his neck, she held herself so close to him they might as well have become one person, joined by lips that sampled and savored hungrily each of the other. Joined just as completely by tongues that twisted together and now seemed unable to draw enough sustenance from each other.

"Claire!"

They couldn't go on this way.

Couldn't, no matter how much either of their minds might insist they could. They still had to come up for air. They still had to acknowledge their own needs. Their own undeniable, pressing, urgent physical needs that had to be satisfied. *Must* be satisfied.

She leaned her forehead against his. Snugged her arm more securely around his neck, the better to hold him where she wanted him, the better to keep him at her absolute mercy. "What?" she asked, and he marveled at the way she packed so incredibly much meaning into such a very small word. She packed in so many layers upon layers of meaning, each of them powerful enough and sultry enough to excite a man past the point of losing his mind. Instantly. Thoroughly. Irretrievably.

"Do you want me to do it right here?"

"Hmmm...mmm." Her laughter steamed. Sizzled. *Burned.* "What something might that be?" she inquired sweetly enough. But at the same time the hand at his jaw dropped. It skimmed lightly yet purposefully, brushing its destructive way across his shoulder. Seeming to leave wide and barren trails of char wherever it passed. And then it dropped again. Then it dropped still lower, to blaze a similar perversely pleasurable track across the planes of his chest. A track that seemed to dissolve whatever it touched...dissolve shirt, and flesh, and muscle, and the bone beneath that muscle. A track that seemed to render living flesh toneless and formless, leaving it utterly senseless. Utterly defenseless.

"I think you know what." The soul-shaking tremors inside him grew stronger when her hand meandered from the territories where it had laid such complete waste to other, much more susceptible and much more vulnerable territories below.

Closer her hand drifted, to the place Eli knew it was going to end up. Closer and always closer, but never fast enough. Never *close* enough.

"And if I do know?" she inquired in a new and altogether breathless tone. "Even if I do know what 'it' you're talking about, do you seriously expect me to believe you'd really do it here?"

"Hmmm." Laughing, catching her tardily lingering hand, Eli forced it to drop again. He urged it toward the swollen, still swelling agony she'd started between his legs. And then he held it there. Just in case she might get the wrong idea. Just in case some weird and twisted sense of propriety should spring up at this late stage of the game to grab hold of her and make her decide she needed to withdraw. Before he was in any way ready for withdrawal. Of any kind. "You don't believe I wouldn't, do you?"

"But...*here*?"

"Hmmm." Eli pressed her hand harder against him...harder against the cock that had grown enormous. Painfully and riotously enormous, even though every instinct he possessed warned it had scarcely begun to grow at all.

This time she really did try to pull her hand away. "Now? Eli..."

"Hmmm," he said again. "You started this. And now you think you're going to stop before you let me finish?"

"But the twins are upstairs!"

"With Nanny." He refused to allow her to do a single thing he knew she wanted. Refused to allow her to pull away, move away, move her hand away. "And that woman's a drill sergeant. You know she is. You know as well as I do that she's..."

"I thought you liked Nanny."

Chuckling, he tightened his arms around her. Tightened more too in other places. The hardness of him thrust upward with renewed vigor, reaching for the soft flesh at the underside of Claire's thigh. "I love Nanny. I'm ecstatic about having Nanny on the premises. But the point is, she'll keep the twins occupied. She's got a Program…got their every move planned, probably up until the day they graduate high school. Which won't be for a few years, by my calculations. So I don't think we'll have to worry about…"

"Well, what about my mother?" She wasn't struggling to escape his determined clutches. Not exactly. But what she *was* doing, whatever he might choose to call that continued, eager wriggling, was in its turn doing all kinds of things to him. All kinds of the most delightful, most provocative and suggestive things.

"What about your mother?"

"What if she were to walk in on us? The shock of seeing us…you know…right in the middle of the music room might…"

"A bomb couldn't tear your mother away from the TV while her soaps are on."

"Well, then, what about Hannah?" Claire wriggled again. This time she shoved at his shoulders as she made another attempt to rise out of his lap. To escape what was absolutely, positively not going to be escaped. And all that wriggling and twisting did nothing to help the situation. It only inflamed the way it had before. It only lit a hot and scorching fire inside what had been pretty damned intolerably hot before.

All that wriggling and twisting only made Eli that much more determined to hold her right where she was. No matter how hard she might struggle.

Spluttering all the while in protest, Claire continued to wriggle long after it should be obvious she was no match for the strength in his arms or the determination in his heart.

"What about Hannah?" she insisted a little more strenuously than before. "Hannah could come strolling in here any second, Eli. There's nobody watching over her and planning her day. She doesn't watch the soaps either. Told me once she thought they rotted your brain and turned it to mush. And if you think I want her to find us rolling around on the floor together like a couple of…of…"

Eli nuzzled her ear. Nuzzled it much the same way she'd been nuzzling his lips a little while before…with soft strokes designed to inflame her and set the inside of her as badly aquiver as she'd long since set him. "You're just full of arguments. Aren't you?"

She gave up. Quit her struggling with a sudden ease that only made him suspicious. Certain of ulterior motives.

Just in case, he firmed his grip on her even more.

"We can't do it here." She *sounded* like she'd pretty much given up, too.

But Eli wasn't about to be fooled. He knew a few of Claire's little tricks. He'd seen them before, and this was a situation that screamed at him to pull her deeper into the circle of his arms. As deep as he could, and then ordered him to wrap them as tightly around her as he could.

Just for good measure, once he'd done all that, he gave the long and sloping curve of her neck a just-as-soft nuzzle.

In his arms, she shuddered.

Need had risen in her too. It was still rising, as swiftly and precipitously as it continued to rise in him. He could *feel* it in the sudden shimmer of softness that overtook every part of her body. Not by slow and torturous degrees the way the softness most often stole over her and through her.

This softness came all at once. It came in a single massive and surging rush that surely was the cause of her sudden submission. Her sudden lack of struggle that could be explained in no other way that made any kind of sense.

Softer than soft in his arms, pliant and supple, openly ready for whatever plundering he might decide to carry out, for whatever they might be, she went suddenly limp. Suddenly twice as pliant as ever before, her breathing twice as ragged as he'd heard it before.

Of course Eli hadn't yet decided what kind of plundering he'd like to inflict. He hadn't even started…hadn't in all honesty thought much beyond this one single moment in which delight and anticipation mounted exponentially. Mounted without end and without limit in flesh that never seemed to have room for more. Flesh that somehow always did.

He didn't want to waste his failing energy thinking about anything other than the fact that he loved her. The fact that he loved Claire like it had never been possible for him to love anyone in his life. Like he now knew, without room for even the smallest or most niggling of doubts, he'd never in his life be able to love anyone else.

He loved her so much he felt like he'd lost his way. Lost his soul. Lost himself. He loved her so much he didn't want to find himself anytime soon. Or maybe ever if it meant he'd have to risk the terrible, frightening, unendurable distance popping up again to separate them.

He wasn't going to be able to take much more of this…torment.

Because that was all it was. Pure, needless and yet utterly necessary torment that wasn't to be borne another minute. Another instant, another micro-fraction of an instant.

But Claire had been absolutely right about one thing.

"We're in too much danger of being interrupted here," he breathed into her ear, nuzzling aside a lock of shatteringly fragrant hair that threw itself into his path.

"What do you think I've been trying to tell you?" Her voice shook as badly as the inside of him. Unsteady partly with laughter and partly, almost entirely, with the simmering tide of her audible and unassuaged need, the sound sent another kick, this one of extreme urgency, splintering through him. Making him laugh as oddly as before. As damned near hysterically.

"It's time for us to find a nice spot," he murmured into her delectable, irresistible ear. "I think we need to head on out in search of a door with a good, sturdy lock and a room with a nice, comfortable bed. Right this minute."

And was pleased to note he heard no protest at all in return.

About the Author

A native of a small town not far from Pittsburgh, Pennsylvania, Evelyn Starr always had a passion for the glamorous, the exotic, the sensuous. And she's always been willing to travel the world in search of them. Among her favorite places are Boldt's Castle in the Thousand Islands, Tasmania, Australia's tropical Queensland, and all the nooks and crannies of the Rocky Mountains she now calls home.

Like her wanderlust, Evelyn's fascination with words and stories began at an early age. She remembers being able to read and write before she started school, and by the time she'd finished first grade, she was writing her own little one-page stories. Following graduation from high school, she left her small-town home and hasn't looked back. She majored in journalism, romance, and adventure, and eventually married her college sweetheart, who remains the most romantic, and the most adventurous, hero of them all.

e-Books available by Evelyn Starr at:

www.extasybooks.com

A Little Bit of Tina
Absolute Jasmine
Bamboozled
Bedazzled
Bird of Paradise
Dancing in Dreamland
Dark Pleasures
Elmwood
Haunted Hearts
Mystic Falls
Neptune's Daughter
Nothing but Trouble
One Night in Bangkok
Pirouette
Sherry don't Go
Snow Fever
Sweet Little Lies
Sweetie
The Day After Summer
The Love Charm
Where Magic Dwells
Three Weeks 'til September
Wild Blue
Witch Kissed
You Know You Make Me Blue

For other great books, visit our website.

Anthologies available both in print and e-Book

Made in the USA